Praise for the novels of Libby Fischer Hellmann:

"Libby Hellmann can get into the mind of a character, whether the character is a mentally ill man or a teenage girl. I kept reading after the first brutal and fascinating pages because I . . . wanted to know what would happen to the good, the bad, the beautiful and the ugly people . . . This is good stuff, very good stuff."
—Stuart M. Kaminsky, Grand Master, Mystery Writers of America

"Hellmann's done her homework here and it shows: the writing is assured, the voices authentic . . . [Georgia] Davis' arrival on the mean streets is long overdue."
—Sara Paretsky, author of the V.I. Warshawski series and *Bleeding Kansas*

"She's indisputably crossed the line into the realm of great crime fiction writers. There's no going back now."—Jen Forbus, *Crimespree*

"A true page turner with suspense and a compelling need to forgo a good night's sleep."—*Beyond Her Book* blog, *PublishersWeekly.com*

"A story with enough twists and turns to keep you reading to the end. Highly recommended."—*Library Journal* (starred review)

"Just what's needed in a mystery . . . Depth of characterization sets this new entry apart from a crowded field."—*Kirkus Reviews*

"Hellmann knows how to distill the essence of a character in a few unadorned but dead-right sentences."—Dick Adler, *Chicago Tribune*

"Hellmann's cool style and sleight-of-hand plotting draw you in deep before you know what's happened. This one will keep you up at night."
—SJ Rozan, author of *In This Rain*

"Exciting plot development and a strong heroine . . . If you enjoy gritty noir mysteries, this one is highly recommended."—*Midwest Book Review*

Also by Libby Fischer Hellmann

SET THE
NIGHT
ON FIRE

Libby Fischer Hellmann

 ALLIUM PRESS OF CHICAGO

Allium Press of Chicago

www.alliumpress.com

Book design by E. C. Victorson
Cover design by Miguel Ortuno
Front cover image courtesy of Chicago Park District

ISBN: 978-0-9840676-5-7 (Paperback)

978-0-9840676-6-4 (Hardcover)

To my ever-loving, Sixties-loving, hippie girl Robin

ACKNOWLEDGEMENTS

So many people helped "birth" this novel it's difficult to know where to start to express my gratitude.

First, many thanks to Steve Bunting, Senior Forensic Consultant at Forward Discovery, Inc., for the tutorial on steganography. Thanks also to Austin Camacho for the referral.

Thanks go to Chicago attorneys Bob Egan and Christina Egan for the legal ramifications of a crime committed forty years ago. Likewise to Dr. William Ernoehazy, Dr. Arnold Tatar, and Dr. Doug Lyle, for their medical expertise about the symptoms and treatment of tuberculosis forty years ago. And a special shout-out to attorney and neighbor Dan Franks, who turned me onto the book *Rads* (see below).

Don Whiteman and Cathy Jaros were extremely helpful about venture capitalists. And Zoe Sharp and Andy Butler were indispensable for their wealth of information about motorcycles.

Northfield Fire Chief Mike Nystrand, Agent Rick Witt of State Farm, and Bill Riordan, of Riordan and Scully, all spent an untold amount of time explaining arson and insurance issues. And thanks to Marcus Wynne who introduced me to the HideAway knife.

Judy Bobalik, Sean Chercover, Michael Dymmoch, and David Walker have always supplied inspiration and support, and put up with my whining. Marianne Halbert, in Indianapolis, helped brainstorm the ending. And Alison Janssen had a terrific idea for a revision. Lee Child not only gave me a generous blurb, but corrected my misinformation about southpaws.

And a special thank you to Allium Press, and Emily Victorson, who saw the potential of *Fire* and helped bring it to life.

It goes without saying that any mistakes remaining are mine, not those of the good people cited above. To that end, I admit I took liberties with the Women's Health Clinic described in the book. In reality, the Chicago Women's Health Center opened in 1975, not 1970. Artistic license made me move it.

Several books and articles were very helpful. Among them is *California Power and Light*, by Don Winslow, whose description of an arson fire is unparalleled. Another helpful text was *Rads: The 1970 Bombing of the Army Math Research Center at the University of Wisconsin and Its Aftermath*, by Tom Bates.

Finally, a 2002 article in *The Washington Post*, titled: *I Was a Terrorist. Where Did It Come From, the Hatred That Led Pampered Americans to Want to Bring Down the System in the 1960s?*, by Jonathan Lerner, was fascinating.

Thank you, all.

Try now we can only lose
And our love become a funeral pyre
Come on baby, light my fire
Try to set the night on fire

Light My Fire, The Doors, 1967

Set the Night on Fire

Part One

The Present

ONE

November

Dar Gantner was surprised when Rain showed up at the restaurant. He hadn't counted on her to return his call. After a while he wondered why he'd even tried. His life had been a series of failures. Grandiose plans but flawed execution. No follow-through, no "closure," as they called it now. It wasn't for want of trying. God, or fate, or whatever you called the monkey upstairs, obviously had a plan for him. It just wasn't the same plan he had.

She wasn't the first person he called when he got out. That honor went to Teddy. He hadn't gotten through, of course. He left a message and gave them the number of the cell he'd bought with his first paycheck. Good for a month, they said. Then you threw it away. He remembered exiting the big box store, appalled at how disposable capitalism had become. At the same time, he was fascinated by phones smaller than a pack of cigarettes. Dick Tracy's wrist-phone come to life.

Rain hadn't been hard to find, once he remembered her real name. She'd returned his call a day later and after a shocked silence asked where he was. He'd come first to Old Town, the only part of Chicago he knew well, but the prices were too steep so he ended up in Rogers Park. He heard the pity in her voice when he said he was washing dishes. But he might be promoted to waiter or even bartender, he said, hoping he sounded cheery. Then he asked for a favor.

"Can you track someone down for me?"

"Depends who it is," she'd replied.

Four days later she appeared at the restaurant just before closing. He'd been scouring a large pot, thinking about the instantaneous global connections Thomas Friedman described in *The World is Flat*. He'd always been a voracious reader, and while reading was a poor man's substitute for experience, he had a hole of four decades to fill. He glanced up as she pushed through the swinging door.

She immediately picked him out. "You look exactly the same, Dar."

Dar had never been vain, but he knew she was flattering him. Tall but stooped from years of inactivity, he had a paunch, no matter how many sit-ups he did. His dark hair, now salted with gray, had thinned, and age spots freckled his skin. Only his eyes looked the same, he'd been told. Deep-set and so smoky you couldn't tell where his iris ended and his pupil began. Eyes with such a piercing expression that people figured he was as crazy as a loon and crossed the street rather than walk past him. They had helped him inside, those eyes. People generally left him alone.

Now, he and Rain exchanged one of those half-hearted hugs you give when you don't know what else to do. Rain was smaller than he remembered, but in blue jeans and a sweater she still cut a trim figure. Her ashy hair was still long and straight. But her face was lined, and her glasses, which she'd worn back then, too, seemed thicker.

She glanced around the kitchen. Disappointed, he figured. She had a point. Paint was peeling off the walls, the floors were chipped linoleum, and most of the equipment was circa 1950. "How 'bout I wait for you in the Golden Nugget on Lawrence? It's open twenty-four-hours."

"Okay," he said. "I'm off in twenty minutes."

"You won't disappear again?"

He flashed what he hoped was a reassuring smile. "Wild horses . . . "

She smiled weakly and went back out.

Half an hour later, he passed underneath the yellow sign outside the Golden Nugget restaurant. A video camera tilted down toward the sidewalk. He'd noticed them in stores, office buildings, parking lots, street corners. Big Brother was now ubiquitous.

Inside, the staff outnumbered the customers. Two waitresses chatted up the short order cook at the pass-through behind the counter. Rain, in a booth at the back, waved him over. As he sat down, one of the waitresses shuffled over and asked tiredly what he wanted.

Rain peered at him over her glasses. "It's on me."

He nodded his thanks, not even bothering to muster a show of pride. He was short on cash, and she knew it. Then again, that was nothing new. He ordered a BLT with fries and coffee. Rain shook her head when the waitress turned to her, "Nothing."

Rain waited till the waitress poured his coffee and went away. Then she announced, "Alix's brother lives in Michigan. In their old summer home. A big ass house on the lake. Near Grand Haven."

"Thank you." He put down his cup. "I guess I'm not surprised."

Rain shrugged. "The house is on a private road. There's a gatehouse, and they won't let you in unless you've been cleared in advance."

Dar thought about it. Then, "How'd you find out?"

"It wasn't hard. I Googled him."

He sank back. He'd only just discovered Google, at the library, but he was fascinated by its reach. The waitress brought his sandwich.

"Why do you want to know about her brother?"

Dar explained.

"Have you called Casey?" she asked. Rain had always been blunt, he remembered.

Dar chewed his food. "I didn't think he'd want to see me."

"Casey isn't a bitter man."

"Have you been in touch with him?"

"Only once. When Payton . . ." She cut herself off. "I hear about him, though. Casey, that is. He's very successful." She paused. "What about Teddy? I don't expect you'd want to hear from him."

"Actually, I put in a call to him the other day."

Rain set down her cup so hard that it clattered on the saucer. "Why . . . I don't . . . why did you do that?" she sputtered.

Dar speared his pickle with his fork. "Teddy and I have unfinished business."

Rain had been a woman who'd shown no fear, even when she was arrested during the Convention in '68. But now she looked small and vulnerable and scared. "Dar, does he know where you are?"

Dar thought back to the message he'd left. Did he mention he was in Chicago? He had. "Why?"

She squeezed her eyes shut.

"What's the problem?"

She opened her eyes. "You need to watch your back, okay? You remember what we used to think about Teddy?"

"What you used to think."

"Listen to me. About fifteen years ago I got a package in the mail."

Dar looked over, interested.

"Small. Carefully wrapped. No return address. Just a note with it that said, 'You were right.'" She paused. "Took me a while to figure out who sent it and what it meant."

"And?"

"It was from Payton. And it contains something that . . . well, it has to do with Teddy."

"What?"

She shook her head. "Not here. Not now. But it's important, and it's in a safe place. If anything—ever—happens to me, you need to know that."

"Still the theatrical one." He smiled. "The Sixties are over, Rain."

Her gaze hardened. "You can't tell me you haven't thought about it over the years."

"I've had forty years to think about everything."

"Yeah, well, a month or so after I got the package, Payton had that fatal car 'accident.'"

Dar laid his fork down.

"Like I said, watch your back."

TWO

The next day Dar headed to the Army-Navy Surplus store and bought a pair of faded khakis, a blue shirt, and a pea coat. Then, wearing his new clothes, he boarded a bus for Grand Haven. The ride around the eastern shore of Lake Michigan took over six hours, with stops in Gary, St. Joseph, and Holland. He'd grown up near Detroit, and although Grand Haven was on the other side of the state, he was familiar with the area. One of the most popular resorts in Michigan in summer, the town now looked November bleak. A gunmetal sky threatened snow, and an icy lake breeze penetrated his jacket.

He tried to hitch a ride to the estate—Rain said it was off the road to Ferrysburg. But traffic was thin, and no one picked him up. He ended up making the three-mile trip on foot. He kept the lake in his sights to guide him, its angry whitecaps a grim reminder of why he had come. He was rounding a bend when he had the sensation he was being watched. He spun around. Nothing—except the desolate landscape.

It had been a while since he'd hiked this far, and he had to stop to catch his breath. His eyes watered. He had no gloves, and he'd forgotten how bitter the wind off the lake could be. Part of him wanted to catch the bus back to Chicago. Despite the gassy smell and cramped seats, it would be blessedly warm.

It took over an hour to reach the estate. He halted in front of a double iron fence. On one side was a small wooden gatehouse. Rain had said there was a twenty-four hour security guard, but no one was there. He grasped one of the iron bars and pulled. Nothing. He blew on his hands and tried again. Still nothing.

He walked to the gatehouse. It was unlocked. Inside, the booth wasn't heated, but there was some shelter from the elements. He stamped his feet, then slid onto a metal stool beneath a window. His nose had started to drip, and he rubbed his wind-burned skin, wondering if he would ever be warm again. All his energy had been devoted to getting this far; now that he was here, he wasn't sure what to do. He looked around for a phone or intercom. There was nothing inside the gatehouse, but a small box was attached to the opposite side of the gate. He sighed. He wasn't anxious to go back out.

He closed his eyes, willing his mantra into his thoughts. Forty years ago he'd taken up transcendental meditation, and he still used it occasionally. It relaxed him, and at the same time fueled him with energy. The inherent contradiction of the mind. He started to mentally chant the syllables. A moment later the crunch of wheels on gravel made his eyes fly open.

A black Cadillac rolled to a stop on the other side of the gate. Two men were in the car. Both wore dark suits. The driver wore shades, though there was no sun. The man in the passenger seat held a phone to his ear. Neither seemed to notice Dar. The man in the passenger seat nodded. As he did, the gate swung open and the Cadillac glided through.

Dar waited until the car had turned onto the main road and was out of sight. Then he jumped off the stool and hurried out. The gate was swinging shut. He slipped through before it closed.

He trudged another half mile past a colorless wooded area. Tree branches shivered in the wind, producing sharp angles of black against the sky. As he drew closer, he smelled the faint scent of evergreens— white pine, he thought.

The woods ended unexpectedly, and a house came into view. It was old, and irregularly shaped, as if it had been added onto several times. Gabled roofs were pitched at different angles, and the occasional turret sprang up at their intersections. There seemed to be three main wings, but they folded back on each other so that it was difficult to tell where one stopped and the next began. Landscaping concealed much of the exterior, but the walls he could see were a faded white.

He walked up to a red door, the only bit of color he'd seen since he got off the bus. There was no buzzer, so he lifted a brass knocker and let it thump against the wood. Footsteps sounded almost immediately, as if someone was waiting for him.

The man who opened the door was about six feet tall and slim. He had a full head of thick white hair, but his eyes were small and hooded, and puffy pockets of skin lay underneath. He wore tailored wool slacks, and his gray sweater looked so soft and warm Dar wished he could wrap himself in it.

"What did you forget?" he asked irritably.

Dar spread his hands. "Sorry?"

Startled, the man stepped back. "You're not . . . " As he inspected Dar, his eyes turned quizzical. "Who are you? How did you get in here?"

"My name is Dar Gantner, and I came through the gate when the Cadillac went out."

The man didn't move, but his eyebrows rose in what looked like mild surprise. After a moment, he said, "Well, well. We finally meet." He looked Dar up and down. "You look frozen. Why don't you come in?"

Dar nodded. "Thank you."

As he stepped inside, the man said, "I'm Philip Kerr. But you already knew that." He turned around and pressed a buzzer on the wall beside the door. "Manuela, please bring tea for us in the study."

A heavily accented female voice replied through the intercom. "Hokay."

Kerr turned around. "Follow me."

Dar was surprised. Based on the one dinner he'd shared with Kerr's father many years ago, the son wasn't what he expected. Then again, he didn't really know the Kerr family—or Rain or Casey—any more. He followed Kerr down a long hall. Kerr's shoes clacked on the terracotta floor. Dar's sneakers were silent. Kerr led him into a small, cozy room with a view of Lake Michigan. He motioned to two comfortable leather chairs in front of the window. "Please. Sit."

Dar sat and gazed out the window. A lonely pier extended out from the shore. Angry waves pounded its moorings. He could get lost in those waves.

Kerr cleared his throat. "So, what can I do for you, after all these years?"

Dar brought his focus back. "I'm grateful you're seeing me. I don't think your father would have been as civil."

Kerr let out a small smile. "I am not my father."

"I see." Dar straightened. "I don't think I need to go over my past. You know it. But I got a letter while I was inside, and I wanted to ask you about it."

Kerr cocked his head.

"It was from Joanna Kerr."

Kerr froze for a moment. "My ex-wife."

Dar nodded. "The letter said that Sebastian Kerr changed his will on his deathbed. That he always regretted the way he treated his daughter. And that he wanted to make amends and willed half his fortune to Alix's children."

Kerr tilted his head.

"The letter also said that you covered it up. Made it all go away."

Kerr looked like he was going to say something, but the maid came in balancing a tray filled with a teapot, two cups and saucers, and a plate of shortbread biscuits. She set the tray down on a small table between the chairs. Her face was an empty mask. Hired help were like that, Dar knew. Hiding their bitterness or ambition or resignation under the guise of servitude.

"Thank you, Manuela," Kerr said, with just a touch of superiority.

The woman retreated.

"You were saying?" Kerr took a bite of a biscuit.

"I'm not here for myself, you understand," Dar said. "Or the past. I'm here to advocate for the next generation."

Kerr took his time pouring the tea. He placed a biscuit on both of their saucers. He stirred his tea, picked it up and sipped. "In that case I'm afraid your trip has been a waste of time, Mr. Gantner."

Dar eyed Kerr as he picked up his own tea. "How so?"

Kerr set his cup down. "My wife and I divorced several years ago. It was a . . . well . . . it was contentious. She made all sorts of accusations

8

about me that weren't true, in an effort to ensure she got what she believed was her due. I'm afraid that was one of the charges." He took another bite of his biscuit. "It was all made up. Total fiction. We never had any children, you know. Maybe that played a role in her . . . behavior. You know, the barren mother." He sighed. "In any event, it became clear she'd say anything to discredit me. You know how that goes."

Dar winced.

"Pardon me. I apologize." Kerr looked contrite. "It was evident she wanted revenge. For what, I'm not sure. She was . . . unstable."

Dar kept his mouth shut.

Kerr went on. "People are strange, you know? For years, I encouraged my father to make peace with the past." He gave a little shrug. "But he was stubborn. He wouldn't go there."

"He continued to blame me?" Dar asked.

"I'm afraid he did." Kerr gave him another small smile. "Such a waste of energy, don't you agree?" He sighed. "You've come a long way. I just wish I had better news."

What had he expected, Dar wondered on the bus back to Chicago. That it would all fall together without a hitch? He wasn't that naïve. Truth was he'd never responded to Joanna Kerr's letter. At the time he received it, he didn't trust anyone whose name was Kerr. He gazed out the window. At least he had tried.

He thought about calling Rain but decided against it. He didn't sense that she wanted to reconnect in any significant way. She was just fulfilling an obligation. Exhausted, still feeling the cold deep in his bones, he stared at the deepening dusk until the thrum of the bus's motor lulled him to sleep.

Back in Chicago, he walked from the bus station to the El, got off at Loyola, and headed to his lodgings. A small room in a shabby apartment-hotel on Broadway, the place was due to be torn down, which was why he'd been able to snag a room—someone hoping to squeeze out a few more bucks before the building was razed. He didn't mind. The privacy, after so many years of communal living, was priceless.

He pushed through the door and walked past the desk. The place was supposed to have a twenty-four-hour attendant. He occasionally spotted a young African man, a Loyola student probably, who spoke English with a British lilt. Tonight, though, no one was there. He bypassed the rickety elevator and climbed the stairs to the third floor. He should have picked up something to eat, but he was too tired and cold to go back out. He fished out his key and inserted it into the lock.

The door was unlocked. Dar clearly remembered locking it before he left.

He pressed his ear to the door. He heard nothing, but that didn't mean someone wasn't on the other side. He tried to recall who knew where he was. Rain, of course. Casey, if Rain had told him. He'd left a message for Teddy, too.

Uneasiness rippled through him. Maybe it was the street gangs. He knew they were a problem in neighborhoods like this. Maybe they'd broken in. The conveniently AWOL desk attendant might be their accomplice.

He bent down, looking for a telltale sliver of light under the door. Nothing. If someone was in his room, they were in the dark. He straightened. If he threw the door open, he'd have the element of surprise. He grabbed the doorknob, turned it, and shoved open the door. It swung wide. The light switch was to his right. He snapped it on.

No one was there, but someone had been. His mattress was pulled off the frame, half of it now slumped on the floor. Bits of orange clung to it. Drawing closer, he saw they were tufts of foam rubber. Someone had slashed through it, and the stuffing had spilled out. The drawers to the bureau were pulled out, too, and his few items of clothing were balled on the floor. The backpack he'd picked up a few days ago was in a corner. In the bathroom, the door to the medicine cabinet was open, his toiletries scattered.

He leaned against the wall, willing his pulse to slow. He had nothing of value. They certainly hadn't made a secret of their visit; they hadn't even locked the door when they left. Maybe they wanted Dar to know they'd been here. That they could—and did—find him.

But why?

He took another breath. He was exhausted, hungry, and wanted to sleep. Instead, he picked up his backpack, threw in his clothes and toilet articles. He added the two books he'd checked out of the library. He dropped his key on the bureau. Slinging the backpack over his shoulder, he exited the room and crept down the steps. The desk was still unoccupied. He walked to the front door, then changed his mind and turned down a hallway. He pushed through a side door into the alley.

As casually as he could, he strolled back to Broadway, all the while searching the shadows. His left hand brushed against his cell phone in his pocket. He pulled it out. The screen indicated two missed calls. There was some kind of tracking device in cell phones these days, he'd read. With the right kind of equipment, you could figure out exactly where the cell phone—and its user—were. Across the street he spotted a large metal dumpster at the mouth of another alley. He crossed over. A couple was walking down the sidewalk, arm in arm. Neither paid any attention to him. He glanced around. Then he lifted the dumpster's metal cover and dropped in the phone.

THREE

December

You can't un-ring a bell, Rain thought, as she pulled up to Casey Hilliard's home. But that doesn't keep some people from trying. The gravel under her wheels crackled as she eased up the driveway. Casey had done well. Something to do with venture capitalism, she recalled. If his house was any indication, this was beyond well. A red brick Georgian with white columns, set back from the road on one of those Winnetka streets you had to know was there in order to find it. Woods hugged three sides of the lot.

She parked her dusty Corolla in between a Jeep Wrangler and a blue sports car and climbed out. It was a frigid night, and a stiff lake breeze swirled the leaves into tiny eddies before they sank to the ground. She buttoned her jacket and padded to the enormous paneled door. Her Birkenstocks hardly made any noise. She smiled. From Birkenstock to Birkenstock in forty years. Like that French saying, "Plus ça change, plus c'est la même chose." Who said that, she wondered. Voltaire? Montaigne? Or some obscure philosopher whose name was forever lost to history?

She ran her hands down her thighs, smoothing out imaginary wrinkles in her jeans. She'd only talked to Casey once over the years, after Payton had his "accident" and they'd agreed to stay below the radar. She took in a breath and pressed the doorbell. She hoped he would see her. He had to. Things had changed.

Casey Hilliard leaned on his cane as he hobbled to his desk. Despite the dim light from a lamp, Rain could see he hadn't changed much. His hair was mostly silver, but there was still plenty of it. Craggy lines weathered his face, but he had the same blue eyes, eyes that always looked cheerful even during solemn occasions. She remembered how he used to make her feel—that life was an adventure and you wanted to share it with him. He was seductive that way. He knew people from all walks of life, and the connections he made were his greatest gift. Look how he'd brought them together.

"When was he released?" Casey asked.

"A few weeks ago." She leaned back in a well-worn leather chair.

"You saw him?"

She nodded.

"How?"

"He found me. I haven't made a secret of my life," she said. "I'm all over the Internet."

"What did he want?"

She ran a hand through her hair—she'd always been vain about it. Her best feature, long and straight, it was an unusual color—an ashy, almost silver, blonde that looked bright or dark, depending on the light.

"It's the color of rain," Alix had pronounced one night, all of them high in the Old Town apartment.

Casey had jerked his head up. "Far out, Alix. You're right!"

"From now on, you are no longer Julie. We dub you Rain." Alix giggled. "Bow your head."

Rain had complied, and Alix touched her shoulders with a stick. "It is done," she said triumphantly.

And it was. From that day on, no one ever called her Julie again. And from that day on, Rain made sure her hair stayed the same color. Even now, forty years later, it was the same silver blonde.

"Rain," Casey repeated now. "What did Dar want?"

"I think he wanted to see you."

Casey didn't react.

13

"I know, Casey," Rain said. It was the closest she could come to compassion. She took a breath. "He also wanted to know where Alix's family was. Something about a letter he got that could change things."

Casey frowned. "Her parents are gone."

"Her brother's still around."

"Of course." He nodded wearily. "Did you tell him?"

She chose her words carefully. "It . . . it was difficult not to."

Casey's eyes flashed. "Did he threaten you?"

"No." She hesitated. "But he said he called Teddy."

A stricken look came over Casey. "Why the hell did he do that?"

"He said they had 'unfinished business.'"

He lowered his head in his hands. "Oh, god."

"You had to know this could happen at some point."

He shook his head. "I thought . . . well, I'd hoped . . . "

"Hope makes you ignore reality."

He shot her a glance, as if she'd overstepped her bounds. It was her first indication that perhaps Casey had changed in some subtle, indefinable way.

"What was he like?" he asked. "Dar, I mean . . . "

"He . . . he didn't say much." She glanced around the room, taking in the antique desk, the fancy computer, the watercolors on the walls. Casey had done very well indeed. "It's strange, you know? For years we thought it was Alix's father. Or Teddy's. We were wrong."

"I guess we can thank Payton for that."

Rain kept her mouth shut. She didn't feel vindicated.

"There's something you're not telling me," Casey said. "What?"

Again she hesitated. "I tried to find Dar again. After we talked . . . but I couldn't."

The color drained from Casey's face. "What do you mean?"

"The cell he'd been using was disconnected. So I drove to the place where he said he was staying. He was gone. No forwarding address. Nothing."

"Jesus. Do you think . . . "

She cut him off. "If they did, they didn't waste any time."

"They can't afford to."

They were quiet for a moment. Then Casey said, "What are you thinking?"

"I'm thinking time doesn't change people, Casey. And when you have something to lose . . . "

"And you have the resources . . . " He sat down at the computer. She could tell his mind was racing. "Rain," he said, finally looking up. "You need to be careful."

"Likewise, Casey." She got up and started toward the door. She stopped and called over her shoulder. "By the way, Merry Christmas."

Rain turned onto I-94 for the drive back to Wisconsin. She'd done the right thing—she owed Casey that much. She'd always been the "go-to" girl, the person who tried to fix their problems. Until the end when everything spiraled out of control. She'd been Alix's friend from the beginning. Alix needed someone to like her just for who she was. God knows it wasn't hard. Despite everything, Alix was a sweet girl. And dogged, once she decided what she wanted.

Rain remembered the night they met at Oak Street Beach. They'd hit it off right away, she and Casey and Alix. They'd met Dar—then Payton and Teddy—later that night in Grant Park, and they'd hooked up for the convention.

She remembered their conversations, discussions that went on all night. How the military-industrial complex had imposed its will on a quiet little country with no provocation. How no one should accept the hypocrisy and corruption of the establishment. How the Movement would transform society into something equitable and wholesome and good.

Everything was possible back then. As long as they were focused on the same goals. And Dar made sure of that. He'd been eloquent. And persuasive. When he spoke, it felt right—the way it should be.

The others felt it too. Together, they were invincible, a bright light rallying against the darkness.

Now, Rain sped past the Mars Cheese outlet, so swept up in her memories that she didn't notice the headlights behind her. She was passing a dark stretch of highway, one of the few not dotted by neon lights and signs, when she looked in the rearview mirror. The headlights behind her seemed higher up than cars'. Must be a truck or a van. She thought she saw a logo of some sort above the cab.

She shielded her eyes. The van was close. Too close. Annoyance flashed through her. "Back off, buster."

She pulled to the right. But the other driver did too, staying on her tail. Who was this jerk? She had half a mind to veer off the road at the next exit. She looked for a highway sign, but—of course—just when she needed one, there was nothing.

The lights drew closer, turning the rearview into a rectangular bar of light. Then something thumped the rear of her car. The Corolla lurched, and Rain nearly lost control of the wheel. What the . . .? Another whack. The car slipped sideways. The jerk was trying to run her off the road!

She floored the gas, but the creep was still locked on her tail. Her pursuer hit the bumper again. The sensation made her realize how light and fragile her Toyota really was.

Shit! She was losing control. She frantically wrenched the wheel to the right, but nothing happened. Somehow the vehicle on her tail was preventing her from turning. Then, without warning, something snapped, and the Corolla veered sharply right. The forward momentum pitched the car over the shoulder to a ditch, where it flipped over. It finally stopped at the edge of a field a few yards from a large "This Property Under Development" sign.

The van slowed and pulled onto the shoulder. A man opened the driver's door, jumped down, and ran back to the Corolla. The engine was still running, but he saw no movement inside. He pulled something from his pocket, lit it, and tossed it. He was heading back to the truck when the car exploded.

FOUR

The Christmas lights are busted." Danny Hilliard pulled the plug out of the wall.

His sister, Lila, sipped her coffee. "They were working last night."

"Well, they're not this morning."

"Weren't you the last person to fiddle with them?"

"Oh. So it's my fault?"

"That's not what I meant."

"Save it for the jury, Lila." Danny's eyes narrowed. "You're always quick to lay the blame on me whenever something gets screwed up. I'm going upstairs. I hate fucking Christmas." He stomped out of the room.

Lila watched his retreating back. Maybe coming home wasn't such a great idea. She hadn't planned to—not because of her father. He needed her, and she loved being needed. But Danny, her twin, was another story. They'd been inseparable as children. "That's what comes of being womb-mates," her father would joke. By the time they were teenagers, though, Danny had become restless, clearly uncomfortable in his own skin. Discomfort turned to self-pity, and Danny turned into a victim, a victim who often made Lila his oppressor.

In fact, she was surprised Danny had come "home" for the holidays. His Evanston condo was only a couple of miles away, but their father liked having his kids under his roof over Christmas. When Danny acquiesced, Lila figured it was a hopeful sign. Maybe Danny was putting away his childhood resentments. Now, she wasn't so sure. She hoped he wasn't into drugs again. It would break her father's heart.

She put down her cup, stood up, and went to the tree, a seven-foot Douglas fir. It had been delivered yesterday. She took one of the strands of lights and inspected the little white label affixed to the wire. Not a UL label—only a bunch of letters and numbers.

She went over and plugged the cord back into the outlet. Tiny bursts of pink and blue and green twinkled through the branches. She frowned. The lights were working now. Must be a short. She looked at the boxes of decorations she'd hauled down from the attic, dozens of ornaments nestled in layers of tissue paper. They were supposed to decorate the tree this afternoon. Hot buttered rum and tree-trimming—it was a Hilliard family tradition. Aunt Valerie would be joining them. Lila decided to drive over to Blaine's and pick up some new lights.

She unplugged the lights and went upstairs. Dad had never redecorated her room when she left. High school mementos were tucked into the corners of her mirror, stuffed animals piled in the corner. A framed eight-by-ten photograph of Gramum sat on her bureau. It had been six years, but she still missed her grandmother. Her death had broken a link in Lila's already tiny universe. Wasn't living supposed to expand her horizons? Bring in new experiences and people? Then why did hers feel like it was constricting?

She threw on a thick sweater, jeans, and boots, then went into the bathroom. She brushed her hair back and pulled it into a ponytail. Dark hair, dark eyes. My little gypsy, Dad used to call her. So unlike Danny, with his light hair and blue eyes. No one ever mistook them for twins; some couldn't believe they were siblings. If she hadn't seen the baby pictures, photos in which Gramum dressed them alike—at least until they were two—she might not have believed it herself.

She washed her face. She was on the wrong side of her thirties; she could use some make-up. She settled for a swipe of lip gloss. That was another Gramumism: "Even when you're in a hurry, try to throw on some lipstick. It gives you a finished look."

She clattered down the back steps to the mud room and pulled her parka off the hook. She went to her father's study and knocked.

"Come in."

She opened the door. Small bars of daylight seeped in around the edges of closed curtains. The only other light in the room came from a computer monitor. Her father was bent over it, his face a pale shade of blue.

"Hi, Dad. Just wanted to tell you I'm going out."

"Okay, sweetheart."

"Do you need anything?"

"I'm fine. I was just checking the news."

She looked around for the newspaper, but didn't see it. A smile tugged at her lips. Along with everything else, her father got his news online these days. Talk about early adopters. He'd been there during the first days of the Internet. He and Al Gore.

"Anything new?"

He shrugged. "The Bulls won. The Bears lost." He looked up, his eyes squinting slightly, as if he was seeing her for the first time. "Where did you say you were going?"

"The tree lights aren't working right. I'm going to pick up some new ones."

"We're trimming it this afternoon."

"That's why I'm going now." She walked over and kissed the top of his head. "Where's Sadie? I didn't see her in the kitchen."

Their housekeeper since the twins were small, Sadie took care of cuts and scrapes, soothed frayed tempers, and had a big lap to curl up in. Best of all, she baked the most delicious pies east of the Mississippi. Lila remembered when she was seven. Her father and brother were away on a camping trip and she'd been invited to a neighbor's house for dinner. But Sadie had made a blueberry pie, Lila's favorite. When it came time for dessert at the neighbors', Lila announced she'd rather go home for Sadie's pie. She got a smart slap on her butt when her father came home. By then, though, she'd had several slices.

"Sometimes she gets stuck in traffic," her father said, bringing her back to the present.

"You sure you don't need anything, Dad?" She pointed to the cane propped up against the desk. "For your hip?"

"For Christ's sake, Lila, I'm not crippled. I just had a hip replacement."

"I know."

"I should have had it done years ago." He shooed her out. "Get out of here. And don't worry about Sadie. She'll be here."

"She'd better. She promised to make blueberry pie."

Her father looked her over. "Tell me something. How do you stay so thin when you're always talking about food? Something you just ate, something you're planning to eat, something you wish you could eat?"

"That's the secret. You burn all your calories thinking and talking about food rather than eating."

Her father waved her out, but he was laughing.

"Can I take the Miata?" Lila didn't want to risk alienating Danny further by taking his Jeep.

He opened his desk drawer, fished out the keys, and tossed them over.

Outside she sniffed the cold, metallic smell that precedes snow. A dirty gray overcast sky confirmed it. A white Christmas wouldn't be so bad. She backed the Miata down the driveway. She had to stop at the corner of Willow Road while a rental truck made a slow turn onto the private lane. Strange, she thought to herself, who moved a few days before Christmas?

Blaine's was a variety store that never changed. Tucked away on a quiet street in Winnetka, it stocked everything people needed, plus things they didn't know they needed until they saw them. The man who owned it, Sam Blaine, had been bought out by his niece a few years ago, but he still showed up for work every day. Now in his eighties, stooped, with white hair, he knew exactly where everything was.

"Hi, Sam." Lila stopped to chat. "Why aren't you in Florida?"

"We're leaving after New Years, honey." Everyone was "honey" to Sam. Had been for fifty years. She doubted he even knew her real name. "Can't abandon the fort during our busiest season now, can I?"

She smiled and asked him where the Christmas lights were. He pointed to an aisle on the far side of the store. She found them easily and picked up two boxes. The store was warm, and she unzipped her parka. She browsed in the aisles, checking out oven mitts, toys, first aid boxes, and cards. She remembered when Danny started a collection of tiny metal cars. He left them scattered all over the house until Gramum, tripping for the umpteenth time, threatened to move out if he didn't put them all in one place.

She paid for the lights, wondering how much longer Blaine's would be around. Prime North Shore property with its own parking lot in back. Developers had to be salivating over the land. If Sam's niece was my client, she thought, I'd tell her to wait for the old man to die, then sell the place and make a killing. But that was the professional voice. Not the little girl who'd happily shopped in what was then a kid's paradise.

She was walking back to the parking lot when she heard a high-pitched, clear voice.

"Is that you, Lila?"

As she turned around, a woman lumbered toward her. She was red-cheeked and plump, and her padding of winter gear accentuated her roundness. Something about her was familiar. Especially her voice.

"It is you!" The woman came closer, her face breaking into a grin.

Finally Lila recognized her. "Annie Gossage! How are you? It's got to be fifteen years."

Annie had lived a block away from Lila. They'd gone to the same schools: Crow Island, Washburne, New Trier. They'd been in Brownies together, then Girl Scouts, until Lila quit after loudly comparing Scouts to the Hitler Youth. Annie's mother had been the troop leader.

"How wonderful to see you!" Annie exclaimed. Fortunately, she didn't seem to hold a grudge.

As a girl Annie had been graceless and self-conscious. That was gone now, Lila noted, a sunny cheerfulness in its place. "You look terrific, Annie."

"You too!" Annie rested a hand on Lila's shoulder. "We really should catch up."

Lila glanced at her watch. Dad was probably still working. Danny was probably sulking. It might be fun to do something spontaneous like catch up with an old friend. Weren't these the life moments she was supposed to savor? "You know, I probably should get home . . . but, hey, what the hell!"

Annie beamed and pointed to a shop on the corner of Elm next to the book store. "Let's get coffee."

Ten minutes later, Lila was sipping a latte, telling Annie about her job at Peabody Stern, a blue-stocking financial management firm in New York.

"Did you major in business?" Annie asked.

Lila shook her head. "Philosophy, which, of course, isn't practical for anything. Luckily, Peabody didn't care. Actually, they don't really want anyone with real experience. Makes it easier to train you in the Peabody Stern tradition."

"So now you're an investment counselor?"

"Financial planner."

"I see."

"I'm just grateful to have a job. In this economy."

Annie nodded. "You always were a whiz at math."

Lila dipped her head. Her life revolved around numbers: P&Ls, financial statements, interest rates, market spreads. Despite the financial meltdown, she trusted them. Numbers were precise, straightforward symbols that people implicitly agreed upon. They offered clarity. At the same time they were flexible. You could make a number sound large or small depending on the context: "Ten thousand dollars would feed a family of four for a year," or "Ten thousand dollars wouldn't even pay for the windshield wiper on an F-16."

"And a vice-president too?" Annie gushed.

Lila's knee pumped up and down. It seemed gauche to dwell on her professional achievements with Annie. She'd achieved a certain success; she'd worked damn hard for it. But she'd paid a price. Her boyfriend thought she was judgmental and cold, so they'd broken up. Now her brother apparently agreed. But Annie didn't need to hear that. Lila hid behind a smile. "What about you, Annie?"

"Me?" Annie waved a hand. "Oh, I'm just a soccer mom. You know, three kids, PTA, dinner on the table by six. Boring stuff."

"What you're doing is much more important than steering someone into the right mutual fund," Lila said, although she wasn't sure whether she believed it. She'd never seen herself as a wife and mother. She didn't "keep house." She hardly even cooked.

"I know. I love my life. I don't want to be any other place." Annie broke off a chunk of coffee cake, stuffed it in her mouth, and chewed with her mouth open. She'd done that in grade school too, Lila recalled.

"How's Danny?" Annie asked tentatively.

She was remembering the Danny from high school, Lila thought. Rebellious, rambunctious, always in trouble. The opposite of Lila: disciplined, conscientious, the girl who colored between the lines.

"Danny's working at Dad's firm."

"How nice for both of them," Annie sounded unenthusiastic. "So . . . " A coy look came over her. "Any men in your life?"

Lila smiled gamely. "Not any more."

"Oh?" Annie chewed more cake.

"There was someone, but we broke up."

"That had to be hard. I'm sorry."

Lila stiffened. What did Annie know about failed relationships? She'd married her high school boyfriend, a chemistry nerd named Ben. And from what she was saying, they were still deliriously happy.

Her thoughts were interrupted by the sound of a siren. A moment later, three fire engines, two trucks, and a rescue vehicle raced down Elm Street.

Annie frowned. "Oh, I don't like that."

"What?"

"Sirens." Annie shivered. "I never like to think of people's houses burning down. Especially over the holidays."

"Maybe it's a false alarm." Lila finished her drink.

"Maybe." Annie didn't look convinced. "Three engines, two trucks, that's an initial alarm. With luck, it'll be the only one."

"What do you mean?"

"The higher the alarm, the more serious the fire. For example, a three alarm fire could be as many as nine engines, six trucks . . . you know, multiples of three."

"How do you know all that stuff?"

"Ben volunteers at the fire department. He loves it."

An uneasy feeling spilled over Lila. She stood up and pitched her empty cup into the trash. "Well, it's been great seeing you, Annie, but I'd better go. Merry Christmas."

Annie nodded, as if she understood they'd exhausted the possibilities of superficial conversation, and it was time to go back into their separate worlds. She stood up and hugged Lila one more time. "I knew you'd go places, Lila. You were always such a go-getter. Give my love to your Dad. And have a great holiday."

FIVE

But Lila never did give her father Annie's love. She drove home, trying to quash her growing uneasiness. She turned on the radio, hoping classic rock would calm her. It didn't. She snapped it off and cracked open the window. As she turned onto Willow Road, she thought she heard a kind of humming, as if a giant machine or pump had been turned on.

When she reached her street, her stomach pitched. Fire trucks and police cruisers lined both sides of the lane. It was impossible to pass. Red and blue lights strobed the air. Tinny voices filtered through radios and walkie-talkies. Firefighters lugged equipment. People, some of them her neighbors, milled at the corner.

She parked on Willow, threw herself out of the car, and sprinted toward the house. A uniformed cop blocked her path.

"Miss, miss . . . you can't go any further. There's a house fire!"

"I live here!" she shouted, and detoured around him.

The cop yelled and started after her. Lila kept going, her heart pumping. Tiny flakes of soot sifted through the air. Smoke started to crawl into her nose, throat, and eyes.

The house loomed into view. For a moment, everything looked the same—the stolid red brick with white shutters, and graceful columns in front. Then a plume of orange-red flame, and then another, shot up from the house, and everything became surreal. Hoses stretched from the fire trucks to the yard. Streams of water attacked the flames. Rolls of brownish gray smoke rose in the air. Men in thickly padded brown uniforms with iridescent stripes across their chests gathered at her front door.

She gazed at the scene, horror-stricken. The adrenaline that had fueled her run evaporated, and she felt dizzy, almost as if she might collapse. The cop who'd tried to block her caught up to her. "Miss, you need to come with me."

"What . . . what happened?"

The cop steadied her with a hand on her arm. "Don't know yet, but fire at this time of year is most likely a Christmas tree."

She stared at the cop. The Christmas tree? She opened her mouth, but nothing came out. The lights. "But I unplugged them."

"What, ma'am?"

"The lights. They weren't working. I went to buy new ones." She remembered pulling out the plug to the Christmas lights. Had they overheated anyway? Or did she just imagine pulling the plug out of the wall? An iron band of pain clamped her head, just behind her eyes.

"Come with me," the cop repeated.

She let the man lead her to another official. He was dressed differently from the others. White collar. Heavy jacket. The fire chief.

"Where's my father? And my brother?"

The fire chief ran his tongue around his lips. It was a subtle move, but it was enough. The band of pain around her head tightened. Something jerked her arm. "What?"

One of the men squeezed her elbow. "Who was inside when you left?"

She couldn't answer. Saying their names would seal their doom.

"Miss, do you understand what I'm saying?" She nodded. "Who was in the house?"

"My father . . . and my brother."

Firemen hurried back and forth, looking like Michelin men. One stood in front of the house barking orders into a megaphone. Everywhere she looked were grim faces. She wanted to start over. Turn back the clock. If she raced back to the coffee shop, found Annie, and started chatting again, it would all disappear.

"Where were they?" the chief repeated. "Bedrooms? Kitchen?"

"My . . . my brother was in his bedroom when I left."

"Where is it?"

Lila pointed to the second floor window. Flames were now licking the glass of his windows.

"And your father?"

"He was in his study. On the first floor. Near the . . . living room."

An even grimmer look came over the fire chief. He turned around and quietly spoke into a shoulder lapel. She couldn't hear the words.

An ambulance arrived. Two paramedics got out and conferred with the fire chief. They went to the back of the van, opened the rear doors, and pulled out two gurneys. Four firemen carried them to the front door and waited.

Lila started to rock back and forth.

Finally, after what seemed like an eternity, a call went out that the fire was under control. The firemen near the front door slipped masks on their faces, picked up the gurneys, and went inside. Five minutes later there was a commotion at the front door, and two firemen emerged with a gurney. A large plastic bag, curled up, lay on top. Something was inside the bag, curled in a fetal position.

Dear God, don't let it be Daddy. But God wasn't listening.

The firemen carried the gurney to the ambulance. One of the paramedics looped a stethoscope around his neck, bent down, and unzipped the bag. Seconds later, he shook his head and zipped it back up. A few minutes later, two other firemen came out with a second bag. She held her breath as the paramedic repeated the procedure. With the same results.

A black van, which somehow skirted the trucks and police cruisers, pulled into the driveway. The words "Cook County Medical Examiner" were stenciled on its side. Two men got out and joined the paramedics near the ambulance. Lila saw them gesture and nod.

A flake of snow swirled down in front of Lila. Then another. She couldn't feel them. Or hear the hum of equipment, the shouting of firefighters. The only sound in her ears was the pumping of her heart. Loud. Accusatory. In her haste to prove she was the responsible child, the child who fixed things and made them right, she'd screwed it all up.

SIX

Lila sat in her father's office in the middle of January, staring out at the night. Hilliard and Associates occupied a suite of offices on the thirty-fifth floor of the Chase building in downtown Chicago. She'd spent most of the afternoon going through her father's will with his lawyer, and now she was here to pick up his and Danny's personal effects.

Her father had started the firm when she and Danny were babies living at Gramum's. It began as a management consulting firm, but her father had a sixth sense about business and the ones that would be successful. Genial and persuasive, he also had a knack for making connections and attracting capital. Within five years his management consulting practice had evolved into financing new ventures.

At the beginning, he'd taken ownership percentages in lieu of fees. It paid off. The business expanded rapidly, and Casey Hilliard grew wealthy. He bought the house in Winnetka and moved everyone, including Gramum, into it. Though the business bore his name, it eventually became a partnership and was a highly successful venture capital firm for early-stage entrepreneurs, seeding companies all over the globe. Only recently, anticipating his retirement, had he begun to wean himself from his work.

It was after eight now. Lila had started sorting through Danny's cubicle, one of a dozen running down the center of the floor. Her twin had objected to his humble trappings, of course, but her father had been adamant that Danny start at the bottom, just like everyone else.

"Lila didn't," Danny had whined one night when they were together for dinner.

"Stop comparing yourself to your sister," their father admonished him. "You two are different."

"Much to your embarrassment," Danny fired back.

Their father shook his head and patiently explained that people rose to their zeniths at different points in their lives. Lila was a rising star, but Danny would outshine everyone, once he settled down.

Judging from the absence of personal items and decorations, though, Danny hadn't settled down. He probably considered the job a way-station, a temporary breather between gigs. Lila wasn't altogether unsympathetic—the cramped space reminded her of a horse's stall in a barn.

The receptionist had thoughtfully supplied several cardboard boxes, and Lila packed his things: a brush, dental floss, a few pens, and a number of issues of *Entrepreneur Daily*. She found a Blackberry in his desk drawer, but when she tried to turn it on, nothing happened.

Story of Danny's life.

She moved into her father's office. His shelves held an eclectic assortment of books, including *The World is Flat*, *Freakonomics*, and a complete set of Shakespeare's plays. A silver golf ball inscribed by someone Lila didn't know sat on a shelf next to a cloisonné bowl that held paper clips and rubber bands. Lila smiled at that—she had the same thing on her desk at Peabody Stern. One wall was devoted to framed photos: her father shaking hands with Arab sheiks, Bill Clinton, Colin Powell, even Donald Trump. She carefully wrapped them before putting them in a box.

On the bottom shelf was a grouping of framed photos of Danny and Lila: as babies in matching sailor suits, eight years old, fifteen, then separate photos of them as adults. Lila's was a posed portrait taken when she joined Peabody Stern. She was wearing a navy business suit and white blouse, her smile cautious. The shot of Danny, taken in happier times, showed him on the deck of a sailboat. He was hoisting the sail and grinning broadly at the camera. He looked like he was attacking life and swallowing it whole. That was Danny. He was either in love with life or ready to throw it back in your face. She couldn't recall smiling that broadly—ever. Work. Discipline. Responsibility. That was her mantra.

But for what? So she could plan funerals for the people she loved? Pack their personal effects in cardboard boxes?

She watched the twinkling lights of a distant plane slowly arc across the night sky, then glide behind a tall building. Columns of white steam, silent and indifferent, rose from the buildings. The smoke from the fire at home had been brown.

She turned back to the desk. A file drawer on the right needed to be emptied. She dumped the manila folders into a box. There would be time to weed out client files and return them later. No one at the firm was applying any pressure, but she sensed they might if she took too long. Like her, they had a future to contemplate—without Casey Hilliard at the helm.

She gazed at her father's computer. The fire had destroyed his laptop; with luck he'd backed everything up here. She'd have to determine which of his files were personal—it might affect the disposition of the estate. She was just booting up the machine when someone knocked at the door.

"Come in," she called out.

A man about her own age peeked around. Sandy hair swept low across his forehead, dark brown eyes, an athletic build. He looked vaguely familiar.

"Hi." He entered, extending his hand. "I'm Brian Kinnear. I worked with your father. I . . . I'm so sorry."

Lila wasn't sure what she was supposed to say. He probably had no idea what it was like to lose a father. Or a brother. Still, he took the time to make the gesture. "Thank you."

"You're here late," he said.

"What time is it?"

"After nine."

"I didn't realize . . . I should go." She massaged her temples. "How about you? Do you always work the night shift?"

"My team has a presentation tomorrow." He shrugged slightly as if apologizing for the fact that life goes on.

She waited.

"Your . . . your father was my mentor. He taught me everything. I just wanted to say again how sorry I am."

Their eyes met. His expression was sad but kind. Now she remembered him. He'd been at the memorial service. Carrying a white handkerchief, which he stuffed into his pocket when he went through the receiving line.

He motioned toward the boxes. "It's going okay?"

All except one was filled. "I still have to download his personal files from the computer." She peered at the monitor and moved the mouse to the *My Computer* icon.

"What will you do with them?"

She looked over. Another decision to make. She'd been making so many: the memorial service—although Aunt Valerie had helped; what to do with the house; how long to stay in Chicago. She didn't know if she could handle another, even one as simple as where to store her father's files. But Brian had a question on his face.

She sighed. "Burn them to a disc, I guess. Or email them to myself." She went back to the computer. There was a disc drive on the tower. She opened one desk drawer, then another. No CDs. She flipped up her palms. "Any idea where he kept blank CDs?"

"Why don't I get you some from my office?"

"I'd appreciate it."

While he went in search of discs, she sat down and moved the mouse to her father's Internet browser. Might as well check her email. A second later, the Hilliard and Associates website popped up. It was the home page on his browser.

She leaned an elbow on the desk. It was a well-designed site, streamlined and graphically pleasing. They'd preserved as much white space as possible, and the font, in burgundy, was subdued but professional. The H&A logo sat inside in a box at the top with a graphic that looked like a Celtic knot. She'd always meant to ask him why he included it in the logo. With its overlapping knots and braids that seemed to lead nowhere, it was, at the very least, unusual. Now, she'd never have the chance.

A list of partners scrolled down the left side of the page, with links to their bios and areas of expertise. The other pages on the website were listed across the bottom of the page. The middle had only two lines of copy, a quotation:

Small opportunities are often the beginning of great enterprises.
Demosthenes (384 BC–322 BC)

She remembered when her father e-mailed her a link to the beta version of the site. He'd searched for the quotation for weeks, he claimed. When she said she liked it, he sounded pleased. And proud. Like a kid.

Brian came back with the CDs and handed them to Lila.

"I guess you'll be taking Dad's name off the website."

"There's no hurry," he answered quickly, but the way he said it made her think the partners had already discussed it. "Our webmaster's in India anyway."

"India?"

He nodded.

Lila frowned. "You couldn't find someone closer?" There were probably a dozen web designers in the Chase building alone.

"Your father wanted it that way. Lots of companies take advantage of offshore companies for customer service and web design. The cost savings are significant."

"Of course." She paused. "Dad was always in the vanguard."

"That's for sure."

Lila took the CDs, fed them into the drive, and started clicking on various icons.

"So what are you going to do . . . when all this is over?" Brian asked.

"I don't know." Lila started to transfer a folder to the CD. "I took a leave of absence from Peabody Stern." The truth was, with the proceeds of her father's estate, she probably wouldn't need to work. But she hadn't quit her job. That would require another set of decisions, which she wasn't capable of making yet.

"You know, if you're interested, you could join us here."

She looked up. He nodded as though to reinforce the offer.

"Come on. I'm not on your level. Not by a long shot." He looked down quickly. She gazed at him. "They put you up to this, didn't they?"

His ears and neck turned crimson.

"Please tell your partners I'm grateful. But I don't need their . . . your pity."

"That's not it. If you have half the skill your father does . . . did, we could use you."

She leaned back and crossed her arms.

"I didn't mean to imply . . . you know, I'm really screwing this up." He hung his head so ruefully Lila almost smiled.

"Okay. You get a pass for first-timer's nerves."

"Poor play preparation. You will think about it, though?"

This time she did smile. "I will. And, Brian . . . thanks."

SEVEN

It was nearly ten by the time Lila finished transferring her father's files. She dropped the CDs into one of the boxes, wondering how she was going to get the boxes home. Fortunately, Brian came back and told her the mail room would ship them wherever she wanted.

She hesitated. "I'm staying at Danny's condo in Evanston."

"We'll have them sent there. Now don't worry about anything more tonight. Just go home and relax."

"Thanks, Brian. You've been a big help."

She shrugged into her coat and took the elevator to the lobby. As it descended, she realized she was famished. She recalled some vending machines in the cafeteria one floor below. She went down, bought a package of Oreos, and shoved it into her pocket. Outside, she put on her gloves, braided her scarf around her neck and headed east to the parking garage.

There was no snow, but a bitter wind threatened to scrape the skin off her face. She picked up her pace, glad she wouldn't have to take the El or a train back to Evanston. She pulled out the cookies and slid one in her mouth. The sensation of dissolving chocolate and sugar made her realize she couldn't remember when she'd last eaten. A bowl of cereal this morning?

She walked briskly, planning the route back to Danny's condo. Lake Shore Drive to Sheridan or maybe Ridge. She was trying to estimate how long it would take when, out of the corner of her eye, she spotted movement across the street. A figure was walking on the opposite sidewalk. A man. Tall. Dark pants, sneakers, what looked like a bulky parka. A wool hat pulled low on his forehead. Walking in the same direction as she.

An uneasy feeling came over her. There weren't any other pedestrians on the street, and traffic was thin. Despite its pretensions as a sophisticated American city, Chicago was essentially a day town, bustling from dawn to dusk. Once night fell, especially in winter, a dark quality descended, rendering the Loop unfamiliar and ominous.

She looked straight ahead, refusing to glance at the figure. What was it about the refusal to make eye contact with a predator? Did anyone really think pretending not to see danger would make it disappear? Maybe it was a primitive instinct, like rabbits that freeze, hoping the fox won't notice them.

When she reached the corner of State and Madison, she stole a glance across the street. The man was matching her pace. Her heart started to race. A friend once told Lila she should carry hair spray in her bag to use as a weapon. She'd laughed it off, but now she thought back to the other things her friend said. Never surrender your wallet. Throw it on the ground as far away as possible, then run like hell. If you had to defend yourself, use your elbow. It was the strongest part of your body.

She started to trot up State. She heard the clatter of the El as it rattled around the Loop. Light spilled from the windows of stores closed for the night. No one would mug her in such a well-lit area, would they? Maybe he wasn't following her. Maybe it was just her imagination.

The thud of footfalls made her twist around. The man was crossing over to her side of the street. She went rigid. She was in the middle of the block. There was no alley to duck into. No store to lose herself in.

Then an idea occurred to her. The Palmer House, a grand old Chicago hotel, was around the corner on Monroe. People would be there. A doorman. She sprinted up the sidewalk, trying to run on her toes. The footsteps behind her accelerated too, but she kept going. Icy air whipped at her. Her heart pounded. She raced the last few yards and barreled around the corner.

Relief flooded through her. Two taxis were idling on Monroe a few feet from the hotel entrance. A canopy of lights under the awning threw bright illumination on the sidewalk. A uniformed doorman was helping an elderly couple out of one of the cabs. As Lila ran past them, the woman threw up her arm.

The doorman spun around. "Hey. What's going on?"

Lila was struggling for breath, and all she could do was point behind her. She threw herself against the revolving door. Thankfully, the stalker was too far away to slide inside behind her. Meanwhile, the doorman hurried through a stationery door and waited for her on the other side.

"What's the problem, miss?" He said crossly.

"Call . . . call the police!" Lila gasped. "A man is following me. Right behind. Please. I'm afraid!"

The doorman rushed back outside past the elderly couple, who hadn't moved since they exited the taxi. Rabbits, Lila thought. She watched the doorman raise his whistle to his mouth peering in one direction, then the other. Then he looked again. Finally he came back inside, shaking his head. "There's no one out there, miss. No one at all."

EIGHT

Lila burrowed under the covers in her brother's bedroom, unable to sleep. She flinched every time the building creaked or the refrigerator motor kicked on. Her eyes raked the darkness, alert to stray noises and movements. She kept the cordless next to the bed, just in case, although calling 911 wouldn't help. If someone broke in, they'd have plenty of time to do what they wanted before the police showed up. Any sense of control the phone gave her was illusory at best.

She checked the clock. The dial read 2:00 A.M. She turned on the light and got out of bed. Danny's condo was in a recently renovated three-story Evanston building a few blocks from Lake Michigan. The view was mostly obstructed by other buildings, but on a clear day you could glimpse slivers of silvery water between the structures. Little details inside the apartment, like decorative moldings and hand-painted woodwork, gave the place some character, but, like his office, Danny hadn't invested in decorating. The furniture was minimal, there was no art on the wall, no blinds covered the windows. Lila had taped up sheets but held off buying anything permanent. She'd be going back to New York.

She made sure the deadbolt was seated, even though she remembered doing it when she came in. She heard the satisfying click as the cylinders dropped. Then she began to wander. She went into the room Danny used as an office and opened the closet door. Tucked away on a shelf was his old baseball glove. He'd played second base. She pulled it out and slipped her hand in. The leather still felt soft and supple. She held it up to her nose, inhaling the faint residue of saddle soap and leather. Danny had squirted shaving cream on the glove right after he got it. Lila thought he was crazy, but Danny swore it was the only way to break it in, and her father said Danny was right.

She clasped the glove to her chest. It was tangible proof that her family had existed. That she had been part of a bigger whole. That there had been a "once upon a time." A photo album would have helped. But Danny didn't have one, and the "official" family album kept by her father was destroyed in the fire.

She put the glove back in the closet. The album had been important for one big reason—it contained the only photo of her mother she'd ever seen. It was on the first page, as soon as you opened it. Lila had gazed at it so often that, years later, she still could call up every detail.

Her mother was fair-skinned with long blond hair. Petite and pretty in a delicate, waiflike way. Her father used to tell Lila that except for her dark coloring, she had inherited her mother's looks. The photo showed her mother from the waist up. She was squinting into the sun but smiling. It had been taken in the summer, and there must have been a breeze blowing, because wisps of blond hair framed her face. She was wearing a white peasant blouse, and there were flowers in her hair. Real ones, it looked like. Behind her was a stand of trees, and if you just glanced at the picture, you'd think she was one of those forest nymphs from Grimm's fairy tales.

Lila remembered asking Gramum about her. Her name was Alice Monroe, Gramum would say, her lips tightening, and she came from someplace in Indiana. Gramum never met her, she would add. Her grandmother wasn't trying to be cruel, but Lila understood that any mention of her mother evoked memories—few of them good. Her father's marriage was something he and Gramum refused to revisit. It wasn't a mistake, mind you, Gramum would say over and over. She and Danny were blessings, and if it hadn't been for their mother, they wouldn't be here today.

Indeed, her mother had died giving birth to them. Her delicate constitution just couldn't bear children, Gramum said, especially twins. Gramum would tell her how they'd named her Lila, from the Aramaic word for "night," because her father had brought them both home in the dead of night. Then she'd change the subject and remind Lila not to bother her father with questions—he was just too busy.

She'd defied Gramum only once, when she was a teenager full of insatiable curiosity. She'd waited until Gramum was in bed, then crept down to her father's study to ask about her mother. He didn't know where her mother's family was, he said; she hadn't been on good terms with them. As far as he knew, they never knew she was pregnant. Yes, it was a shame, he added, but he wouldn't have the slightest idea where to find the Monroe family. With such a common name, they could be just about anywhere. When Lila asked him why he never married again, he said he was just too busy.

Exactly what Gramum said.

She'd even asked her aunt about her mother, but Val quickly changed the subject back to herself. Val—she demanded that Lila call her Val, not Valerie, or God forbid, Aunt Valerie—had been married three times but was childless and currently single. She wasn't evil, and, on occasion, she was fun to be with, but she wasn't what Lila would call dependable. She was always dashing off someplace, traveling all over the world.

Now Lila wandered into the kitchen. She opened the fridge, took out a bottle of wine, and poured a glass. The Pinot Grigio was tart but with an underlying sweetness. Danny did have good taste in wine. Clothes and women, too. She was just about to take another sip when she heard a scratching noise outside the kitchen door.

She froze, the wine glass halfway to her mouth. Danny's apartment was on the second floor, but the back door opened to a porch with stairs down to the street. The scratching stopped. Lila clutched the glass. Her nerves were shot. Was she imagining this, too?

A moment later it started up again. This time it sounded as if someone was lightly scraping against something metal. Not her imagination. Her eyes slid to the phone on the kitchen wall. It would take the police at least ten minutes to respond, but she needed help now.

She heard snuffling and what sounded like labored breathing. Slowly she moved to the kitchen counter, set down the glass, and opened a drawer that housed Danny's knives. Three lay inside. One was a carving knife with a long curving blade. Another, a short paring knife. The third was a sharp, sturdy-looking knife with a six-inch blade. The long knife would be awkward and unwieldy. The short one, too little. She picked up the sturdy one. The handle fit easily in her palm. Like Goldilocks, it was just right.

She edged her way to the door. She had surprise on her side. Would that be enough? What if there was more than one person? She thought again about the scratching. She had no idea what was making it. Her heart pounded. She smelled the fear on herself.

She tore the door open and went out to the porch. Below, at street level, a dog whimpered and trotted away from the garbage cans.

Lila was being chased by a large dog that turned into a snake and slithered faster than she could run. The snake was almost on top of her when she came awake. It wasn't quite dawn, but the blackness outside had thinned, leaving a fog of gray.

She ran a bath, threw in a handful of bubble bath she'd bought at Walgreens, and soaked for half an hour. Afterwards, she flitted restlessly from room to room again, like a fly landing on objects only for brief moments. By the fifth circuit, she realized she was being compulsive and made herself stop.

She thought about calling Rich, her ex-boyfriend. A stockbroker in New York, he would be up by now, maybe on his way to the floor. No. They'd broken up three months ago. What if another woman answered the phone? Or she heard a quiet female murmur in the background? Bad idea.

Maybe she'd call a girlfriend instead. But who? There were women she worked out with, colleagues at Peabody Stern she collaborated with, even women in her building with whom she traded elevator pleasantries. But Lila didn't make friends easily. She wasn't comfortable with "girl talk." She thought about calling Annie Gossage, but pushed away the idea. With her three kids and husband, Annie's life was too busy already.

If Lila called, Annie would make time for her, but she'd feel sorry for Lila, and Lila couldn't tolerate the humiliation of being pitied.

She decided to check her email. Back in Danny's office, she sat at his desk and booted up the computer. She clicked on her email program and waded through the spam cluttering her in-box. After deleting them, only three messages remained.

One was from a grassroots political organization to which she'd pledged twenty-five dollars for Internet neutrality. Not only did the initiative fail, but she was now on every mailing list of activists ever known to man or beast. The second was from her "team leader" at Peabody Stern about an upcoming departmental staff meeting, which she would be missing. The third was a message about a genealogy website. It promised to locate ancestors, make contact with long lost cousins, even run background checks. Lila moved it to her deleted items folder. She was about to erase the folder altogether when something made her pause. She retrieved the message, and read it again.

Death had tagged her and run away, snatching everything she cherished. Her father and Danny were gone. But they were only half of her family. Her mother's family was out there somewhere. If she could find them, connect with them, maybe she could find comfort, even a sense of belonging.

She clicked on the genealogy website.

NINE

"Take these." Val opened her palm. In it were eight or nine little white pills.

"What's that?" Lila asked.

"Ambien. To help you sleep." Her aunt slipped them back into a small brown plastic vial and set it on the table. They were having lunch at Milano's, a white-tablecloth Italian café in downtown Evanston.

Lila held up her palm. Unlike Danny, she was reluctant to take any drug if she didn't have to. "Thanks, Val, but they'd be wasted on me." She smiled weakly and looked out the window. A few snowflakes drifted down, dissolving on contact with the sidewalk, uncertain whether they wanted to be there at all. Chicago winters were like that, she recalled. Furious blizzards followed by periods of apologetic calm.

Her aunt shrugged and dumped the vial back in her bag. Val was as different from Casey as Lila was—had been—from Danny. Tall and statuesque, her aunt cut a dramatic figure, and she usually milked it. She could be amusing, even exciting, but she was often like Auntie Mame on steroids.

Today she was trying for a vintage look, but her shawl was too large, her blouse too busy, and the pants too tight for her middle-aged body. Her thick hair, piled on top of her head, was a rich black this season. Lila suspected a few extensions were woven through it. Her cheeks were as taut as the skin on a drum, the result of two facelifts. Her face would probably vibrate if touched. But Val's blue eyes were large and luminous, and they regarded Lila with curiosity. "How long will you be staying?" she asked.

"I don't know. I took a leave of absence from Peabody Stern."

"Can you do that? I mean, without sacrificing your position? You've worked so hard."

"They said to take all the time I needed," Lila said, a little surprised by the question. As far as she knew, her aunt had never worked a day. She remembered Gramum's scowl whenever the subject of Val came up. Still, Val had managed to accumulate enough income to travel. She also claimed to be an artist, but Lila had never seen any paintings or heard her allude to any work in progress.

"That's wonderful. So . . .," her aunt's voice turned businesslike, " . . . what's going on with the insurance claim?"

The insurance adjuster, Rick Witt, was a man whose trousers and sleeves were too long for his stocky frame. He'd interviewed Lila several times. Each time he'd had a runny nose, and his constant sniffling nearly drove her crazy. "He's waiting for the final report from the fire marshal's office."

"Fire marshal? I thought they just investigated arson."

"Whenever there's a death by fire, apparently, the state fire marshal's office is called in. All I know is that I was interviewed by the local fire department, the state fire marshal, and the insurance adjuster. And then Dad's lawyer said I should hire a public adjuster, just to make sure Midwest Mutual didn't weasel out of its responsibility."

"Have they told you what they think happened?"

"They think the lights on the tree shorted out and started a fire. Which then spread to the curtains and the furniture, and . . . " Her voice trailed off.

"I still don't get it. Why didn't Danny or your father get out? There was a smoke alarm, wasn't there?"

"It wasn't working."

The surprise in Val's voice made raising her eyebrows unnecessary. "Really?"

"Dad was conscientious about that kind of thing. But with his hip replacement and everything, he might have forgotten to replace the battery."

"But don't they keep beeping when the battery goes?"

"I have no idea, Val."

"And don't you think Danny should have gotten him out? I mean, he was more mobile."

Lila hesitated. "They found barbiturates in Danny's system. He was out of it. Probably slept through the whole thing, until . . . "

Val colored, as if she just remembered she'd offered Lila a stash of sleeping pills.

"They say Dad looked like he was trying to get out but was overcome by smoke. His body was by the door."

"Oh god, I'm so sorry, darling."

"The thing is . . ., " Lila's voice wavered.

"What?"

"I thought I unplugged the lights before I left."

Val shot her a look.

"So I don't understand how unplugging them triggered the fire."

"What do the investigators say?"

"Nothing conclusive. In fact, things seem to be dragging."

"I'm not surprised." Val's face took on a knowing expression.

"What do you mean?"

"The fire happened right before the holidays. No one wants to do extra paperwork that time of year."

Lila stared at her aunt.

Val took a long sip of chardonnay. "Lila, darling. I'm going to BA at the end of next week. It's not too late for you to come with."

"BA?"

"Buenos Aires."

Lila thought about traveling with Aunt Valerie, being with her 24/7. She remembered her father constantly rolling his eyes when she stayed with them for a while between her second and third husbands.

"Thanks, but I think I'll hang around here. I . . . I should wait for the insurance report."

"Too bad. Travel is a tonic for me. But I suppose it's different for everyone." She scavenged through the bread basket, surfacing with a soft Italian roll. She broke it in two, buttered half, and popped it in her mouth.

Lila leaned back. "Aunt Valerie, do . . ."

"Val, darling. Val."

"Sorry. Val, do you ever feel . . . well . . . that . . . you're . . . well . . . just treading water while you figure out where you're supposed to be?"

Her aunt stopped chewing and gazed at Lila. Lila couldn't tell if she'd hit the bull's eye or said something so ludicrous Aunt Valerie was struggling to find a courteous response.

"I don't see life that way, darling," Val finally said.

"How do you see it?"

She finished chewing, taking her time. She folded her hands. "Life is a grand adventure," she said. "And I'm the captain, first mate, and boiler room operator all rolled into one. You better believe I know where I'm going."

Funny how traits run in families. When he wasn't feeling sorry for himself, Danny was that way, too.

"Don't be too hard on yourself," Val went on. "You've suffered a horrific loss. Of course you're off balance. You'll bounce back."

Lila fought an achy feeling in the back of her throat. "You lost a brother."

Her aunt smiled. "Yes, but I'm closer to the end than the beginning. You're still at an age where it's a shock to confront death." She pointed her finger upwards. "He and I are becoming more acquainted every day." She picked up her wine glass. "Although we're both taking our time, mind you." She paused. "And, frankly, your father and I were never that close."

"Why not?"

"Different people. Different goals. For example, I could never have built a business the way he did. Or raised the two of you."

"Gramum helped."

Val rolled her eyes. "That too. Living with our mother." She shook her head. "Your father is . . . was a saint."

Lila cocked her head. Val was talking to her like she was an adult. She liked that. Maybe her father and grandmother had been the tiniest bit unfair. Despite the melodrama, her aunt wasn't as superficial or as foolish as they'd led her to believe. Still, Lila gathered her courage before asking the next question. She'd asked it before, but it still felt like venturing out on a high dive. "Did you know my mother?"

Val gazed at her for a moment, then took another sip of wine. She set her glass down carefully. "I never met her."

"How come?"

"She and your father . . . didn't live nearby. And they were . . . well, involved in other things."

"What other things?"

"I told you . . . I wasn't around."

Something in Val's words sounded scripted to Lila. She propped her elbows on the table. "Val, why is . . . was . . . everyone so stingy with information about my mother? Gramum never mentioned her, and Daddy never said anything unless I forced the subject. Why didn't anyone want me to know about her?"

Val tightened her lips, the same way Gramum used to do. "Your father . . . and your mother . . . er . . . got together during a . . ." she seemed to choose the word carefully, ". . . a turbulent time."

"Dammit, Val. What is this wall of bullshit?"

Val studied her. Lila had the feeling she was coming to a decision. Then Val leaned back. "Your father never told you about that part of his life?"

"What are you talking about?"

Val sighed. "For the record, you should know I never agreed with his decision. I thought you and Danny should have been told."

Lila had a sense that Val's next words might change her life. "Told what?"

"Casey . . . your father . . . dropped out of college. After his freshman year."

"Dad dropped out? But he went to night school. At DePaul."

Val made a brushing aside gesture. "After you two were born. But he started out at Michigan."

"The University of Michigan?" Lila straightened up. "In Ann Arbor? Are you kidding?" When Val nodded, she said, "Why didn't he tell us?"

"Probably because he dropped out after his freshman year, and he didn't want you or Danny to follow in his footsteps."

"Why did he drop out?"

Val didn't answer for a minute. "I really don't know, darling. All I know is that he . . . well . . . he did other things."

"What things? Where?"

Val motioned to the waiter for another glass of wine. "Actually, he was living here in Chicago."

"Chicago?" Lila was stunned.

"That's right."

"Did he drop out of school because he met my mother?"

Val shook her head. "He met her here."

"In Chicago? Are you sure?"

"I was about to marry Harvey—that was hubby number one—but . . . your father would call every once in a while, and we'd talk."

"About what?"

A vague look came across her aunt's face. "Oh, you know. This and that."

A wave of suspicion rolled over Lila. "What was he doing in Chicago? Does that mean my mother was here, too? I thought she was from Indiana."

"I guess she was, but . . . as I said, they met here. I'm sorry, doll face. I just don't know any more."

The waiter brought Val another glass of wine and asked Lila if she wanted more iced tea. She waved him off. "When exactly were they here?"

Val's eyes got distant as she tried to work it out. "Let's see. I married Harvey in '69, and that was right in the middle of it. It must have been the summer of '68 through about '70."

"We were born in May, 1970."

"I know."

"There has to be someone who knows about my mother and father and what they were doing here. Two people don't exist in a vacuum."

"I know you want answers, sweet pea. But I don't have any. And I don't know who would."

"What is it about our family?" Lila fumed. "Why are there all these secrets? No one ever talks . . . talked to anyone." Her voice rose, "When I have a family, I'm going to . . ." She cut herself off. She didn't have her own family. And her prospects of having one were dim.

Val's expression said her aunt knew exactly what Lila was thinking, and that she empathized with her. The hot achy feeling in Lila's throat came back.

"Lila," her aunt said. "All I know is that your mother died giving birth to you and Danny. A few weeks later your Daddy showed up at Gramum's in a cab with the two of you in his arms." She drained the last of her wine. "Hey! Did I tell you about my itinerary after BA?"

Lila walked home, sifting a multitude of thoughts. Was she prepared to take on a search for her mother's family? What if she discovered her mother was a heroin addict? Or a thief? Or a prostitute who'd stopped taking her birth control pills? Maybe her mother's parents were so dysfunctional that she'd been forced to escape their clutches before she, too, was destroyed. No. Better not to go there.

She headed south to Church Street. Half way down the next block, she stopped at a bookstore featuring a display of Frank Rich's new book in the window. Rich wrote for the *New York Times*. Lila thought he could be pompous, but his heart was in the right place. She was debating whether to go in to buy it when she was distracted by a reflection in the window. It was subtle, more an impression than an image. Behind her, almost out of her field of vision, something—or someone—moved. A presence had been there, now it wasn't.

An icicle of fear slid up her spine. The day was still overcast; the reflection might be warped. She pulled up the collar of her jacket and focused on the glass. She saw the outline of buildings across the street, a few cars passing. She heard the whine of a motorcycle revving its engine.

She flicked her eyes back to the display. Frank Rich grinned at her from half a dozen book covers. She was an adult. A professional. She made important financial decisions. Whatever demons were plaguing her, she wouldn't let them win. Aunt Valerie would never allow herself to feel intimidated. She would laugh in the face of danger. Lila mustered her courage. Whatever was out there, she would deal with it.

She spun around. No one was there. No pedestrians on this side of the street. No one entering or exiting the stores, no one getting in or out of a car. No one across the street, either.

She'd passed an alley a few yards back. If someone was tailing her, they might be lurking there. She trotted back to the alley and peered in. A few blue dumpsters. The musty smell of rotting garbage. Cracked concrete. Garage doors, all of them closed. The sound of the receding motorcycle. Otherwise nothing. Except the snow. It had started in earnest, big flakes whispering down, coating everything with white.

TEN

The Cherokee Lounge was a place that catered to people who lived below the radar—people who didn't want others to know who they were or where they were going. Maybe they didn't know themselves. Tucked away in the suburb of Schiller Park, it was a brooding, dark bar with blue and red neon signs on the windows, one of them buzzing as if it might take off from O'Hare, only a few miles away.

Dar nursed a beer. This was the second night he'd come in, but nothing was different from the first. The same people at the bar, the same haze of cigarette smoke, the same roar of airplanes shuddering the walls and quivering the glasses. He could feel the apathy in the air.

He'd rented a room in a nearby boarding house. Told the owner he'd been laid off from the O'Hare baggage detail, and his wife kicked him out. The woman eyed him, clearly not believing a word, but rented him the room anyway. Everyone needed cash. He found another job washing dishes, this time in a cafeteria. He hoped it would buy him enough time to figure out what to do next.

He'd spent the afternoon on the computer in the library and discovered that Casey Hilliard had perished in a house fire a few weeks ago. One of the twins, the boy they called Daniel, died in the fire with him. The girl, who wasn't at home, had survived. The news had sent a shockwave through him, and he hurried to a pay phone to call Rain.

He didn't reach her. A distraught man who said he was her husband told him that she'd been killed in a freak car accident on I-94 in December. She was driving back from Illinois when her car unexpectedly swerved off the highway into a ditch, rolled over, and caught fire. The police speculated she'd fallen asleep at the wheel.

"Were you a friend?" her husband asked.

"I'm so sorry for your loss," Dar replied and hung up. He'd started to shiver as if he'd stepped naked into a bathtub full of snow.

Now, hunched over the bar in the Cherokee Lounge, he tried to make sense of the events. An analytical, scholarly mind was one of his strengths. Not like his father, an auto worker with over thirty years on the line, much of it as UAW shop steward. They'd fired his father during a particularly brutal strike, and his subsequent unemployment destroyed him. Men like Will Gantner didn't lose their jobs. Dar, fourteen at the time, was furious. How dare Ford steal his father's self-worth? He tried to tell his dad he could do better someplace else, but six months later his father hanged himself in their basement. Dar vowed never to depend on a corporation for anything.

Now he slid his glass of beer around on the bar, avoiding the whitish stains embedded in the wood. He'd come back to Chicago, called Teddy, met with Rain. He wanted to visit Casey, but went to Michigan to see Philip Kerr. He came back to find someone had rolled his room. Then, a few days or weeks later, Rain died in a car crash, Casey in a fire. Logic told him the string of events was not a coincidence. The link between them was his return to Chicago. He closed his eyes, feeling a weight settle on his shoulders.

When he opened his eyes, he noticed a woman a few feet away. She was wearing a heavy black sweater, jeans, and work boots. Working her way through a double scotch, she was trying too hard to be casual. She had to be on the other side of forty, maybe even fifty. Her hair was unnaturally auburn and pulled back low at her neck, but aside from a little thickness around her middle, she'd kept herself trim.

He studied her face. It was a sweet face, with a widow's peak at her hairline, a small nose, round cheeks, and eyes that looked tired but honest. He kept gazing at her until, as if he'd sent out a magnetic beam, she looked over.

Usually when someone noticed him, he'd avert his face, hoping to fade into obscurity.

For some reason tonight, though, he didn't. They locked eyes. Her cheeks colored, and he saw the beginnings of a smile. He felt suddenly awkward. How long had it been? Almost forty years? He felt a stirring in a part of his body that he'd thought was permanently numb. Christ. What was he supposed to do?

A deafening roar reverberated through the bar, and a series of vibrations splashed beer and liquor on the counter. Dar glanced around worriedly, wondering why no one else seemed to be bothered. The woman who'd been eyeing him pointed a finger upwards. Dar looked at the ceiling, saw the light fixture sway, and realized it was a plane coming in low for a landing. He settled back on his stool, feeling heat on his cheeks.

The woman waited a decent amount of time, then said, "With all the taxes we pay, the least they could do is change the flight path, don't you think?"

Dar gave her a brief nod.

"Sorry, I can't hear you," she said.

Puzzled, he stroked his chin. He'd started to grow a beard when he got back from Michigan.

She shook her head. "It's a joke."

"Oh." He wasn't sure he got it, which made him feel more awkward.

But she vacated her stool and plopped down on the empty one next to him. "I'm Cece."

"Dar." He extended his hand.

She took it with an amused expression that made Dar think the people she knew didn't shake hands. Her skin was warm and soft. "What kind of name is Dar?"

"It's short for Darwin. As in Charles." She shot him a blank look. "The scientist who discovered evolution?"

"Oh." This time, she nodded as if she got it. Dar wasn't convinced. Then again, if she didn't, they'd be even.

He stood there, wondering what to say next, when a man who looked like he was twenty years and thirty pounds past his fighting weight bellied up to the bar. "Hey, doll." He insinuated himself between Dar and Cece.

"Evening, Judd," Cece said.

"This guy hassling you?" He yanked a thumb towards Dar. "'Cause if he is . . . " He let his voice trail off. Cece shook her head. "You sure, babe? 'Cause you know I'm here to look out for you."

"I can look out for myself, Judd."

"I'm not so sure." He eyed Dar suspiciously. "We don't need no strangers around, do we?"

"Judd." Cece's voice went hard. "It's all right."

The guy was shorter than Dar, but twice as wide. He faced Dar. "I dunno. Maybe you'd best be on your way, mister."

"Judd," Cece threw out her hand. "Stop!"

But Judd stood there, his chin jutting out, glaring at Dar.

Dar slid off his stool, hoping his six feet would compensate for Judd's brawn. "The lady thinks it's all right," he said softly. "I'd do what she says."

Judd stared, looked Dar up and down. Then he backed off. He raised his index finger at Cece as he retreated. "You need somethin' honey, you just call."

"I will." Cece watched him go with a straight face. Then she turned and flashed Dar a grateful smile. He smiled back.

Ten minutes later Cece made a show of checking her watch. Dar looked at the wall clock. Almost eleven. She swiveled towards him and looked him over again.

"Okay," she began. "Here's the deal. It's gonna keep snowing, and it's gonna be a long, cold night. We could sit here and bullshit each other for the next half hour, or we could go back to my place now." She tilted her head. "I have a bungalow in Franklin Park."

Dar thought about how long it had been since he'd touched soft skin, pressed his lips against a willing mouth. And now, it seemed so easy—so available, just for the asking. He didn't know where Franklin Park was, but he chugged the rest of his beer and followed her out.

ELEVEN

She'd been a perfect lover, especially when he climaxed right away. She could tell, in that indefinable way women have, that he'd been starved. The second time she took her time, moving her lips slowly over his cheeks, his lips, his chest, his cock. He lasted longer that time, and by the third time the pupil became the teacher. His mouth found her breasts, the soft folds of her stomach, the damp, dark cleft between her legs. When she locked her legs around him, he drank her in, and when he felt her arch up, forcing him deeper, her fire engulfed him. When she finally came, moaning, calling out his name, he thought his head—and the rest of him—would explode.

Now, as he woke up, drowsy and warm beneath a heavy quilt, a long-forgotten peace lulled him. He looked around the bedroom. It was tidy, with hardwood floors and flowery wallpaper he could do without. He recalled her saying, with pride, that she had three bedrooms and a full basement, which meant there was plenty of space. He saw no evidence of kids or pets.

Cece was still asleep, her back to him. He lay quietly, savoring her warmth, her scent, her femaleness. Then he turned and glanced out the window. Three inches of snow coated the window sill, sparks firing in the morning sun. A good sign. He slipped his hands behind his neck and stretched. Cece stirred. When he dragged his gaze from the window, she was looking at him. Her eyes, somewhere between hazel and green, held a serious expression. He smiled uncertainly, but when she didn't return it, he tensed. He wondered whether to say something.

She pre-empted him. "You're in some kind of trouble, aren't you?"

"What makes you say that?" He flicked his eyes to her neck. Her carotid pulsed at her throat. Ba-boom. He touched his fingers to it. She lifted her head to give him more. A simple act, but it spoke volumes. She trusted him. He wondered why.

"You look . . . hunted," she said.

He wanted to ask what a hunted man looked like, then decided he didn't want to know. She stretched again, revealing more of her neck. He ran his fingers up to her chin, the side of her cheek, past her hairline to the tip of her forehead. So soft: her skin, her hair. He felt himself harden again. He rolled on top of her.

When they finally got out of bed, the floor was colder than he expected, and he hopped across it, triggering a giggle from Cece. She had a nice laugh. Musical. He dove back in.

"We should think about getting up," she said. "I have to go to work."

"What do you do?"

"I'm a claims supervisor for an insurance company. Used to be a nurse, but I didn't like the hours." She shrugged. "It's a paycheck."

"Where is your office?"

"Not far. River Grove."

Dar nodded, although she could have been talking about California. He had no idea where River Grove was.

She got out of bed, pulled on her socks, and padded downstairs. He heard a spray of water in the kitchen followed by the clang of dishes and silverware. A few minutes later, the smell of fresh brewed coffee wafted up. Dar got out of bed, threw on his pants, and made his way down to the kitchen. Cece smiled. Opening a drawer, she took out paper and pen and scrawled something. She handed him the paper.

"What's this?"

"My name and phone number. My last name is Wainwright."

"Cece Wainwright."

"That's right."

"Dar Gantner."

She stuck out her hand and giggled again. "Nice to meet you."

He raised her hand to his face and guided it down his cheek.

"You keep doing that and I'll never make it to work."

"Would that be so bad?"

She gently pulled her hand away. The coffee was ready. She poured it into mugs, then, without asking, dumped a truckload of sugar in both. She held out the mug to him. "What about you? Where do you work?"

He sipped the coffee. It was so sweet his teeth itched. He set down the mug. "I wash dishes at the cafeteria. And I don't like sugar in my coffee."

She pretended to pout. "Is this our first fight?"

"Just a request."

She hesitated, then dumped out his mug, poured more coffee, and handed it to him. "You're a dishwasher?"

He kept his mouth shut.

Then, "How long were you inside?"

He took a sip of his unsweetened coffee. "I need a favor, Cece."

"I'm listening."

"I need to borrow your car."

Her eyebrows rose sky high.

"I'm not going to steal it."

"And I know that because . . . "

He looked at her, his mind full of unspoken pleas, rationales. He broke eye contact. "You're right. I did have some trouble. And it looks like it's finding me again. But I've never been a thief."

"You did time." He nodded. "A lot, by the looks of you."

"How do you know?"

"I told you. You have the look." She cupped both hands around her mug. "I can find out who you are and what you did. We have claims investigators, remember? They find out all sorts of things about people. All I have to do is ask."

"I'll make it even easier for you. I'll give you the name and number of my parole officer. If I don't come back with your car, you can have me thrown in jail."

"I just might."

"But just remember . . . if I'm in jail, I won't be able to tell you how beautiful you are and how you saved my soul last night."

She looked as if she wanted to smile but was holding it back. "Are you always such a smooth talker?"

He smiled.

"How long since you've driven a car?"

"About forty years."

Her mouth opened. "Are you crazy? Where do you need to go?"

"Winnetka."

"You have a driver's license?"

He kept his mouth shut.

"Christ! If I do let you borrow it, and assuming you don't total it, when were you planning to bring it back?"

"How about if I pick you up at the end of the day?"

"What makes you think I want to see you again?"

He wasn't fooled. "Because . . . " He stroked her hand, waited for her to put down the mug. Then he raised her hand to his lips. He wondered if she felt the same thrill. " . . . we're not finished."

As his mouth moved over her fingers, she smiled. A real smile, this time. "No." Her voice was husky. "We're not."

It took Dar a few minutes to get the feel of driving again. The car, a black, four-door Honda, was easy enough to maneuver, but the volume of traffic on the road and the speed with which it sped past was unnerving. Where had all these cars come from? Gas cost six times as much as it used to, yet many of the cars were bigger than a VW van. More powerful, too. He'd read about the ocean of debt American consumers were drowning in. These had to be one of the reasons why.

He'd Googled Casey's address at the library but didn't know how to get there. The librarian helped him print out a map, which instructed him to drive north on 294 to Willow, then head east. Thirty minutes later, he entered Winnetka. As he wound through village streets, he gazed at the huge houses, the wide snow-covered lawns, the genteel affluence. This was where the establishment lived. He drove past a street with so many trees that the bare branches made a lacy brocade against the sky. Casey had lived here, in the maw of the enemy. Clearly his old friend had changed.

He headed toward Casey's street. Turning down the lane, he was surprised at how narrow it was. An inverse proposition, he guessed. The bigger your home, the smaller your street.

It wasn't hard to identify the house. The roof had collapsed, and the second story was open to the elements. The exterior walls still stood, but they were stained with soot. The windows were boarded up. He stopped the car. It was winter quiet, as if the fire had obliterated the life force of the entire block. Bits of yellow tape fluttered from the porch. The only thing that seemed untouched was the front door, blood red. It looked like it was supporting the rest of the structure. A lonely sentinel keeping out unwanted intruders.

Dar got out and tramped over ridges of frozen mud to the back. He imagined the place without the snow cover. A broad sloping lawn, big enough for swings, picnics, even touch football. Casey's children had grown up in protected surroundings. That was good. Maybe the only good thing to come out of it all.

He thought he knew who was responsible for the fire. He even thought he knew why. But that didn't make it easier to accept. In the space of a few days, the bridges to his past had been destroyed. Just when he was ready to reconnect with the people on the other side. Teddy. Rain. Casey and his son.

The only one left was the daughter. Lila, they called her. She was out when the house caught fire. If coincidence was the reason she was still alive, would they try again? Then again, why was she in their sights at all? He supposed there was the chance Casey had told the children something unintentionally. Dar imagined how, late at night, Casey might have started to relive the past. He certainly had. Maybe, during one of those reveries, Casey's son or daughter had seen him gazing at an article . . . a photo . . . a letter. He could imagine the child asking, "What's that, Dad?" See Casey dismiss it, with something like, "Oh, that's something you don't have to concern yourself with. It happened a long time ago." But what if one of the children persisted? When a child wants something, it's hard to say no. Or so he'd been told.

He stared at the shell of what had once been a fine home. A bitter wind stung his face. If he was thinking this way, the people who killed Casey and Rain were, too. At the very least they'd be following the girl, checking her movements. Which meant she was vulnerable. Unless he got to her first.

TWELVE

It was nearly dark by the time Lila left the Evanston library. She'd spent two hours researching Alice Monroe from Indiana. Despite all the Internet search engines and databases, she came up with nothing except the writer Alice Munro. The last name was spelled differently, but that didn't stop Lila from wondering if God was playing a cosmic joke on her.

The reference librarian, a chic woman with salon-styled hair, offered to print out lists of all the Monroes in a few cities in Indiana, but Lila told her not to bother. She had no idea where her mother's family was, even if they still lived in the state.

She trudged the few blocks back to Danny's. Almost dark, the snow was still coming down, whitening the sidewalk and muffling her steps. She pulled up her hood. She passed a man shoveling the sidewalk, although the snow filled in as quickly as he tossed it aside. The dry and bitter cold, despite the snow, snatched her breath away. New York winters weren't this extreme.

As she pushed through the door of Danny's building, she found the boxes from her father's office in a corner of the lobby. She went upstairs and changed into jeans and a sweater, then went back down and lugged them up to Danny's condo. Before opening them, she poured herself a glass of wine, and turned on the TV in the living room.

After moving the boxes into Danny's study, she opened the first one. Books and photos. She opened another. More books, but also the CDs she'd made from her father's computer files. She turned on Danny's computer, inserted one in the drive, and waited. She'd titled them—by number, of course—as well as the date she'd recorded them.

This was *Casey 1-011710*. She clicked on the CD icon. A list of files popped up. She scanned them carefully. Some were clearly client files, with names like *Catalyst, Inc,* and *PDT Technologies*. Fledgling companies, probably. PDT sounded vaguely familiar—it must have done well. Others were articles her father had authored on wealth creation and private placement strategies. Still others included links to websites, which, when she clicked on them, dealt with entrepreneurial start-up issues.

A burst of cheering on the TV distracted her. The news was on, and the cheers came from a story about the upcoming presidential election. Something about a candidate who was making people excited about voting. As usual, the media were rushing the process, trying to crown the victor before anyone voted. Elections were like a boxing match, her father used to say, except they lasted fifteen months, not fifteen rounds.

She forced herself back to the CDs. She tried to convince herself she didn't know what she was looking for, but that was a lie. She was looking for something, anything that would unlock the secrets of her mother's family. Her family of origin, as the shrinks liked to put it.

It wasn't until an hour later, after she took a break to scramble some eggs and toast a bagel, that she loaded the third CD. As with the others, most of the documents looked work-related: balance sheets and P&Ls. She sighed. There were only a couple of files left. One was a Word document titled *Tutorial*. She opened it and read: *How to Hide Images In Files*. It was a primer on something called steganography. Lila Googled the word. Steganography was the "science of hiding messages in such a way that no one apart from the intended recipient knows of the existence of the message."

Hiding messages? Why would her father want to know about something like that? She read on. A series of steps had to be performed in order to retrieve a coded message, and the only way to do that was by using special software. She went back to the tutorial file. Whoever created it obviously assumed that her father already had the software—the directions referred to folders he needed to open, links he had to click on. She hunted around for the software on the CD, but it either wasn't there, or it was hidden too, because she didn't find anything.

She rose and went to the window. Apparently, her father's secrets hadn't stopped with his death. She lifted the sheet covering the glass and peered down onto the street. Only a couple of cars were moving, the beam of their headlights illuminating the steadily falling snow. There had to be five or six inches now, and the ground was covered by a mantle that cast a pale glow over everything. The faux daylight was eerie but better than darkness.

She went back to the computer and tried the last file. It didn't have a name, just a number: 082768. She smiled. That was something she would do. Still, before opening it, she right-clicked on *Properties*. The file was a JPEG. An image. It had been created on April 17, 2003. Five years ago.

When Lila opened the file, her pulse quickened. It was a photo of a group of young people, and one of them was her mother. Her mother was smiling at the camera the same way she had in the only photo Lila had ever seen of her. She examined the shot more closely—it *was* the same photo. Her father must have cropped the other people out when he added the photo to their family album.

It was in color, but the colors were harsh and lacked subtlety, like snapshots from a long time ago. There were five other people in the shot: another woman and four men. Her mother and the other woman were in front. The other woman was small, with long, ash-blond hair. She wore a tank top and jeans. A pair of rimless glasses perched on her nose. One shoulder was higher than the other, and it looked like her arm was draped around Lila's mother.

Behind the ash hair was a young man with curly brown hair. His hands rested on the blonde's shoulders. He was wearing a sleeveless brown vest, and a string of beads hung around his neck. Lila stared. Something about this man was familiar. Very familiar. Holy shit! It was her father!

Yes. Now she could see it. The same eyes, the same features, so different from her own. The same challenging expression he took on when he had a strong opinion and wanted you to know it. He couldn't have been more than eighteen or nineteen, but he looked confident, Lila thought. Even brave.

Behind her mother stood another man. He was a good head taller than her father, and had straight dark hair down to his shoulders. Thin and rangy, he wore a t-shirt with the words MOBE MOVES in block letters. In contrast to her father, his arms hung straight at his sides.

Two more young men completed the group, one on each end. The man on the left, small and sinewy, wore jeans and a T-shirt with the peace symbol on it. A red bandana was tied around his blond hair, which reached to his shoulders. The other man, handsome with dark hair and eyes, wore a white, short-sleeved shirt with an alligator emblem on the pocket. Aside from long sideburns, his hair was relatively short. Alligator man was the only one not looking directly at the camera. He was turned toward her father, as if he was talking to him when the photo was snapped.

A canopy of trees formed a leafy backdrop. They were in a park, the breeze making her mother's blond hair float around her head like a halo. Her mother and the other girl were smiling; the men weren't.

Lila checked the file again: 082768. She labeled files by date; if her father did too, the number meant August 27, 1968. Forty years ago. Was that when the picture was taken? Her father would have been in college. At Michigan. No. Not in August. Plus, Val said her father had dropped out at the end of his freshman year. He would have been back in Chicago.

She returned to *Properties*. The photo might have been taken forty years ago, but the file had been created only five years ago. Which meant that was when he'd scanned it into his computer. Or received it from someone else. Or found it on the Internet. She tapped a finger on the mouse. No. That couldn't be. The picture of her mother had been in the family photo album for years. He must have had the photo for a long time and only decided to scan it five years ago. She understood—if this was the only photo of her mother, her father would have wanted to make a digital backup for safekeeping.

Then her eyes caught on something else—the file had been accessed on December 22nd at 10:07 P.M. The night before the fire. Her father had opened this file the night before he died. Did he do that often, to remind himself of his youth and his long-lost love?

Lila gazed at her mother one more time. She was the center of the shot, in more than a physical way. The others surrounded her like the spokes of a wheel, but her mother was at the core. She smiled shyly out at Lila, wisps of hair framing her face, loving her through time. She'd never really missed her mother—how could you miss someone you'd never really known? Still, Lila felt her throat get hot.

THIRTEEN

By morning Lila knew what her next step would be, and the knowledge focused her in a way that had eluded her for weeks. She even hummed as she brewed a pot of coffee. She filled her mug and checked the time. Only 7:30. She drank her coffee, showered and dressed, checked the clock again—8:05. But it was an hour later in Michigan. She turned on the computer and waited impatiently for it to boot up. She Googled the number, then reached for the phone.

"Alumni Office."

A female voice with an expressionless, business-like tone. Probably not a student on work-study. Which would make things trickier. "Hello. My name is Lila Hilliard, and my father went to the University of Michigan."

"How can I help you?"

"Unfortunately, my father passed away a few weeks ago, and . . . "

"My sympathies."

"Thank you. That's why I'm calling. I'm planning a memorial service for him in Chicago, and I wanted to invite some of his fellow alumni. But I'm not sure who or how many to include." She hesitated. "I was hoping you might be able to give me some names and addresses of alumni in the Chicago area."

"What was your father's name and what year did he graduate?"

"Casey Hilliard. Class of . . . er . . . 1971."

"Hold on."

A tinny instrumental rendition of *Benny and the Jets* came on the line. Lila waited. She heard a click, and the voice came back.

"I'm sorry, but we have no record of Casey Hilliard attending the university."

"Pardon me?"

"I checked the Class of '71 as well as two years on either side. He's not in our database."

"I don't understand. I have pictures of him on campus. In fact, I'm looking at one now." Lila was surprised how easily the lie came.

"We only have records of every student who graduated. Is it possible your father . . . er . . . didn't?"

"You mean dropped out?"

"That's one possibility. Or perhaps he transferred to another school."

"I . . . I would be surprised if that was the case. I'm sure his diploma is here. I think he even showed it to me at some point."

"Well . . ., " the woman let the word hang, as if she couldn't be responsible for inaccurate records or faulty memories, "I'm sorry, but if I can't find a record, there's nothing I can do."

Lila got to the point. "Please. He . . . he died in a fire. Right before Christmas. It was sudden. I need to do something. I was counting—I don't know where else to turn. I really want to find people who knew him."

There was a pause, then a sigh. "I understand how distraught you must feel. I'll give you the number of the Chicago alumni club president. Maybe he can help."

"Thank you."

Lila disconnected and called the number she'd been given. A hearty voice-mail welcomed her back to the Maize and Blue at the University of Michigan Club of Greater Chicago. She should listen to the following four options. Lila ignored the suggestions and punched "0" several times, harder than she needed to. She reached another recording, a woman this time, telling her to call back between noon and 4:00 P.M. Perhaps she could find the answer to her question on their website, the voice added helpfully, and cited the Alumni Club's URL.

Lila hung up in the middle of the recitation and took her coffee to the window. The streets had been plowed, leaving neat banks of snow at the curb. The snow was still white, unsullied by exhaust fumes, and a bright sun made it glint and sparkle. Why did the morning after a storm always seem so perfect? As if Nature were apologizing for its wrath the night before?

She turned back to the room. Over the past few weeks she'd learned grief was in the little things: scanning her father's files, making her brother's bed, catching a whiff of his aftershave. But so, too, was joy. Looking outside at a perfect winter day, some of her darkness fell away, and she felt a kernel of hope.

Early that evening, she drove Danny's Jeep down to Chicago's Gold Coast, an affluent neighborhood of million-dollar condos and even more expensive brownstones. She parked in a lot on State Street and walked around the corner to Astor Place. Purple twilight was dismantling the day, but faint streaks of light in the western sky signaled the onset of later sunsets. Still, it was January cold, and people scurried past, thinking, no doubt, about hot meals and cozy evenings at home.

She'd called the Alumni Club back that afternoon, and, through a combination of persuasion and desperation, wangled the name of a Michigan alumnus who graduated in 1971. With a little work on the Internet, she found his address and phone number. She considered calling, then decided just to show up. It was riskier—he might not be home, and if he was, he might slam the door in her face. Still, it would be harder to turn her down in person.

She stopped in front of a three-story brownstone and checked the address. A large bay window extended from the second floor, and light blazed through the drapes. A good sign. A wrought-iron fence surrounded a tiny front lawn, but the gate was unlocked. Another good sign.

As Lila stepped through, a ferocious barking erupted inside. She waited. The racket stopped. She went to the front door and tentatively rang the bell. This time the barking rose to a frantic pitch. She heard a shuffling noise.

The petite Asian woman who opened the door had short black hair threaded with gray. She wore a green silk kimono with a matching obi and bustle in back. On her tiny feet were sandals with two-inch platforms. With her size eight boots, Lila felt like a giant. The woman clutched the collar of a small white Maltese, who was still barking. Lila was ready to talk slowly and use lots of sign language, when the woman held up her palm. She dragged the dog into another room and closed the door. The barking stopped. Returning to Lila, the woman straightened up and spoke in perfect English with a Midwestern twang.

"Hello, there. How may I help you?"

Lila swallowed her surprise. "I . . . I'm sorry to disturb you. I was looking for James Redaker."

"I'm Mrs. Redaker. Was he expecting you?"

"No." Lila felt an attack of nerves. She was good with numbers, not people. Maybe she should go home. But if she did, she'd never learn anything. "My name is Lila Hilliard. It's a personal matter . . . about my father."

Mrs. Redaker looked puzzled.

Lila shifted. "He passed away recently. But he was at Michigan at the same time as Mr. Redaker, and I . . . well, I was hoping Mr. Redaker might have known him."

Mrs. Redaker gazed at her with the same puzzled look. Lila knew she was debating whether to let her in. She fought her desire to flee. Finally the woman nodded. "Come inside, dear. It's cold. My name is Natsumi."

Lila nodded her thanks and stepped in. A gush of clean, comforting warmth blew over her. She could hear the dog snuffling behind the closed door.

Natsumi led Lila into a sitting room. Then she shuffled down the hall, her sandals making a swishing noise. Lila sat in a straight-backed chair that was surprisingly comfortable. The room was full of bamboo: shades, lamps, a floor-length screen. The rest of the furniture was edged in black wood. The floor was white marble, and the faint scents of pine and jasmine hung in the air. In the corner under a spotlight was a yellow and red glass bowl shaped like a large flower. A Chihuly. These people had means. And yet, the clutter she often found in wealthy peoples' homes was absent here, and Lila felt both soothed and energized. Maybe there was something to feng shui.

The murmur of voices floated in from another room. First Natsumi, then a deep, male voice. A moment later, Natsumi reappeared, followed by a man.

James Redaker didn't so much occupy a room as dominate it. About five ten, he had receding blond hair and ice blue eyes. Like his wife, he wore a dark green kimono that almost reached his knees. Pants peeked out underneath. He was wearing sandals, too. But where his wife was small and wiry, he was as wide as he was tall. A jock gone to seed. Lila rose from her chair, trying not to stare at the Nordic-looking bull of a man in a ceremonial Japanese kimono. Beneath her docile Geisha manner, Natsumi must be formidable.

"Natsumi says you have questions about your . . . late father," Redaker said.

"Yes. First, I want to apologize for intruding."

"You've clearly gone to some trouble to find me. The least I can do is hear you out." He waved a hand and sat heavily in a matching chair. She was surprised it held his weight.

Lila sat back down. "My father started at Michigan the same year as you."

He grinned. "Class of '71? Did he tell you about homecoming freshman year? We played Penn State. I was defensive tackle. First freshman from Hartland to make varsity."

The combination of college football and Japanese culture was just this side of bizarre, but Lila kept her composure. "I doubt my father could have made third string."

Redaker folded his hands regally, as if accepting his due. "Yes. Well, you didn't come here to hear stories about the Wolverines."

Lila rummaged in her bag and pulled out a manila envelope. "My father and my brother died in a fire last month. I never knew my mother,

71

. . . or her family. But I'd like to find them now. I have this picture of my parents." She slid it out of the envelope. "There are some other people in the photo as well. I know the chances of you recognizing any of them are slim, but I was hoping you might have a yearbook I could check. Maybe I'd recognize someone who could help me track down my mother's family."

"Enterprising of you." Lila couldn't tell if that was a compliment until she glanced at Natsumi, standing at the back of the room. When she nodded, Lila felt better.

"What was your father's name?"

"Casey Hilliard."

"Do you know what dorm he was in?"

"No."

"Well, let's have a look."

Lila handed over the photo. Redaker stared at it, his eyes squinting into slits. Lila held her breath. Then he frowned.

"These people . . . were all of them at Michigan?"

"I'm . . . I'm not sure." Lila motioned toward the picture. "But my father is the one in the vest. With the beads."

Redaker pursed his lips, making his disapproval clear. "He doesn't look familiar." He twisted around to his wife. "You were there too, Natsumi-anata. Have a look-see." He held out the picture.

Natsumi sidled up and took the photo. Then she looked over at Lila. "Wait here." She shuffled out of the room. Lila could hear her rummaging around in another room. She came back in, holding a college yearbook that said *Wolverines 1968*. She gave it to her husband.

Redaker opened the book and flipped through a few pages. "I remember those days. Hippies, protestors, SDS. Flower children. Most of them from good families, too." His nostrils flared. "They tried to set fire to the research building. Almost tore down the student union, too." He nodded absently. "Strange time to be in college." He looked up at his wife. "You remember, don't you, darling?"

Natsumi nodded, but her eyes were calculating. She took the book from her husband, skimmed a few pages and then stopped. Smoothing the page with her palm, she brought it to Lila and thrust it into her hands.

"Look at this."

A large black-and-white photo was splashed across two yearbook pages. It showed a crowd of students gathered outside. A banner in the background said *Students Against the War.* Some of the students sat on the grass; others stood in knots of three or four. Most of them wore black armbands, headbands, and angry expressions. In the center was a podium on a dais. A young man, tall, with dark hair, stood behind it. He wore a t-shirt and blue jeans, and his fist was raised high in the air.

Lila froze. He was one of the men in her father's photo. The one behind her mother. She compared the yearbook picture with the one she held in her hand. The same dark hair, rangy build, the same brooding expression. It was definitely him.

The caption underneath the photo read: *Student activist Dar Gantner leads a MOBE anti-war rally; Fall, 1967.*

FOURTEEN

By the time Lila headed back to her car, the icy rain that wasn't quite sleet had stopped. Even so, there were few cars on the road, and fewer pedestrians. Lila kept her eyes on the jumble of shoeprints on the snow-covered sidewalk. Usually the sight of random patterns was unsettling, and she'd mentally rearrange the imprints into neat lines and geometric shapes. Tonight, though, they didn't bother her. In fact, she felt buoyant.

It had worked. She had the name of someone who knew her mother. She couldn't wait to get back to Danny's to Google Dar Gantner. She'd track him down and pay him a visit, just like she'd done with the Redakers. He would know something about her mother. He had to.

She hiked to the corner, trying to avoid any hidden black ice. James Redaker obviously didn't approve of Dar Gantner, that was clear. Redaker had been a jock. Jocks and hippies didn't mix.

To be honest, Lila was surprised, too. She'd always believed her father was a practical businessman who, by spotting and growing new businesses, was nurturing capitalism. She'd gone into finance largely because of him. It was hard to imagine him with hippies and war protestors as friends. Then again, a lot of Baby Boomer businessmen claimed to be hippies during the Sixties. Maybe it was her mother's influence. Maybe she'd drawn him into that culture.

And what about Dar Gantner? Was he steeped in the politics of the past? When they met, would he lecture her about the evils of the establishment and the imperialist state? Lila drew herself up. If he had information about her mother, she'd have to deal with it.

The darkness outside was relieved by a pool of light from a streetlamp a few feet away. She was just turning the corner, absorbed in her thoughts, when an engine exploded into life behind her. She spun around. A figure on a motorcycle rode slowly towards her. The bike seemed to have materialized from nowhere. It appeared to be more high-tech than most bikes, with lots of shiny blue metal and gray plastic extending from the front. The configuration almost looked like the beak of a bird of prey.

A helmet covered the rider's head, and the visor hid his features. He was wearing a heavy black leather jacket, leather pants, and black boots. But his hands gripping the handlebars were bare. It was bitter cold. He should be wearing gloves.

Lila turned back and continued down the street. A tall man was walking toward her. He wore a pea coat and jeans. A muffler was tied around his neck, and his face was covered by a ski mask. His hands were in his pockets, and his head was slightly tilted, as though he was watching both her and the man on the motorcycle.

It was then that the incongruity of someone gunning a motorcycle on an icy street hit her. Motorcycles were for warm weather. Summer rides. Fall outings. Why was someone cruising the Gold Coast in the middle of winter?

The whine of the motor intensified. Lila spun around. The rider slowed to a crawl and came close enough for her to see his visor was tinted. He stopped and anchored the bike between his legs. Light spilled onto his visor and split into a shiny rainbow, like an oil slick. She couldn't see his face. He kept one hand on the throttle and slipped the other inside his jacket, which was partially unzipped. When it reappeared, it was holding a gun.

Lila froze. Time slowed, unfolding in a diffident, detached way. The rider aimed the gun. She took a breath, expecting it to be her last. A flash of light tore the night. A loud crack followed. She squeezed her eyes shut, waiting for the pain to rip through her body. Confusion swept over her. She opened her eyes. She was still standing, very much alive. He'd missed. But he was so close. How had that happened?

She ordered herself to move, but her feet were rooted to the pavement. Like a rabbit, if she kept absolutely still she would be invisible. Oddly enough, however, the gunman paused as well. For a split second, he and Lila were motionless, both of them limned in the light from the streetlamp. Then he raised the gun again.

Just as he was taking aim, a presence flew at Lila, knocking her off her feet. A heavy weight pinned her to the sidewalk. She squirmed and wriggled, trying to free herself, but the weight bearing down on her made it impossible. As she gulped down air, another gunshot rang out.

Then came an eerie moment of silence. Lila smelled wet wool. The pea coat. Had someone been hit? Nothing moved.

A sudden growl from the motorcycle broke the silence. She might have heard someone grunt. Then the bike accelerated and sped off, its tires spraying wet snow and slush. As the roar of the bike faded, the man on top of her shifted. He was alive. She lay still. He was trying to get up, but his arms flailed, and his movements were awkward. Finally he pushed himself off and lurched to his feet.

"Are you all right?" Lila croaked. Then she caught herself. What if he was in league with the motorcycle man? Maybe he was there to finish the job his partner had started.

The man hovered above her. The ski mask still covered his face, and the only thing she could see were his eyes. Dark, intense. And something else. Lila wasn't great at decoding feelings, but she thought she saw a gleam of satisfaction. Then he tore his gaze from hers, and, without a word, jogged away.

"Wait! Stop!" Lila yelled as she pushed herself up. "Who are you?"

The man headed east towards Lake Michigan. Before the night swallowed him, she noticed he was wearing sneakers. Sneakers in winter?

She stood up gingerly, stretching and flexing her limbs. Everything seemed to be working, physically, but her pulse was pounding, and she started to shake uncontrollably. She'd never felt so cold. She pulled her coat more tightly around her. She spotted her purse on the ground a few yards away. She was amazed it was still there. She grabbed it and fumbled inside for her cell.

FIFTEEN

So you're not sure if he was attacking or rescuing you?" the cop asked. His partner handed Lila some coffee. She was in the back seat of a patrol car a block away from the "incident," as they called it, in front of a coffee house. Lila would rather be downing a belt of scotch from the bar next door, but she didn't have the chance—or the nerve—to suggest it. She knew from the cops' attitudes that they weren't sure what they were dealing with and didn't much care. Drive-bys were an unfortunate fact of life in Chicago. Even on the Gold Coast.

The cop who'd bought the coffee slid back into the driver's seat and twisted around. Although she'd already told them the basics, she started to explain again. The cop in the passenger seat cut her off with questions. No, she couldn't identify the motorcycle. No, she couldn't describe the rider. No, she couldn't even describe the man who fell on top of her. She didn't know where the bullets or shell casings might be.

The cop in the passenger seat clicked his ballpoint pen. In, out. In, out. The sound of the clicks was mesmerizing. "So what happens next?" she asked. "Do you need me to come down to the station?"

His voice was impassive. "That won't be necessary. We have everything we need. We'll file the report."

She eyed him. "And?"

He shrugged. "You haven't given us much to follow up on. A guy, on a bike you can't describe, shoots at you. Another guy in gym shoes attacks you. A gun goes off that no one else seems to have heard."

She looked at the cop in the driver's seat. "There's got to be other people who heard the shots. I mean, they were loud. Maybe if you interviewed people nearby . . . "

The cop who was clicking the pen replied, "No one called in. We checked. And we don't have the time or manpower to canvas the entire neighborhood. Especially when we don't have a . . . well . . . " His voice trailed off.

A body. That's what he was going to say. She wanted to rip the pen out of his hand. "The problem is I'm still alive, isn't it? If I were dead, you'd be all over this."

"Miss . . . what I'm trying to tell you is . . . "

"Listen." The cop in the driver's seat finally spoke up. "If you feel someone's after you, get yourself some protection. A bodyguard, something like that . . . "

Lila gazed from one cop to the other. "So that's it? As far as you're concerned, it's over?"

The cop with the pen shook his head. "We'll file a report. Beyond that . . . well . . . I'm sorry." He didn't look it.

The cop who brought her coffee got out and opened the door. He walked her to the parking lot. They exchanged cool farewells.

She got in her car, pulled out, and cut over to Lake Shore Drive. She was a financial manager. She'd never had a brush with the law; she'd never even been stopped for speeding. Yet, since she'd come back to Chicago, a fire had killed her family; a man followed her on State Street; she thought she'd been followed in Evanston; and now someone was shooting at her. And she had no one to turn to. Even Val was away. She was alone.

Except for the man who'd fallen on top of her. She glanced out at Lake Michigan. Long fingers of ice extended from the shore, surrendering to the dark, turbulent water. He was somewhere out there, white gym shoes and all. He hadn't hurt her, and she'd seen the glint of satisfaction in his eyes. He probably wasn't the motorcycle rider's accomplice. But how was it he'd been walking down the street at the precise moment a gun was pointed at her? If he really was a good Samaritan, why didn't he stick around and let her thank him?

She gripped the wheel. The heater was blasting, but she shivered. Tonight wasn't just a dog snuffling in the garbage. What if the man on the motorcycle knew where she lived? Could he be there, waiting for her? Maybe she shouldn't go back to Danny's. But where else could she go? She'd become a target. And she had no idea why.

She remembered the movie *Signs*. She'd gone to see it right after she moved to New York. The first half of the film had fascinated her, and she'd concluded the most terrifying thing in the world was to be pursued by someone you couldn't identify, for a reason you didn't understand. In the movie, though, once they discovered the enemy was simply your run-of-the-mill aliens, the story became dull, even tedious.

She wished she'd be that lucky.

Lila did go back to Danny's, but the first action she took when she got there was to take out all the knives and lay them on the counter. Just in case. She checked the phone to make sure it was working. Locked and unlocked the door several times.

She wrapped herself in a dark blue terrycloth robe that belonged to Danny. It still carried the faint scent of Aramis. She grabbed a bottle of bourbon in the kitchen, poured a drink, and tossed it down. It burned her throat, but a few minutes later, a welcome sensation of warmth seeped through her, and she thought she might be able to focus on something else. She ought to try. Distraction would do her good.

She sat down at Danny's computer, turned it on, and entered the name "Dar Gantner" into Google. She blinked in surprise. The listing of websites and links stretched over ten pages. She started to read.

Dar Gantner had grown up in Hamtramck, a working-class suburb of Detroit. His father was a shop steward at Ford, his mother a housewife until his father lost his job during a UAW strike. Then she went to work at a paint factory.

Dar was a good student. He was a National Merit Scholar, and in the fall of 1967, he entered the University of Michigan on a full scholarship.

The same year as her father, Lila realized. That must have been where they met.

Dar majored in history but apparently spent most of his time protesting the Vietnam War. In the fall of his freshman year he went to Washington to demonstrate at the Pentagon. By spring, he'd become one of the campus leaders for the Mobilization to End the War, a national coalition of groups formed in 1967 to stage large demonstrations. A couple of photos showed Dar with Tom Hayden, another Michigan MOBE member, and founder of Students for a Democratic Society.

In August of 1968, Dar helped organize busloads of students who drove from Ann Arbor to the Democratic National Convention in Chicago. During the convention he was swept up in the riots and was beat up by the cops. He was arrested twice. Still, Dar and MOBE claimed they were committed to non-violence. In fact, Dar was quoted as saying he didn't have much use for the Yippies—the Youth International Party headed by Abbie Hoffman and Jerry Rubin—who endorsed more flamboyant, aggressive tactics.

Lila read on. After the convention, Dar went quiet, and information about him was scarce. He dropped out of Michigan. Just like her father. Judging from the Google citations, he might have stayed in Chicago. Again like her father. Lila tapped a finger on the mouse. Were they together? If so, what were they doing?

He resurfaced again in June 1970, about a month after the shootings at Kent State. It was then that everything blew up. Literally. On June 2nd, sometime after midnight, a bomb exploded overnight in the Kerr's department store in downtown Chicago. Along with Marshall Field's, Goldblatt's, and Carson Pirie Scott, Kerr's was one of the bastions of State Street shopping. Although there were no shoppers in the store at that hour, two security guards were killed. A third person, a young woman, was found in critical condition in the rubble. She was taken to the hospital where she died. She turned out to be Alixandra Kerr, daughter of the department store owner. It was unclear how she came to be at the store in the middle of the night. Some speculated she was part of the bomb plot; others said not. One article even theorized that she'd been kidnapped by the bombers.

Lila winced as she gazed at photos of the devastation. The first floor of the store was destroyed. The ceiling had fallen down in large chunks, and beams dangled at odd angles. Glass was everywhere, and a layer of detritus, which had once been leather wallets, cosmetics, and clothing, covered the floor. One photo showed a gauzy haze in the air.

Kerr's was owned by Sebastian Kerr, a political conservative and generous Republican contributor. Although he was grieving the death of his daughter, he vowed to rebuild promptly, and, despite the fact that the store was not in any way responsible for the tragedy, he created a fund to help the families of the dead security guards. "We will not be cowed by thugs and murderers, whoever they may be," he was quoted as saying.

Lila kept reading. The FBI took the lead on the investigation. They scoured the country for leads, conducted extensive and intrusive (at least to civil libertarians) interviews, and kept close watch on anyone who might have had a connection to the crime. Six weeks later, in late July, they arrested Dar Gantner, who'd been hiding out in Lanedo, an abandoned Colorado mining town near Aspen.

Dar was flown back to Chicago and held at Cook County Jail in solitary confinement. Meanwhile a tussle between the U.S. Attorney and the Illinois State's Attorney broke out. The Feds wanted to make the bombing a cause célèbre, thinking that the charges of conspiracy—once they found the other people involved—and the use of explosives would make a dramatic statement. But the Illinois State's Attorney's office, mindful of Mayor Daley's influence, and the fiasco of the Federal "Chicago Seven" trial, fought for the case. Innocent people from our city were killed, they argued, and the monsters responsible ought to be punished.

The state, backed by Daley, won, and an indictment was handed down a week later, charging Dar Gantner with three counts of murder. Punishable by death. He was also charged with arson and criminal damage to property.

The challenge for the prosecution was finding the other conspirators. No one believed Gantner planned and executed the crime alone, and rumors surfaced about a deal to withdraw the death penalty if he gave up his associates. Other rumors hinted at a not-guilty plea, and some journalists were predicting a lengthy trial, one that, hopefully, wouldn't sink to the level of the Chicago Seven.

But Gantner surprised everyone. Two weeks after the indictment, he pled guilty to murder and criminal damage to property. His sentence was one hundred to three hundred years. He made no public statement, and he did not identify his associates. He was sent to Stateville, the maximum security prison near Joliet.

Lila got up from the computer and poured another drink. Why Kerr's? Granted, Kerr was a Republican, and a conservative, but Kerr's only had one store in Chicago. The rest were scattered around the Midwest. If someone was going to make a political statement, wouldn't they bomb Field's, or Carson's, or even Sears, with its reputation as America's foremost retailer? Why target a less known, regional merchant? She went back to Google to find out.

Sebastian Kerr was the son of an Irish immigrant farmer who settled in central Indiana. But Sebastian had no interest in farming, and at eighteen he moved to Indianapolis to work in a small variety store. He eventually became its manager, and when the owner passed away, took out a loan to buy the store from the man's wife. Kerr paid off the loan in three years, then took out a larger loan to expand into clothing for women and children.

He changed the store's name from Green's to Kerr's. It doubled in size, and, a few years later, Kerr erected a six-floor building on Maryland Street. Ten years after that, seven more Kerr's had opened in places like Des Moines, Milwaukee, Minneapolis, Detroit, and the location he called his "diamond"—the Chicago Loop. Kerr was now wealthy, and the family, consisting of Kerr, his wife, their daughter, and a son, bought a summer home on the Michigan shore. Lila couldn't find much information about either sibling online. Someone had done a good job preserving their privacy.

Lila closed the browser. She still didn't know why Dar Gantner and his theoretical friends bombed Kerr's. Like everyone else, she could only speculate. Did Kerr's daughter target her own family? Some radicals during the Sixties did. Maybe Kerr's was easier to get into than Field's or Carson's.

Or maybe, since it was smaller, the bombers assumed the damage would be less severe. Maybe they knew there would be fewer security guards. No. That made no sense. Whether they killed two people or two hundred, they had to know they would spend the rest of their lives in jail. It was the statement. The act. That was the point.

She went to her bag and pulled out the photo of her parents. Was Alixandra Kerr the other woman in the photograph with her mother? The one with granny glasses and long, ashy hair? She studied the faces in the picture, finally resting on the image of Gantner. Any way you parsed it, Dar Gantner was evil. There was no way she could talk to him about her mother. Even though forty years had passed, even though she would be in the well-protected confines of the Stateville visitors' room, she couldn't see herself chatting with a confessed murderer. For the first time since she'd found the photo, she felt a sense of betrayal. How could her parents have befriended someone like Gantner? What did that make them?

She studied the photo again. Perhaps she shouldn't try to track down her mother's family. She didn't have enough time, anyhow. Someone was trying to kill her. She should focus all her energy on finding out who and why. Digging up her mother's past could wait.

She put down the photo and took her empty glass to the kitchen. She remembered how, as a little girl, she was afraid to swim in deep water. Who knew what creatures lurked below the surface, their tentacles ready to capture and drag her down? Her father had spent hours patiently teaching her how to float, to tread water, eventually to swim. He'd shown her how to protect herself.

She rinsed the glass, letting warm water spill over her hands and swirl down the drain. Her father was gone; now it was up to her. She would have to protect herself—from the man on the motorcycle, from stalkers, even from the knowledge that her parents were not the people she thought they were.

But first she would check the locks one more time.

SIXTEEN

It took Dar several days to find Benny Spivak, a fellow inmate at Stateville. Benny had served a twenty-year stretch for dealing meth. A man had been killed during a deal—an accident, Benny argued; manslaughter, said the state. Benny was paroled three years before Dar, and, according to a postcard he sent Dar afterwards, was now running an engine repair shop near Rockford.

Using the Internet and the phone book, Dar narrowed down the possibilities. Once he was sure, he set out before sunrise in Cece's black Honda and headed west on I-90. The dark mantle of sky behind him became tinged with pink. It would be a clear day, but cold.

Periodically he checked the rearview mirror for a tail. He couldn't spot one, but they'd gotten more subtle over the years. Back in the Sixties you'd see two figures in a car, both of them wearing cheap suits, white shirts, narrow ties, or, in winter, a bulky raincoat. They'd be driving a Chevy or Ford, maybe a Plymouth. They'd stay precisely two car lengths behind, no more, no less. These days, though, there were so many cameras and tracking systems on the road that actual physical surveillance was becoming obsolete. Given the right equipment you could tail someone from the comfort of home. Or so he'd heard.

He reached Loves Park, a working-class town twenty minutes from Rockford, before eight. He checked the directions he'd printed out and drove to Prime Motor and Body. It sat in a commercial area off Harlem, near Range, not a backwoods road but not a major highway, either.

He did a slow drive by. The shop wasn't much more than a shack with a corrugated metal roof. The door was locked, and the front window was so grimy the only thing you could see was that it was dark inside. A plastic clock on the door indicated the shop's hours were 10:00 to 6:00.

He turned the corner and parked in front of Sherry's Café. When he went in and ordered coffee—black—Sherry, or whoever was behind the counter, looked disappointed he wasn't springing for a fancy drink. He hesitated. Coffee used to be a staple, one step up from water. Now people made obscene profits dressing it up. He wondered who harvested the coffee beans. He'd read that, in Africa, children were forced to pick cocoa beans under slave labor conditions.

On the other hand, Loves Park was a working-class town. The owner of Sherry's Café didn't give a shit about international coffee cartels. For all he knew, a fancy coffee with its premium price was what helped Sherry feed her family. Who was he to deny a hard-working person her due? He changed his order to a cappuccino. The woman behind the counter beamed.

He took the drink to the car and drove back to Benny's. He wasn't sure how Benny would receive him. Ex-cons were a weird bunch. Those who went straight often didn't want anything to do with their past; those who didn't were often on the lookout for rip-offs, especially from other ex-cons.

He nursed his cappuccino for an hour. Around 9:30, a dark red Toyota pick-up pulled up to the shop. A man bundled up in a wool hat, quilted parka, and thick boots climbed out. Compact but solid like a wrestler, he strolled to the door, his gait a bit bow-legged. Benny.

Dar waited until the inside lights flicked on and the "Closed" sign flipped to "Open." He crumpled his coffee cup, tossed it on the floor, and got out of the Honda.

A metallic smell hit him when he went through the shop door. The residue from oil, gasoline, and glue? Or the dregs of a meth lab? Dar peered over a battered counter with a chipped surface. At the end of a short hall was a closed door. But his entrance had set off some kind of buzzer. A moment later, the door opened, and Benny came out.

He had gray hair, cropped so close to his skull he looked almost bald. He was wearing a faded green sweatshirt and jeans, and he'd put on weight since Stateville. Dar remembered a predatory look on Benny's face, a look that said violence wasn't far from his mind. He didn't see it now.

Benny tilted his head and squinted at Dar. A wide grin split his face. He came around the counter, grabbed Dar's hand, and pumped. "Hey man! When did you get your 12:01?"

"A couple of months ago." Dar let Benny keep pumping. Then, as if he'd just realized he was too familiar, Benny dropped it and rubbed a finger below his nose, like he was stroking an invisible mustache. It was a habit he'd had inside, Dar recalled. Sometimes he rubbed with his finger, sometimes with his knuckle, sometimes his fingernail.

"How'd you find me, man?" Benny asked.

"I made some educated guesses."

"Still the geek."

"Actually, I called here a few days ago asking for you." At Benny's surprised look, he added, "A woman answered the phone."

"Reba," Benny said.

"You weren't around, but she said you would be back. She sounded nice," he added as an afterthought.

"Met her about a month after I got out. Don't know why she's hangin' around me, but . . . " He shrugged and grinned at the same time, looking pleased with himself.

Dar tried to look pleased, too, but his face must have shown something different, because Benny's grin faded. "Hey, what's goin' down, man?"

Dar swallowed.

Benny tilted his head. "You know never to con a con. Qué pasa?"

Dar slipped his hands out of his pea coat. "Things aren't going so well."

"You in trouble?"

Dar nodded. "Someone's after me. But not for anything I've done." He crossed his arms. "God's honest truth."

"Fuck it, you don't gotta convince me. I owe you." Dar had helped Benny compose a letter to the parole board. Benny claimed the letter was what got him out. "What cha' need?"

Dar shrugged out of his coat. "You know motorcycles, right?"

"Is the pope Catholic? Probably ain't a bike on the road I don't know somethin' about."

"I want to describe a bike. See if you know what it is. It was . . . well, unusual."

"How?"

Dar leaned on the counter. "It was higher off the ground than you'd expect. Almost like it was on stilts."

Benny nodded. "Off-road, probably."

Dar went on. "And when you see it straight on, one of the parts near the bottom stuck out at a right angle."

Benny's brow wrinkled.

"And a long, sleek piece extended out in front. Something similar was on the back. A fender of some sort, maybe. With lots of polished blue and gray."

Benny looked thoughtful. "Come on back," he said, leading Dar down the hall to the back room. The chemical smell was stronger here, mixed with stale smoke, but Dar saw no evidence of a meth lab. Shelves loaded with cans of paint, brushes, and other equipment lined two walls. Boxes filled with magazines were stacked against the other two. A bare bulb was screwed into a ceiling fixture. In the center of the room was a rickety card table with three folding chairs. An open pack of cigarettes and an ashtray lay on the table. Benny waved him into a chair, then went to the magazines.

"Lemme see here." He squatted and sorted through the box. "Right angle, you say? A lot of blue and gray?"

"Right."

Benny pulled out two magazines and started flipping through one. "I know I saw an article not too long ago . . . " He dropped the first magazine and started in on the second. A moment later, he stopped at a picture and smoothed out the page. "There you go." He passed it to Dar.

Dar took the magazine, a recent issue of *Motorcycle News*. It was open to a two-page spread of lush photos that made the featured bike look positively sensual. One shot was plastered across both pages, but smaller insets showing different parts of the bike bordered it. Dar studied the photos. He could clearly see some blue and gray materials on the front and back. "That's it!"

Benny snatched the magazine back and studied it. "You sure?"

"Yeah."

Benny whistled.

"So, what is it?"

"It's a BMW. The H2 Enduro. A dirt bike, but very high end. Loaded with high-tech garbage. Lightweight but made for off-road racin'. 'Course, you can throw street tires on it."

"The tires I saw were narrow but . . . knobbly."

"Off-road," Benny said. "You remember seeing a logo on the bike? You know, the black circle—supposed to be an airplane propeller—with the blue and white diamonds?"

Dar shook his head. "It was dark. I was lucky to see as much as I did." He leaned forward. "So what kind of person has an Enduro?"

Benny gazed at the picture again. "A guy who knows his off-road machines. And has money to burn—it costs as much as a car."

"How much?"

"Over twenty grand. And in this weather, all the salt on the roads is gonna ruin the frame. Not to mention the finish and tires. But if the guy's loaded, he probably doesn't give a shit."

"You can ride it in the winter?"

"Absolutely. You get a lot of traction on those tires. And BMW makes sure it handles like a kitten. But only a crazy man would freeze his nuts off in this weather." Benny rubbed his finger across his face again. "Now, pardner, you tell me. Why you wanna know about this bike? My guess is you ain't shoppin'."

From habit Dar looked around, checking for eavesdroppers. Then he told Benny about the incident with Casey's daughter.

Benny shook a cigarette from the pack on the table. He took his time lighting up, then inhaled deeply. "The asshole took a shot at you?"

"Two. Missed both times."

"And he wasn't wearin' no gloves?"

Dar nodded.

"That's probably why he missed." Benny took another deep drag, blew it out. "Goddamn hands were frozen." He shook his head. "Not that it helps you figure out who the asshole is. Got any ideas?"

"Maybe."

Benny started to say something but was interrupted by the buzzer. The front door opened and boots scuffed on the linoleum floor. Dar turned to see a woman come into the back room. She was short and round, and when she took off her wool cap, she shook out a mane of long blond hair. She was wearing a quilted parka, mittens, and jeans, and her skin was so white it looked opaque.

"Hey, babe." Benny stubbed out the cigarette and got up.

"Back at you," she replied. She stepped around Dar to plant one on Benny.

"This here is Reba," Benny said proudly.

She had cool blue eyes and the lightest eyelashes he'd ever seen. Dar shook her hand.

Benny picked up the conversation. "Well, whoever it is, sounds like you're gonna need some protection. Let me fix you up."

"No," Dar answered quickly.

"Listen. I know you want to keep your nose clean. You think I don't remember all your time you spent in that shitty library? But this is the world we're talkin' about. You gotta be a Boy Scout."

"It isn't worth the risk."

Benny grimaced and made a show of sighing. "Well, at least tell me you remember the shit we picked up inside."

Reba unzipped her jacket. "What shit?"

"There was this guy, Johnny V. One of the best street fighters around. He used to talk. You know, in the yard, when the guards let us out for more than ten seconds."

"The one who claimed to be a security contractor?" Dar asked.

"That's him."

"I thought it was mostly first-aid. How to stop a bleeder if you're cut, how . . . "

Benny cut him off. "That was only part of it." He turned to Reba. "It was self-defense too. He showed us how to make the heel of your hand like a weapon." He made a chopping action with his hand. "And how to do a few holds. Like the sleeper hold." He went to Reba. "Here, I'll show you."

Reba straightened her arms in front of her. "That's okay, lover boy. I'll pass."

Benny stopped and slid his hands into his jeans. Reba had him well trained, Dar thought.

Benny turned back to Dar. "Whatever. You sure I can't fix you up with somethin'?"

Dar doubted a time would ever come when he needed a gun, much less a sleeper hold. But then something occurred to him. He threw a glance at Reba.

She caught it. "What is it, darlin'?"

"What if a woman needs to be prepared to fight? Or defend herself? Would you recommend she learn karate? Or judo? That kind of thing?"

Reba and Benny exchanged looks. Reba laughed. "You're shittin' me, right?"

Dar felt embarrassed. "Uh, no."

"You ever hear them martial arts centers called 'McDojo's'?"

Dar shook his head.

"All that shit might sound good on paper, but when you get out on the street, it's worthless."

"It doesn't work?"

"Not in my world. See, it don't matter if I'm a black belt. If my enemy is tall and weighs three hundred pounds, there ain't no way I'm gonna end up on top. I guarantee it." She crossed her arms. "And if he has a gun or a knife? I'm gonna need a shitload more than a karate kick."

"So what do you use? Pepper spray? Mace?"

"Nope." Her eyes with the almost invisible lashes lit up. She dug into her bag and fished out something that looked like a razor blade with a ringed handle. She slid the ring onto her index and middle fingers and slashed it through the air. "I use this."

90

"What is that?"

"I learned about this from a friend. She heard about it at a rape clinic. The woman who designed this was raped and left for dead. She decided that wasn't ever gonna happen again." Reba slid it off her fingers and handed it to Dar. "No woman should be without one. Or two. And now, of course, men've discovered 'em." She looked back at Benny.

Dar fingered the knife. "What do you call this?"

"It's called a HideAway, because you can hold it in your palm and no one can see it. You can open a door, even use your car keys, while you're still holding it in your hand. It's a dandy weapon for close encounters of the human kind. I recommend it to all my friends."

Dar wondered what kind of friends she had, but decided not to go there. "So . . . where do you find one of these HideAways?"

She smiled. "Online, of course."

Dar was working on Cece's laptop in the kitchen when she got home and shrugged off her jacket.

"How did you get home?" he asked. "I was just about to come pick you up."

"I got a ride home with Judy."

"I'm sorry, babe. I must have lost track of time."

"You do that a lot."

He gave her a sheepish look.

"Listen, Dar, there's something . . . "

Dar broke eye contact with her and studied the computer screen. She went over. "What are you doing?"

He clicked the close button, and everything went blank.

Cece peered at the blank screen, then at Dar. "Let's get one thing straight, okay? I might cut you some slack on some things. But I don't do secrets. Even little ones. That's what destroyed my marriage. Got it?"

Dar didn't answer.

"So, I think you and I need to talk." When he didn't respond, she went on. "Not about what you were looking at online. I don't really care: porn, guns, whatever. There's something else."

"What's that?"

"When Judy dropped me off, I saw a rental truck. I think someone's staking out the house."

A ripple of unease ran through him. "What?"

"It may not have been anyone. It's just that . . . we're a pretty close neighborhood. Everyone knows everyone. But no one's said anything about moving. And I didn't recognize the guy behind the wheel."

"What did he look like? What kind of truck?"

"In case you haven't noticed, it's dark out," she said. "I couldn't see the guy's face. But the truck is from Budget. And he's parked about two houses down, across the street."

Dar went to the window above the kitchen sink and peered out.

"For Christ's sake," Cece said. "Why don't you just announce yourself? Send him an engraved invitation?"

"It's okay. He won't bother us."

"How do you know?"

"If he was, he'd have done it already."

"I don't like this, Dar."

Dar kept looking out the window. An engine turned over, the truck's lights flashed on, and it pulled away from the curb. Dar watched as it drove away, but he couldn't make out a license plate. "Problem solved."

"Damn it, Dar. It's not solved. What happens if he comes back?" Cece planted her hands on her hips. "You've been sharing my car, my computer, and my bed. Now someone else is taking an interest in you. And by extension, that means me. I think I'm entitled to know who and why."

He turned away from the window. "I'm sorry, Cece. This shouldn't have happened. I don't want you to be involved. Maybe I should go."

Her eyes challenged him. "Maybe you should."

When she didn't say anything more, he slowly stood up. He was on his way out of the kitchen when she called out. "Hold on there, Gantner."

He stopped.

"Playing Lone Ranger won't work this time. You can't just disappear off the grid and think everything will go back the way it was. They know where I live. Even if you leave, they could come after me."

She was right. He sighed, went back to the laptop, and re-opened the browser. Once he clicked on the website, he motioned her over and scooted the chair back so she could see.

"A HideAway knife?"

He nodded.

"Who's it for?"

He reached around and took her hand. Then he told her about Casey, the fire, and the girl.

When he was finished, Cece was quiet. Then, "Is that why you drove up to Winnetka?"

He nodded again.

"But why is *she* a target? If what you say is true, the fire should have solved the problem. Why are they after *her*?"

"I don't know. I just know she's in danger. The creep on the motorcycle almost killed her."

"Does she know anything about this?"

"I don't know. It's been driving me crazy trying to figure it out."

"The people you've described . . . they sound ruthless. But careful. Why add a new target? It doesn't make sense." She paused. "Unless . . ."

Dar looked over.

"Unless they're using her to flush you out. Maybe they figure if they can get to her, you'll jump out of the bush, too."

"That would make sense, except for one thing."

"What's that?"

He waved a hand toward the window. "The rental truck. They obviously already know where to find me. Why tie up men and resources when they don't have to?"

Cece bit her lip. Dar was learning that was her way of admitting he was right. He gave her a wan smile, then motioned to the image on the computer monitor. "I'm going to order one of these and have it sent to her."

"You think that's necessary?"

"Someone took a shot at her. She needs protection. It might not work if someone's pointing a gun at her chest, but it's better than nothing, don't you think?" When Cece didn't answer, he looked up. "Well, what do you think?"

"I think . . ." Cece's gaze went to the window, then back to the laptop. " . . . I think you better order two more. One for each of us."

SEVENTEEN

L ila was just coming up from the laundry room when the phone rang inside the condo. Hurrying out of the elevator, she dropped the clothes basket and grabbed the wall phone in the kitchen before it went to voice mail.

"Ms. Hilliard?"

"Speaking," Lila said breathlessly.

"This is Carolyn Bauer from Midwest Mutual. I'm the administrative assistant in the claims department. We've completed the investigation into the fire and we're ready to proceed."

Finally. The hours of interviews, walk-throughs, and photography were over. "That's great news," she said.

"We've prepared the sworn proof of loss for you to sign. We also have the subrogation agreement and the settlement draft. I wanted to make sure I have your correct address."

"Subrogation agreement?"

"When a policyholder is injured by a third party, the subrogation agreement allows us to recover costs that we incurred from that third party."

"What third party is that?"

"Well, in this case, EZ Lites, Inc."

"The manufacturer of the tree lights."

"Correct."

"How will you recover the costs?"

"I assume our attorneys will eventually file suit. At any rate, I need your address so I can send these to you. You'll have to get the proof of loss notarized and send it back. Then we'll release the check."

"I'll have my lawyer look it over. Would you mind going over the major conclusions?"

"Not at all." Lila heard a rustling of paper. Then Bauer's voice, monotone, clearly reading. "'The fire that broke out the morning of December 20 resulted in two fatalities. The fire and smoke caused extensive damage to the home. On the first story, only the exterior walls remained standing . . . '"

Lila twisted the telephone cord. First one way, then the other.

"'Local and state investigators determined the cause of the fire was a malfunctioning set of lights on the Christmas tree in the living room. The tree ignited, and the fire spread to nearby combustible materials, including drapes and upholstery . . . '"

Lila twisted the cord more tightly.

"'The fatalities were caused by co-asphyxiation.' That's smoke inhalation," Bauer explained. "'The two occupants . . . '"

Lila knew the rest. "So the official conclusion is an accidental electrical fire."

Bauer sounded surprised. "That was the operative theory from the start. Is that a problem?"

"It's just that I remember telling the investigators I thought I unplugged the cord before I left the house."

"It says here you concluded you could have been mistaken."

"I was in shock. I wasn't focusing."

"The investigators concluded the point of origin was the tree. We found no evidence of tampering, nor any accelerants. And you did admit the lights weren't working properly. In fact, you were out buying new ones when the fire began. Everything points to an electrical fire. However . . . ," Bauer paused dramatically, " . . . if you want to change your statement, we can always reopen the investigation."

The investigation was the only reason Lila had stayed in Chicago. Once the claim was settled, she planned to sell the house and property, as well as Danny's condo, and go back to New York. It made no sense to reopen the case. It would take more time, and if the insurance company determined it wasn't an accident, she might lose the entire payout. "That won't be necessary."

"I see." Bauer paused. "As I said, once we have your signed proof of loss, we'll release the check." Ms. Bauer's voice was noticeably cooler, as if she was reluctant to hand over the company's funds to someone as ungrateful as Lila.

Lila hung up. Despite what she'd told the fire investigators, she knew she'd unplugged the lights. She always turned off lights, unplugged toasters, ovens, coffee makers. She should have been more assertive in the first place, but given the stress of the fire, the memorial service, and settling the estate, she'd let it go. Granted, she didn't know much about electricity, but her theory that pulling the plug somehow sparked the fire seemed far-fetched now, even ridiculous. How would severing an electrical connection cause a fire?

But then, how did the fire start? Had Danny come back downstairs and plugged in the lights? No. He was doing downers in his room. Her father? Unlikely. He was barely hobbling around on a cane. And Sadie, the housekeeper, hadn't arrived that morning.

But according to the fire investigators, not only did the lights set the tree on fire, but the smoke detector wasn't working. Her father was obsessive about changing batteries every six months. She doubted his hip replacement made him forget. The fact that the tree lights shorted out and the alarm was "malfunctioning" didn't make sense.

But then, neither did the man on the motorcycle.

She started to pace. What if the fire wasn't an accident? What if someone tampered with the lights and the alarm intentionally? Her father rarely locked doors—few people did in Winnetka. What if someone was outside waiting for the right moment to sneak in? They could have gone in after she left for Blaine's, disabled the smoke alarm, then shorted the lights. There would have been plenty of time—she'd stopped for coffee with Annie Gossage before she returned home.

Were they trying to finish the job now? Is that what the man on the motorcycle was about? Was there a connection between the fire and the shooting? If so, then someone was trying to kill her entire family. And without the stranger who appeared serendipitously on the Gold Coast, they would have succeeded.

She should call the police. Let them know what she was thinking. Then she hugged herself. She had called the cops after Motorcycle Man shot at her. They didn't believe her and weren't inclined to follow up. Why would the fire officials be any different? They had already decided the fire was an accident. A tragic holiday accident, but an accident nonetheless. And Lila had no proof it wasn't, just an uneasy feeling. Still, she needed to do something. If only to convince herself that she was wrong. But where to start?

Maybe her father's computer files. She sat down at the computer. She would pore over her father's files. She wasn't sure what to look for—a motive? A deal gone bad? Someone who felt they'd been cheated out of financing? Twenty unproductive minutes later, she stopped. The files she was scanning were full of information about companies her father found attractive. Companies he might have acquired or financed. There wouldn't be any disgruntled people in them. They'd be in the files that weren't there. The deals that had never gone through. The deals that fell apart.

She massaged her temples. How would she ferret out her father's enemies? He'd used investigative firms for due diligence work on potential acquisitions. She'd come across a report from one of them, assessing the stability and equity potential of a particular company. Maybe they could help. Where was that file?

She was deep into the files again, looking for the name of the firm, when she came across the tutorial document: *How to Hide Images in Files.* She leaned back. She'd seen it before. But now, given all that had happened to her, she wondered. Why did her father need a step-by-step guide to encryption? What information was so sensitive he felt compelled to conceal it? Did it have anything do with possible enemies? The fire? Even the man on the motorcycle?

No. She was overreacting. Whatever he was encrypting was probably proprietary client information, data that might make or break a deal. Nothing to do with his death. Or Danny's. Or the people who were stalking her.

Still, she had to do something.

"Brian Kinnear."

"Brian, this is Lila Hilliard."

"Lila. Great to hear from you!" He sounded cheerful. Too cheerful.

They traded small talk for a moment, Brian going on about the latest season of *MI-5,* which he'd received through Netflix, until Lila cut him off. "Brian, you worked closely with my father, right?"

"Yes. I told you before. I was on his team."

The idea of working on "teams" in the corporate environment was nothing new—she'd been on one at Peabody Stern. Still, it seemed hackneyed to Lila, given the cutthroat nature of business. When her boss, quoting some management skills manual, said "there's no 'I' in team," she'd wanted to shoot back, "Yeah, but if you play around with it, you'll find 'me'."

Now, though, she said, "Brian, I have . . . well . . . a question. Did my father ever talk to you about encrypting data in digital files?"

He was silent for a moment. Then, "Encryption?"

"Well, actually steganography. Concealing sensitive information in files that he didn't want anyone to access."

"I'm familiar with the process."

"Of course. Sorry." She cleared her throat, wondering just exactly what his familiarity was. "Well, do you know if he did any of that? I mean, I wouldn't be surprised. There's a wealth of information that is—or should be—closely held. I would imagine . . . "

"I never heard him talk about encryption—or steganography—at all. At least on the projects we worked on together."

She paused. "I see." She'd have to come at it another way. "What about . . . enemies? Did my father . . . Do you know anyone who might have wanted him to fail?"

"Everybody loved your father," Brian replied emphatically. "I never heard a word said against him. Why?"

"I . . . I've just become aware of some . . . family history. A long-lost but rather cranky relative." It wasn't a total lie. "I was hoping Dad might have said something or had some documentation about them."

"Aside from you, your father didn't talk much about the family. But he was very proud of you. And, of course, Danny."

Danny—always the postscript, the sibling people felt obligated to mention. "So, you don't know."

"Lila, I was a junior partner. Your father didn't confide in me. Sorry, I know that doesn't help much." She didn't reply. "Listen, Lila, do you think maybe you and I . . . "

She knew where he was going and cut him off. "Brian, do you know anyone who does know about this stuff?"

"What stuff?"

"Steganography," she said impatiently.

"Sorry." Brian was turning out to be rather useless. Then he added, "But your father always said his webmaster was a genius."

"His webmaster?"

"The person who runs the firm's website."

"The guy in India?"

"Yes."

"Thanks."

"Lila . . . "

"I'll be in touch." She hung up and clicked onto the Hilliard and Associates website. At the bottom of the home page was a tiny box with a link that said the website had been designed by Jayanthra Angler, Inc. She clicked on the link. An email address popped up. She composed a note and was just hitting "Send" when her phone rang. Figuring it was Brian, she picked up without thinking.

"Hey. What did you forget?" No one responded. "Brian?" Silence. Then a click.

Lila stared at the phone, then checked the caller ID. "Unavailable." She ran to the window and peeked around the sheet. The street was dark and quiet. Only a few passing cars. She felt cold. She should call someone. But who?

She went to the door and made sure it was locked. Determination was one thing, but stupidity was another. If her pursuers were closing in, she needed protection. A gun was her first choice, but it would take time to get the license and take lessons. Time she didn't have. She hurried into the kitchen, opened the drawer, and took out a knife.

EIGHTEEN

Electronic beeps woke Lila. It was still dark, and she felt disoriented. She checked the clock. Nearly midnight. She was surprised she'd fallen asleep. The beeps sounded again, and she realized it was someone calling her on Skype, the Internet service that turned a computer into a phone. Peabody Stern required all its employees to have their user name as part of their email signature, since one never knew when a call from a trader in Tokyo, an investment banker in Switzerland, or a client on vacation might need to be answered. She'd downloaded it onto Danny's computer when she moved in.

The incoming call had a unique sound, a little like a European police siren but more cheerful. She hurried to the computer. The call was coming from Jayanthra Angler. Her father's webmaster. She slipped on the headphones. "Lila Hilliard."

"Hello, Ms. Hilliard."

"Thank you for calling, Mr. Angler."

"Call me Jay."

"Thanks. You got my email, I assume."

"Yes, and when I saw you were a Skyper, I decided this would be the most convenient way to communicate. How wonderful to make your acquaintance. How is your father?" His voice had a sing-song cadence and clipped British accent.

"You haven't heard?"

There was a slight hesitation. "Heard what?"

She filled him in.

"I am so sorry. I had the deepest respect for your father."

"It's been . . . hard." She swallowed. "Jay, I need your help. I've been going through my father's computer files, and I found a tutorial on steganography. Do you know what that is?"

His reply was slow in coming. "Yes."

Lila sensed there was more. "Would you know enough to have prepared it for him?"

Again a pregnant pause. "I might have."

At last, she was making progress. "Why? What did he want to hide?"

"That I do not know."

Her spirits sank.

"Lila Hilliard, my relationship with your father was a business one. If he asked for my knowledge, I was happy to be of service. But I did not ask questions that were not my place to know."

Lila ran a frustrated hand through her hair.

"Did you read through the tutorial?" he asked.

"Yes. But that . . ."

"From your reading, then, you know you can embed small messages within other data files. Much like a message in a bottle. Except they're hidden. And if you encrypt them, they're practically impossible to detect."

"Those messages . . . they would be embedded in larger files, right? MP3s or digital images, for example?"

"Normally the bigger the file, the better. That way you do not notice a few extra KBs, which would be the text of the actual message." He giggled in that high-pitched way some Indians do. "You see, you do know something about this."

"Not enough. Let's say I think a message has been hidden in a larger file. How would I retrieve it?"

"You would need—in effect—a digital 'key' to unlock it. In this case, the same software that the person who concealed the message used. You'd also need the encryptor's password. And the encryption method they used."

"Did my father have all those things?"

A momentary pause. "I sent him the software and encryption method several years ago. But I would not know his password."

Lila shifted. "Well, assuming I could figure that out, where would I look for the embedded message?"

"That is hard to say. It could be anywhere."

"Where would you look for it?"

Jay was quiet for a moment. "Perhaps someplace obvious. In the open. No one would know it was there, you see, unless your father specifically told them."

Lila considered it. Her father didn't have any MP3 files. Or many digital images. Except one. "Jay, he scanned in a photograph . . . oh, about five years ago. Of a group of young people in a park. I have it on a CD."

"He scanned it in?" Jay asked. "How big was the file?"

She went to the picture and quickly checked the properties. "Says here about 125 KB."

"Not large enough. If something were embedded within it, an image that small would have become unrecognizable."

Her shoulders sagged.

"A larger image, say from a website, for example, would work."

"You mean, like his business website? Hilliard and Associates?"

"It's possible."

"Oh god, I think they're planning to take off everything having to do with my father. Maybe they already have."

"If so, they're using a new webmaster. I haven't been notified about any changes."

She quickly pointed the mouse to the Hilliard and Associates website. It hadn't changed. Thank God. "Jay, I need to find out if my father embedded a message on the website. Can you help me do that?"

He didn't answer.

"It . . . it could be a matter of life and death."

"I can recreate the software I sent him," he said after a pause. "And a new tutorial so you can retrieve it. The encryption would likely not be a problem either. I remember suggesting that he use Triple DES."

"What?"

"It's an encryption algorithm, a block cipher formed from the Data Encryption Standard cipher by using it three times."

"I have no idea what you just said."

He giggled again. "Just remember to enter the words *Triple DES* when you are prompted for an algorithm." He paused. "However, there is still the problem of the password. And where the message might be. If it is there at all."

"Actually, I may know his password. He always used the same one for everything."

Jay sighed. "I warned him not to do that."

"I guess he didn't listen. As usual." It was her turn to laugh. "Tell me, how did you and my father meet?"

"I suppose . . . well, you could say it was a family affair."

"Excuse me?"

"My father knew your father."

She frowned. "How? You're in India."

"That's correct. In Sri Ganganagar. It's not far from Delhi."

"Did your father come to Chicago?"

"Your father came to India."

"My father traveled to India?" Lila couldn't hide her surprise. "When?"

"Let me see. My father lives with us. I will ask."

"Oh, don't wake him."

Another laugh. "It is almost noon here."

"Of course. I'm sorry."

Through her headphones she heard the murmur of voices.

Then Jay came back on. "My father says it must have been in 1968 or 1969."

Lila's shoulders gave an involuntary twitch. Her father had never told her he'd gone to India. "Where did he go? Who was with him? I'm sorry for all the questions, but I had no idea he'd done that."

She heard more soft murmurs. Then, "He came with one other young man. They traveled to Rishikesh."

"Rishikesh?"

105

"It's in Northern India near the Himalayas. It's considered a holy city for Hindus. On the Ganges river. It's where the Maharishi's ashram was."

"Maharishi?"

"Maharishi Mahesh Yogi. He taught transcendental meditation. My father worked at the ashram when your father visited."

Lila dimly recalled reading something about the Beatles and others flocking to India to study meditation during the Sixties.

"Does your father remember the other man who came with him?"

More conversation off mike. Then, "My father can't remember the name of the young man, but says he was tall, with dark hair down to his shoulders. Very slender."

"Was . . . was it Dar Gantner?"

More talk, then Jay came back on. "Yes. My father says that was his name."

Lila stiffened. Dar Gantner had gone to India with her father. Why? Was it just a youthful adventure, kids backpacking through Europe? Or was it something else? "So how did you end up managing his website?"

"Our fathers liked each other. They stayed in touch with the occasional letter and card. Then after I taught my father how to email, they corresponded more frequently. Once my father told your father what I was doing, your father hired me."

Lila nodded to herself. It made sense. Her father always talked about the importance of connections. Circles within circles. Between people, ideas, time. She remembered a BBC series with British science historian James Burke. Burke apparently came up with hundreds of fascinating and clever connections to explain progress and society. Since those were the days before Netflix or OnDemand, she'd had her father's permission to stay home from school if it ever came on TV.

"Jay, thank you so much. I'll wait for the software."

He asked her a few questions about her computer and promised to send it within twenty-four hours.

NINETEEN

T he lobby of Danny's condo building was a tiny room with mailboxes on one wall and a table underneath. Lila crept downstairs the next morning to get the mail. Everything looked normal. No one hanging around the lobby. No one loitering on the street. But a package lay on the table. A small, padded manila mailer. Her name and address were written by hand, and there was no return address. The postmark said Chicago. Her heart started to race. Should she touch it? What if it was some kind of booby-trap? What if it exploded when she opened it? She left it where it was and started back upstairs.

Then she stopped. What if the package contained information about who killed her family? Or who was pursuing her? She went back to the table and stared at the package. Nothing seemed to be ticking, and it looked lightweight. She picked it up by a corner. Nothing happened. She took it upstairs, put it on the kitchen counter, and stared at it some more. She shouldn't open it.

She opened the knife drawer and pulled out the knife she liked. She approached the mailer holding the knife aloft. She took a breath. Then, slowly, gingerly, she sliced through the packing tape covering the ends. Nothing happened. She carefully opened one end. So far, so good. She opened it wider and rummaged inside. Her fingers touched bubble wrap. As she eased it out of the package, a scrap of paper fell out too. It said: *Sharp edges. Handle with care.*

She removed the bubble wrap. A tool of some kind, sheathed in white cardboard. She tore off the cardboard and found another piece of paper inside with the word *Directions*. She put it aside and picked up the tool.

There was a ring at one end, a small, stubby but sharp blade at the other. It looked like a small Exacto knife.

She grabbed the directions, scanning them for an explanation.

"You are now the proud owner of a HideAway knife," it read.

Proud owner?

A sketch of the knife in a human hand followed. She slipped her fingers through the ring. It felt like a pair of scissors. She unfolded the directions. The knife had been invented by a woman who knew from experience that a woman's physical strength might not be enough during a struggle. The HideAway was easily concealed, yet accessible, and you could hang on to it during a fight. Another sketch showed a woman holding the knife aloft. Lila mimicked the sketch and made a few slashes.

Was this a warning . . . or a message? She slid the knife off her fingers. The directions made Lila think that perhaps—just perhaps—the knife wasn't sent by an enemy. But then, who? Aunt Val was in South America. Brian? The insurance adjusters? Her father's estate lawyer? None of them had any idea Lila was in danger.

She started to pace, thinking about the people she'd met recently. The fire investigators, James Redaker, his wife Natsumi. Then there was the man on the motorcycle, and the man who'd thrown himself on top of her. She'd assumed the stranger was just a passerby, a good Samaritan. But what if he knew she was in danger and was there to protect her? No . . . that was crazy. That would mean he knew who she was. Where she lived. Which meant he might have been following her.

She stopped pacing. Someone had been stalking her. In the Loop and in Evanston. She'd thought it was an enemy. But what if it wasn't? She picked up the directions. They included a website for the HideAway knife. She took the paper back to the computer. She would email the website. Insist they divulge who sent it to her.

She opened Danny's browser. His homepage, a news website, was the same as hers. It was the way she assured herself, especially after 9/11, that her world was intact, that no disaster had occurred since the last time she went online. Knowing her twin did the same thing triggered a twinge of regret. Despite their differences, she and Danny did have a connection.

The homepage of the website was crowded with images, headlines, and banner ads. Lila entered the URL for HideAway Knives and was just about to hit "enter" when one of the images stopped her.

It was a photo of a young man with a megawatt smile. Darkly handsome with longish hair and sideburns. He wore a white shirt with an alligator emblem on the pocket. A tennis racket was slung over his shoulder.

She knew that man! He was one of the people in the photo with her parents and Dar Gantner. The photo from forty years ago. She rooted around for the photo on the computer and opened the file. Yes, there he was on one end, standing next to her father. His face was partially in profile, but she could see the same features, sideburns, even the same alligator emblem on his shirt. She went back to the photo on the website and read the caption. "Senator Ted Markham, Democratic candidate for president, as a young man. Click here to read an interview with the candidate's father."

She clicked. Two new photos popped up. The first was an elderly man with stern eyes, bushy eyebrows, and a military bearing: federal judge Stephen Markham. The second was a current shot of Ted Markham on the campaign trail shaking hands. His sideburns were shorter now and nicely grayed. He looked older and more solid, but his face was unlined, and he was smiling broadly. His sleeves were rolled up, and his jacket was slung over his shoulder, like the tennis racket forty years ago.

According to the article, Markham was doing well in the polls but hadn't clinched the nomination. A liberal Democrat, he'd been raised in southern Wisconsin, then attended the University of Michigan—just like her father and Dar Gantner. While on campus, Ted had been active in antiwar politics. He claimed to have been beaten and arrested at the 1968 Democratic Convention. Lila bit her lip. Gantner was, too.

Unlike Gantner, though, Markham found his way back into the system. He entered law school at the University of Wisconsin, and after graduating, clerked in federal court. He moved to the state prosecutor's office, and eventually was elected District Attorney of Dane County. Five years later he ran for the U.S. Senate and won. He decided to run for president three years into his first term.

The senator's father, Judge Stephen Markham, was a former politician, too, albeit with a less storied career. After running—and losing—an election for governor, he decided his skills were best used in the judiciary. LBJ agreed and appointed him to the federal bench in 1966.

Lila rubbed the side of her neck. Too much was coming at her at once. She had to slow down, review where she was. She'd started tracking down the people in the photo in an effort to find her mother's family. She'd managed to identify Dar Gantner, and now Senator Ted Markham. She had no idea of the relationship between them, but Michigan had to be the link—all three, including her father, had been there at the same time.

But that didn't mean either Gantner or Markham knew her mother's family. In fact, it was possible they didn't know her mother at all—they could have all come together just for the photo. How many times had Lila posed for photos with people she barely knew, just to commemorate an occasion?

On the other hand, Senator Ted Markham was a powerful politician. Presumably with powerful connections. If he did know her mother, he could undoubtedly do more for her than she could on her own. But why would he? A man running for president had far more important things to do than help the daughter of someone he once posed with in a photograph.

It all depended on the relationship between Markham and her parents. Which would take time to figure out. Time she didn't have. Someone in a nearby apartment laughed, startling her. She let out a breath. She had to discover who was trying to kill her. She cast an impatient glance at the clock. Where was that software?

The steganography tutorial arrived later that night, along with instructions on how to download the software. Jay had created a special page on his website just for Lila. She saved the software to her computer and brewed a pot of coffee.

Jay had speculated that a message—if there was one—might be embedded on her father's business website. But where? It was a daunting task. Hilliard and Associates' website contained pages and pages about the company's background, bios of officers and staff, plus a series of client case histories and photos.

She decided to start with the images. Opening her father's bio page, she right-clicked his photo and saved it in a new file. Then, following the instructions in the tutorial, she opened the software, then dragged the photo of her father into it. She right-clicked it and selected *Reveal*.

She hesitated when asked for the password. The password he always used was *Casey49*, his name and the year of his birth. He'd disclosed it to her and Danny years ago, in case an emergency called for immediate access to his files. She sucked in a breath, typed in *Casey49* and pressed *Enter*. A command asked her to re-enter it. She did.

A moment later, a command asked for the encryption algorithm. She was elated. The password worked! Brimming with relief, she typed in *Triple DES*. Then, *Reveal*. And waited to see if anything was hidden on her father's photo.

Nothing came up. She sagged, then repeated the same process on another photo of her father shaking hands with a client. Nothing. She did it again on photos of the other partners and senior staff, again with no results. Then she moved to some of the logos of his clients, methodically repeating the same process. Nothing.

Three hours later, hopelessness set in. Lila had no guarantee she was searching in the right place. What if he'd embedded his message on a client's website? Or another unrelated website? Or none, for that matter? She still had no idea if she was looking in the right place. Time was growing short. She checked her email to see if there was a reply from the HideAway people. Nothing.

She stood up. It was after two in the morning. She hadn't been outside in over twenty-four hours. Fatigue and desperation were sapping her energy. She felt like she was looking through the back end of a telescope, the images small and blurry, barely perceptible.

She went into the bedroom and turned on Danny's small TV. It was tuned to CNN. Now that she knew who he was, Ted Markham seemed to be all over the news. Tonight he was marching in a torchlight parade honoring breast cancer survivors and stressing the need for more efficient health care.

She snapped off the TV and burrowed under the blankets, watching the patterns from passing headlights creep across the ceiling. Once this was over, once the danger had passed, she would resume the search for her mother's family, and her first call would be to Ted Markham. She wondered if her father's name would be enough to get her past his handlers. Her father had never mentioned him, which was puzzling. If they'd been close, shouldn't she have heard Markham's name, at least once or twice?

The bedcovers bunched up around her legs. She kicked them off. Her father had so many connections. It was his gift, they said—the ability to bring people together. No question it had helped him grow his business. But over the years the important connections—emotional, intimate ones—had eluded him. For example, he never remarried. As far as she knew, he'd hardly even dated. All those connections, and yet, where did they lead?

Something scraped against her consciousness. The thought was familiar; she'd come across it before. She sat up in bed. Something told her to mentally trace it. She squeezed her eyes shut, willing it to come. Where had she heard it? Connections that led nowhere. Interwoven. Overlapping. Braids.

When she got it, she threw the covers aside and leapt out of bed. She ran to the computer and clicked onto her father's website. The logo of Hilliard and Associates was a stylized Celtic knot. She'd always wondered why he chose it. Its intricate pattern of entwined braids and knots looped back on itself, going nowhere. Looking at the interlaced threads now, though, you could argue just the opposite. That the patterns were circles within circles, with links and connections to everything. Like her father.

112

A burst of energy kicked in, and Lila quickly copied the image and dragged it into the software. She entered the password, typed in the encryption method and clicked on *Reveal.* Something was there! It was the name of a file: *bcinfo.txt*

Her hands shaking, she went back to the tutorial. It instructed her to use the *Save As* command so she could save the file on her desktop. She did, then double clicked to open it. The entire contents of the file was:

www.Hilliardetal.com/bc

Her eyes widened. It wasn't exactly a website, but she was fairly sure she knew what it meant. Her father wanted her to go to a special location on the Hilliard and Associates website. She entered the proper URL, including the slash (/) and the letters "bc."

She was taken to a page containing a PDF file. Opening it required a password. She typed in the same one. The filed opened. It was a scan of an official-looking document. She leaned forward.

Certificate of Live Birth. May 15, 1970. 10:35 P.M.

That was her birthday—hers and Danny's. And 10:35 was the time her father said she was born. Danny had come two minutes later. This was her birth certificate. She read on. She barely registered the sudden whine of an engine outside.

Female. Northwestern Memorial Hospital.

She squinted. In the box where the father's name was required, "Casey Hilliard" was printed. In the box for the mother's, the name was "Alix Kerr."

She gasped. Alix Kerr? Her mother was Alice, not Alix. Monroe, not Kerr. She stared at the document, blood shouting in her ears. Sebastian Kerr was the department store mogul whose store was bombed by Dar Gantner forty years ago. Alix must be Alixandra, his daughter. The girl who was killed when the bomb went off at the store.

She went to the kitchen in a daze and filled a glass with water. She was just taking a sip when the world exploded.

TWENTY

The waves gently rocked Lila. She was floating somewhere dark and warm. She was surprised at how content she felt—deep water usually frightened her. Far away, up on the surface, a bright watery light beckoned. She decided to swim towards it and started a slow breast stroke, the way her father had taught her. But as she drew closer, the light exploded into a shimmering mass of ripples. Too much. Too harsh. She sank back into the darkness. She'd try again later.

This time she was near the surface, and the light was closer. But something was blocking it, protecting her from the worst of the glare. And there were sounds. A rustle here, a whisper there. The current was pushing her closer. But to what? She didn't know, and she didn't want to leave the blackness.

"I think she's coming to," a woman's voice said.

Lila crashed through the surface and instantly wanted to dive back down. Fiery pain stung her. Her skin felt like it was crawling with biting red ants. The pain demanded all her attention. She wanted to scream, but her mouth wouldn't obey. The noise came out as a moan.

The woman's voice again. Calm but concerned. "Easy does it, baby. I know it hurts, but you'll handle it. It won't get any worse. Try to let it roll over you. Meanwhile, I'm going to spray your skin with something."

A cool and soothing sensation misted her face. For a few seconds, the pain retreated, and she relinquished the tight grip on her consciousness. A minute passed. Or was it five? Her eyelids began to flutter. Slowly she opened her eyes. A woman's face swam into view. Blurry, out of focus. A widow's peak on her forehead. A kind expression.

"Hello, Lila." The woman's brow smoothed out. "I'm Cece, and we've been worried about you." She lifted a hand, and for a moment Lila thought she was going to brush her fingers against her forehead. Don't, she wanted to cry out. Hurts too much. The woman's hand halted in midair, as if she'd heard her.

"I'm not going to touch you. You've got some mean abrasions on your face. But they'll heal, and you'll be just as pretty as ever," the woman said. "You're at my house, in Franklin Park, by the way, and I used to be a nurse."

Lila made a croaking sound.

"Dar, bring her some water."

For the first time Lila was aware of someone else in the room. She tried to turn her head to see, but the effort was too great. She fell back against the pillow.

"Don't try to move, sweetheart," the woman said. "The best thing you can do is sleep. There will be plenty of time to talk."

Lila closed her eyes. She heard an uneven tread of footsteps. Someone was dragging a foot. Limping. "How is she?" A man's voice. Soft. Worried.

There was a beat of silence. "As well as can be expected," the woman replied.

"Here. Open your mouth." Lila felt a straw slide between her lips. "This is water. Take a sip."

She did.

"Good girl. Now go back to sleep."

She did.

When the motorcycle pulled up to the curb, Dar was climbing out of Cece's Honda. He'd taken to staking out the Evanston condo at night, convinced whoever had shot at Lila would be back. Cece wasn't happy about it, but he always got the car back to her by dawn.

The night was sharp and clear; the moon looked glued onto the dark sky. Arctic air bit through his clothes. Dar stayed on the street until his fingers and toes went numb. Then he went back to the car and blasted the heater.

If her pursuers were whom he thought, they wouldn't give up. They would be as relentless as they'd been with Casey, Payton, and Rain. But Lila was an innocent. She hadn't even been alive when everything went down. Why target her?

Five minutes. That's all the time he would give himself to thaw. He pulled his gloves back on and was back at the building when the motorcycle pulled up. A high-tech design, blue and gray plastic extending from the front. A BMW Enduro. His stomach pitched. He knew that bike.

Dar ducked into the gangway next door but kept the man in sight. The rider swung his leg off the bike and studied Lila's building. Then he started around to the back. Dar crept out of the gangway, his gym shoes muffling his steps. Enduro Man mounted a set of stairs that led up to porches on the upper floors. Lila lived in the second-floor apartment on the left. Inside, a shadow passed across a window. She was up. Walking around the kitchen.

Enduro Man stopped at Lila's landing. Unzipping his jacket, he slid his hand in and fished out a small object. Dar gasped. Dread shot through him. He sprinted across the yard.

Too late. Enduro Man pulled something from the object he was holding and tossed it onto Lila's porch. A grenade! Then he wheeled around and raced down the steps. A thunderous bang split the night. Lila's door blew in, glass shattered, flames erupted. At the base of the steps, the goon stopped and looked over his shoulder. To admire his handiwork, maybe? Twisting around, he caught sight of Dar. He froze.

Dar froze too. He knew he should make the first move. Tackle the guy, try one of those holds he'd learned in prison. But he couldn't make himself initiate a fight. They faced off, staring at one another, each knowing the other was an enemy. Then Enduro Man bolted across the yard and disappeared around a corner. A moment later an engine roared to life. Tires screeched.

Dar charged up the steps, hoping they would support him. But when he reached Lila's porch, most of the floor had collapsed. The blast had ripped away big chunks of floorboards, exposing the joists underneath. The back door had been blown apart: the top half hung at an angle from its hinge, while the lower half was in pieces. Flames licked the walls, and the smell of char and burnt plastic wafted out.

Dar strained to hear a sound, any sound that would indicate Lila was alive. Except for the crackle of flames, it was silent. But it would be a short-lived silence. Already lights were snapping on. Soon sirens, radios, and the jangle of emergency equipment would fill the air.

What would the police do when they found an ex-con on the site where a hand grenade had exploded? An ex-con who once killed several people with a bomb? Was that why the man on the motorcycle used a grenade?

Common sense said he should flee. Get out before he was discovered. Help would be arriving in less than a minute. She'd probably be okay. He should put a lot of space between himself and Evanston.

No. Not this time. If he let the paramedics take her, the killers might try again. If she was still alive.

He stepped carefully from the landing across what was left of the porch. His balance wasn't what it used to be, and one foot landed in a large gap. He slipped and fell. He broke his fall with his hands, but sharp pain shot through his ankle. He waited for it to subside and tentatively circled his foot. The movement produced a fresh stab of pain, but the fact he could move it meant it wasn't broken. He dropped to his hands and knees and crawled the rest of the way to the door.

A sprinkler gushed water from the kitchen ceiling, and most of the flames had died. Still, a curtain of black smoke hung in the air. He stripped off his pea coat and threw it over his head. Lila had to be nearby —he'd seen her shadow moving before the grenade went off. His eyes raked the debris.

There! Near the sink, under a layer of rubble that might once have been a table, was a leg. An arm protruded nearby. He crawled to her. Her torso and face were partially covered by rubble, and she wasn't moving. He sucked in a breath. But when he looked more closely he saw the shallow rise and fall of her chest. She was alive. He allowed himself to exhale.

A siren whined in the distance. Gently he wiped debris from her face. An ugly gash marked one cheek, and her forehead was bleeding. Lacerations scored her hands. He got to his feet, then bent down and scooped her up. His ankle screamed in pain. He struggled toward the front door of the apartment.

The impact of the blast diminished the further away he got from the kitchen, and by the time he reached the door, there was no damage and little smoke. He opened the front door. Thankfully, there was a small elevator in the hall. He punched the call button, and when the elevator came, he staggered inside and propped Lila against the wall.

By the time they descended to the lobby, his ankle was on fire. Sweat beaded his brow. The sirens sounded closer. Lights blazed up and down the block. He limped outside, with Lila in his arms. Cece's car was under a streetlamp. Could someone identify the license plate? It didn't matter. He had to get her in the car.

He lurched to the car and fumbled the door open. He laid her gently on the back seat. As he pulled away, a police cruiser and fire truck turned onto the block.

TWENTY-ONE

The next time Lila opened her eyes she felt logy, as if her brain was still underwater. She was on her side, the covers over her, a pillow under her head. A man sat in a chair beside her. He was wearing white gym shoes. An Ace bandage was wrapped around his left ankle. She blinked. White gym shoes in winter. Where had she seen those?

She forced herself to roll onto her back. Arrows of pain shot through her, but she studied him. Dark hair salted with gray. Dark, smoky, worried eyes. A long, gaunt face. The lines on it told a story of a hard life. He looked familiar.

"I know you," she croaked.

He nodded.

She willed the connection to come. When it did, an icy recognition flooded over her. "You're the one who fell on me the night I was shot at!"

He nodded.

"Why?"

"To protect you."

"Why? Who are you? How do you know me?"

The man cleared his throat. An odd look crept across his face. Sorrow, she thought. She squinted. He looked much too familiar. The night on the Gold Coast wasn't the only time she'd seen this man. The connection fired. "Are you . . . oh my god! You're one of the men in the picture with my mother. You're Dar Gantner!"

He nodded again.

Recognition turned to panic, and Lila looked wildly around the room. She struggled with the bedcovers thinking she needed to escape. But all she managed to do was tangle the sheets. Her throat was raw and hoarse. "Who . . . what do you want?"

Cece came running. "It's okay, sweetheart. He won't hurt you. He saved you."

Lila recognized the soothing voice, the widow's peak. But her pulse was still racing, and she felt hot and cold at the same time. Nothing made sense. This woman was good. Dar was bad. And yet, he had "saved" her? "What the hell is going on?"

The man got up and started to pace. He was limping.

The woman sat on the edge of the bed. "Someone threw a grenade into your apartment. Dar was there when it happened. No . . . " She held up her hand. "He didn't do it. But he saw who did. You're hurt, but nothing's broken, and you're going to be okay. Good thing you were wearing sweats. They helped protect you."

Lila tried to process what she was hearing. The bandages tugged her forehead and made it hurt. "They're Danny's," she said absently.

Dar stopped pacing. "Daniel," he murmured

Cece went on. "Your face took the brunt of it. They're superficial, but you won't want to look in the mirror for a while. Your hands are torn up too, but the pain should lessen soon."

Lila looked at her hands, which were wrapped in gauze. But Cece was right—the pain had dropped a few notches. Now she just felt achy and sore. She didn't have the strength to flee. She turned to Dar. "You still haven't told me why you saved me."

He seemed to be wrestling with his thoughts. He came back, sat down, and clasped his hands together. "You already know my name is Dar Gantner. What you don't know is that I am your father."

Part Two

1968–1970

TWENTY-TWO

"C asey, you're a Celtic knot." Alix giggled as she passed Rain the joint. The smoke Casey had been holding in exploded out of his lungs. He coughed long and hard, drowning out the chorus of *People are Strange* by the Doors.

"Are you all right?" Rain squinted through her granny glasses.

Casey nodded, his throat so raspy he couldn't speak.

Rain crossed her legs Indian-style and took a hit off the J. She held it in, exhaled quietly, then passed it to Dar.

"What do you mean, Alix?" Casey finally croaked.

Alix tucked a lock of blond hair behind her ear. The six of them were on the living room floor of the apartment, a shabby space with yellowed shades, torn linoleum, and cracks in the walls. "You're always making connections," she said. "With people, places, events. You twist things all together. Like a Celtic knot."

"Aw, man, you're just stoned." Payton wiggled his fingers and sang along with the music.

"Cool it, Payton." Dar raised a warning hand.

"It's all right." Alix gently stayed his hand and took the J from his fingers. She passed it to Payton. "Actually, a Celtic knot is a symbol for the complexity of the universe. No matter how our lives play out, we're all intertwined. Twisting and weaving and overlapping. No beginning. No end. Here, I'll draw it."

"Alpha and omega," Teddy said. He lay spread-eagled on the floor.

"Right." Alix got up slowly.

"You all right?" Dar and Casey said it together.

She giggled again and grabbed the back of the couch. "Trippy. I guess I'm a little high."

Dar's eyes, always dark and brooding, were edged with concern. He looked liked he wanted to rescue her, Casey thought. He usually did.

"Just sit," Casey said before Dar had the chance. "Don't draw anything."

But Alix shook her head and went to a large leather satchel in the corner. She fished out a pad and ink pen and started sketching. A minute later she brought it back and handed it to Payton. "See? It folds back on itself. Nothing lost. Very economical."

Payton stared without comment, took another hit, and passed the J to Teddy.

Casey peered at the sketch over Payton's shoulder. He saw a circle with lots of overlapping lines and squiggles. "Far out," he said appreciatively.

"That's you. Symbolically speaking." Alix plopped back down beside Dar.

"Hey. This is good shit." Teddy exhaled and passed the joint back to Casey. "Where'd you get it, Payton?"

Payton scratched his forehead underneath his rolled up red bandana. "Uh . . . some guy."

"Casey scored it," Rain said. "Not Payton."

Payton shot her a dark look.

"Well, he did. We were in Old Town, looking for copies of *The Seed* —you know, the special one with the psychedelic 'Yippie' on the cover— and we met this guy. Casey started rapping with him, and a few minutes later, we walked out with an oz."

Alix splayed her hands. "Connections. See what I mean?"

Dar took Alix's outstretched hand. She snuggled closer to him.

Casey tried not to notice. "Where's the hemostat?"

Teddy sat up, found it, and handed it to Casey. Casey clipped it to the roach, took one last hit and passed it back to Teddy, who took another toke, then dumped the hemostat and roach into a large ashtray.

Payton sighed. "So what's the program, group?"

"*I Love Lucy,*" Teddy said.

"*Star Trek.*" Casey blew out the last of the smoke.

"*The Flying Nun,*" Alix said.

"Fuck it." Payton shook his head. "And you call yourselves activists?"

"We boldly went where no man has gone before," Teddy said in a stagey, TV voice.

"And met some very spacy creatures," Casey added with a laugh.

"We've done our part," Alix said.

"Wrong. 'There can be no peace until every soldier is out of Vietnam and the imperialistic system is destroyed.'" Payton scowled. "Quick. Who said that?"

Casey rolled his eyes. "Give it a rest, Payton."

Payton persisted. "Who?"

"Rennie Davis," Dar cut in.

"Give the man a medal," Payton said.

Alix and Dar exchanged looks. "Alix has a point," Dar said. "We brought thousands of people to Chicago. Discredited the government . . . and the party that got us into this mess."

"So we brought the war home for a few days." Payton shrugged. "The war didn't take a few days off. And the pigs are still in control."

"You can't run the world according to Mao's little red book, Payton," Rain sniffed. When Payton arched his eyebrows, she added, "I saw you leafing through it the other day. That's dangerous."

"Shit, Rain." Payton ran a hand through his long blond hair. "We invade a country, dump bombs on the people, and risk the lives of millions. All in the name of 'Peace with honor.' Now *that's* dangerous."

"Hey man, Payton's right," Teddy said, coming to his defense. "Look what happened last week. Troops in the street. Fucking bayonets and tear gas. Mass arrests. This isn't America. It's Nazi Germany." He pulled out a cigarette from a crumpled pack, struck a match to it, and took a long drag.

Alix frowned. "I thought we all agreed it was time for a break. And you shouldn't put that poison into your lungs."

Teddy took another deep drag. For spite, Casey figured.

He went to the window, only half-listening to the bickering. Below was the intersection of Sedgwick and Willow, a few blocks north and west of the heart of Old Town. The neighborhood was in transition from an artists' community to a home for hippies, and some of the buildings were abandoned factories that had been divided up into apartments. Theirs wasn't much more than a few rooms with bare bulbs and the occasional cockroach, but the rent was reasonable, and at night you could imagine you were on the Left Bank of Paris or Greenwich Village.

Casey had never thought of himself as a connector. Then again, over the past week they'd formed their own personal collective, Payton called it—and it had been Casey's doing. His and Alix's.

TWENTY-THREE

C asey and Dar had come on the bus from Michigan on Sunday, August 26th, the day before the convention started. Teddy was on the bus too—Casey vaguely recognized him from campus demonstrations. They struck up a casual conversation, and when Teddy asked where they were staying, Casey told him he was from the North Shore but wouldn't be staying at home. His parents didn't understand. He and Dar had heard about a youth hostel somewhere in Lincoln Park. When Teddy asked if there might be room for him, Casey said, "Why not?"

They arrived just in time for the Yippies' *Festival of Life* concert and spilled into Lincoln Park along with five thousand other people. An hour later, Casey hooked up with Eric Payton. He'd hitch-hiked from Iowa City where students were into corn more than politics, he said. One of the few activists on the Iowa campus, Payton claimed he'd heard about Dar through the Big Ten inter-campus grapevine.

The four of them hung out that afternoon. The sky turned overcast, the PA system wasn't the best, and you could hardly see the singers, but they were grooving to the togetherness, the free dope, and the sheer numbers of people.

Then somebody tried to bring in a flatbed truck to use as a stage, but the cops refused to let it in. People started throwing rocks—so the cops said. Casey never saw anyone throw as much as a pebble, but he heard taunting and shouting and lots of profanity. The cops retaliated by sweeping into the park to bash heads.

Looking back, he supposed it was inevitable. Everyone knew there was going to be trouble. Hell, the Movement had been encouraging people to come to Chicago to disrupt the convention. The four of them had hung back. This wasn't an organized protest, Dar said, and he didn't like unplanned demonstrations.

"We might not embrace a capitalist society," he'd said in his authoritative campus-leader voice, "but we're not anarchists. Chaos is not an alternative."

Payton looked like he wanted to argue, but Casey stared him down. Payton kept his mouth shut.

When the 11:00 P.M. curfew rolled around, a crowd of people moved south from the park to the area between Stockton and Clark. Police rushed in with clubs and tear gas, pushing the crowd further south into Old Town. Casey saw a news reporter get clubbed by cops just for asking a few questions. His anger flared, and he glanced over at Dar, certain Dar was feeling the same way. But the light was spotty, and Dar's expression was unreadable.

Then a line of cops moved in, squeezing them from the rear. Casey heard a pop and a clink as something hit the ground. A metal canister rolled toward him, sizzling as it turned over. A fog of white billowed up from it.

"Tear gas!" someone yelled. "Back off!"

Enveloped in the gas, Casey's eyes began to sting. He felt as if flames were crawling up his nose. He wanted to squeeze his eyes shut, but a flood of tears poured out. His throat started to burn, and he couldn't stop coughing. He staggered back, trying to hold his breath. He wanted to cover his face with his hands, but touching his skin made things worse. He stumbled over a curb. He heard shouting. He was yelling for Dar. Dar didn't answer.

A slice of light cut an open space through the fog. He lurched forward, gasping for air. That's all he wanted. Clean air. If he took in little breaths instead of big gasps, he discovered the pain wasn't as intense. He stumbled toward the sliver of light.

"Hey, you." A girl's voice came out of the darkness. "This way. Come this way."

The streetlight pooled on the pavement, but all he could see was a silhouette. A girl. Slender. Not tall. He squinted through his tears. She was making big circles with her hands, beckoning. He started towards her but tripped on the curb.

She helped him up and led him down an unfamiliar street. At the corner she turned right and went behind some buildings. He had no idea where Dar and Teddy and Payton had gone. The walk and the fresh air helped—his vision was still blurred, but the fire in his throat was subsiding. The girl cut across a lawn, down an alley, into a building. Then up two flights of stairs. He could still hear the din from the riot, but the shouting was a few decibels removed, the sirens less shrill.

Inside the apartment, she made him lie on a ratty sofa and gently washed his face, arms, and hands. When he started to feel human again, he thanked her.

"That's cool. Glad I was there," she said.

"I'm Casey. Who are you?"

"Alix Kerr."

"Where are you from?"

"Indiana. I came in for the convention."

"I came in from Michigan." He propped himself up on his elbows. "We have a . . . well . . . I go to the Michigan shore sometimes."

Casey nodded and looked around. "How did you find this place?"

"Um . . . a friend from home hooked me up with the man who owns the building. There's a film studio on the first floor. The guy let me crash for next to nothing. He said the lights would make people think twice before ripping off his equipment."

When she got up and went into the kitchen to rinse the cloth she'd been using, Casey took a good look at her. Long, wispy blonde hair framed her face, and her blue eyes were huge. Her nose was long, but her lips formed a perfect bow when her face was in repose. But that rarely happened, he came to realize. Her mouth twitched when she was amused. Which was often. And when that twitch turned into a dazzling smile, as was the case now, Casey's heart cracked open.

Once he could breathe again, they went out to find the others, doubling back through side streets and alleys. People were gathering at Grant Park, they learned, so they headed south along the lakefront. The weather cleared, and a silver moon slid across the night sky, trailing a veil of sparks on the waves. By the time they reached Oak Street Beach, with the twinkling expanse of water on one side and the lights from the buildings on the other, Alix said she'd never seen such a beautiful city. Casey felt a swell of pride.

A crowd of about a hundred people huddled on the beach around a campfire. As they passed, Casey called out for Dar and Teddy. They heard a few shouts back of "Not here, man," and "They're waging the revolution." Then a female voice called out, "Teddy Markham? Are you looking for Teddy Markham?"

Casey's pulse quickened. "You know him?" he yelled back

A girl disengaged herself from the crowd and trotted over. She was small, with long silvery blonde hair that glinted in the moonlight. She was wearing a denim jacket, jeans, and granny glasses. A camera encased in a macramé sling hung from her shoulder. "I haven't seen him, but we went to high school together."

"In Madison?"

"Yeah."

"Who are you?"

Rain hesitated. "Julie."

"Cool." Casey nodded.

Alix stepped forward. "I'm Alix."

Julie started to sway. Alix grabbed her arm. "Are you okay?"

"I was gassed earlier. I guess I'm still kind of messed up."

"Me too," Casey said. They exchanged nods. Then Casey said, "So have you seen Teddy?"

"You know, it's weird. I hadn't seen him in over a year, but I thought I saw him earlier. In the park. He's got long sideburns now, right?"

"That's him."

"But that was hours ago. I don't know where he went."

"Okay. Thanks. Peace." Casey turned to go.

It was Alix who intervened. "Hey, Julie. You have a place to crash tonight?"

She shook her head.

"You want to stay with us? We have a place in Old Town. Running water and everything."

Casey, elated that Alix had used the pronoun "we," sidled closer to her. Alix didn't seem to notice.

Rain did, though. Casey could tell. But all she said was, "That would be far out."

The three of them walked to Michigan Avenue and caught a bus to Grant Park. Searching the crowd, Casey spotted Dar and Teddy and Payton. They'd marched to police headquarters at 11th and State, but the cops had forced them back to Grant Park.

Casey made introductions.

That was a mistake, Casey thought now, as he stared out the window in the apartment. From the moment Alix and Dar met, he didn't stand a chance. It didn't matter that they were totally mismatched: Dar, tall and brooding, from blue-collar Detroit; Alix, fair, petite, almost ethereal, from the wheat fields of Indiana. They couldn't take their eyes off each other.

Rain saw it, too. Although she pretended to be excited about reconnecting with Teddy, Casey saw her glance at Dar and Alix when she thought no one was looking. Teddy seemed restrained, but whether that was because he'd unexpectedly hooked up with someone from high school, or because of the vibes from Dar and Alix, Casey didn't know. The only one who seemed oblivious was Payton.

Dar made sure he sat next to Alix on the bus back to Old Town, and he offered her his arm—almost tenderly, Casey thought—as she descended the steps. Back in the apartment, when Casey finally crashed in one of the bedrooms, Alix and Dar stayed in the living room, talking softly. Casey tried to deny it, but envy gnawed at his gut.

The convention was marked by flashes of exhilaration and moments of fear. There was no master plan. Demonstrations erupted opportunistically—someone wanted to march to Grant Park, someone else wanted to liberate the Amphitheater, someone else to overrun the Hilton. Squads formed and split off, only to be stopped by the cops who overpowered them with billy clubs and tear gas. If not for the injuries and arrests, it might have been funny, in a black-comedy, Lenny Bruce kind of way, Casey thought. Everyone was playing their assigned role.

Through it all, though, Dar was their leader. If he ordered them to march, they marched. If he ordered them to hang back, they hung back. Casey understood Dar's need to right the wrongs of the system and insure that every member of society had a piece of it. That system had failed his family—his father had killed himself after losing his job, he'd told Casey. He didn't want it to fail others.

"Isn't that just another word for Marxism?" Teddy said one afternoon when they were relaxing in Lincoln Park between demonstrations.

"Not necessarily," Rain said. It had only been a day or two, but Dar seemed to exert a pull on the rest of them. Rain and Alix hung on his every word; Rain even mimicked Dar's language. "There used to be a balance in this country between social conscience and militarism," she said soberly. "But we let the military-industrial complex throw it out of whack. We need to restore that balance, and the first step is to stop the war."

Payton was different. He had a reckless streak and favored bold, flashy moves. Like the night he convinced Rain and Alix to sneak into the Hilton where a lot of convention delegates were staying. Their mission was to throw open the doors so protestors could overrun the hotel. Alix and Rain had gone to a Salvation Army store for second-hand high heels and cocktail dresses and nervously presented themselves at the hotel's entrance. When questioned, they claimed to be meeting Humphrey campaign staffers in the bar. The doorman seemed inclined to let them in until a security guard demanded IDs they couldn't produce, and they were kicked out. Later that night a crowd of protestors smashed through the bar's plate glass window.

There were quieter, peaceful moments, too: a rally in Grant Park where they listened to Dick Gregory, Allen Ginsberg, and Norman Mailer . . . the night Alix anointed Julie "Rain" because of her silvery hair . . . the afternoon when Rain found someone to take pictures of the six of them together.

When the convention ended, Dar decided to stay in Chicago. He would have more impact working for change on the street, but everyone knew he wanted to be with Alix. Alix would stay also. She'd never been much of a student, she said. Her parents wouldn't be happy, but she could handle them. Payton had dropped out and would be staying, too. Universities were the handmaidens of the establishment, he said, sucking your life-blood and turning you into corporate drones.

Casey was torn: he enjoyed campus life, but Dar was his best friend, and loyalty trumped school. He decided to stay too, but couldn't tell his parents—they'd try to talk him out of it. Instead he confided in his sister, Valerie. She'd tell them. She owed him, anyway—he'd covered for her abortion six months earlier.

Rain couched it in political terms. Her father would be angry, but going back to campus life would rob her of the chance to change society. Her mother, a long-time labor activist, would understand—Rain was practically a red diaper baby.

Teddy wanted to stay as well, but knew his father would be furious. So he decided simply not to tell him. By the time he discovered Teddy wasn't back at Michigan, it would be a fait accompli.

Alix talked to the guy who owned the film studio and came back with good news. They could all live in the Old Town apartment, provided they chipped in thirty dollars a month per person for rent. No phone or TV, but those were the earmarks of a materialistic society anyway. They didn't need superficial contrivances.

That's the way it started, Casey thought. People sharing their homes, their money, their beds. Together they would change the world.

TWENTY-FOUR

D ecked out with turrets, Roman arches, and even a few Gothic touches, the Chicago Coliseum looked more like a fortress than a convention center, Rain thought. Maybe that was because the building's façade once belonged to a Civil War prison in Richmond, Virginia, and had been transplanted, brick by brick, to Chicago.

"Spooky," she said, as the six of them gathered outside the building at 16th and Wabash. "Why does SDS want to have their convention here?"

"It's the only place that'll have them," Casey said. The Students for a Democratic Society had tried to find a venue for weeks, but no other spot in the city was willing to risk the violence they feared would accompany the proposed gathering.

"I think it's romantic," Alix said. "Like something out of Shakespeare. Or King Arthur."

It was a few days after the Democratic Convention, and they'd taken the bus to the national SDS office on the west side. Rain wasn't thrilled about it, invoking the Groucho Marx rule that any club that wanted her was not a club she wanted to join. But she made an exception out of respect for Dar.

The two-room office was small and patchy, with a few battered desks, a couple of second-hand typewriters, and a mimeo machine. The walls were covered with posters glorifying the Black Panther Party and Ho Chi Minh. Two men and a woman with brown waist-length hair were perched on desks. Rain didn't know their names, but she was sure she'd seen them on TV. The woman, talking on the phone, didn't appear to see them.

"There's no question that the FBI is trying to infiltrate," she said. "They're probably listening in right now." Her voice rose. "Hi, Feebies. Hope you're having a good day." She laughed. "Of course, it's a hassle. Hoover's a rabid dog. And Daley's right there with him. The twin dogs of war." She paused. "No shit!" She covered the phone with her hand and spoke to the two men. "Do you believe it? Congress is planning hearings to find out whether there was Communist subversion during the Convention. Like it matters." She laughed again and went back to the phone. "Sure. Bye." She hung up.

One of the men, his back to them, said to the woman, "You know we're fucking sitting ducks."

"That's why we need to cement our relationship with the working class. Build some defenses . . . " She swiveled around and caught sight of Rain, Dar, and the others. "Hello. Who are you?"

Dar introduced himself.

"From Michigan, right?"

"You know him?" Rain jumped in.

"Heard the name." She looked them all over. "You're all friends?"

"We're a collective," Payton jumped in.

She frowned. "Why are you here?"

"We want to help. I'm Eric Payton. From Iowa."

If Payton thought he'd be recognized, he had to be disappointed, Rain thought. The woman made no sign that she knew him. "Well, well, that's far out." But she didn't look pleased. She looked suspicious. She pushed a shirtsleeve above her elbow. "Well, if you're serious about helping, there *is* something that needs doing."

"Anything," Payton said.

"We need someone to case the Coliseum. They're willing to let us have our national convention there next June, and we want to make sure it's cool."

"Isn't that where the Doors show was a few months ago?" Casey asked. "And where Hendrix is coming next month?"

"That's right."

135

"How about we check it out then, like from backstage?" He grinned hopefully.

A sour look was her answer. The woman spotted Rain's camera, which was slung over her shoulder. "Is that a 35 millimeter?"

Rain nodded. "It's a Minolta."

"Cool. Could you take some shots of the place? It would really help us figure out the lay of the land."

And keep us out of your hair until you check us out, Rain thought. She glanced over at Dar. He was watching her. Probably thinking the same thing. She turned back to the girl and shrugged. "Sure. Why not?"

"Damn. My lens isn't wide enough." Rain stopped snapping pictures of the exterior, which occupied the entire block of Wabash between 16th and 17th. "I'll have to take a series and bracket them."

"Where's the door?" Payton asked.

She pointed to an entrance with an overhanging canopy. "Right in front of you."

"Let's go in."

They filed into a huge, cavernous arena with a gently arched ceiling. It looked bigger than two football fields, not including the balcony that ran around the perimeter.

Payton whistled. "I bet you could fit fifty thousand people in here."

"Probably," Casey said. He scanned a flyer he'd picked up near the entrance. "Did you know both Republicans and Democrats have held conventions here?"

"How many is SDS expecting?" Rain asked.

"I've heard ten, maybe twenty thousand."

They climbed up to the balcony. Rain framed the widest shot she could manage and clicked. "We're becoming a force."

"Maybe." Dar leaned over a railing.

"Maybe?"

"The convention was one thing," Dar replied. "But now everyone's trying to figure out what direction SDS should take. There's a lot of politics and saber rattling."

"What do you mean?" Rain asked.

"Some people want to forge an alliance with blue-collar workers. Convince them it's in the financial interests of the powerful to keep the war going. Encourage them to take action."

"Stand over there," Rain ordered. "With Payton and Teddy." She took a shot of the three of them together, the hall in the background. "So?"

They headed back down the steps. "Other people want to open channels with the Black Panthers." Dar glanced at Payton. "And others want to organize on the community level, using the Methodist church or other grassroots organizations, like Saul Alinsky."

"It's all bullshit," Payton cut in. "The next step should be direct action. Confrontation."

"There's that too," Dar said.

"Hold on, Payton," Alix spoke up. "Just because things aren't perfect doesn't mean you have to destroy them."

"That's counter-revolutionary thinking," Payton said.

Alix crossed her arms. "Actually, it seems to me we have a choice whether to see things in political terms or not. That's the beauty of living in this country. I choose to think you can improve things without annihilating them."

"Spoken like a true member of the ruling class," Payton sneered.

Rain finished shooting her roll of film, rewound it, and popped it out of the camera. Alix didn't look happy.

"Issues and agendas are created for all sorts of reasons," Dar offered, clearly trying to calm the waters. "You have to look at their motives. Most SDS members aren't from the working class. They aren't oppressed. They aren't even poor."

"Like us," Alix said.

"Well . . . " Dar hesitated, as if the answer was obvious.

"Are you saying it would be better if we'd been born poor?"

"Not necessarily. When you have an organization with factions splitting off in different directions, there can be a vacuum of leadership. No matter where you come from." He paused. "They didn't coin the term 'divide and conquer' for nothing."

"Like what the FBI is doing to us," Teddy said.

"It's not just them," Dar said. "We're starting to do it to ourselves."

"What do you expect, man?" Payton shook his head. "You can't just wish change. Or pray for it. Someone has to take a stand."

"Dar was arrested twice at the convention," Casey said. "I think that's taking a stand. What about you?"

"Just because the pigs didn't get me doesn't mean I'm not committed." He looked around. "Do I have to be a martyr like Gantner?"

"No one's attacking you, Payton," Dar said peaceably. "All I'm saying is that this might be a good time for me to shift gears."

"You're gonna do a Timothy Leary? Just drop out?"

Dar started back toward the front door. The others followed. "Actually, Alix has convinced me I've been neglecting my spiritual side. I'm going to India."

Payton rolled his eyes. Teddy looked shocked.

"What the fuck's in India?" Payton asked.

"Maharishi Mahesh Yogi," Dar said.

"The dude the Beatles went to see?" Teddy asked.

"He teaches transcendental meditation. Which is supposed to help you achieve a higher level of consciousness, creativity, and energy." Dar smiled at Payton. "How about you, Payton? Want to come with?"

"I have all the consciousness I need. I don't have the time—or the bread." Payton frowned. "Hey. How can you afford it?"

"I'm lending him the money," Alix said quietly.

Payton looked at Casey, then Dar. He started to say something, then stopped.

"Is she going too?" Teddy asked.

Dar shook his head.

"Well, you can't go alone," Casey said. "I'll go with you."

"You?" The surprise in Payton's voice was genuine. "You're about as spiritual as Teddy's tennis racket."

"There's always a first time," Casey said. "You've got enough commitment for the rest of us, anyway." He turned to Rain. "What about you?"

"Actually, I think Payton's right. There is work to be done here. I met some people who work for *The Seed*." She held up her camera. "I'm gonna be their photographer."

"What about you, Mr. Markham from Madison?" Casey asked.

Teddy scratched his cheek with his little finger, an oddly feminine gesture, Rain thought. "I think I'll help Payton mobilize the Black Panthers."

TWENTY-FIVE

October 1, 1968
Dear Alix,

Well, we made it! It took us over twenty-four hours to get to Delhi, what with changing planes in New York and Frankfurt. When we got to Delhi we didn't know whether to take a train or hitch— Rishikesh is about one hundred fifty miles north. We ended up taking the train. Which was freaky. You know how they say you can set your watch by the trains in Italy because they're always on time? Not in India. It was four hours late—which someone told me afterwards was par for the course—and then it made all these stops. Took us all day to get here.

Rishikesh itself is beautiful. They call it the gateway to the Himalayas because the Ganges River flows out of the mountains right through the center of town. In fact, mountains ring the city everywhere you look. I've been taking lots of pictures. Maharishi's ashram is practically on the river, and it's a peaceful place. In fact, the whole city is full of religious significance, if you're Hindu. It's supposed to be the place where Vishnu vanquished the demon Madhu, and there are tons of temples and ashrams.

Oh—it turns out the Beatles wrote most of their new album while they were here. It's coming out in October, and they're calling it the White Album. *Maybe you should reserve a copy at the record store.*

People are heavy into meditation here. You'll be walking and see someone clasp their hands and close their eyes, right in the middle of the sidewalk. There's also lots of time to think. I remember what you said about me being a "connector." Meditating helps me realize you're right. I wonder if that will be my life twenty years from now. Hard to imagine, since I usually don't know what I'll be doing twenty minutes from now. But I'm trying to go with the flow. Focus on my consciousness and all that.

We met Maharishi once, but he's been gone most of the time. We were initiated into TM by a monk named Bansal. "Monk" isn't really the right term, but I don't know what else to call him. He works here. He's very spiritual, but still grounded, if you know what I mean? And he has the patience of a . . . well . . . a monk. He tells me that, if I meditate twice a day, I'll be much more creative and live a longer life. We promised to keep in touch after we come home.

Hi to Rain, Teddy, and Payton. And of course, you.

Peace,
Casey

October 8, 1968
Dear Alix,

Maharishi says an unlimited source of cosmic life energy is at our disposal. We have only to begin to connect our individual minds with the universal and we will gain eternal freedom. That is what I am learning in Rishikesh. I wish you were here and that we could expand our minds together. To be one, in more ways than merely physical. Although that is pretty special too. Almost holy. I know you were afraid you wouldn't understand TM, but Maharishi says you don't have to understand the theories in order to benefit from them.

We were initiated the day after we arrived. It was a lovely service. The student being initiated brings a small offering—I brought flowers—to a room with a table. There were candles, dishes for water, rice, sandal paste, incense, and camphor on the table. There was also a picture of Guru Dev. He was Maharishi's teacher. I put my offering on the table, then our teacher, a guy named Bansal, sang something in Sanskrit. After that, I was given my mantra, and he told me how to meditate. We do it for twenty minutes twice a day. We repeat the mantra over and over. If we do it long enough and can block out any unnecessary thoughts, we're supposed to gain consciousness.

TM is not a religion, really, although some people think so. The main doctrine, from the Advaita Vedanta, is that the true self is the highest and ultimately the only Reality. Sometimes this Reality is called "God," though it is not a personal being but an unchanging Absolute, an impersonal state of consciousness. Through meditation we become one with the Absolute Being, which Maharishi calls "God-consciousness."

He is persuasive. I can almost believe there is a primal source of all happiness and energy, from which spreads all the happiness in the world. If it's there, I want to find that happiness, Alix. I want to live in that energy and serenity. And I want you to live there with me. I love you.

Your soul mate through time,
Dar

October 15, 1968
Dear Alix,

Well, I think we're about to come home. We just found out that Maharishi may not be the guy we thought he was. Remember when Mia Farrow came here to meditate after the Beatles were here? Well, apparently, Maharishi came onto her. WHILE THEY WERE MEDITATING! He put his arms around her and tried to kiss her. He claims it was just affection. She says it felt sexual. I kind of believe her. Whenever you ask him something he doesn't want to answer, or he doesn't know the answer to, he giggles. Like a little kid. Shit! It's really disappointing. I thought we were onto something. Dar says the guy's a dirty old man.

Still, it hasn't been a total loss. I really like Bansal, the guy I told you about before. When I told him about Maharishi, he shrugged and said, "Isn't it all in the eye in the beholder?" I suppose that's true. But it is a shame. Especially for Dar. I'd never seen him so peaceful. Wearing his white robes, making flower necklaces. He was even smiling. At least twice every day! This will be a major disappointment for him. I miss the apartment and all of you.

Peace,
Casey

October 22, 1968
Dear Alix,

We will be home soon. India has turned out to be just another place on the map. You are what matters. Here is a poem I wrote.

Falling into Alix

What would it be like,
I used to wonder,
Tumbling from a plane into the body of a cloud?

Soft like milkweed silk?
Bouncy like a box spring?

I don't wonder anymore,
For I've fallen into Alix,
And every dream of cloud
Has been fulfilled or surpassed.

Now, when I look up at the blue sky above,
At the cotton clouds there,
It's Alix that I see.

And I understand why they call it heaven.

TWENTY-SIX

On a Saturday afternoon in late September, Rain and Alix walked past the Irish bar on Wells to the head shop two doors down. A song by Gary Puckett and the Union Gap pounded out from an open door. A group of thick-necked, rowdy white guys crowded in front watching college football, and as Rain passed the bar's window, she caught a few leers and smirks.

For the few taverns still hanging on, while Old Town evolved into Hippie Central, the clash between the cultures was palpable. The straights were jealous of their freedom—hers and Alix's. They dressed the way they wanted, wore their hair the way they wanted. Rain had happily thrown away her rollers, bobby pins, and the hair dryer that looked like a shower cap with a hose attached. They were natural. Authentic. Working at things that mattered. No bourgeois affectations for them. No living in "little boxes made of ticky-tacky."

And to think, only a year ago, Rain would have gone inside the bar to flirt, with the hope of meeting a guy who'd put her in one of those boxes. Not anymore. She did a little shimmy as she passed, making sure that her boobs jiggled and her hips swayed through her shirt and bell-bottoms. You can look, but you can't touch.

As they walked into Up Against the Wall, Bobby, the owner, nodded at them. He was gaunt and morose-looking and always dressed in black. The smell of grass overlaid with patchouli oil wafted through the shop.

Rain planted herself at the counter, but Alix started browsing. Hearing her gush over the hookahs, day-glo posters, and clothes, Rain realized Alix was a shopper. Not Rain. She couldn't deal with crass materialism. She'd go in, buy what she needed, and leave.

"This is better than Woolworth's." Alix picked up a beaded bag decorated with a psychedelic design and fringe. Fringe was everywhere: on pillows, jackets, vests, bags. She smiled at Bobby.

"You better believe it." Bobby smiled back. When Alix smiled, even a stone returned it. "Looking for something in particular?"

Alix looked over at Rain, who answered for her. "Maybe."

Bobby threw her a quizzical look.

"Alix is an artist."

"Far out."

"It's very far out. She's working on jewelry now, and her designs are incredible. We think you should sell them."

They'd brainstormed the idea the night before. Next month's rent was looming, and everyone had to fork over their share. Payton and Teddy promised to come up with their thirty dollars, although they didn't say how. Rain figured she would sell *The Seed* on the street. But when Rain asked how Alix would make rent, she just shrugged.

"She paid the whole thing last month," Teddy said. "She should get a pass."

Payton frowned. "That's not the way a collective works. No one gets special treatment."

"Then we should pay her back for last month," Rain said. "Pro-rated, of course."

"Don't worry about it," Alix said quietly. "I understand where Payton's coming from. I'll pay my share. I'll find a job."

"I thought you had plenty of bread," Teddy said. "Well, enough, to send Dar to India, anyway."

Alix's cheeks colored. "I . . . well, I had this trust fund. But it looks like . . . "

"Trust fund?" Payton's eyes narrowed.

"When I turned eighteen, I got control of the trust fund my parents set up for me. But . . . "

Rain stared at her. "You're a trust fund baby?"

"I thought . . . Dar said he would tell you . . . " Alix's voice trailed off.

Rain searched her memory. Alix Kerr. Where did she know that name? Who was her family? She sucked in a breath. "Holy shit. Are you Kerr's department store? On State Street?"

"Guilty," Alix said softly.

"Well, consider me totally freaked out," Teddy said.

"Dar said he'd tell you." She shot them an imploring look.

"Well, he didn't." Rain averted her gaze. "And to think I was feeling sorry for you because you couldn't pay the rent."

"Hold on. Before you go around making judgments, you need to know what happened." Alix's voice strengthened. "I called and tried to get money yesterday . . . for the rent . . . but some woman at the bank told me I didn't have the authority. Someone—my father, probably—blocked my access to it."

"Isn't that illegal?" Teddy asked.

"I don't know."

"You should."

"Well, I don't. And rubbing it in won't help."

"Why would your father stop you from using your own money?" Rain asked.

Alix looked down. "Because he doesn't approve of my staying in Chicago."

"You told him?" Teddy sat up.

"I called my mother. She said he freaked out. But that's okay." Alix shrugged. "Why? Isn't your family pissed off?"

Teddy scratched his cheek. "They don't know."

"Shit, Teddy," Rain said. "What's the good of taking a stand if no one knows you're taking it?" She glanced over at Payton. He'd been quiet since Alix dropped her bomb. "What do you think, Payton?"

Payton didn't say anything at first, then, "We're a collective. Everyone works. Everyone shares. Including Alix." He looked at everyone in turn.

"But it's not necessary to break off contact with your parents. You never know when they might prove useful." He paused. "So, Alix," he asked in a distinctly kinder voice, "what kind of work are you going to do?"

Now, in the store, Bobby arched his brows and crossed his arms. He might be hip, and he might have the hots for Alix—didn't everyone, Rain sighed—but he was still a businessman. "Got any samples?"

"Not yet," Alix said a little too quickly. "But I will. I've been designing . . . er, for a while."

"Well, when you have them, bring 'em in. I'll take a look."

The door opened and two young women walked in, arms around each other.

"Peace," one of the women said. Her short hair was the color of straw, and though it was a hot September day, she was wearing a black leather jacket and jeans.

"What's happenin', Donna?" Bobby said.

"Not much." She squeezed the shoulder of the other woman, who had long, straight brown hair and was wearing a paisley granny dress. A gold cross hung from a chain around her neck.

Rain made it a point not to stare, but Alix's frank examination of them was embarrassing. They're just lesbians, Rain wanted to tell her. Stop gawking.

Bobby seemed to sense the awkwardness. "Alix and Rain, meet Donna and Linda."

"We're getting married," Linda giggled. Her feet were bare, and she looked high enough to take off from O'Hare. She leaned over and kissed Donna on the lips.

"Far out," Rain said, not knowing what else to say.

Linda didn't seem to notice her unease. "We found this little park, right around the corner," she said dreamily. "We're going to have the ceremony there. And we know this far-out guru—he's really old, but he's spiritual, you know? He said he'd marry us. At the end of the month. Then we're all going back to our place to pig out. You're invited, Bobby." She faced Rain and Alix. "You too, if you want."

"Um . . . well . . . " Rain stammered.

Bobby glanced at Alix, then the two women. "You lovebirds get a ring yet?"

Donna shook her head.

Rain arched her eyebrows, and Bobby stared hard at Alix. When she didn't respond, Rain gave her a little shove.

Alix got it. "I . . . I make jewelry," she said tentatively. "Maybe I could make you a ring."

"For real?" Donna looked over.

Alix nodded and flashed them a shy smile.

Donna nudged Linda. "What do you think?"

"Far fuckin' out," Linda said dreamily.

"What are you looking for?" Alix asked.

Donna and Linda took a minute to confer. Then, Donna said, "We want to do our own thing, you know? Something different. Unique."

"Something that symbolizes our love and commitment," Linda cut in. "That we're two people becoming one." She gazed up at Donna.

"Bobby, do you have a piece of paper and pen?" Alix asked. Bobby handed them over. She leaned over the counter and started drawing. A moment later, she held up a sketch of a ring with a braided design. It looked like a simpler version of the Celtic knot she'd drawn for Payton.

Donna and Linda inspected it. Then Linda handed it back. "Far fuckin' out!" She beamed. Even Rain, who didn't know the first thing about jewelry, smiled.

Donna straightened up. "How much?"

Alix turned to Rain. "Well, uh . . . I hadn't really . . . "

"You want real gold?" Rain cut in.

Linda and Donna exchanged glances, then nodded.

Rain did some calculations. "Fifty dollars." Even with a cut to Bobby, that would more than pay Alix's share of the rent.

"If you can deliver it by the end of the week, you got a deal," Donna said.

"Really?" Alix asked eagerly.

Donna nodded, and they exchanged addresses—neither Donna nor Linda had a phone—and promised to return to the store for a fitting in three days. After the two women left, Alix started to thank Bobby.

He held up a warning finger. "These are my friends. It's gotta be good," he said.

"Don't worry," Alix breathed. "It will be the best piece I've ever done."

It'll be the only piece you've ever done, Rain thought.

After leaving the store, Rain headed south on Wells. Alix trotted after her. "Hey, wait up, Rain." Rain slowed. When Alix caught up, she said, "Thanks for your help. I couldn't have done it without you."

"I did it for all of us," she said in a flat voice. "You know, the collective."

"I get it. Hey, do you realize this will be the first time I'll ever been paid for my work?"

"No way. You did some babysitting, right? Sold Girl Scout cookies? Had a lemonade stand?"

Alix shook her head.

Rain picked up her pace. "That's right. I forgot. You're rich."

"Rain, wait," Alix said. Rain kept going. "Don't be that way. Please, talk to me."

Rain wheeled around. "Okay. Here it is. You've been pretending to be one thing, when in reality you're another. In my book, that's about as hypocritical as it gets."

"That's not true. I told Dar the night we met. I was scared to tell the rest of you. He said he would."

But Rain was adamant. "You're part of the ruling class. You're everything we're . . . well . . . trying to destroy."

Alix took a breath. "Listen, Rain. Just because I come from money doesn't mean I don't care about the war. Or the society we've become. If you shun me, you're doing everything you say you don't want to. Everyone's welcome. As long as they contribute. Isn't that what you and Payton believe?"

"But . . . but . . . you know nothing of the struggle."

"And you do? And Payton? Or Teddy? Come on. We're not laboring in the rice paddies of Vietnam. Or struggling in the ghetto. We're kids whose parents could afford to send us to college. Except for Dar."

She had a point, Rain conceded. Still. Just because Dar considered Alix his reclamation project didn't mean *she* had to. "Why aren't you back with mommy and daddy in Indiana?"

Alix's face closed. "It was time for me to take a stand."

"What kind of stand does a rich girl take?"

Alix looked around, saw a bench at a bus stop and sat down. She patted the empty space next to her. "I want to tell you a story."

Rain reluctantly joined her.

"Earlier this summer—I'd just gotten home from college—a boy I used to know came to my house. His name was Jimmy Smith. We went to public school together from kindergarten 'til sixth grade—before my parents switched me to private school. Our house was right across the street from the school. It was a big white house. With a swimming pool in back. Jimmy lived a mile away in . . . well . . . it wasn't a great neighborhood.

"So, the doorbell rings, and I open it. And there he is in his full dress army uniform. Hat, brass buttons, those little colored flags on his pocket, the whole thing. Right out of the blue. After we said hi, he tells me he just came back from a tour in Vietnam. And re-enlisted for another. He wanted to share that with me."

Rain felt her eyes widen. "What did you say?"

"I asked him why me? And you know what he said?" Alix blinked. "He said he'd had a crush on me ever since kindergarten. And he wanted me to know he'd amounted to something."

"And he figured he'd accomplished that by enlisting?"

Alix nodded. "After that, how could I say anything? I just smiled and told him I was proud of him." Her eyes got a faraway look. "Six months later he was killed."

Rain didn't say anything.

"We need to let people know what this war is doing to boys like Jimmy Smith. Boys who really believe in this country. Who want to better themselves by doing their duty. That's why I came to Chicago." Alix's gaze focused. "What about you? Why did you come?"

Rain made a soft noise in her throat. "My boyfriend was asked to be the youth coordinator for Bobby Kennedy's campaign. He . . . we . . . were going to drop out of school for a semester and do it together. I was so excited. I mean . . . to work on a national campaign . . . and for Bobby Kennedy! Then Kennedy was killed, and nothing mattered any more." She looked up. "We have to stop this war. Bobby would have."

Alix was quiet. Then, "Where's your boyfriend?"

"We broke up," Rain said tersely. She got up and motioned for Alix to follow.

"Where are we going?"

"The El."

"Why?"

"You're gonna need supplies for your jewelry. I know a place on Jewelers Row."

"Really? I've never been on the El."

"Then this is your lucky day."

TWENTY-SEVEN

There's a period of time in the Midwest that is relentlessly gray and gloomy, as if nature is taking a break after the fire and splendor of autumn—it's called November, Casey thought. He and Dar came back from India at the beginning of the month.

Consciousness raised meant that consciousness could be lost. Dar meditated twice a day, but otherwise was at loose ends. He made no effort to reconnect with the Movement and took a job at a Wells Street bookstore. Casey didn't know if his disenchantment was triggered by the trip or by Alix.

Since their return, the two of them were inseparable, often disappearing into the bedroom and closing the door. When he wasn't at the bookstore, Dar seemed content to help her with her jewelry business, which, to everyone's surprise, was thriving.

Casey had never been much of a political animal. He took a job at a nearby Chinese restaurant. Rain was working twelve hours a day, taking photos for *The Seed* and selling the newspapers on the street. Payton, who kept pressuring them to read *Soul on Ice*, claimed to be working with the Black Panthers. He didn't seem to have a job, at least one that Casey knew about, but he always seemed to come up with cash at the last minute. Casey figured he was dealing. Teddy was in and out, never really saying what he was up to, but money didn't seem to be a problem for him either. Casey wondered if he was getting ready to take off. People were always coming and going—dropping in, crashing, then heading out, usually to Berkeley or the Haight. Or drifting back into the straight world.

For Casey the presidential election was almost an afterthought—a burp in a parallel world that had little to do with them. Neither candidate was acceptable, they all agreed, but Humphrey was marginally more tolerable. Still, neither Humphrey nor Nixon would make much difference in terms of the war, and when Nixon won, no one was shocked.

The weekend after the election Teddy asked Casey, Dar, and Payton to go to Wisconsin.

"Why do you want to go home?" Casey asked, slurping the won ton soup he'd brought home.

"The school called when I didn't show up last semester. My father's pissed, and he's demanding we have a face-to-face." Teddy leaned against the kitchen wall. "Payton says we shouldn't cut our ties to family. He says they can be useful."

"How do you figure, Payton?" Casey asked Payton, who was lying on the couch. "We're doing exactly what they don't want us to."

"If we play our cards right, his father could supply us with provisions, shelter, maybe even money," Payton answered. "And what's he going to do to Teddy if all of us are with him? He'll be outnumbered."

And might not be able to talk Teddy into going back to school, Casey thought.

Payton addressed Dar, who was on the floor sorting beads. "You're coming too, right?"

Dar looked up. "Depends what Alix is doing."

"She hawks jewelry on Maxwell Street every weekend."

Despite the fact he'd been in India for a month, Dar looked puzzled, even a little irritated that Payton knew more about Alix's life than he did.

"You need to get back with the program, man," Payton said. "A weekend in the country is just the ticket."

The four of them arrived in Madison late Friday night. The traffic out of Chicago was miserable, and the bus seemed to stop at every town along I-90. Teddy, usually the talkative one, was quiet and jiggled his feet the entire way.

They took a cab to the house. On a private beach by Lake Monona just outside the city, the house was all redwood and glass, with balconies on three levels. You had to drive through a strip of woods to find it. The Markhams probably weren't in Alix Kerr's league, Casey thought, but they more than met the establishment's criteria for affluence.

Judge Stephen Markham greeted them at the door. He looked like a man with little else but power to recommend him. Watery blue eyes, bushy eyebrows, hair just turning gray. He was only about five ten, but held himself ramrod straight. Either he'd served in the military or he had a very stiff pole up his ass.

He and Teddy didn't hug, just nodded at each other. After introductions, the judge led them down a long marble hallway lined with large windows that overlooked the lake.

There was no Mrs. Markham—his parents had divorced years ago, Teddy said. The judge's housekeeper, a cheerful heavyset black woman, cooked for them, heaping roast chicken, mashed potatoes, peas, and gravy on plates in the kitchen. She had the whitest teeth Casey had ever seen. Payton wanted to smoke a joint afterwards, but Teddy said they were expected in the study.

"Expected?" Payton's eyebrows arched.

"It's time for our audience," Teddy said, trying to be cool, but Casey heard the edge in his voice.

They filed into a room that could have been a movie set. Dark wood, soft lighting, heavy drapes, oil paintings of ships in rough seas. Judge Markham sat at a polished mahogany desk in a leather chair, watching TV. He zapped the set off when they entered and put down a remote control. Casey was impressed. Not many people had the new TV controller. As the judge swiveled to face them, he picked up a pipe, then made a show of tapping the edge against a glass ashtray, filling and lighting it. The scent of cherry tobacco gradually filled the air.

"I trust you boys were well fed."

Teddy cleared his throat. "Chassie cooked a great meal."

The judge nodded and focused on each of them, lingering first on Payton, whose hair was in a ponytail and who was wearing a denim jacket and jeans. "You are who?"

"Eric Payton."

The judge puffed on the pipe and slid his eyes to Dar. "And you?"

"Dar Gantner."

"I'm Casey Hilliard," Casey said when the bushy eyebrows lifted in his direction.

"And you are all friends of my son?"

"We work together," Payton said.

"And where would that be?" He blew out a cloud of smoke.

"In Chicago."

The judge looked at his son. "I see. So that's where you've been?"

Teddy swallowed.

"I assume you were at the convention?" When Teddy nodded again, he asked, "Did you get arrested?"

"No."

Judge Markham scanned the rest of the group. "Did any of you?"

"Dar was busted twice," Payton offered.

"I see." Markham looked back at Teddy. "I wondered where you'd gone."

Teddy's face reddened. He looked at the floor. "I . . . I was going to tell you . . ., " he stammered.

Judge Markham put down his pipe. "What sort of work are you doing?"

"We're social activists," Payton said.

"Social activists," he said disdainfully. "And that entails what exactly?"

Casey tried to make eye contact with Teddy, but Teddy kept staring at a spot on the carpet. Payton's eyes were veiled as well. Only Dar looked back at the judge, as if he hadn't expected anything except hostility. A warning bell went off in Casey's head.

"There's a powerful movement out there, Judge," Payton was saying. "Young people won't tolerate a repressive society."

Markham picked up a bottle of vodka on the edge of the desk and poured two fingers into a highball glass. "In what way is society repressive?"

Here it comes, Casey thought.

"The capitalist system," Payton said, "with its focus on progress and the accumulation of wealth, is inherently repressive. In fact, we do ourselves a disservice when we use the word . . . 'progress.' What we're really doing is exploiting our resources, people, and power. The prime example of that is the war in Vietnam, which . . ."

"So progress is undesirable?" Markham smiled mirthlessly. "Somehow I think you'd have a hard time selling that to most Americans."

Payton turned to Dar with a look that said he needed help.

Dar jumped in. "Judge Markham, have you heard of the philosopher Herbert Marcuse?"

The judge's eyebrows knit together. "Of course."

"Well," Dar continued, "Marcuse says that progress breeds guilt. He says it actually inhibits happiness and fosters a sense of alienation. All it does, he says, is perpetuate and rationalize the prevailing system."

"And what does Mr. Marcuse suggest we do?" Markham asked. "Become Marxists?"

"Not at all. He's as unhappy with communism as he is with capitalism. He believes in a true socialist society."

"And how are we to achieve this?"

Dar didn't like patronizing questions, Casey knew. Still, he answered with only a splash of contempt. "Marcuse advocates something called the 'great refusal'—an attempt to foster oppositional thought and behavior through radical thinking."

"I see." Markham tossed down more vodka.

Payton tensed and tapped his foot, as if he was gearing up for a fight. But Dar remained calm. Unflappable. Dar's cool and Payton's heat made for a potent mixture. Meanwhile, Teddy didn't say a word. But this was his father's turf. That would crimp anyone's style.

The judge cleared his throat. "Interesting. But there's a significant flaw in your analysis."

Careful, Dar, Casey thought. The old man is baiting us.

"Where do you think oppositional thought and behavior leads?"

Dar cocked his head. "Ultimately, to change."

"No." Markham shook his head. "It leads to violence. And crime. I've been on the bench for years. Before that I was a prosecutor. I've dealt with vast numbers of men—and women—who 'practiced' oppositional behavior. In every case, there's a stiff price paid. Their lives are ruined, their families' too. Oppositional behavior leads to retaliation, punishment, and more repression. Not change."

"Bullshit!" Payton fired back. "That's because there hasn't been a model of what could be. Over time, as more of the populace becomes . . ."

"When you're perceived as a hooligan hell bent on destruction," Markham said firmly, "you don't do yourself—or society—any good. You've simply unleashed your innate impulses toward aggression. And those, as Konrad Lorenz pointed out, are what man needs to control if the species is to survive."

I'll call your Marcuse and raise you a Lorenz, Casey thought.

"We've tried to work through the system," Payton said passionately. "But the system has abandoned us. This has been the bloodiest year of the Vietnam War. How much longer do we beat our heads against the wall?"

"What would your father say?" The judge picked up his glass.

"My father ran out on us when I was five."

"What about yours?" He turned to Dar.

Dar hesitated. Then he said quietly, "My father killed himself when I was fourteen."

Markham froze, his glass in the air, but only for a moment. "I'm sorry." He put the glass down.

"He really is," Teddy said.

"You don't need to rescue me, Ted," Markham said. "I am a public servant. Offering my views on what makes society work. Public service is a Markham family tradition. We've done more for . . . yes . . . progress . . . than many others."

He means us, Casey thought.

"And we will continue to." Markham leaned back. "On that note, gentlemen, if you'll forgive me, I would like to talk to my son for a moment. Privately." He paused. "This has been a fascinating conversation."

Payton raised his eyebrows. Teddy gave him a brief nod. Dar, Payton, and Casey put on their coats, went outside, and strolled down to the beach. Though a thin layer of clouds covered the moon, it shed enough light to see.

"Well, he was a trip." Payton fished out a joint and lit it.

"He's dangerous," Dar said. "Smart, articulate, and arrogant."

Casey said, "I can see why Teddy doesn't want to stick around."

Dar turned to them. "Have you really talked to Teddy? Do you know what he stands for? I tried once but didn't get far. I just couldn't get a reading. He was . . . well . . . slippery. I got the feeling he was telling me what I wanted to hear."

"Don't worry." Payton brushed it off. "Teddy is fine. He's part of the solution. It's his father who's the problem."

Casey stared at the lake, the choppy waves forming whitecaps visible even in the dim light. He didn't know if people were problems or solutions. All he knew was that a thick layer of ice would soon cover much of the lake's surface, turning it into a frozen, deceptive calm. Underneath, though, the water would be churning, cold and heartless, threatening to pull them down.

TWENTY-EIGHT

The crowd on Maxwell Street was smaller than usual. Then again, it was a chilly November day. Most of the fair-weather shoppers were gone, but the merchants still showed up, and Alix felt lucky to find a space. She didn't have a stall and didn't want one—she didn't have the money—but she was able to muscle a table into a spot between an appliance dealer and a couple who sold leather goods.

She was by herself today. At first Rain had come with her; Dar too, once he was back from India. But Rain was doing layout for *The Seed*, and Dar was in Wisconsin. Alix didn't mind. The routine was familiar—she'd even mastered the El—and she was starting to enjoy the independence that came with making her own way. If her parents could only see her: the girl who'd gone to prep school and cotillion, raised to wear white gloves and diamonds, selling jewelry on Maxwell Street. The irony was it wasn't so far-fetched. Her father, a self-made man, had earned a fortune in retail. She was just following in his footsteps.

She gazed down Maxwell Street, checking out the faces. Blacks, whites, Orientals, hippies, vets, all hoping to snag a bargain. Maxwell Street was the Ellis Island of Chicago, a place where, for over a hundred years, newcomers poured in to buy and sell and deal and barter. The cheerful chaos, somewhere between a church bazaar and a street festival, was especially active on Sundays, when stalls lined both sides of the street. They said the end of Maxwell Street was coming, that Mayor Daley had sold the land to the university, and the university would be expanding. Alix hoped not. Everything was so cheap and available here. As long as you didn't ask what truck it fell off.

She nodded to a Blues guitarist playing a riff as she set out necklaces, rings, and bracelets. She'd been using silver and 24-carat gold wire in her designs, often incorporating a variation of a Celtic knot. Then Bobby showed her a ring made of several bands that seemed to be braided together but could be separated at will. She'd tried casting her own version. If it sold today, she'd make more.

By afternoon she'd sold a few things, including the ring, and she was famished. She made it a habit to try something new every weekend. Grilled sausage, fresh-baked pastries, gyros, food she'd never find in Indiana. She asked the owners of the appliance stall to watch her table while she went to Nate's Deli for a pastrami sandwich.

The wait was longer than she expected, but finally she exchanged a smile with the black man behind the counter, and headed out with her bag, inhaling the tang of pastrami and pickle. Halfway across the street, she spotted a man with dark hair in a denim jacket and jeans at her table. He'd been lurking earlier, she recalled, watching her surreptitiously. Now he looked both ways, scooped up a few necklaces and rings, and stuffed them into his pocket.

"Hey!" She yelled. "Hey you! Stop! That's my jewelry!" She started to run.

The man spun around. A kid, not a man. Fine black straight hair tied back in a ponytail. An impossibly high forehead and cheekbones. But a baby face. He couldn't be more than fifteen. When he saw her, a look of panic broke across his face, and he bolted in the opposite direction.

"Stop him!" Alix shouted. "He's stealing my stuff!"

Two beefy looking men near the appliance stall took off. The kid wasn't fast, and they managed to tackle him before he'd gone very far. As they piled on top of him, Alix caught up. A crowd started to form. The kid's eyes were squeezed shut, and his breath came in short little gasps.

She grabbed one of the men's shoulders. "You can get up. He's not going anyplace."

The guy threw her a look, then planted himself more heavily on the boy. A muffled moan escaped the kid. He was having trouble breathing. Someone in the crowd yelled, "Right on. That'll show the punk!"

"Really, thank you," Alix repeated. "I can handle it from here."

The guy refused to get up. "Goddam Injun," he hissed. "Never shudda let 'em off the fuckin' reservation."

Alix remembered a discussion in the apartment about hippies and Indians. Payton claimed they were natural allies. The tribal culture could teach them how to live close to nature, how to barter, thus bypassing a materialistic society, how to chew peyote for spiritual gain.

"Sure, Payton," Teddy had replied. "Try selling that to the tribes up north. Most of them are unemployed, sick, or alcoholics. I bet they'd just love to hear how much like us they are. Shit. The government screwed them more than the blacks."

The discussion became heated, Alix recalled. She had to calm them down by passing the hash pipe. Which, Payton said, only proved his point.

Alix tugged again at the man holding the kid down. "He can't breathe. Let him up." This time the man slowly rolled off and stood up, brushing himself off. The kid didn't move.

"I'll get the cops," the other guy said, pointing to one end of the block. "They're down there." He started down the street.

The kid turned his head to the side. He was coughing, and Alix saw scratches on his face where he'd hit the asphalt. Fear still contorted his face, but something else was there too. Guilt. He was ashamed of himself.

She made a split-second decision. "No cops!"

The beefy guy whirled around.

"It's okay. I just want my stuff back."

The guy tried to talk her out of it, but she stood her ground. She thanked both men and offered them a necklace. They refused. One of the guys still looked like he wanted to beat the kid to a pulp, but after a while he walked away. The crowd started to disperse.

The kid was still on the ground, but he was breathing more easily.

"You can get up," Alix said.

He didn't move.

"It's all right." She started to pull him up. He struggled awkwardly to his feet. Underneath his thin denim jacket he was wearing a t-shirt. His jeans were threadbare, and he was so skinny that his face looked too big for his body. The bruises on his cheeks were already turning purple. He started to shiver.

The guilt Alix thought she'd seen on his face turned into a dogged, almost defiant expression. It was the look a kid on the outside would throw. A kid who'd been ignored or bullied but wouldn't allow you to pity him.

"I'll take my things now," Alix said.

He fished his hands into his pockets and came up with the chains, which he handed to Alix.

"And the rings." He dug them out of his pocket and dropped them into her hands, refusing to look her in the eye.

Alix put them in her bag. One of the stragglers in the crowd called out. "Lady, you should press charges. Can't have trash like him thinkin' he can get away with it."

Someone else said, "What do you expect? He's an Indian."

The kid flinched, but the wind hurled a chilly gust their way.

"What's your name?" she asked. He didn't answer.

"I'm Alix," she continued as if they were having a friendly chat.

His back straightened, but the movement caused him to cough.

"I'm not gonna call the cops."

The few remaining bystanders melted away. It was just the two of them.

"I just didn't want you to rip off my stuff. I paid for the materials, and I worked really hard on the designs." The moment she said it, she wondered why she sounded defensive. He was the thief. She'd done nothing wrong.

When he still didn't answer, she shrugged. "Well, I'll be going now. See you around." She headed back. She didn't feel like sticking around. She was folding her table when a reedy voice called out.

"Billy."

She looked up. The kid was in the middle of Maxwell Street, hands in his pockets.

"My name is Billy Two Feathers."

TWENTY-NINE

R osebud," Billy said between spoonfuls of pea soup. "I grew up on the Rosebud rez." They sat on a stoop on Maxwell near Halsted. The buildings sheltered them from the worst of the cold, but the wind still whipsawed, making Alix sniffle. She'd gone back to Nate's and spent most of her day's earnings on soup. From the way Billy was spooning it down, this was probably his first meal in days.

"South Dakota, isn't it?"

"Right. I'm Lakota."

"I don't know much about Indians," Alix said apologetically. It was an understatement. The only thing they'd taught her in Indiana was that Indians were kind, gentle creatures who'd shared their corn—no, maize— with the Pilgrims. "When'd you leave?"

"Last summer."

"Why?"

"My mother died. And my father . . . well . . . " He shrugged. "My uncle told me if I wanted to survive, the best thing would be to get away. My brothers and sisters, too."

Alix had a brother, Phil, but they weren't close. He was five years her senior and five years was tantamount to a generation during the Sixties. She was envious of people who came from large families. "Why Chicago?"

"I know some Lakota here. Up on Montrose."

Alix studied him. Something about him—his voice, maybe, so clear and matter-of-fact, or the way his eyes were like magnets, drawing her into his thin face—reminded her of Dar. Or maybe it was his acceptance, at such a young age, that life was full of pain.

"Are you staying with them?"

He hesitated. "Yeah."

As he scooped up the last of the soup, a little color crept back into his cheeks. For some reason, that made her happy.

"Your stuff isn't bad," he said, motioning toward her jewelry.

"Thanks."

"But it could be better."

Alix was taken aback. "What do you mean?"

Billy wiped the back of his sleeve across his mouth. "You need to work with stones more. And real metal, not just wire. Like that ring you had earlier. Try silver. It's easier than gold."

She felt the stirrings of professional jealousy. "How do you know?"

He leveled her with a "how dumb do you think I am" look, the kind only a fifteen year old can master. "My mom—before she got sick—made jewelry. I helped."

"Is that so?" When he nodded, Alix thought about it. "Maybe you could help me."

"You mean like a job?" When she nodded, he cocked his head. "How much can you pay?"

"More than you'll get stealing."

Billy showed up at the apartment a few days later. Rain was suspicious, especially after Alix told her how they'd met, but Dar said he'd hang around to make sure Billy didn't rip them off. Aside from an unusual interest in their food, which he eagerly consumed when invited, he didn't exhibit any sticky fingers.

It didn't take long for Alix to find out that the "friends" on Montrose he was supposedly staying with didn't exist. He'd been living hand-to-mouth, crashing at hostels, YMCAs, sometimes sleeping in the park. She told Casey, and a day later, he found Billy a room in a boarding house a few blocks from the apartment. The landlady, a frequent patron of the restaurant where Casey worked, would charge ten dollars a week. Alix made sure he had enough to cover the rent.

It turned out Billy knew a lot about jewelry. Alix had taught herself the basics of casting and soldering, but Billy showed her how to water cast to create unusually shaped pins and pendants. He also showed her how to metalsmith in a way that didn't require many tools. Over the next few weeks, in addition to beading and wirework, she began to experiment with more sophisticated designs in silver and gold.

Bobby sold them as quickly as she and Billy produced them, and between going downtown for supplies, casting the jewelry, and taking it to the head shop, Billy was hanging around several days a week. He usually managed to show up at mealtime, and Alix made sure there was food. Rain kept proclaiming the benefits of organic food, but it tasted like cardboard and cost a fortune, so Alix learned how to make spaghetti, tuna casserole, and, much to Rain's chagrin, macaroni and cheese. Billy began to look better, Alix thought. His eyes grew clearer, his skin smoother. He may have even put on a pound or two.

The most unexpected—and gratifying—aspect of Billy's presence was his relationship with Dar. Dar perked up when Billy came around, and they hit it off in some macho, guy way. Alix figured they must see parts of themselves in the other. She did: the same lean bodies, coloring, intense expressions. After Dar gave Billy some of his old sweatshirts and jeans, they even started to smell alike. In fact, Dar fussed over Billy almost as much as Alix, making sure he ate, bathed, had a decent winter coat. Once in a while, when it was too cold or snowy, Dar made him spend the night at the apartment.

For his part, Billy clung to Dar and Alix. Rain didn't like it. "You can't just adopt a person like a pet. What are you going to do when you get tired of him? You'd be better off with a dog."

Alix bristled. "You and Payton keep saying we should reach out to oppressed people. Seems to me Billy qualifies."

"But this is a collective. We make decisions equally. You and Dar can't play house by yourselves."

Alix turned away from the stove where she was stirring spaghetti sauce. "I'm paying for his food. Dar's giving him clothes. Aside from inviting him to spend the night occasionally, which you and Teddy and Payton do with your friends, we're just looking out for a runaway who otherwise would be on the street. It's not playing house; it's charity."

Rain arched her eyebrows. "Kind of bent out of shape about this, aren't you?"

"No," Alix lied, "I just don't understand why you have to be so . . . so political all the time. Why can't we go a day without talking about the 'system'? Why can't we go to shopping? Or even . . . God forbid . . . a movie? Isn't there more to life than . . . than ranting against the establishment?"

Rain peered at her oddly, then unexpectedly backed down. "It's a free country. Do what you want."

That was Rain. Always testing, nudging, uncovering motives. She'd take you right up to the edge of conflict, have you hanging over the precipice and then backpedal, as if she'd just realized she didn't like what it said about her. Not like Payton, who'd race everyone to the edge, fling himself over, and take down as many with him as he could.

Casey's fears about Teddy turned out to be unfounded. Teddy came back to Chicago after the weekend in Wisconsin. In fact, something about seeing his father seemed to rekindle his commitment to the Movement. Before, he only occasionally spent time with them. Now, he stuck close to Payton, accompanying him to the south side where Payton had started hanging out with the Panthers.

Dar had stopped TM, but with Billy and Alix filling his life, he didn't go back to Movement politics. Casey didn't mind. He wasn't sure how they'd sustained their anger and energy for so long, anyway. Sometimes it was exhausting. Casey came to love the pools of calm when Payton and Teddy—and even Rain—were gone.

He enjoyed the lightness Billy brought to the apartment, too. For all the hard knocks he'd endured, Billy was still a kid. He had a sly sense of humor, and he liked corny jokes. He and Casey discovered a mutual love of comic books, so Casey started to bring home the latest R. Crumbs, *Bijou Funnies*, even *Mad* magazine. Payton frowned on such superficial reads, of course, so Casey would slip Billy the comics in a brown paper bag, preceded with raised eyebrows and furtive gestures, like they were secret agents.

One cold February night all of them except Rain were in the apartment. Alix made dinner, which Casey supplemented with egg rolls and fortune cookies from the restaurant. Afterwards, Casey sprawled on the floor reading *Fritz the Cat*; Payton and Teddy were on the sofa rolling joints. While Alix washed dishes, Dar tried to teach Billy how to play chess.

Casey watched over the edge of his comic book. Listening to Dar's instructions on how to move the knight, Billy absentmindedly fingered a turquoise and silver pendant around his neck. His mother had made it for him, Alix said. He wore it all the time, refusing to take it off even when he showered.

Casey had never seen Dar so content. When Billy moved his knight correctly, Dar leaned over and ruffled his hair. Billy grinned back. They were all becoming a family, Casey thought. A weird, unconventional family, but a family. Sure there were a couple of rambunctious siblings, who went off half-cocked. But didn't that always happen? Alix and Dar managed the nest. The others ventured out to flap their wings, but always came back to roost.

"Good job," Dar said to Billy, who'd gotten his knight across the board. "You get it."

Billy flushed in pleasure.

"Now let's talk strategy."

Payton licked a rolling paper. Content was not a word to describe Payton. He was always in motion, tapping his feet, rolling a J, scrutinizing everything. Payton didn't say much about his background, but Casey knew he'd grown up in a small Iowa town near the Nebraska border. His father had split when Payton was an infant, and his mother worked two jobs to make ends meet. Payton had more or less raised himself. He was smart—he'd gone to Iowa on a full scholarship, at least until he dropped out. But he was angry: at his father for cutting out; at his mother for not spending time with him; and at the world, for letting him down. Casey watched as Payton struck a match and took a hit. Holding in reefer as long as he could was the only time he sat still.

"Gantner, what's happened to you, man?" Payton blew out a haze of white and passed the J to Teddy.

Dar looked up from the chessboard. "What do you mean?"

"You used to be . . . shit . . . you used to be Dar Fucking Gantner! We heard about you all the way in Iowa. No one could speak like you, organize like you. I mean, next to Hayden, you were SDS. Now look at you." He waved a hand.

Casey tensed, but Dar seemed unperturbed. "I guess I'm moving on, Payton. You have to keep growing."

Teddy jumped in. "Dar, the only reason I got on that bus for Chicago last summer was because of you. You convinced me we could make a difference. That we could stop the war. Create a new order. But now . . ." Teddy, who was wearing an ID bracelet he'd brought back from Wisconsin, shook his wrist. The chains on the bracelet clinked.

Alix appeared at the kitchen door. The strains of Crosby, Stills and Nash on the radio broke the silence.

"What's your point?" Dar asked.

"We need you back, man."

Dar put down the rook he'd been holding and looked at Payton. So did Billy. Alix folded her arms. All the attention was focused on Payton, Casey noted. Just the way he liked it.

"For what?" Dar asked.

"Well, for one thing, you know the SDS leaders."

"So do you."

"But you really know them. You have clout. I need your help. For the SDS convention."

"That's not until June," Dar said.

"I know."

"What do you need?"

Casey watched Alix. Her face was blank.

Payton went on. "Okay. Here it is. You know who Fred Hampton is, right?"

"Yeah."

Billy looked confused.

"He started the Chicago branch of the Black Panthers," Dar said.

Payton nodded. "He's an amazing brother. Came over from the NAACP, you know. Was gonna be a lawyer but started doing community outreach in Maywood. He reminds me of you, Gantner. He's really smart. And committed."

Dar looked interested. Payton wasn't stupid. He was playing to Dar's ego.

"He's started the Free Breakfast Program. And he wants to start a health clinic. After-school programs, too. You know what he's into now?" Payton didn't give Dar time to answer. "He's trying to broker a peace between the street gangs in Chicago. The Panthers, Young Lords, Blackstone Rangers. Think about it . . . if the gangs aren't fighting each other, they can fight the system. Together. It's fucking brilliant."

"And long overdue," Dar admitted.

"But that's not the best part," Teddy cut in. "He wants to reach out to us."

Dar arched his eyebrows.

"He's creating what he calls a 'Rainbow Coalition.' He wants us to be part of it."

"It's an intriguing idea," Dar said, after a pause. "But do we really have the same goals as the Panthers?"

"How can you even ask, man? We're all oppressed. White, black, even red . . . " He gestured toward Billy, who ducked his head.

"I get it," Dar replied. "But beyond the war, what's our mission? Theirs is to improve conditions for black people in the ghetto. What's ours?"

"Mission?" Payton's ponytail bounced as he shook his head. "You know our fucking mission. People are sacrificing their lives for a society that refuses to meet their needs—and discriminates against them on top of it." An irritated look came over him. He took another hit off the joint. "Why are you hassling me, man?"

"A lot has gone down since the convention," Dar replied evenly.

Payton threw a chilly glance at Billy. "I see."

Dar followed Payton's look. "I still don't know what you want from me." This time there was an edge to his voice.

"We want Hampton—and some of the Panthers—to appear at the convention."

"Why?"

"Because . . . " Payton spoke slowly as if he was talking to a child. "People need to know who their real brothers are. Come on, man. The Panthers start a breakfast program for kids, and the next day nineteen of them are busted. On trumped up charges. You don't think it's connected? They're being systematically oppressed, and we need to show solidarity. Here . . . " Payton rose and grabbed a few flyers off the coffee table. "Read these."

Casey scanned the flyer, a mimeographed plea to send money to the Black Panther Defense Fund. It was co-signed by the Black Panthers, the Young Lords, and SDS.

"The least you can do is grease the wheels for us. Convince SDS we need the Panthers at the convention. To show a united front. You owe us. The collective, remember?"

Dar looked down at the chessboard. "I'll see what I can do."

Payton's face smoothed out, and he actually smiled. "Far out. Hey. I'm going to Weiss's for a brew. Anyone want to come with?"

THIRTY

The Chicago Eight were indicted on the first day of spring. Rain had given up her organic food kick and was teaching Alix how to fry chicken. She held forth while heating a frying pan filled with oil. "You should have been there, Alix. Judge Hoffman already has his mind made up. It's a fucking joke. We need to stop it. *The Seed* is printing up posters announcing a mass protest."

Following Rain's lead, Alix coated a piece of chicken with a mixture of flour, salt and pepper and dropped it into the pan. "Is this right?"

"Not bad," Rain said. "We'll make a working woman out of you yet."

"That's bullshit," Payton called from the other room.

"What?" Rain said acidly.

"Protesting against the trial. It doesn't fucking matter. So what if they go to jail? You can't jail the revolution."

Rain rolled her eyes at Alix. A second later Payton appeared in the kitchen. "You can roll your eyes—I saw you—and plan demonstrations, but you and I both know the only thing that will make any difference is direct action."

"You mean violence?" When Payton shrugged she added, "That's not the answer—even in a repressive society. You've been spending too much time with the Panthers."

"There is no choice. It's the only thing the pigs understand."

"That isn't what SDS is all about. Ask Dar."

"Dar doesn't know shit any more." He glared at Alix.

Alix gave Payton her back.

"Wake the fuck up," Payton went on. "Student riots in France and Mexico. An uprising happens in Prague. This is a fucking international guerilla movement. SDS needs to be a part of that."

Rain started to say something but was cut off by the sound of the intercom. Alix went to it and pushed the button.

"It's me," a thin voice said. Billy.

Alix pressed the buzzer while Payton kept blathering on. She went to the door and let Billy in. It was an icy, blustery night, and although Billy was wearing Dar's old pea coat, he was shivering. Alix walked him into the warmth of the kitchen. His shoulders relaxed as the heat hit him. Then he started to cough. Long, wracking coughs that wouldn't stop.

"Are you okay?" Alix asked.

"It's just a cold." He coughed again.

"Hold on. I'll get you some cough medicine." On her way to the bathroom she brushed by Payton, still leaning against the kitchen wall. He tugged at his ponytail, his expression flat, as if he was jealous of Alix's attention to Billy.

Alix brought the medicine back to the kitchen. Billy's shoulders were hunched, and he was still coughing. She poured the red syrup into a spoon and held it out. "Open up, champ."

Billy gave the medicine a once-over.

"Come on. It'll help."

Billy opened his mouth and swallowed. He grimaced. "Stuff tastes like shit."

"Don't be such a baby." She laughed. "And don't say 'shit.'"

Billy leveled a withering look her way. Rain, watching them, fought back a smile.

"Can I have some water?" he asked.

"How about tea?" Alix filled the kettle and put the flame on.

Billy started to take off his coat.

"It's a mean night," Rain said. "Why don't you keep it on 'til you're dry?"

"I'm fine," Billy said.

Rain eyed him. "Keep it on anyway."

173

Billy grumbled but kept the coat on.

"Dinner will be ready in twenty minutes," Alix said.

"I'm not hungry."

"You will be. Rain's chicken is not to be missed." Alix picked up a pair of tongs and turned the chicken over. "And now I have the recipe."

Billy shrugged and went into the living room. She heard him ask Payton if there were any new comic books.

Payton sighed dramatically. "When are you going to stop wasting your time on that trash, my little warrior?"

"When you stop acting like you know what's best for everyone," Billy shot back.

In the kitchen Alix suppressed a giggle. Even Rain managed a grin.

The chicken crackled, sending a hearty aroma through the apartment. Alix was draining a few pieces on paper towels when Rain said, "Alix, we need to talk."

"About what?"

Rain turned from the stove. "Have you ever wondered why we're the ones always cooking and cleaning, and the guys don't do shit?"

"That's just the way it is."

"Well, it shouldn't be."

"What do you mean?"

"We've been organizing down at *The Seed*."

"Organizing what?"

"A women's caucus. We do all the grunt work. But men make the decisions and take the credit. That has to change."

Alix reached for the spatula. "What does a women's caucus do?"

"It will start to raise consciousness that women are just as oppressed as—the blacks, say—and need to be liberated."

"Oh, come on, Rain. Black people and women are equally oppressed?"

"Come on, you. Who's in the kitchen frying chicken? Do you see any of the men helping? We aren't much more than cooks to them. Or wombs."

"You can't change biology."

"Biology gave us brains as well as vaginas. We are half the population. Have you ever thought what the world would be like if women had an equal voice? We need to create our own power base."

After a pause Alix said, "I don't know, Rain. You know I'm not political."

Rain's glasses reflected the light, making them sparkle. "This isn't politics. It's survival."

"I just don't know. Between Billy, and the jewelry, and Dar . . . "

From the living room, Billy coughed again. Alix stiffened.

Rain turned back to the frying pan. "Oh, never mind. You're hopeless."

THIRTY-ONE

Alix and Billy were selling jewelry on Maxwell Street on a warm Sunday in June, well past the end of flu season, when Billy started coughing again. He picked up a white paper napkin and covered his mouth, the way Alix had taught him, but when he balled it up and pitched it in the trash, the napkin was pink.

Alix, who'd been laying out turquoise necklaces, straightened up. "How long has that been going on?"

Billy bent over the table. "I don't know."

"I thought the cough was gone."

He wouldn't look at her. "It's only been a couple of days. It's not bad." He started to arrange the necklaces in straight lines. "How many necklaces did you bring?"

Alix knew she wasn't supposed to be over-protective. Dar had told her a kid like Billy needs to feel independent. That, in a strange way, he'd earned it by running away and forging his own path. But Alix felt responsible. "Well, if it keeps up, we'll have to do something about it."

He shot her an impatient look. "How many necklaces?"

"Seven." She finished laying out the jewelry. "So, what do you want to eat? A Polish? They have these kielbasas on a stick. Or a burrito?"

Billy shrugged, which meant he didn't care. She settled on the Polish, but when she brought back two hot dogs, loaded with fixings, he only took a bite of his. "You don't like it?"

"I ate breakfast late."

That was a lie—Billy always ate when she or Dar fed him, which made her think he ate poorly—or not at all—when they weren't around. In fact, now that Alix was studying him, he looked pale under his olive skin. And thin. Part of that was his clothing. It was June—he wasn't bundled up in bulky sweats or sweaters. Still, she insisted he come home with her.

The apartment was empty when they got there. The SDS convention was due to start in a few days, and Dar, making good on his promise to Payton, was meeting with the leaders to discuss an appearance by the Panthers. Teddy was with them, and Rain and Casey were at their jobs.

Alix told Billy to hole up on the sofa while she heated soup. Maybe the food on Maxwell Street was too spicy. He only took a few spoonfuls of soup but drank the 7-Up she poured. He fell asleep on the sofa almost immediately.

Over the next two days Billy didn't get better. He was still coughing, sometimes bringing up specks of blood. Alix made him stay at the apartment and dosed him with aspirin and cough medicine. He didn't complain but was lethargic and slow. He wasn't even interested in comic books.

"We need to take you to a doctor," Alix said the next day.

"No!" His answer was emphatic.

"Billy, there's something wrong. A doctor can fix it."

"I don't like doctors. I'll get better. I promise. I'll take all my medicine."

Billy's mother had died after a long illness. Although he'd never admit it, Alix figured he associated doctors and hospitals with death. Dar told her later that distrust of "white man's" medicine was embedded in Indian culture. She sighed and gave him more cough medicine.

By Wednesday, though, he still wasn't better. Alix knew he had to be seen, but she wasn't sure where to take him. Back in Indiana, Dr. Dougherty made house calls, usually bringing medicine with him, or writing a prescription her mother promptly filled. Alix had only been in a hospital once, when her tonsils were removed. She didn't remember much about it except for ice cream and Jello.

Here in Chicago, though, there was no Dr. Dougherty. And no money if he had been. In fact, being young, healthy, and full of energy, the idea of getting sick had never occurred to her. She wanted to talk it over with the others, but, except for Casey, they were all at the SDS convention. Even Rain was covering it for *The Seed* and crowing about her press pass—the establishment media had been banned.

The Moon Palace, where Casey worked, was only three blocks from the apartment. She told Billy she'd be right back and hurried over. It was a hot, sticky night, and by the time she got there, sweat clung to her neck and shoulders.

Casey was in the kitchen, washing dishes. When Alix pushed through the door, the clatter of dishes and machines was overlaid by Jimi Hendrix's guitar, making it impossible to talk. Casey's face brightened when he spotted her, and he shouted, "Alix! What's doing?"

It was hotter here than outside. She blew a breath upwards to fan her face. "I'm worried about Billy."

He turned off the spray of water and turned down the radio. "What's wrong?"

"I think he should see a doctor, but I don't know where to go."

Casey loaded the dishwasher with the blue and white plates every Chinese restaurant seemed to use. "How about the emergency room?"

"Yes, but which one? I . . . I don't have any experience with hospitals . . . at least in Chicago."

Casey shrugged. "Northwestern would be good. Or maybe Children's Memorial."

"Billy's almost sixteen."

"Then take him to Northwestern." He stopped. "Wait. Fullerton Hospital is only a few blocks away. That's the place to go."

"He's not going to be happy. He hates doctors."

"Have Dar go with you."

"He's at the convention."

"Can't it wait till he gets back?"

"Casey, he's coughing up blood."

He turned on the dishwasher and wiped his hands on his apron. Then he reached up and snapped off the radio. The quiet was unnerving. "Why don't I come with you?"

"Really? Will you?"

"I'm off at eleven."

She let out a relieved breath.

Fullerton Hospital's emergency room was all white walls, fluorescent lights, and color-coded stripes on the floors. A stout nurse with a peaked cap, sat behind a high counter doing a crossword puzzle. She wiped sweat off her face with a tissue. "Can I help you?"

"He needs to be seen." Casey motioned to Billy.

"Name?" She put down her paper and slid a clipboard toward Alix.

"Billy."

"Billy what?"

"Billy Two Feathers," Alix answered.

The nurse frowned imperceptibly as she wrote down his name. "What is his problem?"

"He's coughing. It won't stop, and there's blood in it."

"How much blood?"

"Enough to turn a Kleenex pink," Alix answered.

"How long has this been going on?"

"About four days. Although . . . " Alix stopped short.

"Yes?"

"He was coughing a couple of months ago. But it went away."

"I see." The nurse tapped the pencil against the counter. "And what is your relation to him?"

"Relation?" Alix asked.

"That was the question."

"He's . . . "

"Nephew," Casey cut in. "He's our nephew."

"Your nephew." Her gaze swept over them. Alix's throat tightened. They were only a few years older than Billy. Casey's hair was down to his shoulders. She was wearing a "Stop the War" t-shirt. Not to mention they were white, and Billy was an Indian.

The nurse narrowed her eyes. "Does your . . . 'nephew' . . . have insurance?"

"No."

"Who is going to be responsible for the charges?"

Casey's jaw worked. "We will."

"You."

Alix and Casey exchanged a glance. Casey nodded.

The nurse looked at Billy, then back at them again. Alix waited for her to kick them out. To tell them she knew they were lying. But all she did was let out a long-suffering breath. Then she passed them a form. "Fill this out."

Relief washed over Alix. She took the form and led Billy over to a chair in the reception area. When Casey joined them, she whispered, "Why'd you say he was our nephew?"

"I didn't think they'd see him otherwise."

Alix bit her lip. The threadbare carpet, institutional chairs, and dingy walls didn't speak to the hospital's prosperity. Still, the room was filled with people: black, white, even some Orientals. Some were doubled over in obvious pain, others had the vacant expressions that come with long waits and hopelessness. She'd never seen suffering like this back in Indiana. She'd always dealt with it from a distance: school-sponsored canned goods drives, wrapped presents for the "unfortunate" at Christmas. The despair and misery made her heart ache.

"I want to go home," Billy said.

Alix brushed her hand across his forehead. He was sweating. She got up, got him a tissue, then started filling out the form. "When's your birthday?"

"I don't like this place," he said.

"Neither do I. When's your birthday?"

"Why?"

"We have to write it down for the doctor."

He shrugged.

"Billy . . . please."

"October 20th," he finally spit out.

"You'll be sixteen, right?"

He nodded.

Alix checked the form, then tugged on Casey's arm. "What do I put here?"

Casey looked. "Address?" He paused. "Use ours."

"You're sure?"

"I feel better." Fear tightened Billy's features. "Let's go home. Please."

That's when it dawned on her why Casey was lying. And why Billy didn't want to be here. He was a runaway. If they found out, they could take him away. She let out a breath. Sometimes she was as dumb as a box of rocks. She grabbed Billy's hand and gave it a squeeze. She wouldn't let that happen.

It was three hours later before another nurse in a white uniform came out, clipboard in hand. She cleared her throat. "Billy Two Feathers?"

Casey and Billy had been napping, but Billy woke with a start and dug his fingers into Alix's arm. She patted his hand to calm him, ignoring the indentations on her skin.

The nurse led them through a set of doors into the main ER. Several desks, pushed together, took up most of the room. They were surrounded by about eight curtained areas. The smell of disinfectant was strong. A closet off to the side was open. Inside was a crush of equipment: oxygen masks, metal instruments, bandages, and bowls.

The nurse showed them into one of the curtained areas. "Are you family? If not, you can't stay here."

"We're his aunt and uncle," Casey said, with more bravado than Alix felt.

"Really." The nurse let her gaze linger on them just long enough to let them know she knew they were lying. Then she turned to Billy. "Take your jeans off. And your shirt." She handed him a gown. "Put this on." Billy shrank back, as if the gown was contaminated. The nurse looked at Billy, dropped the gown on the gurney, and left.

Fifteen minutes later there was a commotion on the other side of the curtain. Alix pushed it aside. Across the room several nurses and two men crowded around two curtained-off areas. One of the nurse's uniforms was streaked with red. Everyone was shouting. Above the voices, Alix heard groans.

"Casey, what's going on?"

Casey got up to look. "I don't know."

They waited another thirty minutes before a young doctor in surgical scrubs hurried in, carrying a clipboard. His name tag said Schindler. He looked from the clipboard to Billy, who was dozing on the gurney. "What's the problem?" he asked brusquely.

Billy woke up. His brows drew together, eyes wary.

Alix explained.

Schindler asked the same questions as the intake nurse. As Alix answered them, the noise in the main room grew louder, more frantic.

"What is it?" Casey asked.

Schindler turned around. "Someone got shot. Bullet's lodged in his spine. We're taking him up to the OR."

Alix recoiled. "Someone was shot?"

The doctor looked at Alix as if he wasn't sure what planet she was from. He turned back to Billy with an expression that said he'd rather be dealing with the gunshot wound than a young boy's cough. "Fever?"

"Off and on," Alix said.

The doctor took out his stethoscope, bent over, and placed it on Billy's back. "Breathe." The doctor moved the stethoscope. "Again." After more repetitions, he straightened up. "We're going to need an X-ray. I'll let them know." He nodded. "And I'll get you some antibiotics. That should take care of it."

They waited another hour. Nothing happened. No X-ray, no antibiotics. The noise and commotion in the ER subsided, and they could hear static from a police radio. Casey went out to check the time. "It's practically dawn," he said when he came back. "We've been here for five hours."

Alix pushed the curtain aside and stepped into the ER room. No one was there. She walked back into the reception area. Only a few people were waiting, and someone had turned on a radio. Easy listening. A new nurse sat behind the counter.

"Excuse me, but we've been waiting all night for antibiotics. We're in curtain area five. Dr. Schindler said he would bring them to us."

The nurse consulted a sheet of paper. "Schindler went up to the OR. But he's off now." She must have seen Alix's distress, because her next words were surprisingly kind. "Let me see what I can do."

Ten minutes later, yet another doctor walked into the curtained cubicle. Alix didn't bother to check his name tag. "Sorry for the wait. It's been pretty busy around here." He looked at Billy's chart and frowned. "Looks like he's been diagnosed with bronchitis."

Alix ran her hand through her hair. She was losing it. "He was coughing up blood."

"But not that much."

"How much is too much?"

The doctor shot her a patronizing look. "Let's start with antibiotics. If it doesn't go away in another week, he should be seen again."

She tried once more, "You were supposed to give him an X-ray."

Billy piped up. "I want to go home."

The doctor looked at his watch. "The technician's off. If you want an X-ray, you'll have to wait at least two hours for the next shift."

Alix covered her eyes for a moment, then dropped her hand. "Okay, I give up."

Billy smiled for the first time that night.

THIRTY-TWO

By the time Alix woke up, late afternoon sun was sneaking in around the edges of the shades. She and Billy were alone. She woke him, then scrambled some eggs. After making sure he ate and took his pills, she fell asleep again.

She didn't see the others until that night when Rain and Dar came back from the SDS convention and Casey got home from work.

"Where are Payton and Teddy?" Alix asked.

"Don't know," Rain said. Her ashy hair shimmered in the light, and her eyes were shining. "You should have been there, Alix."

"What happened?"

Rain made herself comfortable on the sofa. "Well, you remember how huge it was, right?"

"The Coliseum."

"Right. Well, picture a ring of tables around the perimeter for groups like the Young Socialists, Marxists, even Maoists. All of them piled with flyers and literature and other crap. People milling around, connecting, making plans." Rain chuckled. "It reminded me of Maxwell Street in a way. Then they called the meeting to order. Which was when the fireworks started."

"What fireworks?" Casey asked.

"You haven't heard?" Rain looked incredulous. She wriggled further down on the couch. "Well, they passed out this essay that originally was printed in *New Left Notes*, the SDS newsletter. It was written by the 'action faction,' and it was a call for direct action."

"Isn't that what Payton keeps yammering about?" Alix said.

"Right. So it ends with this quote from Dylan. 'You don't need a weatherman to know which way the wind is blowing.'"

"*Subterranean Homesick Blues*," Casey offered.

Rain nodded. "Turns out the people behind it are Mark Rudd and Bernadine Dohrn, among others—they're leaders of one of the factions."

"The RYM . . . you know—the Revolutionary Youth Movement," Casey said, sounding impatient, "the one Payton's involved with. So?"

Rain was taking her time. "I'm getting there." She glanced at Dar. "See, there's this other faction . . . the Progressive Labor Party. Basically, they're Marxists who see the revolution as class war. They want blue-collar workers to get involved."

"You predicted that, didn't you?" Alix asked Dar.

Dar shrugged.

"Well," Rain said tartly, "then the Panthers came into the convention and trashed the PLP."

The door to the apartment opened, and Teddy came in.

"Hey, man," Casey said. "What's happening?"

Teddy looked at each of them in turn. For some reason, Alix thought he looked nervous. Then he took a breath and shook his head. "Not much."

"I was just telling them what happened at the convention," Rain said.

"Oh . . . right."

"Where have you been?" she asked.

"Took a while to get out of there."

"Where's Payton?"

"Don't know."

"Sit down, Teddy." Alix waved a hand. "Rain was just telling us what happened when the Panthers came in."

Teddy sat. Rain picked up her story, "So, the Panthers start lecturing. Telling everyone they don't know what they're doing. One of them called the PLP counter-revolutionaries. Then he started calling women cunts. He even started threatening the PLP members."

"You're kidding!"

"It got heavy." She glanced at Teddy, then Dar. "The Panther leader started in and said they were black, we were white, and they would never authorize us to speak for them. Meanwhile, there were all these huge, armed guards everywhere." Rain paused dramatically. "Everything went up for grabs after that. People started shouting at the Panthers and each other. No one was listening to anyone. Some people were yelling: 'Power to the People!'; others 'Fight Male Chauvinism'; still others 'Ho Ho Ho Chi Minh/NLF is Going to Win!' She looked at Casey. "Someone even shouted 'Let's Go Mets!'"

Casey laughed. Teddy didn't crack a smile.

"It was crazy. Then Bernadine Dohrn walked out with a bunch of people, including Payton." Rain looked around. "She said the convention was over. That the RYM was withdrawing from SDS and starting a new movement. They're calling themselves the Weathermen—you know, for the Dylan song—and they're taking over the Chicago SDS office. The other faction—the student workers—are going back to Boston."

"That is heavy," Casey said. He turned to Dar. "What about you, Dar? Where are you with all this?"

"Nowhere." He raised his hands, palms out. "Things have changed. New leaders, new strategies, new tactics. We've created a Hydra, and each of the heads wants what they want. But I'm done. A lot of people I know are out too."

"Not Payton," Teddy said. "He's really wired into things."

Everyone looked at Teddy. A flush crept up his neck. "Well, someone has to keep the faith."

"Well, I guess we know which group you're going with," Casey quipped.

Teddy shrugged.

Alix got up and went into the kitchen. Dar followed her. "Is it true, Dar? Are you really finished with the Movement?"

He went to her. "The whole time I was at the Coliseum, all I could think about was you and Billy. Casey told me you went to the hospital. I should have been there."

Alix told him about the ER: the wait; how the doctors didn't know one patient from another; how they gave Billy antibiotics but never did a chest X-ray. Her eyes started to fill. "I can see why Billy hates doctors." She shook her head. "If he doesn't get better, I don't know what we'll do."

Dar cupped her face in his hands. "We'll get him the help he needs. Together."

She allowed herself a weak smile.

THIRTY-THREE

obby, the owner of Up Against the Wall, lived above the shop in a small apartment and owned something they didn't: a TV. Rain hadn't watched in months and didn't miss it, but today was an exception. This was the day the astronauts were supposed to land on the moon. She'd wheedled and pleaded with Bobby to have a 'moon party'; eventually, he agreed. Casey brought food from the Moon Palace, which was only appropriate. Rain brought soda and wine. Teddy brought weed.

By afternoon all of them, except Payton, were on Bobby's living room floor, watching a blurry, black-and-white telecast of what looked like two Michelin men hopping around a rocky terrain.

"This is FFO." Casey's eyes narrowed into slits. He'd already finished off a joint.

"Two hundred thousand miles far fucking out," Bobby said in a gravelly voice.

Rain lowered her camera and squinted at the TV. She'd been snapping pictures of the telecast as well as shots of them watching it. "They look like they're on pogo sticks."

Dar laughed. Billy, who had come with them, did too. Despite the frustrations at Fullerton Hospital, the antibiotics seemed to have worked, and Billy's cough had subsided.

Alix looked more carefree than she had in weeks. "It's so amazing to see pictures . . . live . . . from the moon. How do they do that?"

"The miracle of progress." Casey glanced at Teddy and Dar.

"Progress, eh?" Dar smiled at Casey. "Where's Payton when we need him?"

Teddy frowned. "What?"

"Remember our discussion in Wisconsin about 'progress'?" Casey said. "Payton tried to convince your father that progress wasn't in the best interests of society."

Teddy shook his wrist. His ID bracelet clinked as it settled. "Yeah, well, answer me this. How do we know it's really happening?" He motioned toward the TV.

"Huh?" Casey asked.

"What if that's just a Hollywood set we're watching? A TV show they created to make us think they're on the moon?"

"Why would anyone do that?" Alix asked.

"To divert attention from the war," Teddy said.

"How do you figure?" Rain asked.

"The government doesn't want us to question the war, so they create this TV show that purports to show astronauts landing on the moon. But in reality, it's just a bunch of actors and props on some back lot in Hollywood. We don't know that, of course, so we're all excited about our 'progress' . . . ," he said, glancing at Casey, " . . . conveniently forgetting all the killing and bombing and repression."

"You're saying this is all just a big conspiracy?"

"It could be."

Rain rolled her eyes. "You know what, Teddy? You're right. In fact, I'll bet the Kennedys produced it. You know, to take the pressure off your namesake and Mary Jo Kopechne." The girl's body had been discovered in the senator's car near Chappaquiddick two days earlier.

Teddy nodded solemnly. "I was wondering about that myself."

Rain stared. "Jesus, Teddy. You're serious!"

He shrugged and pulled out a Marlboro. Rain watched him strike a match, light the cigarette, and take a drag.

She took a shot of him exhaling smoke. "You're getting weird, you know?"

"You've been hanging out with the wrong people, Markham," Casey added. "Your mind is turning to mush."

Bobby reached for an egg roll, broke it in half, and popped one half in his mouth. "Do you think it's gonna be the end of his career?"

"Kennedy's?" Dar asked. "Don't know. But I guarantee you won't see him running for president."

"That's probably not a bad thing," Casey said. "They say he's the stupid brother."

"Which is why he'll survive in the Senate," Dar said.

Teddy kept his mouth shut but jangled his bracelet.

A knock on Bobby's door interrupted them. "Oh. I forgot to tell you. I invited a few other people." He got up and went to the door.

"Linda and Donna?" Alix asked.

Bobby shook his head, but something in his expression made Rain's antenna go on alert. Meanwhile, Bobby opened the door to a guy in a t-shirt, cut-offs, and sandals. Bobby introduced him, but Rain didn't catch his name. He got a plate and loaded it with sweet and sour chicken, an egg roll, and rice. Rain waited for Bobby to settle back on the floor.

"So, Bobby," Rain said. "How are Donna and Linda? Everything okay?"

This time the head shop owner's face reddened, and he looked everywhere except at Rain.

"What happened? Did they break up?"

"Not exactly."

Sensing a story, Rain leaned forward. "Well?"

"It's . . . it's complicated," Bobby said. And looked at Billy.

Dar stood up. "Hey, Billy," he said, "come into the kitchen with me. I need your help."

"Wait. This is gonna be good," Billy said.

"Billy . . .," Dar's voice was stern.

"You never let me hear the good stuff." Everyone laughed, but Billy reluctantly got up and followed Dar out.

"So?" Rain asked when they'd gone.

"You know how Linda and Donna were . . . lovers, right?" Rain nodded. "Well, it wasn't always that way." Bobby grabbed his legs and rocked back on the floor. "See, Donna used to be Don."

Rain gasped. Alix's mouth opened.

"He was on his way to becoming a woman. Had the hormone shots. Started dressing and acting the part. The only thing left was the surgery." Bobby hesitated. "But then he/she met Linda."

"Oh, god!" Alix said. "Don't tell me. He decided he'd rather be a man after all?"

"That's right. They went someplace in California so Donna can turn back into Don."

Now Rain's mouth dropped open. For a moment neither she nor Alix spoke.

Alix recovered first. "Wait a minute. How does Linda feel about it? She's the one who's gay."

"She's okay with it." Bobby flipped up a palm. "They're in love."

Rain covered her face with her hands and shook her head. Alix looked blank. Then a huge smile broke over her face, and she started to giggle. Rain started to laugh, too. Bobby glanced over, then joined in, too. Before long the three of them were roaring. Casey, Teddy, and Bobby's friend offered polite smiles but mostly looked bewildered. Even Dar poked his head out from the kitchen.

"Everything okay?"

Alix was laughing too hard to speak, but Rain waved a hand to signal they were fine. "Help! I can't breathe!"

"Me either," Alix wheezed.

Billy appeared briefly, threw them a scowl, then returned to the kitchen.

Eventually, their laughter subsided, and they sat exhausted, but happy, the way friends do after they've shared something that's brought them closer. Bobby lifted his chin towards the kitchen. "How's the kid doing?"

"He's a lot better. I guess it was just bronchitis," Alix said.

Bobby's friend looked up from his plate. "What was wrong?"

"He was coughing up blood. I took him to Fullerton Hospital a few weeks ago, and they gave him antibiotics."

"Blood?" When Alix nodded, he asked, "Did they do a chest X-ray? Or a TB test?"

"No. Why?"

"There's a high rate of TB on Indian reservations."

Concern flared on Alix's face. "I thought it had been wiped out."

The guy shook his head. "The government wants you to think that, but in some places it's still rampant. Nobody talks about it, of course."

"TB's contagious, isn't it?" Rain asked.

He nodded.

"Billy doesn't have TB," Alix said. "Look at him. He's fine."

"Sometimes you can have the infection, but if it's not in an acute phase, you might not know it."

"How do you know so much?" Alix ran a nervous hand through her hair.

"I'm in med school." He went back to his plate. "Hey, don't worry about it. It's probably nothing. But if it happens again, make sure a doctor sees him."

Billy bounced back into the living room, all smiles. "Hey, Casey, I told Dar you had a new Fritz the Cat. He said I could read it."

"It's back at the apartment," Casey said.

"Can I go back to get it?" Billy pleaded. "Please?"

Alix smiled at Billy, then turned to Bobby's friend. "Thanks for the advice. But I doubt we'll need any more help."

Rain lay on the sofa reading. Alix was already in bed, Casey was at work, and Teddy was off somewhere with Payton. Dar swept the kitchen. Of the four men, he was the most willing to help out with "women's work." When he was done, he put the broom and dustpan away and went out to the living room. Rain made room for him on the couch.

He laced his hands behind his head and closed his eyes.

"Tired?" Rain asked.

"Not really. Just thinking."

"About what?"

"Life. Love. The universe. You know, everything." He opened his eyes.

Rain closed her book. "It's all changing, isn't it?"

Dar tilted his head.

"Everything's getting fucked up," Rain said, "and ugly."

"How do you mean?"

"Nothing's the same. You've changed. Casey too. And now Teddy's getting weird."

"I noticed."

"He's been hanging around Payton too long."

"Maybe he's just more committed. People find themselves at different times."

Rain twirled a lock of hair. "I don't know. Teddy and I went to high school together, remember? He was . . . well . . . he moved in all the right circles. Tennis team. Debate Club. He was part of the 'in' crowd. Concern for the oppressed wasn't a priority."

"That doesn't mean anything. Abbie Hoffman graduated from Worcester, and Kathy Boudin went to prep school. Sometimes the privileged develop the keenest sense of justice."

"Or guilt."

Dar gave her a sharp look.

"Rich, white America exploited plenty of people over the years," she said.

"Guilt might be the reason why you got involved in the Movement, but that's not the case for me. Or from what I can tell, Teddy."

"So why did he get involved?"

"I don't know."

"That's my point . . . , " she persisted, "we don't know. By now, though, we should. Tell me—what happened when you went to his house in Wisconsin?"

"What happened? Nothing. Why?"

"That's when he started to change." Rain stopped twirling her hair. "Look . . . I don't want to get paranoid, but do you think he might be an informant?"

Dar gave her another sharp look. "You mean for the FBI?"

"Something like that."

"You're kidding, of course."

Rain shook her head. "His father is a judge. He has a lot of connections. Maybe he got talked into it."

"It makes no sense. Why?"

"I don't know," Rain said. "Why does anyone turn? Maybe . . . "

Dar cut her off. "No. You can't do this, Rain. You can't go around accusing people. Especially without evidence."

"I've been watching him, Dar. There are things that . . . well . . . are really weird. Like his whole rap today about the moon landing conspiracy."

"You think he's covering for himself?"

"Maybe. There are all these times he just disappears, sometimes for hours. No one knows where he's gone. And he never volunteers a thing."

Dar was quiet for a minute. "Don't do this Rain," he said softly.

She felt a stab of resentment. "I'm just trying to protect us. In case . . . " She saw his expression. "Oh, never mind." She picked up her camera and went to the window. Sliding onto the window ledge, she looked at the fat shadows squeezed between pools of light from the lampposts. "July 8th was Ringo's birthday, you know."

"Huh?"

She framed a shot and took a picture. "When I was in junior high, I used to talk about the Beatles with my best friend for hours. We were . . . oh . . . about fourteen, and we'd spend hours on the phone. She loved Paul. I liked Ringo. We read about them in trashy magazines, books, anything we could get our hands on. We knew everything—Paul's birthday was June 18th, Ringo's was July 8th." She took another shot out the window. "We used to fantasize about going to a concert. We would be the only girls who weren't screaming. Of course, the Beatles would notice, and they'd send us a note to meet them backstage after the concert."

She turned around to face Dar. "We were so innocent back then. Maybe even silly. But now the Beatles might break up, Payton and

Teddy are doing God knows what, and you and Alix are . . . " Her voice trailed off.

Dar lowered his chin. "Alix and I are what?"

"You're all caught up with Billy . . . pretending you're a family."

"Is something wrong with that?"

Rain slid off the window ledge, put the camera down, and came back to the couch. "I just don't . . . Let me ask you something." She sat down. "Are you sure Alix loves you as much as you love her? Is she always going to be there for you?"

"Of course I'm sure." Anger flashed in Dar's eyes. "Why? What are you getting at?"

"I don't know. Her background . . . her values . . . they're so different from yours."

"That's not true. We agree on a lot. Anyway, it's what's in here that's important." He tapped his chest. "Not here." He tapped his forehead.

Rain angled her head. "You know, of course, that Casey's in love with her."

"What?"

"Haven't you seen the way he looks at her when he doesn't think anyone's watching? How he's always doing things for her? Like taking Billy to the hospital when you weren't around. Making sure she has all her jewelry supplies. Buying Billy comic books. It's almost sad how grateful he looks when she doles out a smile. Like a dog waiting for a bone."

Dar crossed his arms. "Casey is my closet friend. And Alix is . . . my soul mate. That will never change."

"Are you sure, Dar? Are you sure she'll always be there for you?"

Dar narrowed his eyes.

"I would," Rain said softly.

Dar looked at Rain. Then his face took on a knowing expression. He looked like he was groping for a response.

Rain immediately regretted what she said. She'd always sworn to hide her true feelings, and she wasn't sure why she'd blurted them out. To make things worse, the length of time it was taking Dar to reply confirmed her worst fears. She'd been stupid. She tried to backpedal. "As your friend, of course."

Dar didn't say anything, but there was a catch in his eyes.

"Never mind." Rain got up, went to the radio, and snapped it on. The announcer was still talking about the men on the moon. "Let's listen to more of those giant steps for mankind, okay? 'Course, he should have said 'humankind', don't you think? At least 'men and women.'"

THIRTY-FOUR

Billy's cough came back in August, worse than a smoker's hack. He was coughing up blood again, and this time the Kleenex turned red. He seemed tired, and he was losing weight. At night, he sometimes ran a fever.

Alix went to the health food store on Wells Street. The owner recommended a combination of echinacea, garlic, licorice, and eucalyptus, all of which would fight respiratory infections. He also told her about something called *Arsenicum album* for cough and chest pain. He didn't have any but could get some. She put in an order.

She took the bus to another health food store in Lincoln Park. The woman behind the counter suggested *Calcarea carbonica* for chills, sleepiness, and night sweats. She also suggested Alix talk to a homeopathic doctor who would prescribe something tailored exactly to Billy. Alix wrote down the doctor's name.

Despite the remedies, Billy didn't get better. He was still bringing up blood and sputum, his chest hurt, and he was hardly able to get out of bed. Alix got a used mattress from Goodwill and moved him from the boarding house into a corner of their bedroom. She told Dar they needed a doctor.

"How are we going to pay for it?" he asked. The bill for their visit to Fullerton Hospital came to over two hundred dollars. It would take months to pay it off. "And what will they do? Make us wait another four hours for a vial of antibiotics?"

"We have to find a doctor who will see him for free."

Alix and Dar combed through the phone book and, through a stroke of good luck, found the American Indian Center on Wilson Avenue. The

197

organization had sprung up more than ten years before to help Indians who'd relocated from reservations. The center referred them to a doctor in Uptown who, when they showed up at his storefront office, looked a little like Robert Young from *Father Knows Best.*

He examined Billy in a small cramped room, took a chest X-ray, and after studying it, called Alix and Dar into another cramped room for a consultation. Billy had TB, he told them. It was a difficult disease to diagnose conclusively because it was tricky—and took too much time—to culture the bacteria in the lab. But he pointed out what looked like tiny bubbles on Billy's x-ray that he said were incidences of cavitation—little holes—in his lungs.

They were obligated to report it to the Chicago Health Department, the doctor said. "But that isn't a bad thing. They can set you up with the MTS."

"What's that?"

"The Municipal Tuberculosis Sanitarium. He needs to be institutionalized while he's recovering."

"In a hospital?" Alix asked.

"That's his best chance for a full recovery," the doctor said.

"How much does it cost?"

"I don't know, but I think they have a sliding scale." The doctor wrote down the name on a scrap of paper. "There's probably a waiting list, though. What about a private sanitarium?"

Dar and Alix exchanged glances. "I . . . I don't know," Alix said tentatively. "Even if we could afford it, Billy hates hospitals. He'd probably run away."

The doctor paused. "Well, there *is* another possibility." His tone made it clear he didn't think it was the best solution.

"What's that?"

"The MTS and Chicago Health Department have clinics around the city. He could go there for his medicine. They'll make sure he takes it, and they'll supervise his overall health."

"That sounds perfect," Alix said.

The doctor rubbed a finger below his nose. "He'd have to go there every day for eighteen months, you realize."

Alix's eyes widened. "Eighteen months?"

"That's the standard course of treatment. There are some new protocols that are only six months, but they're not available yet."

"He can hardly take medicine for eight days, much less eighteen months."

"It's either that or a sanitarium." The doctor handed over the slip of paper. "You'd better get him on the waiting list."

While Alix was still processing the information, Dar asked, "How contagious is TB?"

The doctor inclined his head. "It's not as contagious as people think. It can be spread by coughing and sneezing, but you can't spread it by touching, for example. Still, you need to take reasonable precautions. Wear a mask when you're with him . . . actually, he should, too. Wash your hands after being with him. Keep him quiet and isolated in a room with good ventilation. And keep the door closed. And make sure he always uses a tissue when he coughs or sneezes. Once he's been on the medications for a few weeks and the active part of the disease goes into remission, he won't be contagious."

"Do you have any idea how he got it?"

"Probably on the reservation."

"His mother died last year, but he never explained why. I thought it was cancer. Now I wonder if she had TB," Alix said.

"It's possible. It's also possible he's been infected since birth. Most people who are infected don't develop symptoms, and their X-rays remain negative. The disease only turns active when the individual's immune system or general health is compromised. Like it might be on the rez." The doctor paused. "And there's always the chance it might have become active in the past and was misdiagnosed as a cold or flu."

Alix recalled their trip to the ER. "Or bronchitis?"

"Get him out of here," Payton demanded when Alix told them about Billy's TB. "And burn the fucking mattress he's been sleeping on."

"But he's not that contagious," Alix began. "And I'll make sure . . . "

"Payton's right, Alix," Casey cut in. "Billy can't stay here. It's not fair to the rest of us. Even if he's not contagious."

"But we have no idea when he's going to get into the MTS. Where's he supposed to go?" Alix asked.

"If we're lucky, he can hole up in his room at the boarding house," Casey said soothingly. "We'll do everything the doctor says."

Alix turned to Dar. "That's not good enough. He needs to be in a private sanitarium. I'm going to call my father."

Dar stiffened. The phone calls she'd made to her parents over the past year had ended badly—her father had been full of dire predictions about her "drug-crazed, hippie" lifestyle. He reminded her of that.

"But this is different. It's for Billy."

"He doesn't know that, Alix. And he's been looking for a way to drag you out of here. The minute you ask him for money, you're giving him power over you. What if he puts conditions on it?"

"Like what?"

"What if he won't give it to you unless you go back to Indiana?"

"He can't make me."

Dar shrugged. "And you can't make him give you money."

Alix massaged her temples. "So what do we do? Billy needs help."

"I have an idea. Give me a day."

"That's about all we have," Alix said more sharply than she'd intended.

Dar spent most of the next day on the pay phone at the corner of North Avenue. He came back looking dejected.

"Where were you?" Alix asked.

"Trying to talk to the BIA." At her puzzled look, he added, "The Bureau of Indian Affairs. But, between getting transferred to people on vacation, and those who didn't know what I was talking about, I didn't get far." He squared his shoulders. "The only thing to do is to show up down there."

"Where?"

"At the BIA field office."

"Billy can't go. He's too sick."

"I'll go by myself."

Alix softened. "If someone looks after Billy, I'll come too."

Casey agreed to watch Billy, and the next day Dar and Alix took the El downtown. The BIA office was tucked away on the seventh floor of a faceless government building in the Loop. They would have missed it altogether if Alix hadn't noticed a small sign halfway down a long hall.

The door opened to a windowless room with no pretense at decoration. Two men sat behind standard issue metal desks covered with paperwork. One of the men, whose five o'clock shadow was noticeable though it was well before noon, looked up.

"Yes?"

Dar pointed Alix to the chair beside his desk and made her sit down. He stood behind her and explained the situation. The man listened without interrupting. Dar finished by saying, "So we're looking for some financial help so he can be admitted to a sanitarium."

Alix stole a glance at the other man, who was leaning back in his chair, listening.

The man Dar had talked to cleared his throat. "Unfortunately, you've reached us at a difficult time. Our programs are in transition."

"What does that mean?"

"BIA used to have jurisdiction over every aspect of Indian affairs, but Congress 'reassigned' some of our duties. Indian health care, for example, is now the responsibility of HEW. Health, Education and Welfare."

"Which means what?"

"You'll need to talk to them."

Dar took in a breath. He was trying to stay calm. "And where are they?"

"In the Government Services building. Across the Loop." The man frowned. "Although, as far as I know, most of the Indian programs are on the rez. There's not a lot going on here."

"So what do we do?"

The bureaucrat opened a drawer, withdrew a pencil, licked it, and started writing. "Try Medicaid. The state of Illinois gives medical care to children through AFDC—Aid to Families with Dependent Children. Is he your son?"

"Well . . .," Dar began.

Alix cut in. "Yes."

The clerk threw them a skeptical look. "I thought you said he was Indian."

"He is. Lakota Sioux. He's adopted."

"I see." Alix knew he didn't believe her. "Well," he said slowly, "if you're on welfare, you can get Medicaid."

"We're not on welfare," Alix said.

"Oh." He pursed his lips. "Well, then, I . . . "

"How long would it take to sign up?" Alix asked.

He tapped the pencil against his desk, then opened the drawer and dropped it back in. "I wouldn't know." He slid the drawer closed. "Not my department." He scraped his chair against the floor and stood up.

Alix stayed in her seat.

"Sorry I can't be more helpful," he said in a clipped tone that clearly indicated the meeting was over.

Alix didn't move.

"Alix." Dar prodded her shoulder. "Let's go."

"No, not yet." She looked at the bureaucrat. "There's got to be something you can do."

An irritated look came over his face. "I'm sorry, but there's . . . "

The man at the other desk cut in. "There is one other thing."

"What?" Alix twisted around. A photo sat on his desk, he and a woman grinning at the camera, the woman cradling a baby. A good sign.

"We have a relocation program. For Indians between eighteen and thirty-five. If he wants to join, we could help him with transportation, job placement, and subsistence funds until his first paycheck."

Alix deflated. "He's only sixteen, and he can't work. He has TB."

"But that's what I'm saying. If he relocates formally, and we can look the other way when he fills in his age, he might be able to get health benefits."

"He needs help now. Not in two months or whenever the paperwork goes through."

The man spread his hands. "Then I'm sorry. I just don't have any advice."

Alix and Dar walked past Kerr's State Street store on their way back to the El. The windows, festooned with artificial autumn foliage, featured manikins dressed in earth-toned fashions. Alix looked away as they passed, but Dar gazed silently at the building with an odd expression, almost as if he was seeing it for the first time.

They didn't speak on the El back to Old Town. It was only after they took the steps down to the street that Dar said, "I'm sorry, Alix. I tried."

She placed a hand on his arm. "It's not your fault."

He took her hand and gently removed it. His expression darkened. "If you still want to call your father . . .," he paused, " . . . go ahead."

Alix hesitated. Then she said, "I already did. They'll be here tomorrow. They want to have dinner."

Alix wasn't surprised her father suggested a steak house—he was a meat-and-potatoes man. But she was a little surprised he'd chosen Gene and Georgetti's. His tastes ran more toward Bing Crosby than Frank

Sinatra, and she didn't think he would like a place where anyone from the mayor to a mob boss might drop in. It wasn't until she was nearly there that she realized he'd probably chosen Gene and Georgetti's because he didn't want to be seen at the fancy, white-bread establishments he usually went to in Chicago—that he might be embarrassed at his daughter—and her boyfriend.

Tucked away under the El tracks, the restaurant was loud, rambunctious, and crowded. It sported lots of paneling, celebrity pictures, and a high-gloss bar, all rendered a little hazy by a curtain of smoke. Alix gave her name to the maître d'.

"Ah yes." He spoke with an Italian accent, stretching the word "yes" into two syllables. "They're already here." He pointed them upstairs.

They went up to a room of tables covered in red and white tablecloths. An elaborate chandelier hung from the ceiling. Her mother's face lit up when she spotted Alix. She rose and threw open her arms. "Oh darling, it's been too long!"

Renee Kerr had given Alix her cloud of blond hair, light coloring, and slender build. She wore a conservative pink suit. St. John, probably. You could never go wrong with St. John, she always told Alix. She was pretty but had a slightly vacant look, as if she wasn't quite plugged into life. The look disappeared when she was with Alix, but tonight Alix thought she looked even more remote. For the first time since she'd moved to Chicago, Alix felt a pang of guilt.

Alix turned to her father. Sebastian Kerr was a big man just turning to flab. Since she'd seen him last, his waist and chest had thickened, and his cheeks were forming soft jowls under his chin. His starched collar bit into his neck, but his tailored suit and tie looked new. Thin strands of gray hair were brushed back from his face. Only his eyes, a cold blue, were hard.

Alix kissed him on the cheek, then smoothed out her secondhand black dress. She'd borrowed an iron from a neighbor, but she wasn't used to ironing her own things and hadn't done a very good job. She'd tried to press Dar's clothes too, which she'd picked up at Goodwill. He didn't want to wear a tie and jacket, but she'd insisted—they had to make a neat impression.

She was aware of her father checking them out, taking in their clothes, their shoes—scuffed secondhand heels for her, sandals for Dar— and Dar's hair, which though shorter than before, still hung below his collar.

"Alix, you're too thin, darling," her mother blurted out. "You must have lost ten pounds."

"I'm fine, Mother. I eat vegetarian most of the time," she lied.

"Well, maybe you should change your diet," her father said. "Eat more wholesome things like bread and meat."

"It's the processing, Daddy. Manufacturers add all sorts of things to bread and meat that aren't good for people."

"It's good enough for most people." He motioned to a waiter in a black jacket and bow tie a few feet away. "Two vodka gimlets."

He didn't ask her mother what she wanted, Alix thought. Just ordered for her. She'd forgotten that.

Her father focused on Dar. His probing gaze, always measuring and assessing, more than compensated for her mother's detachment. "I don't suppose you want a drink."

"No sir, but thank you."

Her father broke eye contact with Dar, as if he couldn't stand to look at him. Folding his hands on the table, he frowned at Alix. "Did you hear about that carnage out in California a week or so ago? The movie star murders?"

"Sharon Tate?" Alix asked.

"That's the one. Apparently, they found the word 'Pig' scrawled in blood in her house." Her father's expression turned icy. "They're saying a bunch of hippies did it." He glanced coldly at Dar. "And then there were those thousands of people who went to upstate New York for that concert. No bathing. No plumbing. Just rain, mud, and drugs." He waved a hand. "I tell you, our society is falling apart. There are no limits any more."

"I agree, sir," Dar said. "About the horror out west."

Her father's eyebrows shot up.

"But Woodstock . . .," Dar smiled, " . . . was unique. They say over half a million people showed up, but there was no violence for the entire weekend. We would have gone ourselves if we could have."

Kerr's eyes narrowed. The waiter brought their drinks. Alix's mother and father lifted their glasses at the same time and took a sip. The waiter passed around embossed menus in thick leather folders. Her father ordered a sixteen-ounce steak for himself and veal medallions for her mother. Alix ordered fish. So did Dar.

When the waiter left, Alix's mother leaned in. "Alix, do you remember Steven Frederickson? He was a year or so ahead of you in high school."

"Vaguely."

"Well, he was just accepted to Harvard Law School. His parents are thrilled. Isn't that marvelous?"

"That's lovely."

"And what do you do?" her father asked Dar. "Are you in college?" Alix tensed.

"Not any more, sir. I went to the University of Michigan, but I'm not sure formal education is what's important. At least for me."

"And what is?"

"I want to create a better social order. One that provides the services people need from their government."

Her father's expression tightened.

A new round of drinks arrived with their food. Her father concentrated on his steak, but her mother filled the gap with chatter about neighbors, the coming fall fashions, and old school friends of Alix's. Alix tried to appear interested, but she was aware of the tension around the table, and her stomach clenched. She hardly touched her meal.

When the waiter finally cleared the dishes, her father folded his hands on the table again. "Now, tell me why you need money for a hospital." His eyes were veiled. "You're not . . . pregnant?"

Alix flinched. A muscle worked on Dar's jaw. "No, Daddy. It's something else. There's this young boy. Well, a teenager. We've been . . . kind of . . . mentoring him. He's Indian, and he's sick. He has TB."

"Oh my god. TB?" Her mother's mouth dropped open. "You're not . . . interacting . . . with him, are you?"

"Of course we are. But that's not . . . "

"You can't do that!" Her mother's voice was shrill. " You . . . you'll get sick yourself. Alix, darling. You must stop. Use your common sense."

"I've done a lot of reading, Mrs. Kerr," Dar cut in. "And we talked to his doctor. TB isn't really as contagious as you might think. Especially if it's not in the acute phase. Believe me, we're taking reasonable precautions."

"Reasonable precautions?" Her father's voice went cold. "You have no formal education, yet you're making medical pronouncements about TB?"

Dar kept his mouth shut.

"Do you have a job at all?" He didn't wait for Dar's answer. "No, don't answer that. I don't want to know." His knuckles turned white. "I did not raise my daughter to live . . . in squalor."

"She doesn't." Dar put his arm around Alix. "Your daughter has created a home for all of us. She is one of the most generous, beautiful women . . . "

Sebastian registered Dar's arm motion and leaned forward. "Don't talk to me," he scowled, " . . . as if we're on the same level, discussing an employee at one of my stores. This is my daughter. You may have happened to catch her fancy—for what reason I can't fathom—but I will not permit you to talk to me like that."

"Daddy, stop." Alix threw up her hand. "This isn't about Dar. Or me. Billy needs to be in a sanitarium. We don't have the money. I need to get at my trust fund."

Her mother wrapped both hands around her vodka gimlet. She looked like she might cry.

Her father drained his glass and set it down. "Let me get this straight." His voice was quiet but filled with rancor. "You want money to care for an . . . an Indian boy . . . who has no blood connection to you. Or us."

Alix started to feel panicky. "It's not . . . as simple as that."

"But I'm close," he barreled on. "I assume you know that TB takes forever to cure. If it can be cured at all. Between the doctors, the sanitarium, and his medicine, his needs—and expenses—could stretch out indefinitely." His expression hardened. "Are you prepared for that?"

Alix raised her chin. "Yes."

"Because he's . . . he's important to you. You and your . . . " He couldn't seem to bring himself to say the word, "boyfriend."

"Sir, I'd like to say something," Dar interjected. "This boy is . . . well, he's like . . . "

"Your son?" Her father raised his voice. "Is that what you were going to say?" He flicked his wrist. "You have no idea what it's like to raise a child."

Alix felt a headache coming on. She massaged her temples.

"But, sir . . . " Dar removed his arm from the back of Alix's chair.

"Don't 'sir' me." He glared. "I'll tell you the truth. I didn't want to come here, but my wife said we should make an effort. Maintain our ties to our daughter, however flimsy. I've done my part. But what I'm seeing . . . well, we'll never agree on what's important. Therefore, there's no use prolonging the inevitable. It's time for us to go."

"Daddy . . .," Alix made one more stab. "Please. Billy needs help." She took a long breath. "If you help, I . . . I'll come home."

"Alix!" Dar breathed.

Her father sat back. Her mother's lips parted, and she leaned forward. Neither of them spoke for a moment. Then, her father said, "It means that much to you?"

Alix avoided looking at Dar. "Yes," she whispered.

Her father picked up his glass. "Nothing would give me more pleasure, Alixandra, than for you to come home where you belong. And it's admirable that you feel that strongly. For that, I owe you an honest answer." He took a swallow. "My stores contribute to charity on a regular basis. I'm sure we already contribute to Indian causes. If not, I'll make sure we do. But that's all. There's a reason why only the strong survive. You can't change that, Alixandra." He looked at Dar. "And neither can you."

THIRTY-FIVE

When Casey got home from work that night, Dar joined him in the living room to smoke a J. Casey could tell Dar was upset, but he didn't want to pry. He knew Dar had gone to dinner with Alix's parents. Casey kept the conversation light. If Dar wanted to talk, he would.

They were still up when Payton came in an hour later. He'd had been spending more time away from the apartment, coming back only to shower, change clothes, and sleep. Tonight, though, he grabbed a can of pop and stretched out on the floor.

"You've been scarce." Casey relit the roach and passed it over.

"Lots to do. You know how it goes. Or went." He glanced at Dar while he took a hit.

Dar looked away.

"It's okay." Payton held in the smoke, then blew it out. "We have a bunch of committed volunteers. Even Teddy is coming around. In fact, we're going up to Wisconsin this weekend."

"To see the judge?" Casey asked.

Payton shook his head. "Teddy wants to show me something."

Casey was suspicious. "What kind of something?"

Payton placed a finger on his lips. "You never know who's listening." Then he smiled. "You ought to come with, Dar."

"For what?" Casey repeated. If Payton didn't want them to know, he wouldn't have brought it up.

But Payton was being cagey. "I can't talk about it." He passed the J back to Dar.

"So you're keeping an eye on Teddy?" Dar asked.

Payton frowned. "What are you getting at?"

"Nothing. Forget it."

"Whoa . . . you just can't let something drop."

"You just did."

"That's different. State secrets."

Dar shrugged.

"If you're talking about Rain's theory, she's already come to me."

"She did?"

"She's paranoid. Has been from the start."

Casey looked from Dar to Payton. He felt left out. "What is she paranoid about?"

"Rain thinks Teddy's an informer," Payton said.

"What?" Casey sat back, startled.

"Exactly."

"Why would she say that?"

"Who knows?" Payton flicked his eyes to Dar. "Maybe she wanted to ball him but he didn't reciprocate. So she decided to get back at him."

"Bullshit," Casey said. "Rain's not like that."

"What do you say, Gantner?"

"Forget it, Payton," Dar said. There was a catch in his voice.

"Why? Can't stand a little heat on the reservation?"

Dar shifted. "What does that mean?"

Payton tilted the can of pop to his mouth and took a long swig. "Just that you're too busy with your girlfriend and your sick little Indian brave to do anything for anyone else."

Just then Alix appeared in the hall. She was wearing Dar's shirt, and her hair was tousled.

"I didn't know you were up," Dar said.

She rubbed her eyes. "What are you talking about, Payton?"

"I was just talking about your boyfriend's commitment. You won, you know. You've turned him into a political eunuch."

"You know something, Payton? You can say whatever you want. I don't care," Alix said. "There are more important things than the fucking Movement."

Both Casey and Dar stared. Alix never used profanity.

"That's why the best you can hope for is a safe house," Payton fired back.

Alix planted her hands on her hips.

"When the revolution comes, you'll have to leave the heavy lifting to others. But you can have a safe house if you want. That's what you've been doing with this place, isn't it?"

"That's a shitty thing to say," Dar said. "You've been living in her 'safe house' for over a year."

Payton shrugged, as if that just proved his point. But whatever was fueling Alix suddenly evaporated. "It's all right," she said tiredly and sat next to Dar.

Casey got up and turned on the radio. The DJ introduced a song called *Wooden Ships* from an upcoming Jefferson Airplane album. A good song usually softened his innards. This time, though, he couldn't shake off a premonition of doom.

"Turn it off," Payton snapped. "You shouldn't listen to establishment media."

Casey tensed. "What are you talking about, man? It's *The Spoke*. FM."

"AM–FM, it doesn't matter. They're all owned by corporations. What you hear is what they want you to hear."

"That's not true. *The Spoke* plays an entire side. With no commercials."

"You're naïve. Music is only fodder for ads. And fantasies that pass for entertainment. It's designed to suck you in. Distract you. The only thing worth listening to is the weather forecast."

No one said anything. Then Casey deadpanned, "I hear they missed you at Woodstock."

Everyone laughed, except Payton. But it did ease the tension. Temporarily.

"You know what your problem is?" Payton asked. "You've all allowed the system to corrupt you. What we need are some self-criticism sessions around here. To reorient your thoughts."

"My thoughts are just fine," Alix replied.

"Said like a true member of the privileged class," Payton shot back.

"Lay off, Payton," Dar said. "It's been a tough day."

"Every day's a tough day for the oppressed."

"Hey, guys. How about we go up to Wrigley tomorrow?" Casey said brightly. "The Cubs are closing in on the pennant."

THIRTY-SIX

With no money for a private sanitarium, and a six-month waiting list for the MTS, Billy began treatment at a city clinic on Division not far from the boarding house. The regimen was long, slow, and highly specific, with pills that had to be taken at precise times each day, every day. At first, Alix and Dar took Billy there.

"Hey, I'm not a baby," he complained after a week of being chaperoned. "I can go by myself."

"It's only for a little while," Dar said. "When you're stronger, you'll go on your own."

Alix wasn't counting on it, though, and said so to Dar. "Billy's still a kid. When he starts feeling better, he's going to think he's cured and stop going."

"We'll have to make sure he doesn't."

"How are 'we' going to do that? And what if he starts to freak out? He could bolt. Or even lie about going."

"So what do you propose?"

"I'll keep taking him."

"That's a huge responsibility."

"There's no other choice." She shrugged. "The jewelry business will have to slide." She sighed. "It'll make a significant dent in our income."

Dar kissed the top of her head. "I'll pick up an extra shift at the bookstore, and see if they'll put me on as a delivery man at the Moon Palace."

Alix would have preferred that he help out with Billy.

In September Payton and Teddy went downtown to the Chicago Seven trial. The roster of defendants had been reduced from eight to seven after Bobby Seale was separated from the others. Supporters weren't allowed into the courtroom, but they demonstrated outside as a show of solidarity. By October 9th the National Guard was called in to control the crowds. Payton and Teddy came home with stories about uptight guards and imminent brutality, but nothing ever materialized.

October also brought the "Days of Rage," billed as a massive revolutionary anti-war action. The Weather organization expected thousands of people to gather and show their contempt for the "state," but only about five hundred did. They stormed a few neighborhoods, caused some property damage, and fought with police.

One of the protestors was tackled by Richard Elrod, the city's "law and order" attorney who happened to be on the street during the event. The cops said Elrod was kicked and beaten with an iron pipe; the Weathermen, including Payton and Teddy, claimed Elrod fell. Regardless of whose story you believed, Elrod broke his neck and was temporarily paralyzed. The Chicago papers gushed with sympathy for Elrod, and what little support the Weathermen had eroded. The group began to be shunned, which made them shift even farther left.

But the defining moment of late 1969 was the assassination of Fred Hampton. On December 4th the Chicago police raided the Black Panther leader's apartment on Monroe Street in the middle of the night. Hampton was killed, and several other Panthers were wounded. The cops claimed they'd been attacked by "violent" and "vicious" Panthers and offered photos showing bullet holes made by Panther fire.

But this was the Chicago police, and no one bought their story. An internal police investigation exonerated the officers involved, but most people saw it as part of an orchestrated strategy to destroy the Black Panther Party. Over five thousand people attended Hampton's funeral, including Payton, Teddy, and Dar. Rain covered it for *The Seed*, and even Casey felt an injustice had been done.

"If they were gonna assassinate someone, he was the one to hit," Rain said the night after the funeral.

Casey was lying on the couch, one arm flung over his forehead. "How do you figure?"

"He was smart, articulate, and charming. Tons of charisma. The Bobby Kennedy of black people . . . "

"In other words, he was a threat."

Rain nodded.

"The cops claim it was a fire fight."

"At four in the morning, with everyone in bed?" Rain snorted. "How much you want to bet the cops had a little help?"

Casey propped himself up on an elbow. "The FBI?"

"Hoover had to be involved. He's been trying to get the Panthers from the beginning." Her eyes turned sad. "I guess he's finally succeeding."

Casey fought a sense of despair. He had the feeling everything was unraveling.

On New Year's Eve Alix wanted to take Billy over to Bobby's to watch the Times Square ball drop on TV, but Bobby refused to let him in. She talked about borrowing a TV from the guy who owned the film studio and setting it up in Billy's room, but Payton kept criticizing her for sinking to the level of the masses, so she gave up rather than argue. Instead, she ordered Chinese food from the Moon Palace and took it to Billy. Dar was making deliveries, but Casey had the night off and came with her.

While Alix set out the food on a tray in the landlady's kitchen, Casey went up to Billy's room. It was a small, cramped space on the third floor of an old house on Eugenie Street. Billy had tacked up a few psychedelic posters as decoration, but his mattress was threadbare, the bureau wobbled, and a sour smell hung in the air.

Billy still looked sick. His face was pale, and his breathing was labored. He'd lost so much weight that his eyes dominated his entire body. Casey put on a mask from a stack at the door. Billy had been taking his medication for over three months now—shouldn't he be showing improvement? Casey was relieved they hadn't taken him to Bobby's. He tried to conceal his concern. "How you doin', man?"

Billy shrugged. His mouth and nose were covered by a mask as well.

"Alix has enough Chinese food downstairs to feed an army."

Billy gave him a listless nod.

"And look what I got." Casey pulled out a paper bag from under his jacket and tossed it on the bed. Billy peeked in and slid out a new R. Crumb comic and the new *Mad* magazine.

"Thanks, man." Billy's eyebrows smoothed out and the muscles under the mask shifted. He was smiling.

Casey smiled back, hoping it didn't look as forced as it felt.

Billy was watching him. "Casey, I need a favor."

"Sure, pal."

Billy rolled off the bed and retrieved a paper bag from the floor underneath the mattress.

"This is for Alix. It's her Christmas present." He held up a silver chain with heavy links, like an ID bracelet. "It's kind of like the one Teddy always wears, you know?"

Casey was surprised Billy had noticed. "But I want to work some turquoise into it," Billy said. "I've got the turquoise . . . " He fished in the bag and pulled out the turquoise pendant he used to wear—the one his mother gave him. "But, see, the thing is it needs to be reshaped. I can't do it. I don't have the right tools, and I can't borrow Alix's 'cause it's supposed to be a surprise."

"So what do you need?"

"Go down to Jewelers Row on Wabash and talk to the guy we buy from. He can do it. I've got the bread. I've been saving up."

"That's all?" When Billy nodded, Casey smiled. "I thought it was something tough."

THIRTY-SEVEN

But Casey never got the turquoise reshaped for Billy. Two weeks into the new year, on a blustery, frigid evening, Alix and Casey found Billy coughing up massive amounts of blood and struggling for breath. They rushed him to the ER in a cab. The ER attendants took one look at him, slipped him onto a gurney, and raced through the double doors. Casey and Alix were sent to the waiting room. Dar met them there.

A few minutes later, a nurse gestured to them from the corridor.

"He's not good," the nurse said. "They're trying to intubate him, but he's bubbling up blood, and they're having a hard time getting it in. They think he might have ruptured a bleb in one of his lungs."

"What does that mean?" The waiting room was warm, even stuffy, but Alix shivered.

The nurse pretended not to have heard Alix's question. "The doctor wants to know what drugs he's been taking."

Alix told her.

"Has he been taking them every day?"

"I've been taking him to the MTS clinic on Division for three months. Why?"

The nurse shook her head. "I have to go back. The doctor will come out when he can."

"Please." Alix grabbed her arm, her face a sea of grim anxiety. "You have to tell me what's happening."

The nurse sighed. "We could be seeing a drug-resistant form of the disease. Or maybe the medication isn't doing its job. Sometimes the quality of the pills isn't what it should be."

"We're getting them from the city health department."

"Or," the nurse said, "it might be that it's just too little, too late. The type of TB he has is usually due to a flare-up of a previous infection."

"What are you saying?"

"He's probably had the disease since he was young. If we'd known earlier . . . if he'd gotten the right kind of help six years ago . . . even six months . . . " She threw Alix a compassionate glance. "You need to prepare yourself."

"No!" Alix cradled the sides of her face with her hands. "Don't let him die."

But an hour later, in the winter-gray period before dawn, Billy took his last breath.

Dar stayed at the hospital to make arrangements and try to contact Billy's family—or what was left of it—at Rosebud. Casey took Alix back to the apartment, where she went into her bedroom and shut the door. Dar came back an hour later, spoke to no one, and went into their room.

A minute later Alix came out and sat on the sofa. Her face was blank, her gaze vacant, but Casey could feel her grief gust in like cold air through an open window. He knew she was torturing herself with recriminations and might-have-beens. He draped a blanket around her shoulders. She made no sign she knew he was there, but for the first time since she and Dar had been a couple, Alix slept on the couch.

The memorial service was quiet and sad. Alix went through the motions with a glazed look that never quite came into focus. Bobby, the owner of Up Against the Wall, asked the man who'd married Donna and Linda to deliver a eulogy, and Rain made a surprisingly eloquent speech about the immortal life of the spirit. Payton showed up, which surprised Casey—Payton had disapproved of Billy and his relationship with Alix and Dar. But there he was, in a clean pair of jeans and a white shirt. Teddy, too. Dar was there, of course, but he didn't talk to anyone.

For days afterwards the sound of Alix's weeping through the bedroom walls sliced through Casey like shards of glass. When she wasn't crying, she wandered around the apartment peering into space, as if seeing Billy's ghost. For his part, Dar fled the apartment every morning and stayed away all day. They must have been feeling the same grief, the same remorse, the same guilt, but they avoided each other, unable to share. The silence when they were both in the apartment was heartbreaking. The core of their extended family had collapsed. The others were upset, too, although they didn't admit it. Rain tiptoed around, and Payton and Teddy were uncharacteristically quiet.

It was Casey who went through Billy's things at the boarding house. He took the bracelet Billy had been making for Alix, as well as the turquoise pendant his mother had given him and gave them both to her. At first she clasped them to her chest, but then she handed them back. "I can't handle these. You keep them."

One night Dar didn't come back to the apartment until dawn. Alix was still in bed but wasn't asleep—she rarely slept more than an hour or two at a time. She lay staring at the ceiling, as usual, waiting for her nausea to subside. It had started about a month ago, mostly in the mornings. She figured it was the stress of taking care of Billy. She looked towards the door as it opened.

"Alix?" Dar whispered. He stood in the doorframe silhouetted by the light from the hall. "Are you awake?"

She nodded.

He walked in, closed the door, and came to the edge of the bed.

Alix gazed at him. He looked tired and thin and sad. He needed a shower. "I'm glad you're here," she said. She got out of bed.

"No. Don't." His hands shot up as if he was warding off danger. "We need to talk."

She shushed him with a finger against his lips, and then pulled him close. At first he tried to pull away, but she slipped her hand under the waistband of his bell bottoms and kissed him, teasing his lips with her tongue. He relaxed then, and kissed her back, his fingers tangling in her hair. She leaned closer, and his tongue moved down to her throat, her neck, her collarbone. He knew her body so well. She arched her back.

She helped him take off his sweatshirt and tossed it on the floor. She saw the longing in his eyes. She watched as he took off his pants. He was ready for her, but she pushed him onto the bed and slowly unbuttoned the shirt she wore at night. His breath came faster. She slipped off her panties and straddled him, guiding him in. She rocked back and forth, riding him hard. When she came, a shudder wracked her body. Then he took over.

Afterwards she lay beside him listening to his breathing. She'd seduced him. But he'd made all the right moves, whispered all the right things. Still, a seed of doubt had sprouted during their love-making. It wasn't anything obvious, just a slight hesitation, a subtle shift from passion to awareness. The problem was she didn't know if it was coming from him or from her.

Dar was putting on his clothes when Alix woke a few hours later. "Alix, we need to talk."

She stretched and gave him a smile. "Good morning."

"Alix, I'm leaving. Payton and Teddy are moving out, too."

Alix's stomach twisted. A dull pain gathered at her temples. "Why?"

"I tried so hard to make it work," he said softly. "You. Billy. Everything."

She got out of bed and went to him. "We both did." She started to brush her hand across his forehead. "It wasn't your . . . "

"No." He pushed her hand away. She froze. Dar had never rejected her before. She didn't know what to do with her hand.

"At first I thought it was my fault," he said. "That I'd failed you. That if I could have done more, been more attentive, made more money, Billy wouldn't have died."

She let her hand drop. "I feel the same way, Dar. I . . . "

He held up his hand. "No. Listen to me Alix. The thing is, it wasn't me. Or you. It was the system that failed Billy. He was fucked from the beginning."

"The system?"

"The first screw-up at the ER. The fact that we couldn't get him the right treatment until it was too late. There should have been procedures in place to protect Billy. Months before he got so sick. There weren't." He sighed. "Alix, I've decided Payton is right."

A sudden memory of Billy grinning when he mastered the chessboard flew into Alix's mind. "About what?"

"We need to change society. Deep-seated, radical change. What happened to Billy should never happen again."

"But you said the Movement had spent itself. Too many factions. Foolish tactics. Divide and conquer."

"I know," he admitted. "But I've been rethinking it. I'll be an even bigger failure unless I try again."

Alix began to shiver, the way she had in the ER the night Billy died. "Try what?"

"It's better that you don't know." He paused. "Rain was right, you know. We're . . . very different."

"That's not true. Dar, I need you."

"I'll tell you what the truth is," he said slowly. "The truth is that you loved Billy more than me."

"You're wrong. I loved Billy because he reminded me of you. And then when we were caring for him together, I felt like we were . . . "

"A family?" He turned an anguished face to her. "What kind of family? Alix, you told your father you'd go back to Indiana if he gave you money for Billy."

"What else could I do? I had no other options."

"Options." He paused. "Yes. That's a good word. Then you understand why I have to go. I have no other options."

"No!" Her eyes filled. "At least, tell me where you're going. I can't bear the thought of not being in touch with you."

He cupped her chin in his hand, gazing at her as if recording her features. Then he kissed her softly and walked out of the room.

She was suddenly cold. Achingly cold. She hugged herself. Maybe he was still on the other side of the door. Waiting for her to beg him to stay.

"Dar?"

There was no reply.

THIRTY-EIGHT

C asey came awake all at once. For a moment he thought Payton and Teddy were having a conversation, but he was alone. Strange to have this much privacy after sharing for so long. Gradually he realized that Alix and Rain were talking in the hall outside the bathroom. They kept their voices low, but he heard the tension. When he heard the word "clinic," he roused himself and stumbled through the door.

Rain was standing against the wall, arms akimbo. "You have to go. What if it's TB?"

"I don't have TB, Rain. I'm not coughing."

Rain shook her head. "You don't know that. Do you want history to repeat itself?"

"What's going on?" Casey yawned. "Are you sick, Alix?"

Rain's face was tight. "She needs to see a doctor, but she keeps saying no."

Alix leaned against the other wall. "I'm all right."

Casey brushed his hair off his face. He'd tried to encourage Alix to go back to her jewelry business, but her heart wasn't in it. Aside from the occasional trip to the grocery store, she wasn't doing much except reading and, now that Payton wasn't there to criticize, listening to the radio. Part of it was mourning Billy. Part of it was mourning Dar. And part of it was the brittle Chicago winter. Last year, their combined energy had fueled their souls and their bodies. This year, he'd started to notice how the cold seeped in, leaving a chill in every room.

But Alix did look pale and listless. Casey couldn't take a chance. "Rain is right. You're going to a doctor. We'll take you. No argument."

"And what did you have in mind?" Alix said. "It's not like we have money for a Michigan Avenue practice."

"The Panthers' free clinic is down on 16ᵗʰ Street. We'll go there."

"Uh, excuse me, but I think Alix just might be the wrong color for that," Rain said.

"Mention Payton to them, and they'd probably treat her." Casey shrugged. "But if that's a hassle, I guess we can go to the ER."

"No," Alix answered quickly.

"Wait." Rain held up her hand. "*The Seed* was just doing an article about a new clinic in New Town. Let me check it out."

Alix and Rain emerged from the Women's Health Collective at the corner of Sheffield and Clark the next afternoon. Located in a squat building, the clinic had been started by feminists who wanted to provide women with an alternative to the male-dominated health care system.

Casey was waiting at a coffee shop across the street. He threw fifty cents down on the counter and hurried outside. "What happened?"

Rain's expression was enigmatic, but Alix looked dazed. "I am so stupid." She shifted her feet.

Casey looked from Rain to Alix. "Did they do a TB test?"

Alix said something, but the clamor from a passing El train drowned out her reply.

Casey motioned to the train. "What?"

Alix dug out a card from her bag. When the train had passed, she said, "The doctor did the test. I'm supposed to check my arm over the next three days for any of these things." She handed him the card, which had four squares with various bumps and drawings of what she should look for. "But the doctor doesn't think that's the problem."

"What is it, then?"

"She thinks I'm pregnant."

Casey took a startled step back. His mouth dropped open.

"I should have known. I mean I was putting on weight, even though I was hardly eating."

"And the nausea," Rain added.

Alix nodded. "So they did a pregnancy test. I'm supposed to call next week."

Casey hung back, still speechless.

But Rain was already making plans. "If you *are* pregnant, there are places that can take care of you. A couple of girls at *The Seed* told me about one in Lincoln Park. Very clean. Almost a hospital."

"Take care of me?" Alix looked surprised. "You mean an abortion?"

Rain nodded. "It's gonna be legal one day. Has to be."

"I don't want one," Alix said quietly.

"What do you mean? Of course you do."

"No, Rain, I don't."

Rain waved one hand over the other. "Are you crazy, Alix? This isn't just a fifteen-year-old boy who wandered into your life for a year or two. This is a baby. It will change your life. Forever."

For the first time since Billy died, a genuine smile spread across Alix's face. "I know, Rain. But it's our baby, Dar's and mine. Don't you see? Now he'll have to come back."

A week later the clinic confirmed that Alix was nearly four months pregnant. When she went in for a follow-up appointment, she received another surprise. The doctor detected two heartbeats. She was carrying twins.

"Casey, we have to find Dar. He needs to know."

Casey's lips tightened. "I don't know where he is."

"But you're his best friend."

"And you're his girlfriend. Doesn't mean we know what he's up to."

"There must be some way to find out," Rain said.

"Are you sure you want to?"

225

Alix looked worried for a moment. Then her forehead smoothed out. "Don't worry, Casey. It's going to be fine. We're going to be parents."

She was already talking about turning the back bedroom into a nursery. And even though the babies weren't due until July, she was making plans to shop for blankets and cribs and two little mobiles to hang over them.

Casey ran his tongue around his lips. "Alix, what if he doesn't? Come back, I mean?"

Her smile wavered. "Why? Do you know something I don't?"

"Of course not. But I don't want . . . "

"He will. These are his babies."

Casey and Rain exchanged glances. Then Rain asked, "Have you called *your* parents? They should know."

Alix bit her lip. "Not yet."

It took Casey three weeks and several trips to Weiss's, the local hippie bar at Belden and Lincoln, to find someone who knew someone who could make contact with Dar, Payton, or Teddy. All of which made Casey nervous. Why were they so deep underground?

Finally, on a crisp, sunny February morning, the same day most of the Chicago Seven defendants were convicted of crossing state lines to start a riot, Casey found a message in their mailbox. Scribbled on the back of a piece of brown cardboard was the following:

The record store on Wells at 9. Listen to Volunteers in the booth.

Casey felt a spit of irritation. This wasn't a James Bond movie. But he'd promised Alix, so that night, at ten past nine, he showed up at the record store a few doors down from Up Against the Wall. He was the only customer in the shop, and he browsed through bins of records, studied the album covers on the walls, smelled the incense. The guy behind the counter, a black guy in a dashiki with dreadlocks and lots of gold in his mouth, watched him carefully.

Finally, Casey went up to the counter, feeling foolish, and mumbled, "I'm looking for the Volunteers album."

The guy grunted and pointed to a curtained-off booth at the back of the room. "I'll bring it to you, mon."

Casey went inside the tiny booth, where a turntable and speakers lay on a waist-high counter. A stool sat in front of it. What was he supposed to do now? He sat on the stool, drumming his fingers on the shelf, wishing he could leave and go home.

A minute later, the guy behind the counter knocked on the door. When Casey opened it, he slipped him the Volunteers album. A scrap of paper was taped to the cover, directing him to an alley near Clybourn and Division, about a mile away. He sat for a moment, wondering if he was expected to play the album before he left. He decided not to and exited the booth. He dropped the album on the counter. The guy manning the store was nowhere to be seen.

Rain and Alix were waiting outside.

"Well?" Alix asked.

Casey explained. "This is a stupid idea. It isn't safe," he added.

Rain said she was happy to forget the whole thing and go back to the apartment, but Alix insisted. "Please, guys. Do it for me. And the babies."

Casey capitulated. It was a cold night, but there was no snow and the wind was calm. They could walk.

The three of them headed down Wells. This part of Old Town was safe and well-lit. The Ambassador East, a luxury hotel, was a few blocks away. As they turned west, though, the neighborhood changed. Once they passed Sedgwick, the sidewalk became cracked, and there were slippery patches of ice. The streetlights were dim, and angry shadows loomed between buildings.

Two minutes later they reached the alley. It was bricked along most of its length. Someone had made an attempt to banish the darkness with a weak floodlight, but it looked gloomy and sinister. The smell of decay wafted out from a dumpster. They quietly crept past it, Casey starting when a cat streaked across their path. Rain shivered and pulled her parka close. Only Alix—the girl who'd been protected and coddled all her life—marched fearlessly.

At the far end it made a surprising ninety-degree turn, opening onto an abandoned snow-mottled field. The field was littered with trash and bottles and tires, but new buildings surrounded it, and Casey suspected it wouldn't be long before it too was developed. He stepped gingerly, trying to avoid broken glass. He didn't want to think about what else might have been dumped there.

A streetlamp splashed a watery pool of light onto the field. Casey saw a tall form emerge from the shadows behind it. Dar. Alix spotted him, too, and started to sprint toward him. Half way there, she slowed, as if she'd just realized she was pregnant and had to be careful.

Casey watched as Alix threw her arms around Dar, who let his arms sag, but then, as if he couldn't help himself, he hugged her back. She buried her face in his coat. Though Dar wasn't that close to them, the coat looked unfamiliar. Casey wondered what had happened to his pea coat.

He couldn't hear their conversation, but he watched as Alix made wide gestures with her hands. At one point, Dar straightened and reared back, as if surprised. Then there was more talk, after which Alix lifted the wool serape she was wearing because she couldn't button her coat, and placed Dar's hand on her stomach. Covering it with her own, she looked up at him. Casey could see her cloud of blond hair escaping the hood of the serape. He imagined her hopeful expression.

Then Dar withdrew his hands and shoved them in his pockets. Alix went still. She said something. Dar shook his head. A moment later she held out her arms one more time, but he stepped out of reach, and disappeared into the shadows.

Alix watched him go, not moving, her solitary figure etched in the weak light. Then she turned around and trudged slowly back to the alley.

When Alix reached Casey and Rain, she spoke only one word, "No."

That one word held all the sadness and despair that comes with the end of a dream.

On the street, at the far end of the field, the dome light of a car snapped on. Casey caught a glimpse of Payton in the driver's seat. Someone was in the back—he was sure it was Teddy. Dar slid into the passenger seat, the door closed, and the car sped off.

THIRTY-NINE

I t was a stormy spring. News of the My Lai massacre became public and triggered a fresh wave of outrage. In March, a bomb accidentally went off, leveling a townhouse in Greenwich Village and killing the three Weathermen who'd been assembling it. Closer to home, at the end of March, a bomb went off in a recruiting office on Chicago's north side, shattering windows and destroying furniture. A month later Nixon announced he'd sent forces into Cambodia.

Casey found it all hard to absorb. Time seemed to have accelerated, compressing events into a procession of shocks with no distance or perspective between them. On one hand he felt battered and desensitized; on the other, he was hurtling toward oblivion.

He wasn't alone. The breaking point for Rain came on May 4th when the National Guard opened fire on a crowd of student protestors at Kent State University, killing four and wounding nine others. That night Rain stalked around the apartment in a cold fury. "It's bad enough we're killing the Vietnamese. But when we start killing our own, I'm . . . I'm ashamed to live in this country."

"What are you going to do?" Casey asked.

"I'm done. It's over. I'm going back to Madison. I want to study something that has nothing to do with society. Or politics. Maybe I'll go to Europe."

"What about *The Seed?*"

"It's not gonna be around much longer. The Weathermen have scared away our advertisers. They think we're committed to the violent overthrow of the government." She flipped up her palms. "No ads, no articles, no paper."

Alix came out of the kitchen. "I never thought of you as someone who gave up."

Since the night they'd seen Dar, she hadn't mentioned his name. It was as if he'd never existed. All her energies were focused on the babies. She bought Dr. Spock's *Baby and Child Care*, as well as a book of baby names. She'd made lists of all the equipment she needed, and even made Casey go with her to Kerr's to comb through racks of baby clothes.

"I'm not giving up," Rain answered. "You know the Byrds' song, *A Time for Every Purpose Under Heaven*? Well, it's time for me to find a new purpose."

Alix looked stricken.

Rain let out a breath. "Look. When we started living together, we thought we could do anything. We were special. Cooler, more daring. Our words, our parties, even our sex was more meaningful." She pasted on a sad smile. "But we've been fooling ourselves. We've been pulled along by the current, hoping to grasp a branch along the way that would give us a sense of our own importance. The truth is we're no better—or more important—than any other generation."

Casey sensed something inevitable about Rain's words.

"We're never going to change society. Not in any meaningful way. So it's time for me to accept it, fold up my tent, and hit the road," Rain said. "What about you, Alix? What are your plans?"

She was getting huge; it was difficult for her to get around. Even climbing the two flights of stairs to the apartment was a chore.

"My purpose is to have my babies and take care of them right here."

"You seem so . . . sure of yourself," Rain said. "Why here? Why Chicago?"

"It's become my home. And I can't wait to be a mother. For real this time."

Rain arched an eyebrow, as if surprised by Alix's insight into Billy's role in her life. At least she seemed to be done with mourning. That was a good thing.

Rain turned to Casey. "What about you?"

"I'm going to stay with Alix. At least until the twins are born."

"You've always been here for me, haven't you, Casey?" Alix got up and headed to the bathroom, complaining that was all she ever did any more.

Rain waited until the bathroom door closed. Then she said, "Well done, Casey. How does it feel to get what you want?"

Casey tilted his head.

"Dar is gone, but you're still here. With Alix. All your waiting paid off."

"Alix needs me. I'm glad I can help."

Her smile was knowing. "I guess at least one of us should get what they want."

The toilet flushed, and Alix came back.

Rain stood up. "You're due the end of July, right?" When Alix nodded, she said, "Well I guess I can hang around 'til then. Be nice to have new life around here."

FORTY

O nce they homed in on the target, the rest was surprisingly easy. The hard part had been the decision—they'd discussed it for weeks, the conversation at times turbulent. Dar was dead set against it, but Payton and Teddy were relentless. Given the police state they lived in, they were compelled to make a statement. The target they had chosen, a symbol of rampant materialism, was appropriate.

Payton took pains to say no one would be hurt. It was the establishment they were striking against. He'd cased the place. After midnight, it went dark. No one was there. Bricks and mortar were the objective, not people. Workers were the oppressed victims. In a way, they would be releasing those workers from bondage. Symbolically. "We've tried everything else, and it hasn't worked," Payton said. "An armed attack against the imperialist state is the only choice left. We've got to carry this through."

For his part, Dar was desperate to do something—anything—to reclaim his sense of purpose. Watching the sun rise over Lake Michigan, after yet another night of Payton's rhetoric, he reluctantly agreed. It would be easier to shake up a complacent nation than to face his own limitations.

Payton ripped off a copy of *The Anarchist Cookbook* from an alternative bookstore. The first step, he said, was to secure a supply. Ammonium nitrate powder was the ticket—it was commonly used by farmers as fertilizer. When combined with fuel oil, it made an excellent explosive. Plus, it was widely available and cheap. He and Teddy bought large amounts from rural vendors, paying cash up front.

They couldn't take delivery, however, until they had something to haul it in, so the next step was to find a truck or van. Payton decided they should steal a VW van. They'd have more choices in Madison, a center for students and hippie culture, so they cased the streets around Mifflin until they found one parked on the street. They returned at three in the morning, and Payton hot-wired it, a skill he'd picked up as a teenager. "Like taking candy from a baby," he joked as they drove off.

The next morning Teddy insisted they file off the van's Vehicle Identification Number.

"Why?" Payton asked. "The van'll be totaled."

"I just think it's a good idea."

"It's stupid. So what if they figure out it's stolen? They can't trace it to us."

"I just want to be on the safe side." When Payton frowned, Teddy explained. "Look. I'm from Madison. I just don't want anything . . . well, you just never know. Humor me, okay?"

Payton shrugged. "Fuck it, man. Do your thing. But you'll have to buy some shit to take it off with. And make sure you're disguised when you go to the store. You don't want anyone remembering you."

Teddy nodded. That afternoon he came back with a screwdriver and a pack of razor blades. Opening the driver's-side door, he located the VIN on what looked like a decal attached to a strip of metal at the bottom of the doorjamb. Rivets on both ends held it down. Dar watched as Teddy pulled out a blade and started sawing and scraping the decal.

"It should come right off." Teddy frowned. "How come it's not?"

"You're trying to cut through metal. Seems to me you might need a hammer and a cold chisel," Dar said.

"No." Teddy shook his head. "I'm just trying to get the decal off the metal strip."

"You have to take off the whole piece, asshole," Payton said. "Try the rivets."

"Yeah, okay. But it's not . . . Shit!" He jerked his hand.

"What's wrong?"

"Fuck it! I sliced through my thumb."

Dar looked over. Blood was oozing from Teddy's left thumb. A few drops landed on the doorjamb.

"Goddamnit!"

"I warned you," Payton said.

"Doesn't look too bad," Dar said.

"To you, maybe," Teddy said.

Dar watched the blood drip onto the VIN decal. "Maybe it's a sign."

Teddy gave Dar the finger and sucked his thumb.

Payton laughed. "If you could see yourselves . . . "

Teddy went back to work on the VIN with no more success. "The fucking thing won't come off."

"Shit. You're useless." Payton grabbed the screwdriver and pried up the rivets. A second later, he held up the bloody decal. "Satisfied?"

Teddy eyed him, then nodded. "You're going to get rid of that, aren't you?"

Payton slipped it into his pocket.

"I mean, torch it or something?"

"You think I'm a retard?"

Teddy kept his mouth shut.

After they picked up the ANFO and loaded it into the van, Payton said, "Okay. One more step and we're ready to rock and roll."

"What's that?" Dar asked.

"We need us some nitromethane."

"What? Why?"

"For a little extra kick." Payton grinned.

"I've never heard of it."

Payton snorted. "Figures."

"Are you sure you know what you're doing?" Teddy asked.

"You can get it at any racing parts store. And yes, I know what I'm doing. You assholes are really turning out to be pansies, you know?"

FORTY-ONE

The intercom buzzed around ten the next morning. Rain answered it. "Yes?"

"We want to talk to Alixandra Kerr," a man demanded.

"And you are?"

"Special Agents Dalton and Stevens. FBI."

Rain spun around. "What do we do?"

Casey's heart started to pump like a jackhammer. A year ago he—or Dar or Payton—would have told the pigs to take a hike, leave them alone. But now he spread his hands. Some hero.

It was Alix who went to the intercom. "Of course. Come up."

Casey watched Alix open the door to two men in gray suits, narrow ties, and the shortest hair he'd seen in a long time. One was tall and skinny, the other tall and burly. Alix motioned them to the sofa.

The skinny man introduced himself as Dalton. "Which of you is Alixandra Kerr?"

Alix rested her hands on her stomach. "I am."

He gazed at her belly in surprise.

Casey wanted to ask how they'd found out where she lived. Then he realized anyone could have told them: Bobby, the Moon Palace, even someone at *The Seed*. After almost two years, they were known in the neighborhood.

"What can I do for you?" Alix asked placidly, as if they were having tea.

"We're following up on some information that came our way." His eyes swept over them. "We want to talk to you one at a time."

Rain spoke up. "About what?"

"You'll see."

"Hold it. It's our right to know. So we know if we want to take the Fifth."

"Does that mean you have something to hide?" the agent asked.

"You know that's not the way it works."

Rain was brave, Casey thought. He didn't have the guts.

The agent stared at Rain, his expression blank. "Tell you what. If this is a problem, we can always go downtown and talk."

That was the quid pro quo, Casey thought. Spill your guts now and we won't run you in. Great choice.

"All right." Alix sat and folded her hands. "Rain, you and Casey wait in the bedroom."

Rain and Casey got up and shuffled into Rain's bedroom. His nerves were jangling. Rain closed the door.

"Shit," Rain groaned. "What's going on? What have we done?"

"I don't know, but I don't like it." Casey put his ear against the door. He heard the murmur of questions being asked, Alix calmly providing answers. He stared at a spidery crack in the wall. How could Alix be so cool? She had to be under enormous pressure.

Fifteen minutes later, Alix came in and gestured to Casey. "Your turn."

He ran his tongue around his lips.

"Don't worry," Alix said. "It's about Payton. And Dar. Just tell them the truth."

When Casey went into the living room, Dalton was on the couch. Stevens was perched on the windowsill, in Casey's favorite spot. Dalton asked Casey if he had a job.

Casey said, "At the Moon Palace. A few blocks from here."

"Is there someone who can verify that?"

"My boss, Mrs. Lee." He gave them her number.

"How long have you known Dar Gantner?" Dalton asked.

"About three years."

"Where did you meet?"

"We were freshmen together at Michigan."

Dalton nodded and continued to ask questions about Dar—what kind of person he was, how committed was he to the Movement, was he prone to violence.

"Dar is the least violent person I've ever met," Casey answered. "He lost his father when he was a teenager, and I think it gave him a deep respect—almost a reverence—for human life. He would never be violent." He hoped he sounded more convincing than he felt. The truth was he hadn't seen or talked to Dar in months. Dar was a stranger to him now. But he wouldn't share that with the FBI.

"But Gantner was active in anti-war activities at Michigan. As were you."

They'd done their homework. "But when we . . . I mean . . . Dar met Alix, he pretty much dropped out of the political scene. His relationship with Alix was more important."

"A relationship her father strongly disapproved of," Stevens cut in.

Of course. They'd talked to her father before coming. "I don't know anything about that. But I do know that Alix and Dar were very much in love. She's going to have his children."

"Is that so?" Dalton asked.

Casey bit his lip. He shouldn't have given that up. They'd report back to her father. Dalton went on, "Tell me about Eric Payton."

"Payton talked big," he admitted, "but underneath, I think it was just that. Talk."

The agents grilled him about Payton, then started in on Alix. How did Casey know she wasn't political? Didn't she harbor a grudge against her father because of her father's disapproval? Wasn't her "peace and love" demeanor just a cover for a rebellious nature?

"Absolutely not. Alix was—is—an artist. She makes jewelry. Things of beauty. She would never approve of anything violent or destructive."

"Didn't you have an Indian boy living with you?"

Casey swallowed. They knew everything. "Yes. He died."

"How?"

"He had TB."

Dalton nodded, his face about as expressive as a clock. Then, "What about the other girl? The one who takes pictures for *The Seed*?"

As Casey answered questions about Rain, Dalton scribbled on a notepad. They'd clearly known the answers to most of their questions before they came. Why pretend? What did they want? Casey's stomach knotted.

"Back to the men . . . ," Dalton went on, "you said they moved out. When did they leave? Where did they go?"

"In January. I don't know where."

"Did they ever talk of any places, refuges you can recall? Somewhere in Wisconsin, perhaps?"

Casey shook his head.

"And you're sure you have no idea where they are or what they're planning?"

"Do you?" Casey cocked his head.

The agent kept his mouth shut, but ran his hand up and down the sleeve of his jacket. Doubt or frustration, Casey wondered. Maybe both. "All right. Send in the other girl."

Casey went back to the bedroom. "We're screwed. They think Payton and Teddy and Dar are planning something. And they think we know what it is."

"Fuck, fuck, fuck," Rain moaned.

"Both of you calm down, okay?" Alix said. "I don't think they know anything. Maybe a rumor here or there. They're just fishing."

But Rain didn't look convinced. She looked haunted. Exactly the way Casey felt.

"Just tell them the truth," Alix repeated.

Rain squeezed her eyes shut, then trudged into the other room.

Casey and Alix sat on Rain's bed, trying unsuccessfully to overhear her conversation with the agents. Ten minutes later there were footsteps, and Rain came back in.

"They want the photos I took of everyone at the Coliseum way back when. And at Bobby's when the men landed on the moon."

Alix gave her the briefest of nods. "Hand them over. They need to think you're cooperating fully."

Casey stared at Alix, astonished at her composure. No. Not just composure. Alix was radiating power. Had she been this way all along and he just hadn't seen it? Or was it something she'd kept bottled up until now? For the first time since he'd known her, he saw how formidable she was.

Rain opened the bottom drawer of her dresser and pulled out a manila envelope. She slid it under her arm and went out. A moment later, she called out, "They want you to come back now."

Casey followed Alix back into the living room. He stood next to Stevens while the agents studied Rain's photos. Stevens' jaw twitched when he saw a shot of Teddy. It was a tiny gesture, but Casey caught it.

Dalton looked up. "Did any of your roommates have an interest in race cars?"

"You mean like stock cars?" Casey asked.

"Any type of automobile racing."

"Not that I know of," Casey said. "No one mentioned it."

"Do you know what ammonium nitrate is?"

They exchanged glances. Casey did have an idea, but Alix shook her head. He followed suit.

They asked a few more questions, then, as unexpectedly as they'd come, they left.

Rain sagged against the door and ran a hand through her ash-blond hair.

Alix flicked her hand. "You did fine. We all did."

"No, we didn't," Casey said. "We folded like an accordion."

"We didn't have a choice," Alix replied.

"Payton wouldn't have told them anything."

"You don' t know that." Alix's expression softened. "And you're not Payton."

"I want to know what's going on. What are they up to? Dar and Payton and Teddy," Rain said.

Casey said, "I want to know what the feds are up to. They didn't show up 'cause they had nothing better to do. They suspect something."

Rain's eyes held a far-away expression. "Did you notice how that agent—Stevens—reacted to the picture of Teddy?"

Casey nodded. "Almost as if they recognized him."

"They know him—I'd stake my life on it." Rain straightened up. "And now that I think about it, they never really asked any questions about Teddy. They were focused on Dar and Payton."

"Same here," Casey said. They exchanged glances.

"It's Teddy," Rain said. "I told you he was an informant."

"But who would he be informing on?" Casey asked. "And about what? I work at a Chinese restaurant. You take pictures for *The Seed.* Alix makes jewelry."

"Not us." Rain slid her eyes to Alix. "It's something else. Something big."

Casey hesitated. "Um, I didn't tell the truth about something."

"What?"

"Ammonium nitrate. You use it when you're building a bomb. An ANFO bomb. They used to talk about it on campus at Michigan. The last resort. That kind of thing."

"Oh, god." Rain pulled on her hair. "What do we do?"

Alix had been standing next to the couch, still composed. But she was pale. And quiet. Too quiet. A strange expression came across her face. She started to say something, then suddenly cried out. Clutching her belly, she staggered and fell on the couch.

"What's the matter?" When she didn't answer, Rain shouted, "Alix?"

"Oh, god." Alix gasped. "I think the babies are coming."

FORTY-TWO

S omething was wrong. The babies weren't due for six weeks. Alix shouldn't be going into labor. And while Casey knew nothing about childbirth, he didn't think it was supposed to be this painful so soon. But Alix kept crying and complaining of sharp pains. Her forehead was beaded with sweat, and she was bleeding.

They debated calling an ambulance, then decided to take her to the ER themselves. While Rain went downstairs to hail a cab, Casey dragged the mattress Billy had used out of the closet. When Rain came back up, they put Alix on it and slid it carefully down the stairs like a toboggan. The cab driver helped get her inside. They left the mattress on the sidewalk.

The closest hospital was Fullerton, but Casey told the driver to head to Northwestern. By the time they arrived, Alix was barely conscious. The ER attendants rushed her inside. Casey and Rain went to the waiting room.

Twenty minutes later, a young man in surgical scrubs came into the waiting room. "Who's here for Alixandra Kerr?"

Both Casey and Rain jumped up. The man spoke to Casey. "Are you her husband?"

"Why?"

"I'm the resident on duty. We took her up to the OR. She's presenting with placenta previa."

"What's that?"

"The placenta, which usually attaches itself to the inside of the uterus along the side or back wall, is attached over her cervical opening instead. It wasn't a problem until she went into labor. It's preventing the fetus—in this case, fetuses—from passing into the birth canal. But now it's starting to rupture, which is why she has such severe pain."

"What are you going to do?"

"Usually, we'd do an emergency Caesarean, but she's hemorrhaging badly, and she's in shock. The doctor isn't sure her body can take it."

Casey's skin felt damp. "What happens if you don't?"

"They could all die. The fetuses . . . and the mother." The intern paused. "The fetuses are still quite immature."

Rain grabbed Casey's hand. He barely felt it.

"The surgeon wants you to know that we're going to do our best. You're her husband right?"

Casey felt Rain watching him, reading his thoughts. He took a breath. "Yes."

"Well, you might want to call another family member. Someone should be here. In case."

By six o'clock that evening the babies and Alix were in intensive care, and the doctors were cautiously optimistic. The babies, still quite small and premature, would have to remain in the hospital for a month at least, but they were breathing on their own, which everyone considered a good sign. Alix was young and strong and would bounce back quickly.

Casey came to the hospital every day, sometimes twice a day, to check on Alix and the twins. He hung around the nursery so much that the nursing staff taught him how to give the babies a bottle and burp them.

Alix was released ten days later. She was still weak but forced herself to come back to the hospital every day to feed the twins. After the fifth day she returned to the apartment exhausted.

"This is more than I can handle," she said. "I need help."

"I'm here," Casey said.

"I know." Alix gave him a sad smile. "And I'll always be grateful to you, Casey. But you have your whole life ahead of you. You can't help me forever."

Casey kept his mouth shut. She should only know.

"It shouldn't be you, anyway."

He sighed. "Alix," he said gently. "Stop dreaming. Dar's gone."

"I don't know about that." Her smile grew hopeful. "If I put it out there in the universe, it could happen. If I believe hard enough."

A few weeks later, on the night of June 2nd, the doorbell rang. It was past eleven, and Alix was already in bed. Rain was out with her latest boyfriend. When Casey opened the door, he stepped back in surprise. It was Dar. Looking haggard, disheveled, and drawn.

"What are you doing here, man?"

"I want to see them."

"They're not here."

"Why not?"

"They were premature. They're still in the hospital."

"Is Alix okay?"

"She's fine. She's asleep."

Dar nodded and turned toward the door of the room he and Alix had shared.

"Dar, the FBI was here. They're looking for you. All over Chicago. You need to split. Right away."

"Don't tell me what to do, Casey."

Casey spread his palms. "Dar . . . "

"I know you're in love with her. I know you want her for yourself, okay? But don't tell me I can't see my children. Or their mother. Ever."

Casey threw up his hands. "Fine. You're on your own, Dar. I'm out of here."

He grabbed a jacket, opened the door, and clattered down the stairs. When he got back an hour later, everything in the apartment was quiet. He thought about looking in on Alix, but he didn't want to know if Dar was still there. He went to bed.

FORTY-THREE

On the morning of June 3rd—a warm, summery day that made people think about ditching work and heading up to Wrigley Field—Chicago woke up to the news that a bomb had exploded in the early morning hours at Kerr's department store on State Street. Most of the devastation occurred on the first floor. The ceiling of the lobby collapsed, columns leaned at strange angles, glass counters shattered. A blackish residue of soot covered everything, and clumps of dark matter were splattered on the walls. Fortunately, the store was thought to be empty, and there appeared to be no injuries.

According to the news reports, teams of investigators from the Chicago Police Department's Bomb and Arson squad, the FBI, and the ATF moved in immediately, setting up huge arc lights so they could work. By daylight they'd found pieces of metal near the loading dock that turned out to have come from the engine mount of a vehicle. An hour later, the parts were traced to a VW van that had been stolen three days before in Madison, Wisconsin. They hadn't found the VIN from the door frame, but the number was duplicated on the engine mount.

Investigators set up a perimeter so they could continue working without interference. Extra shifts of police were called in to control the mass of people who thronged to downtown to bear witness to a small piece of history. Hot dog and ice-cream vendors wound through the crowd.

After most of the debris was hauled away, investigators discovered a shallow crater in the alley next to the loading dock, evidence the blast had occurred there. A residue of organic material was found on the exterior walls, raising the possibility that an agricultural fertilizer may have been the explosive.

A reward of one hundred thousand dollars was offered for information leading to the arrest of the offenders.

Rain heard about the bomb on her way to *The Seed* later that morning. She'd spent the night at her boyfriend's but rushed back to the apartment. It was quiet inside; Casey and Alix must still be asleep. She woke Casey. "We have to go to Bobby's."

"Why?" Casey asked sleepily.

"A bomb went off at Kerr's department store last night."

Casey sat up.

"It's bad, Casey," Rain said. "They totaled the store. I'll wake Alix."

"Okay." He got out of bed and threw on some clothes.

Rain came back a moment later. "Where's Alix?"

"What do you mean?

"She's not in her room. Did she go to the hospital to feed the babies?"

Casey ran a hand through his hair. "I . . . I don't know."

Rain planted a hand on her hip. "Earth to Casey. What did she tell you before she went to bed?"

A queasy feeling spread through Casey's gut.

"What's wrong?"

He grimaced. "Dar was here last night."

Rain's eyes grew as wide as plates. "What?"

"Around eleven. He said he wanted to see the twins. Then he went into her room. I . . . I didn't want to hang around, so I went out for a beer."

"What happened when you got back?"

"I don't know." He couldn't meet Rain's eyes. "I went straight to bed."

"So you don't know if she—or Dar—was still here."

"I . . . I guess not."

"Oh shit, Casey. I don't like this." Rain blew out a breath. "Finish dressing. Fast. We gotta go."

As soon as they got to Bobby's, Rain and Casey glued themselves to the TV. Coverage was continuous, and Bobby closed the head shop so he could watch with them. He even brought breakfast in from the diner on Wells.

The TV commentators reported that Sebastian Kerr was on his way to Chicago to personally assist in the clean-up and investigation. By afternoon the experts on TV began to speculate that the bomb was made from ANFO, a mixture of ammonium nitrate and fuel oil, long used by farmers instead of dynamite to blow up stumps and clear ponds. One man said the enormity of the blast indicated that as much as twenty-five hundred pounds of fertilizer could have been used. Someone else said an additional element could have been mixed in to strengthen the blast—nitromethane, for example. All the materials were cheap—fifty pounds of ammonium nitrate only cost a couple of dollars—and widely available.

Most of the bomb, the theory went, was assembled in barrels, then driven to Chicago in the stolen van. The van was parked near the loading dock of the store, probably sometime after midnight. Once it was in place, the nitromethane was added. Then the detonator, blasting cap, and primacord were rigged up.

Casey and Rain exchanged glances. Rain beckoned him into the kitchen.

"The FBI," she whispered. "That's what they were talking about, remember?"

Casey nodded.

"I don't like where this is going, Casey. Do you think Dar and Payton and Teddy . . . "

"No," Casey cut her off. "I can't believe that. Alix would never approve of it, either."

"Well then, where the fuck is she?" Rain asked.

Casey didn't have an answer.

They went back into the living room. The anchorman on TV was interviewing a Bomb and Arson official when the station interrupted with a special bulletin. The news show cut to a reporter on the scene looking somber. "There has been a grisly discovery among the debris at Kerr's department store. It was thought at first that the blast, which occurred between midnight and two o'clock this morning, did not cause any injuries. Sadly, it is now clear that this was not the case. The bodies of two men were found near the guard's station in the lobby. A third individual was found near the loading dock. It appears to be a female. She has been transported to Northwestern Memorial hospital in critical condition."

Casey's throat went dry. "Do you think . . . "

"We better find out," Rain said.

As they tore out of Bobby's, Casey heard the announcer grimly say, "It would seem, ladies and gentlemen, that what was a frightening destruction of property is now—at least—a double homicide."

Neither Rain nor Casey said a word on the way to the hospital. Rain bought a copy of the *Daily News* and read it in the cab. It was the only time Casey had ever seen her read an establishment paper.

"What do you think?" Casey asked.

"The same thing as you," Rain said from behind the paper.

"It had to be an accident. Dar would never kill anyone."

Rain put the paper down. "What planet are you from?"

"Where do you think they got it?" Casey asked.

"There are plenty of places near Madison."

Casey thought about it. "It must have been when Payton and Teddy made that trip up to Wisconsin. Remember? The one where they wanted Dar to go with them?"

Rain put a finger to her lips. And motioned to the cab driver.

Casey stopped talking.

A minute later, though, she whispered, "Why the fuck did they make Kerr's the target? There are a lot of other places they could have chosen to make a statement."

Casey looked at her sideways. "Isn't it obvious?"

"She would never have let them." Rain tightened her lips.

"What makes you think she had a choice?"

When they got to the ER, they discovered that the unidentified woman from the bomb site had been taken into surgery. They approached a uniformed nurse behind the desk. Rain cleared her throat.

"Look, we think . . . well, we may have an idea who the woman is."

The nurse cocked her head. "Who?"

Rain swallowed. "Our roommate. Alix Kerr."

The woman did a double take at the name, then picked up her phone.

Rain went to a seat and continued thumbing through the newspaper, but Casey knew she wasn't reading. He started to pace.

A few minutes later two men, one beefy, one skinny, hurried into the waiting room. After checking with the nurse, they came over. One held up a badge. "I'm Detective Rizzo, Chicago police. Tell me why you think the woman is Alixandra Kerr."

Casey watched the cops study him. He was wearing jeans and his sleeveless vest. Rain was in a granny dress. They clearly looked like hippies. Hippies and cops didn't mix. Casey wasn't surprised by his next statement.

"Listen, we're not playing games. If you don't play ball, we can charge you with obstruction of justice."

Casey and Rain were taken to an empty room where they told the police everything, including their visit from the FBI. After repeating the chronology several times, Casey asked, "How is she? Can we see her? Is she going to be all right?"

The detectives looked startled. "I thought you knew," Rizzo said. "The victim died in surgery. She's gone."

FORTY-FOUR

C asey didn't want to stay, but he didn't want to leave either. He didn't know what to do. Neither did Rain. Dazed and subdued, they stayed in the ER waiting room. Finally, Casey checked the time. It was after seven in the evening. They'd been at the hospital over eight hours. He leaned forward, propping his elbows on his thighs.

"I should go up and see the babies."

"What's going to happen to them?" Rain asked.

"I don't know," he said bleakly. He stood up. "Coming?"

Rain shook her head. "I'm going home."

"Rain, please stay."

She played with a strand of her hair, uncertain. "I don't know the first thing about babies. They make me nervous."

"You don't have to do anything. I just don't want to be alone. Please stay."

Reluctantly, she nodded. They went up to the nursery. The babies lay in their tiny bassinets, oblivious to the fact that both their parents were gone. Alix had named the boy Daniel, and the girl, Lila. Casey waved to the night nurse, who gazed at him with a sad expression. She knew. Probably everyone in the hospital knew. In a way that was good. He didn't have the energy to explain.

Casey gave baby Lila a bottle, watching how greedily she sucked down the formula. She had dark hair, and lots of it. From Dar, of course. The nurses said lots of hair on an infant was good luck. He brushed his fingers across her cheek. Daniel was as bald as Dwight Eisenhower. The nurses had said every baby looks like Ike. He remembered how he and Alix had giggled. It was just last week, he thought. A lifetime ago.

"See, this is what you do. You just . . . ," Casey said to Rain when Lila finished her bottle. He was rubbing tiny circles around the baby's back the way the nurses had taught him. He stopped when he heard noises outside the nursery.

The doors to the room swung open, and a big man swooped in. He was trailed by several men who looked like FBI agents, and another man whose white coat indicated that he was a doctor or hospital official. The big man's eyes swept the room as he made his way to the nurse in charge, but when he spoke his voice was surprisingly soft.

"I'm Sebastian Kerr," he said to the nurse. "I want to see the infants. Now."

The nurse waited a beat, as if to say he might be important, but his authority didn't extend to her nursery. Then she looked at the man in the white coat who'd come in with Kerr. When he nodded, the nurse motioned to Casey. "Over there," she said quietly.

Kerr turned around, his eyes taking in the room. When his gaze landed on Casey, Casey felt his cheeks get hot. He got up and handed the baby to one of the nurses, then went over. Rain came with him.

"Mr. Kerr, I'm Casey Hilliard."

Casey was five ten, and Kerr towered over him. "Do you have some connection to my daughter?"

"We . . . we're roommates. We live . . . lived together." Casey motioned to Rain. "She does, too."

"The last man I saw her with was tall and dark. An unemployed bum. Who are you?"

Casey tried to restrain his anger. "I'm her . . . a close friend."

"Does that mean you slept with her, too?"

Rain's mouth opened. "You can't talk that way, Mr. Kerr. You have no right . . . "

Kerr turned to Rain. His voice was soft but his tone was rock hard. "I have every right. She was my daughter."

Rain's fury exploded. "But you're implying she's . . . that she was . . . that we don't know who the father is. That's not true."

251

"Young lady," Kerr said, as if a lady was the last thing he considered Rain to be, "frankly, I don't care who the father was. Or is. Those babies should never have been . . . conceived."

Casey flashed back to the tiny mobiles Alix had ordered for the cribs. He'd gone with her up to Lazar's, the baby furniture store on Devon, to shop for them. "Mr. Kerr, you have no idea how much your daughter loves . . . wanted them. These babies were the only thing she cared about."

Kerr wheeled around. "Alixandra didn't know what she wanted. Or what was best for her. And now it's too late . . . So if you'll excuse me. I've seen enough." He started toward the entrance and turned to the official in the white coat. "All right, here's what we're going to do." He lowered his voice, and Casey couldn't hear what he was saying.

As Kerr and his retinue left, Casey's stomach knotted into a ball of rage. Rain was so angry she started to stalk out too.

"Where are you going?" Casey asked.

"To smoke a cigarette."

"You don't smoke."

"I do tonight."

Twenty minutes later, Rain was back. Casey finished giving Danny his bottle, but when the nurse took the baby from him, she avoided making eye contact.

"What's wrong?"

The nurse shook her head.

Casey frowned. "Carla, something happened . . . I can tell. What is it?"

Finally she peered at Casey with a gloomy expression. "I shouldn't be telling you this, okay?" the nurse whispered. "He claims you're not the twins' father. And have no rights over them . . . or the mother. He's planning to airlift the mother's body out of here tomorrow. He rented a private jet." She paused. "The twins will not be going with him."

"What?" Casey's voice cracked.

Rain's jaw dropped. "He can't do that!"

"I'm sorry. I shouldn't have told you." The nurse settled Danny in his bassinet. Casey and Rain lurched back into the hospital corridor.

Rain dug her fingers into Casey's arm. "We've got to stop this. What's going to happen to them? We have to do something!"

"What, Rain?" Casey felt desperate. "What can we do? The man is a monster."

Rain looked past him. "Casey…"

But Casey wasn't listening. "A monster who's out to ruin their lives."

"Casey." Rain grabbed his arm, her voice insistent.

He turned around. Sebastian Kerr was standing in the corridor just behind them. Casey wondered if Kerr had heard him. He didn't care.

Kerr stood against the wall, arms folded. "We will be flying my daughter's body back to Indiana tomorrow morning. We will not be taking the infants."

"If Alix knew, she would never forgive you."

Kerr dropped his arms. For a moment, the shell of his face cracked and a shadow of something almost compassionate passed over him. "Alix was young. She had her entire life ahead of her." Then Kerr's face closed, and his features resumed their cold fury. "Believe me, some childless couple will be thrilled to have twin newborns. Unless they are separated, in which case, two couples will be blessed."

"You can't abandon your grandchildren. They're your heirs."

"They are not my grandchildren. They are bastards. That is not a burden my family needs to shoulder."

"God damn you!" Casey's fury spiked. "They're Alix's children. Not yours. I won't let them be thrown in the trash like yesterday's newspaper. I . . . I'll take them myself."

Kerr's eyebrows shot up. "Do you know what you're saying?"

Casey nodded defiantly.

"Are you prepared to say you're their father?"

"Would it make a difference?"

"Are you?"

There was no time to think about it. Casey sucked in a breath. "Yes, I am their father, damn you."

"And your name will go on their birth certificate?"

"That's right."

Kerr didn't say anything for a moment. Then, "You're a fool." He leaned in so close that Casey felt Kerr's breath on his face. "I don't know who you're protecting," he said softly, "or why. Or if any of this is tied to the bomb that destroyed my daughter. And my store." Kerr straightened. "But as for the infants . . . if you take them with the self-indulgent hope that you will one day make a claim on my estate, or reveal whose babies these are, let me tell you what will happen. You—and your girl friend . . . ," he motioned toward Rain, "will be arrested and charged with the explosion at my store. As well as the murder of two security guards and my daughter."

"You can't! I . . . we had nothing to do with the bomb!"

Kerr stared at Casey.

"We weren't there. You have no evidence."

"Are you sure?"

Casey's insides churned. He thought about the FBI agents who'd come to the apartment. Had they taken something besides the photos? Somehow slipped something into their pockets that would incriminate him and Rain? It was possible.

Kerr looked as if he knew what was going through Casey's mind. "You understand, of course, that there is no statute of limitations on murder."

Who would raise Alix's babies if he was arrested or—God forbid—prosecuted? Casey saw a dark hole opening up with everything he knew and loved slipping inexorably into it. Dar. Rain. The babies. Alix. His future. All because he wanted to do the right thing.

"I understand," he said softly.

"Good." Kerr cleared his throat. "Now, I am not an unreasonable man. In return for your silence, I am prepared to write you a significant check which can be put toward the welfare of the infants."

"I don't want your money."

"Again, I ask are you sure?"

"I don't want a goddamned dime from you."

"The more fool you." Kerr sighed. "But, if that is the case I believe our conversation is now over."

Kerr gave him a cold smile and started down the hall. Casey watched until he was out of sight.

Two weeks later Rain lifted her knapsack onto her shoulders.

"Is that it?" Casey asked. She didn't have much more than she'd come with.

"I travel light."

"You'll keep in touch?"

"Sure," she said.

Casey didn't believe her. He looked around the apartment one more time. The furniture was still there, and the utensils, but Rain had packed up Alix's things and donated them to the Salvation Army. Casey did the same with the few things Dar, Teddy, and Payton had left behind.

"When are you leaving?" she asked.

"As soon as the twins can travel."

"Wilmette isn't that far."

He didn't answer.

"Do they know? Your parents?"

"Not yet."

"Are you sure about this, Casey? You're taking on a huge responsibility."

He smiled. "Surer than anything I've ever done."

"Well then, I guess this is it." She shuffled toward Casey and awkwardly put her arms around him. Casey hugged her. He looked away so she wouldn't see his face. "Alix was right, you know."

He drew back. "How?"

"You're a connector, Casey. You brought us all together. And now . . ."

"It wasn't me. It was her."

"Believe what you want. But I know the truth." Her hand brushed his cheek. She went through the door, letting it close it behind her.

Casey heard Rain clatter down the stairs. The downstairs door squeaked as it opened, and he heard the hum of traffic outside. He waited a moment, then followed her out to the pay phone around the corner. He dialed the hospital's number, talked to a nurse, then hung up. He dropped another dime in the slot and dialed a familiar number.

"Mom? It's Casey."

"Oh my god!"

"I'm coming home. Tonight. And I have a surprise for you."

Part Three

The Present

FORTY-FIVE

L ila Hilliard didn't believe Dar. She was still woozy from the painkillers Cece had given her—maybe she had misheard. People living together in a commune. Working for the "Movement." Innocent lovers torn apart by events beyond their control. The death of one at the hand of the other. On some level, it sounded like a hippie version of Romeo and Juliet. With her father as the arch-villain. And yet she felt a tenuous connection to the story, as though questions she'd never articulated, but had been gnawing at her, were finally being addressed.

If it was the truth.

She forced herself to focus. She trusted numbers, not people. People lied. Shaded the truth for their own agendas. She didn't know either Gantner or Cece. She had no reason to trust them. Especially if he was the one who killed her mother. If she wasn't injured, she'd probably try to run away from them before he killed her, too.

On the other hand, why would he have told her a preposterous sounding story if he wanted to do her harm? In fact, now that she was thinking about it, this man, father or not, murderer or not, had saved her life. Didn't that warrant a fair hearing?

She blinked several times. "My father . . . ," she said. "It's Casey's name on my birth certificate. Not yours. How did that happen?"

Lila wasn't sure whether Dar was surprised by her question or grateful that she hadn't dismissed him altogether. "Your father . . . Casey . . . ," he said, "was my best friend. He was also the most honorable man I've ever known. At the time, putting his name on your birth certificate was the right thing to do. For your mother . . . and the two of you."

"But why didn't he ever say anything about it? And why did he tell me her name was Alice Monroe, not Alix Kerr?"

"To protect you."

"Why?"

He hesitated before answering. "Your grandfather—Sebastian Kerr—didn't want anyone to know that you and Danny were his daughter's children. He put Casey in a no-win situation."

"But there had to be other people who knew the truth."

"There were. The six of us in the apartment knew. And Bobby." He explained who Bobby was. "And your grandparents. Alix's brother, Philip, too. But Rain and Casey were the only ones around when you were born. And once Casey decided to keep you, he probably never said another word about it to anyone. "

"Even to my grandmother?"

"Even her."

A wave of confusion washed over Lila. Coming so soon after her father—Casey—and Danny's deaths, this was too much. She couldn't absorb it. Either Dar was lying, which made him no better than a con man, or he was telling the truth, which made him a monster. "How do you know all this? Why should I believe you?"

Dar swallowed and lowered his head for a moment. Then he looked up and took a breath. "Because it's the truth."

Lila fell back against the pillows, recalling a dim memory from her childhood. She'd awakened from a bad dream one night and went down to her father's office to be comforted. The door was closed. She could hear her father's muffled voice, "No. We can't do that."

She opened the door. He was standing, the phone in his ear, an anguished expression on his face. Now she realized it was fear, but at the time, she only knew whatever it was made her uncomfortable.

That night was one of the few times her father had ever been sharp with her—he'd told her to go back to bed and stop snooping. She thought she'd done something terribly wrong and crept up the steps, humiliated. He came up a few minutes later to apologize, but he never said to whom he'd been talking or why. Did that conversation have something to do with his secrets?

Still.

She refocused on Dar. "Even if it's the truth, why should I trust you? Or forgive you? You killed my mother."

A shadow passed over Dar's eyes. He kept his mouth shut.

"Well?"

"You're right," he said slowly, a look of pain clearly etched on his face. "I've had to live with that for forty years."

"How did it happen?"

Dar was quiet.

"You owe me," Lila said.

Cece, who was standing behind him, squeezed his shoulder. He twisted around. She nodded. He turned back to Lila and took a breath.

"I went to see your mother right after you were born. You were still in the hospital, you'd been born prematurely. I didn't know that, of course. I just wanted to say goodbye. To all of you. But . . . " His eyes filled. "Alix—your mother—wouldn't let go. She begged me to stay. She wanted to work it out. I couldn't. I told her. So I left. I took the El down to the store. The thing was . . . " He bit his lip. "She followed me. I didn't know until I saw her dart into the alley, right before the blast went off. She started running toward the van. I was across the street with Payton. I wanted to run after her, but there wasn't enough time. She got caught by the full blast of the explosion."

No one said anything.

"So, yes. Because of my recklessness, I killed the only good thing I'd ever had in my life. Until now."

Lila stiffened. He couldn't woo her with words, no matter how prettily he made them. "If I weren't injured and weak, I'd get away from you as fast as I could. You destroyed my family. What makes you think I want anything to do with you?"

"I understand. I don't expect anything from you. But I needed to try."

"Try what?"

"To save you."

"From what?"

"Whoever's trying to kill you." He hesitated. "I think I know who it is."

"Who?"

"One of the men who planned and detonated the bomb with me." He paused. "Senator Ted Markham," he said softly. "The man who's running for president."

Maybe that was why she and Danny always felt so unsettled, Lila thought the next morning as she came awake. If Dar Gantner was telling the truth, the detachment she'd always felt—the feeling of skating around the periphery of life—was not just the deprivation of a lonely, motherless child but a biological reality. She really was a separate being, not part of Casey Hilliard's DNA.

They said children sometimes had a sixth sense about those things, and despite the blanket of security which Casey and Gramum had thrown over them, she must have felt it. Danny, too. Her brother had dealt with it through drugs and booze; she'd coped by over-achieving, dismissing her isolation as the result of some deep-seated character defect. She lay in bed, trying out her new knowledge. Knowing she hadn't been crazy all those years was, in an odd way, satisfying.

The murmur of voices floated upstairs. "We can't stay here indefinitely," Cece was saying.

"You don't like sleeping on the couch?" Dar replied.

"Come on. You know what I mean. Whoever lobbed that grenade is still gonna be after her. They have to know she's disappeared—her picture's all over the news. Everyone—the police, ATF, and God knows who else, is looking for her. Unless you're prepared to explain it to the world, we need to leave."

"The cops will never believe me. Especially since it was an explosion. They'll yank my parole faster than you can say 'hand grenade.' Which means whoever planned this knew who they were dealing with. They wanted me to be implicated."

A guilty realization hit Lila. Despite her ambiguous feelings about the man, her presence was complicating his life. She thought about getting up and leaving. Maybe she should go to the police herself and explain what happened. They'd believe her.

Except Dar had a point. The only person she could identify at the scene was him. With his track record, they'd never believe he'd saved her. They might even think he'd flip-flopped—tried to kill her, and when he realized she was still alive, pretended to save her instead. The same thought had crossed her mind.

She bit her lip. She wasn't sure how she felt about Dar Gantner, but there was another problem. The cops couldn't—or wouldn't—protect her from Teddy Markham. Who in their right mind would believe a presidential candidate was trying to kill her? They might even press charges against her. Could you be charged with making reckless accusations against a public figure? And, in the unlikely event they did give her any credence, they'd probably tell her to hire a bodyguard, like the Chicago police did the night Enduro Man shot at her on the Gold Coast.

She lay back, feeling helpless and weak and frustrated.

Cece's voice cut into her thoughts, " . . . Well, then . . . we don't have a choice."

"Can she travel?"

"Her injuries are mostly superficial. She should be able to." There was a pause. "You have someplace we can go?"

"Yes."

Cece drove west on I-90 under a flinty sky. Lila was propped in the back seat surrounded with pillows and blankets. A gusty wind threatened to push the black Honda across lanes, and even though traffic was light,

Cece kept both hands on the wheel. When Lila cracked the window, the air pressure inside the car changed, and her ears popped. She rolled it back up.

Dar looked back at her. "You okay?"

Lila nodded.

He nodded, too.

"Why did you do it?" she asked. "The bomb?"

He took his time answering. "Because I didn't say no."

Lila felt her expression harden.

"I know that isn't much of an answer. The others had already planned it. I probably could have dissuaded them. But I didn't try."

"Why not?"

"I didn't care by that point. Your mother and I were finished. The Indian boy we'd been taking care of was dead. Nothing mattered. I was even thinking about suicide." He hesitated. "It's a family tradition."

Lila tilted her head.

"My father—your other grandfather—hung himself."

"I'm sorry." She paused. "But this was your girlfriend's father's store. The mother of your children. How could you betray her like that?"

"I didn't see it in those terms. I thought I was striking a blow against the capitalist system. I assumed we'd be caught, but we'd go out in a blaze of glory. And usher in a tiny part of the apocalypse. In retrospect, it was incredibly reckless and selfish. And narcissistic. But when you're young, you don't think about the consequences. At least I didn't." He focused on her. "One thing, though. I never intended to kill anyone. You have to believe that. There wasn't supposed to be anyone in the store that night. And I certainly didn't know that your mother was in the alley."

Lila hugged her chest. She didn't know what to believe. "Was . . . was . . . my father involved?"

"No. Your father wasn't political to begin with, and he'd dropped all his activities by then."

"Who was?"

"It was mostly Payton. Although Teddy became more enthusiastic." A faraway look came over Dar. "It was Teddy who found the VW van we

264

ripped off. And filed off the VIN so it couldn't be traced. Except they did, anyway. He didn't realize the number was also mounted on the engine block."

"Why were you the only one charged? The only one who went to jail?"

"After the blast, I ran off to Colorado. To an abandoned town called Lanedo. Payton and Teddy were the only two people in the world who knew where I'd gone. One of them must have told the feds where I was because they found me pretty quickly. When they did, I figured they'd already picked up the other two. It was only after they arrested me and no one else surfaced that I realized what I was up against."

"Which was . . . "

"Let's just say I realized powerful interests were aligned against me. The system wasn't going to work in my favor. That's one of the reasons I pled guilty."

"What happened to Payton and Teddy?"

"Payton went underground . . . so far off the grid no one ever found him."

"For forty years?"

"About seven years ago I got a letter from Rain saying he'd resurfaced. That he'd changed his name to William Kent and was teaching school in New Mexico."

"Why didn't you tell the authorities? There's no statute of limitations on murder."

"I never got the chance."

"Why not?"

"He died in a car accident a few weeks later."

Lila was quiet. Then, "What about Teddy?"

"Teddy?" A small smile played on his lips. "Teddy went to law school. Became a DA. Got elected Senator. Decided to run for president."

"So he was the one who set you up."

"Rain always suspected Teddy was an informer. I didn't want to believe it. But yes, Teddy set me up."

"You spent forty years in jail because of him."

"No." He swallowed. "I spent forty years in jail because I detonated a bomb that killed three innocent people. Including your mother. It's just that Teddy and Payton didn't do the time with me."

She shook her head. "How can you go on knowing he got away? He . . . he robbed you of your life. Climbed on your back to get ahead. If he was capable of that forty years ago, what's he going to do if he's elected president?"

"I'm not convinced he's evil. Just weak." He draped his arm over the back of Cece's seat.

"You're being naïve," Lila said.

"Maybe." Dar absently caressed the back of Cece's neck. She stretched, giving him more of it to stroke. It was a subtle gesture, but Lila was struck by how willingly Cece yielded to his touch. Despite everything he'd done, this woman trusted Dar. Lila felt a stab of envy. She wondered if she would ever trust Dar that much. Would ever trust *anyone* that much.

Dar cracked the window. Cold air whistled in. He rolled it back up. "It's funny. For the longest time, I thought Sebastian Kerr was behind it all."

"Because he threatened my father?"

"Exactly."

"He's been dead for over ten years."

"I know." Dar twisted around. "Since Payton died seven years ago, and Rain and your father a few months ago, it couldn't have been him."

"So . . . " Lila said slowly. "The fire that killed my father and brother wasn't an accident."

Dar nodded. "Markham is taking out everyone who could connect him to the bomb. Your brother was probably collateral damage. You would have been too, if you'd been there."

Cece glanced into the rearview mirror, frowned, and switched lanes.

"I don't get it," Lila said. "I had nothing to do with any of this. I wasn't even born. Why is he still after me?"

Dar sighed. "I made a mistake. When I got out of jail, I called Teddy. I shouldn't have. I think that call triggered the new spate of killing."

"Why did you call him?"

"I wanted to give him a chance to tell me why he'd left me holding the bag. In retrospect I see how naïve that was. Even arrogant. As if I could exert any influence on him forty years later." He looked down. "His people wasted no time coming after me. Remember . . . I'm the only one left alive who knows what really happened back then. Once I realized it, I knew I had to disappear."

Lila thought about it. "So he's coming after me just to flush you out?"

"Either that or he suspects Casey or I might have told you the truth, which, of course, would be unacceptable."

"Either way, when he finds us, he'll kill us."

"Which is why we need to protect you."

Lila frowned. "Except that by running you're doing exactly what he wants."

"I don't see any other options."

Lila leaned back against the seat. Something deep within her was loosening, like a rusty lock that had been oiled. Tumblers were falling into place. "Well, maybe we should find some."

Cece glanced in the rearview mirror again. "Um, guys . . . I hate to break up your fun, but we're being followed."

FORTY-SIX

I don't see a motorcycle." Dar squinted through the back windshield. Cece shook her head. "It's a rental truck. Budget. It's been on us for the past mile or so."

"How do you know it's following us?" Lila asked.

"Because one just like it was staked outside my house a couple of weeks ago," Cece said.

Dar straightened up.

"What do you want me to do?" Cece asked.

Lila cut in. "How close is the next exit?"

"I don't know," Cece said worriedly. "And we have less than a quarter tank of gas."

Lila leaned over the armrest between the front seats. The red line on the fuel gauge hovered near the bottom. "This car gets about thirty miles to the gallon, right?"

"Sometimes more."

"And the tank holds about thirteen gallons?"

Cece nodded. "About."

"We're good for at least another hundred miles. Go for it."

"How do you know?" Cece asked.

"I know numbers," Lila said.

Cece stomped on the accelerator. The Honda hesitated, then surged ahead. Lila tightened her seatbelt and bunched the pillows on her stomach. Dar dug his fingers into his seat. Cece whipped around traffic, passing cars in both lanes. Highway markers passed in a blur. Telephone and utility poles raced by in staccato succession. Cece glanced at the rearview. "Damn. He's still there."

"Bastard," Dar said. "How far to the next exit?"

Cece pointed to the glove compartment. "There's a map in there. You tell me."

Dar tried to lean forward, but the Honda hit a bump and he was thrown against the seat. Lila checked the speedometer. They were doing over eighty. A moment later Dar fished out the map. "Anyone have an idea where we are?"

"I saw an exit for Route 25 a while back," Lila said.

"That's near Elgin," Cece said.

Dar fumbled the map open. "That's still a ways to Loves Park."

"Is that where we're going?" Lila asked.

"Not any more," Cece deadpanned.

"Route 31 should be coming up," Dar said. "Just on the other side of the Fox River."

"Good." Cece looked into the rearview. "He's closing."

Both Dar and Lila twisted around.

"Can you see who's driving?" Cece asked.

Lila craned her neck, but the reflection of the sky on the truck's windshield made it impossible to see. All she could make out was a form behind the wheel. "No."

"What about a license plate?"

Dar shook his head. "Nothing. At least in front."

"Figures." Cece's face was flushed, and her eyes were bright. She was enjoying this. "Well, I'm not going to make it easy for the asshole. Hang on, kids."

Cece started to swerve between lanes, passing one vehicle, then veering sharply back to pass another. The truck tried to follow, but the Honda's tiny size was an advantage. The truck swayed, careening off balance, while the Honda nimbly darted in and out.

"Look!" Lila pointed to a sign. The exit for Route 31 was two miles ahead.

"We're there," Cece said.

Cece floored the accelerator. The speedometer rocketed past ninety. Lila turned around. They'd pulled away from the truck.

"Exit coming up," Dar said. "One mile and closing."

Cece nosed the Honda into the left lane. A massive eighteen-wheeler was barreling down on their right. Lila's chest went tight. How in hell was Cece going to get past the truck and over to the exit ramp? She could see it about a quarter mile away. A sign and arrow pointed towards McHenry.

Dar clutched the edge of his seat.

The ramp loomed closer. Cece was still abreast of the giant semi. If she didn't move, Lila thought, they'd never make it.

Suddenly, Cece pumped the accelerator and swung the wheel. The Honda swerved into the semi's lane, barely a few feet in front of it. The driver let loose with an angry blast of his horn, but Cece kept going. The ramp was right beside them. Lila's stomach twisted. They weren't going to make it. Cece gripped the wheel. Lila squeezed her eyes shut. She heard the scream of metal scraping concrete. Felt the Honda bang and lurch. When she opened her eyes, they were speeding up the ramp. They'd made it! Lila looked back. The eighteen-wheeler was still blaring his horn, but the Budget truck had overshot the exit and was heading past them down the interstate.

"Oh my god!" Lila was breathless. "How did you do that?"

Cece slowed the car, allowing herself a small smile. "Damned if I know."

Dar ruffled her hair.

Watching their easy intimacy, Lila felt another jab of envy. They were driving down Route 31 toward McHenry. On one side of the road was a cemetery, its sign proclaiming "River Valley Memorial Gardens." In the flat gray light the gardens looked desiccated and brown with patches of dirty snow on the earth.

"It's probably not over," Lila said. "If I were Budget, I'd double back at the next exit and hunt us down. We need to disappear."

"And get the damn car fixed. The engine sounds like a sick duck."

"I can help," Dar said. "The place where we're headed . . . that's what the guy does."

"Excellent." Cece relaxed her grip. She turned left on Boncosky Road.

"No!" Lila cried out. "Not this way. He might pass us if he backtracks from the next exit. Turn around and head east. To the Fox River."

"Good point." Cece made a left into a driveway and turned around. "Aren't there new housing developments over there? Maybe we can get lost in one of them for a while."

Lila fell back against the seat and took a breath. The adrenaline that had been pumping through her subsided, leaving her exhausted, but oddly contented.

Dar smiled at her.

"What's so funny?"

"It's just . . . you look so much like your mother right now."

She looked away, annoyed. It was too much, this intimacy. Too much and too soon. This man had killed her mother. She changed the subject. "Cece, where'd you learn to drive like that?"

"My brother always wanted to drive NASCAR. I guess he taught me a thing or two."

FORTY-SEVEN

Benny Spivak's home in Loves Park was four miles from his shop. A small ranch on a street of indistinguishable houses, its best feature was a path from the back yard into the surrounding forest preserve.

Three days later, on a crisp February morning that hinted of spring, Lila, Cece, and Reba ventured down the path. For Lila it was a test: most of her wounds were scabbed over, her bruises yellowing. She pushed up the sleeves of her borrowed sweatshirt, enjoying how the air kissed her skin. She breathed in the tangy scent from the evergreens. "I'll never take my health for granted again."

Reba laughed. "Amen to that, girl. When you got here, you looked like you were in a fight with a porcupine, and the porkie won."

Lila had taken an immediate liking to Reba, a small, plain-spoken, unpretentious blonde. The woman didn't seem surprised when they'd arrived at the shop after dark, tired, anxious, and hungry. She promptly locked up, led them to the house, and hustled them inside. Then she covered the Honda with a tarp so it couldn't be seen from the street, went out, and returned with a bag of tacos.

"So what is your next move?" Reba asked now. "I mean, we love having you here, but we know it's not for long."

"I'm not sure," Cece said.

"I am," Lila said.

Reba and Cece looked at her.

"I've been thinking. We've been lucky the guy in the rental truck hasn't found us. But that doesn't mean he won't. It's not safe for us here.

Or for you." She bent down and picked up a stone. "The man on the motorcycle is still out there, too."

Reba nodded. "Your dad told us about him."

The word "dad" rolled over Reba's tongue so easily, Lila noticed.

"I reckon you should consider that a back-handed compliment."

"What?" Lila palmed the stone.

"That you're so hard to pin down they have to send two teams." The path they were on made a sharp turn left. Reba followed it, then stopped. "One thing don't make sense, though."

"What?"

"We know why they're gunning for Dar. The question is why they're trying to kill you."

"Does it really matter? The end result is still the same. We have to stay one step in front of them. Until we stop Markham."

"How?" Cece asked.

"I don't know." Lila made the turn on the path. "But I'm not going to let some politician control whether I live or die." She rolled the stone in her hand. "I do want to know why they're suddenly using a rental truck. Compared to a motorcycle, it's slow and awkward."

"I guess it depends what's inside," Reba said.

"You think they stashed something in back? Like weapons or explosives?"

"Or a motorcycle."

Lila raised her eyebrows. "A Trojan horse."

"Or someplace to squirrel you away once they get you," Reba said.

"If it's a rental," Cece asked, "couldn't we track down who signed for it?"

"Unless it's really not a rental, and they just painted it to look like one," Lila said.

"If that's the case," Reba said, "it would be a huge time suck to try."

"Plus give them more time to find Lila," Cece added.

"Markham would have the resources to pull off something like that, don't you think?" Lila pocketed the stone.

"I think." Reba stopped at a low-hanging branch. She bent back a dead branch, but it was too thick to snap off. She dug her hand into her jeans pocket, pulled out her HideAway knife, and started sawing through it instead.

When Lila saw the knife, she froze. "Where'd you get that?"

"Why?"

"Someone sent one just like that to me."

"Now, is that a fact?" Reba turned around slowly. She and Cece exchanged glances.

Lila caught it. "It was you! You sent it. How . . . "

"It was Dar." Cece corrected her.

Reba nodded. "He wanted to know all about 'em when he was here. I told him no woman should be without one."

Lila spread her hands. "I left mine at Danny's apartment. With everything else."

Reba kept hacking at the branch. Finally it snapped off. She stripped off the smaller twigs, turned it upside-down, and started using it as walking stick. "Well, then, I'd better teach you how to use mine."

After dinner that night, Benny and Reba went into the kitchen to wash up. Cece started a load of laundry, while Dar and Lila stayed in the living room, watching the local news. The search for the "missing Evanston woman" was no longer the top story, but a reporter, citing the recent deaths of Casey and Daniel Hilliard, followed so quickly by Lila's disappearance, couldn't help speculate about the "star-crossed Hilliard family."

Lila squirmed. "Maybe it's time to go to the press."

"With what?" Dar asked.

"The fact that we've been stalked. And shot at. There is the police report from the Gold Coast."

"Which they can explain away as a drive-by."

"What about the house burning down?"

"A tragic accident."

"And the grenade?"

"Dar Gantner, himself convicted forty years ago of using explosives . . . " Dar shrugged. "It's too risky. And circumstantial. We need more solid evidence."

Lila frowned.

Dar muted the TV. Commercials whizzed by in a dizzying series of cuts and colors. He was about to turn it off when Lila said, "Wait."

He looked over.

"I just remembered something. From the day of the fire, when Danny and my father . . . " She cut herself off.

"What?"

"There was a rental truck outside the house before it happened. It was on the street when I went to the store to get Christmas lights. I'm sure of it."

"I should never have called Teddy. That's what set this chain of events in motion. I was unbearably stupid." He lapsed into a stony silence.

"It wasn't a mistake," Lila said finally. Dar looked up. "Calling Teddy. He would have come after you—and my father—at some point anyway. He can't risk having anyone alive who knows what he did."

"You don't have to bail me out."

"I didn't say it to bail you out. I said it because if we're going to stop him, we have to know how he thinks."

"Stop him?"

"Three people were killed in the original bombing. And over the years, he's killed at least two others—Casey and Danny."

"Don't forget Rain and Payton," Dar said.

"You see?" Lila tightened her lips. "Four people have been killed— and that's only the ones we know about—in order to cover up the past of a man who might be the next president of the United States."

"You don't know the forces arrayed against us. Hell. We used to talk about Hoover having tentacles that stretched everywhere. Compared to Markham's organization, Hoover ran a nursery school."

"So you'd rather let them win?"

He started ticking off one finger at a time. "Like I said, we can't go to the press without solid proof of a conspiracy. Which we don't have. And never will. Any reports or documents—anything that mentions Teddy and the time he spent in Chicago—are probably locked up and will never be declassified. Or were destroyed years ago."

"So we find something else."

"Proof of a crime committed forty years ago?" Dar made snorting sound. "Sure. There's a bunch of DNA waiting to be found. Just like on TV." He ticked off a second finger. "Second, we can't leak anything without revealing who and where we are, which, of course, would draw their fire. And third, who's going to believe the word of an ex-con? We have no leads. No angles. Nothing."

"Ah, but you're wrong." Lila smiled. "We do have a lead."

"What?"

"Me."

Dar looked startled.

"I'm Sebastian Kerr's granddaughter. I can use that to open doors and dig around. Say I'm looking into the troubled times around when I was born and the bomb exploded. People do that all the time. Search for their roots. Maybe I can even talk to some of the officials involved in the investigation."

"What about the fact that no one knows that you exist?"

"They will. I'll get a copy of the birth certificate from Dad's website." She went on, "I'll tell the truth . . . that I just found out who I am and that I want to know my family history."

"Lila, you can't march into the FBI or the Chicago police and demand to look at an investigation they did forty years ago."

"You don't know that."

Dar crossed his arms. "You'd be painting a giant bulls-eye on your back. What makes you think you'll find anything after all this time? And how long do you think it'll be before Markham finds out you're poking around?"

She stared at him. "Two months ago I would never have imagined doing anything like that. But two months ago I wasn't being stalked. Or shot at. Or attacked with a grenade. Sure, I want my nice, boring life back. But to get it back, I have to fight."

Dar shook his head. "Too dangerous."

"First off," she said, mimicking him, "you can't stop me. And second, it might not be that dangerous . . . if I go in the back door."

"Now what are you talking about?"

She explained what she had in mind. Dar listened, then said, "What if the person guarding the front door finds out you're coming in the back?"

"Is it any more dangerous than doing nothing?"

Dar stared. She'd never reminded him more of Alix.

"We have to try," she went on. "Not just because it's the right thing to do." Her voice caught, but so quietly it was easy to miss. "We have to do this . . . for everyone in the family."

Dar's throat thickened. The family. She'd said "the family."

FORTY-EIGHT

Mavis Dietrich had no illusions about the nursing home. Her kids considered her a problem, and a nursing home was the easiest way to solve it. As far as they were concerned, she was a doddering half-wit put out to pasture. She sniffed. Her children always thought they knew best. Part of the baby boomer generation. No respect for their elders. Or anyone who disagreed with them.

She stared at the TV. Damn thing was always on, even when no one was watching. Just noise and light, like ugly wallpaper you tried to ignore. She'd worked full-time after Samuel had the accident, and in those thirty-five years, she'd never whined like they did on TV: "It's because I was poor that I slept around" . . . "cheated on my husband" . . . "murdered my sister-in-law." Just fill in the blank.

She picked up her knitting. She was making mufflers for her grandchildren. It was comforting, doing something with her hands. Although the arthritis was slowing her down. She wondered how long it would be until she had to give it up, like Marion, who, bless her soul, left this world two months ago. During the entire year before she passed, she just sat. Couldn't knit, crochet, or draw. Near the end, she couldn't even talk. Mavis hoped like hell that didn't happen to her. Better to end it somehow, before it got that bad.

The clack of footsteps made her look up. One of the aides was coming down the hall with a young woman. She had long dark hair, dark eyes, and except for too much make-up, she was attractive. Mavis wasn't sure but she thought the make-up might be covering up bruises. Was she one of those abused women she'd seen on TV? At least she was dressed properly. Navy pants, jacket, low-heeled shoes. Mavis approved.

"Mrs. Dietrich, you have a visitor," the aide said with a cheery smile.

Lila stepped into a large square room with linoleum floors and cheap paneled walls. It smelled of urine and lemon-scented air freshener. A sign announced that Bingo would be moved from Friday to Sunday because the caller had suffered a heart attack. The TV was on, but the sound was low. Otherwise it was quiet, many of the residents in chairs staring into space.

Now that she was here, she felt nervous. What if she couldn't pull it off? They'd talked it over, decided how to approach things. She'd driven Cece's car, although they were reluctant to let her, in case Markham's goons were on her tail. But she insisted—it would only be for a few hours. She'd be back that evening.

She wanted to go back to Danny's to retrieve some of her clothes, her cell, and the HideAway knife, but Dar and Benny refused. The police were still looking for her. If she unexpectedly showed up, alive and healthy, they'd bring her in for questioning. Hell, they might decide she had something to do with the blast, even her own disappearance.

So she went to Target and bought an outfit, then stopped by a phone store and bought a disposable cell. One of Benny's friends made her a fake driver's license, and they all chipped in some cash. Reba loaned her the HideAway.

Now she walked toward the old woman on the sofa. The woman had to be almost ninety. Her hair was snow white, her skin crepy. Her fingers were gnarled, and her back stooped, but her eyes were intelligent, and they were studying Lila with suspicion. Lila had picked up a small bouquet of flowers: daisies, baby's breath, and a lily or two.

"Hello, Mrs. Dietrich. These are for you."

The woman grabbed them so tightly Lila thought they might wilt before they hit water. "Have we met?"

"No, but I know you used to work at Kerr's department store. You were the Chicago manager's secretary."

"How do you know that? Who are you?"

"I called the store. My name is Lila Hilliard."

Mavis's lips pursed into a petulant frown. "They're not supposed to give out that information."

"I got lucky." Lila smiled. It was the truth. When she'd called the store's Human Resources Department the day before, the phone was answered by a young girl who apparently had just started at the store. When Lila asked her to look up the records of clerical staff in 1970, the girl promptly tapped a few keys and came up with three people. Two of them were now dead, but after hours of phone calls and Internet searches, Lila located Mavis Dietrich.

"You're probably one of the few people still alive who worked at Kerr's when the bomb exploded," Lila said.

Mavis nodded. "Estelle passed about ten years ago, and then Helene . . . about three or four now, I think." A distant look came over her. Then she roused herself and focused on Lila. Frown lines creased her forehead. "Who are you again? Why are you here?"

"My name is Lila Hilliard, and I was hoping you could give me some information."

Mavis sniffed the flowers. "Are you a reporter? Because if you are, I have nothing to say."

"No, I'm not a reporter." She forced herself to smile. People tended to let their guard down when you did. But Mavis's expression didn't change.

"What do you want?"

Lila sat down. "I'm Sebastian Kerr's granddaughter."

She and Dar had debated about whether Lila should reveal herself. It was a calculated risk, but she decided to go ahead, reasoning that most people wouldn't talk to her otherwise. Of all the potential dangers Lila would be facing, identifying herself to a woman in a nursing home seemed to be on the low end.

Still, Mavis's eyebrows rose. "Mr. Kerr had grandchildren?"

"Two. My brother and me. Unfortunately, my brother died two months ago."

"Really? I thought Philip didn't have any children."

"Philip?"

"Mr. Kerr's son."

"Of course." Lila hastily tried to cover her mistake. "I just found out myself. I . . . I was adopted." She braced for Mavis's reaction. She'd blown it. Big.

But to Lila's surprise, Mavis nodded and a knowing expression came across her face. "My aunt Isabel had an illegitimate child when she was sixteen. Had to put her up for adoption. Wouldn't you know . . . the girl showed up at Christmas eighteen years later. Nearly gave my aunt a heart attack."

Lila gave her a sad smile. "You are very compassionate."

Mavis straightened. "Well now, of course, it's none of my business . . . " She threw her a glance, clearly hoping Lila would decide it was.

Lila went back to the script. "You worked at the store when they were investigating—after the bomb."

"Oh, yes. There were interviews and meetings, then more interviews and meetings. We were all devastated. Especially Mr. Kerr. Such a waste."

"Mrs. Dietrich, I'm looking for the names of any police officers or FBI officials who were part of the investigation. Would you happen to remember any?"

"Why?"

"Maybe for the same reason your aunt's illegitimate daughter showed up at her house. It was a volatile time for my family. I want to understand it. Make peace with the past."

"Why don't you call the police? They must have records."

"I . . . I'd rather not."

Mavis threw her a cagey look. "Why?"

"Because . . . well . . . " Lila leaned forward. "They're only going to tell me what they want me to know. Not what really happened. And . . . " She lowered her voice to a conspiratorial whisper. "They said at the office you knew everything about everyone."

Mavis looked away, as if she was thinking about it.

Lila held her breath.

Then, "As it happens, part of my job was to manage the conference rooms—make sure they were available. And that there was fresh coffee. I kept track of all the meetings in a Day-Timer. You know, one of those little black spiral-bound books. Had one every year I was there. Almost thirty of them, all told, by the end."

"Would you have jotted down any names in those books?"

"Maybe." A gleam came into her eyes. "But no more cock and bull stories about your past. You didn't go to all the trouble of tracking me down after forty years—and bringing me flowers—because of family history. Who are you, and what do you really want?"

Mavis Dietrich was no pushover. Lila chose her words carefully, "I'm trying to right a wrong that was committed."

"What kind of wrong?"

"The man who was charged with the crime, Dar Gantner, may not have acted alone. I have reason to believe others were involved and equally culpable."

"Why is that important after all this time?"

Lila folded her hands. This she couldn't—wouldn't—reveal. "From everything I know about my grandfather, he wouldn't have approved of a rush to justice. I want to make sure that didn't happen, or, if it did, to undo the damage. I don't believe his daughter would have approved either, if she'd lived."

Mavis sat back and crossed her arms. She was quiet for a moment. "I always respected your grandfather, but he wasn't an easy man to work for." She paused.

Lila met Mavis Dietrich's gaze.

Finally, the older woman said, "I might . . . I say might . . . help you. On one condition."

"What's that?"

Mavis took her time standing up. "Most of my things are in storage. Over on Elston Avenue. But you have to take me with you. I need to get out of this place."

To Lila's surprise, she enjoyed Mavis Dietrich's company. First they drove to the storage locker where Mavis easily found the 1970 Day-Timer in a cardboard box labeled "Kerr's." "I think you'll find what you're looking for in here," she said.

Lila wanted to pore through it right away, but Mavis slipped it into a large purse she'd brought with her. "First things first." She directed Lila to a tavern a few blocks away. Inside, Mavis tossed down a shot of Johnnie Walker Black. Neat. Lila ordered a glass of wine.

An hour later, Lila knew all about Mavis's marriage to Samuel and the automobile accident that paralyzed him. Mavis had gone to work full time, raised two kids, and taken care of Samuel. "I got no truck with women on the TV who complain about doing it all," she sniffed. "Or look for excuses why they did something wrong. They don't have a clue."

Lila sipped her wine.

"Now you . . . ," Mavis squinted, " . . . I got a feeling you're different. Am I right?"

"I won't be going on Jerry Springer, if that's what you mean."

Mavis laughed, as if Lila had just cracked the funniest joke in the world. A few minutes later, she pulled out the Day-Timer and handed it to Lila. "I hope this helps. Whatever you want it for." She wiggled her shoulders cheerfully. "This has been a good day."

After Lila dropped off Mavis, she automatically checked her rearview mirror. She couldn't spot a tail, but she made a wide loop around the block anyway, then headed north on Pulaski. Satisfied that no one was following her, she headed to a Walgreen's on Foster and turned into the parking lot.

The Day-Timer, about five-by-eight inches, was on the front seat. She opened it. The spiral binding and black leather-like cover were intact, and the paper, while musty and fragile, wasn't as yellow as she'd expected.

She carefully turned the pages. Most of the notations were in black or blue ink. Fountain pen, not ball point. The penmanship was a careful, delicate cursive rarely seen anymore. Lila remembered laboring for hours in school over swirls of O's and A's and capital G's. Mavis Dietrich had it down.

She skimmed the pages up to June 3rd, the morning the bomb went off. There was no reference to the explosion, but where there'd been, perhaps, one or two meetings a day in the conference room before the 3rd, afterwards there were four or five. She pored over the rest of the week. Emergency staff meeting. Emergency board meeting. Then something indecipherable, in a different penmanship. Someone besides Mavis must have entered a meeting. The careful penmanship returned the next day: At 10:00 A.M., Special Agent Dalton, FBI. At 2:00, Detective Liotta, CPD Bomb and Arson.

Lila closed the book and slipped it into the bag she'd bought at Target. Were either of those men still alive? Maybe she should try to find them. She pulled out her cell. She was about to call Benny's to check in, when it occurred to her she hadn't checked her own messages in weeks. New York seemed like another universe now. She probably wouldn't go back to Peabody Stern. Still, Manhattan had been her world for ten years.

She started to tap in her phone number, then remembered Benny's warning to use the cell only in an emergency. She pressed "end" and slipped the cell back into her bag. A pay phone stood at the edge of the parking lot. She climbed out of the Honda and went to it. She didn't have any change and had to reverse charges, which took some persuasion, but at last, she heard her voice, clipped. Brisk. All business. "It's Lila. Let me hear from you."

She punched in her code. The machine beeped twice, then started to play back her messages. Two hang-ups, a call from the cleaners reminding her two suits hadn't been picked up since December. Then a message. From two weeks ago.

"Lila Hilliard, my name is Joanna Kerr. I used to be married to Philip Kerr, whom you may have heard of. I'd appreciate a call back at your earliest convenience." A number with a 619 area code followed. Lila memorized the number. Philip Kerr was her uncle. Alix's older brother. What did his ex-wife want with her? How had she found her? She disconnected and dug around in her pockets. No change. But Kerr had called Lila—she'd call the woman back collect.

It took time—and several mysterious clicks—to get past whoever was screening Kerr's calls. Eventually, though, a female voice came on the line, "This is Joanna Kerr. I'll accept the charges."

More clicks, then Lila said, "Hello, Ms. Kerr. Sorry to call collect, but I'm at a pay phone in . . . well, at a pay phone."

"That's all right. I was starting to believe you might be in some trouble. I called over two weeks ago."

"I'm . . . I'm fine." Where was she going? "Sorry about the delay. I've been . . . traveling." Lying was definitely becoming easier.

"Well . . . I know you must be surprised. I assume you know who I am?"

"Actually, this is very curious. I just found out that Alix Kerr was my birth mother."

"That's correct," Mrs. Kerr said, as if she'd been testing Lila and she'd passed. "By the way, I realize how unusual this situation is . . . Lila. I may call you Lila, I hope?"

"What is it that you want, Mrs. Kerr?"

"Of course. You have no idea why I'm calling."

"Go on."

The woman sighed. "Your grandfather died of pancreatic cancer years ago. Maybe seven now." She cleared her throat. "I was still married to Philip, Alix's brother, at the time."

"Yes . . ."

"Before he died, he made . . . well . . . I suppose you'd call it a death-bed decision."

"What?"

"He always regretted not acknowledging you as his heirs. Especially as he aged."

Lila's heart pinged.

"He often talked about you both toward the end. Philip and I never had any children, you know. I guess you and your brother became his legacy. The only blood kin, aside from Philip, that he would leave behind."

If he hadn't died, maybe they would have met, Lila thought. Maybe she would have had a second grandparent. A wave of sadness washed over her.

"So he changed his will."

Lila gasped.

"There wasn't a lot of time. He was very sick." Kerr's tone softened. "He instructed his lawyer to make sure you and your brother inherited half of his assets."

"Are you serious?"

"Completely. But . . . you see . . . my ex-husband wasn't happy about it. He stood to lose fifty percent of what he thought was . . . well . . . it was a considerable fortune. He's a greedy son of a bitch. I had to drag him into court just to get a modest settlement." She cleared her throat. "But that's another story. Now listen carefully. I don't know what happened or how he did it, but I do know that the will your grandfather revised was not the will that was presented after he died."

"What are you trying to say, Mrs. Kerr?"

"Your grandfather had me witness the revised will. And he made me put a copy of it in a safe place."

"Is it still there?"

"Of course it is. I reread it just the other day. Lila . . . your grandfather's will was very specific. Half of what he had was supposed to go to you and your brother. Of course, I don't know what might happen now. I just know that, if it hadn't been tampered with, you'd be a very wealthy woman."

Lila didn't know what to say.

Joanna Kerr kept going, "I wrote your birth father in prison to tell him about it. But I never got a reply. I don't know whether he even got the letter."

Lila's head was spinning. "Why are you telling me this now, Mrs. Kerr? Isn't it too late? Why didn't you get in touch when my grandfather died?"

"Two reasons. For one thing, it took a while to track you down. Your grandfather couldn't remember your father . . . I mean . . . Casey Hilliard's name. I promised I would try."

"How?"

She laughed. "That's what private detectives are for."

"And the other reason?"

"The brakes went out on my car a week or so ago. No one was hurt, thank God. But it scared me. Then I heard about the fire and how you lost your family." She paused. "Let's just say I decided to fly under the radar for a while." She paused. "And knowing my ex-husband, I strongly suggest you do the same."

FORTY-NINE

om Reimer heard the car before he saw it. At seventy-three his eyesight was horrible, he had sciatica, and he had to pee all the time. For some reason, though, his hearing was still sharp. It wasn't just the high or low tones, which eluded Jeanie, his wife. Tom heard everything. Maybe the good Lord had dulled his other senses to improve his hearing. Whatever the cause, he heard the idle of the engine as soon as it pulled up. A little ragged and tinny, like it needed a tune-up.

He raised the shade in the front room. He didn't recognize the small black car, and at this distance he couldn't make out who was behind the wheel. He thought it might be a woman.

There wasn't much happening today. He'd be in court tomorrow, up in Skokie, handling a speeding ticket for his nephew. He was winding down a modest career as an attorney. No big bucks for him: his biggest matter was a wrongful death suit, which the insurance company ultimately settled. Still, he'd managed to eke out a living. At least Jeanie knew he'd be coming home at the end of the day.

The leather in his chair crackled as he stood up. If the driver of the black Honda was a new case, he'd probably take it. It was nice not to have to work twelve hours a day, but extra money was nice, too. Especially since Jeanie had recently retired. He was just straightening up when the doorbell rang.

Lila's finger had hesitated before she pushed Tom Reimer's doorbell. After her conversation with Joanna Kerr, she'd called Dar. Kerr had sounded grim. And scared. She ought to find out if there was any truth to her story. But no one answered at Benny's, so she stopped by a library where she Googled FBI Agent Dalton and Detective Liotta, the names she'd found in Mavis Dietrich's Day-Timer. She found Dalton's obituary in the *Tribune*—he'd died of cancer twelve years ago. But Tony Liotta seemed to be alive, and she found an address for him in Sauganash, one of the more upscale residential neighborhoods on the far north side. When she rang the bell, though, no one answered. She tried several times, then went to a neighbor's. An elderly woman told her the Liottas were snowbirds spending the winter in Florida. They wouldn't be back until the end of March.

Dejected, Lila trudged back to the car to take another look through the Day-Timer. The first round of meetings after the explosion was followed by more two days later. But the names of the attendees were penned in an illegible scrawl that clearly wasn't Mavis Dietrich's. Lila thumbed through more pages. Finally, about a week after the explosion, she found another notation: 3:00 P.M.: Det. Tony Liotta and Officer Tom Reimer, Bomb and Arson.

During a second trip to the library she discovered an attorney named Tom Reimer in Park Ridge. A search revealed he'd once been a Chicago police officer. She checked the time: after three o'clock. She'd promised to be back in Loves Park by nightfall. Instead, she printed out directions and drove west on Touhy. A few more turns and she was in front of Tom Reimer's house.

When she finally did ring the bell, he answered right away, almost as though he was expecting her.

He seemed cheerful enough, but his eyes were the saddest blue she'd ever seen. His hair was mostly gone, except for little white tufts ringing a shiny crown. Still, after the suspicious Mavis Dietrich, Reimer was a relief. Maybe too much of one. He invited her in for coffee and told her how he'd grown up on the west side in a lace-curtain Irish neighborhood. He'd transferred the décor to Park Ridge: doilies covered the arms of the furniture, which was all dark and heavy. Lila tried to steer the conversation her way, but Reimer nattered on about his grandsons in high school and a granddaughter who worked for City Hall.

After the second cup of coffee, she finally blurted it out. "Mr. Reimer, I'm here because I have some questions you might be able to answer."

"Of course. At least I'll try." He shifted, all business now.

"Were you once a Chicago police officer?"

He leaned back, raised his eyebrows. "How'd you know that?"

She replied cautiously, "One of the secretaries who worked at Kerr's department store when the bomb exploded forty years ago kept records of people involved in the investigation. Your name was on one of the lists."

He put on an unreadable expression. His police officer face.

"You worked the case—at least for part of the time—didn't you?"

Reimer's good humor disappeared. "I was deployed temporarily to Bomb and Arson during the investigation. But what does that have to do with your legal problem?"

"I don't have a legal problem, and I'm not looking for a lawyer, Mr. Reimer. I'm doing some . . . research into the past."

"Research?" His eyes narrowed. "I'm afraid I can't help you, miss." His chair scraped against the floor.

Lila raised her palm. "Please. Don't kick me out. Someone I'm close to was involved in the case. We're trying to resolve some 'loose ends.'"

A knowing look came over him.

He knew something. She was sure of it. She sat straighter. "Dar Gantner was the only person prosecuted. But it was a massive explosion. It required careful planning, advance work. It's only reasonable to assume he had help."

Reimer kept his mouth shut.

"I know that two other individuals were involved." She went on, "One of them is dead. But the other isn't."

Reimer went stiff. Then he did stand up. "Miss, you need to leave."

Lila stayed where she was.

"Miss Hilliard, I was expecting a client with a property dispute, a divorce, something like that. This . . . well . . . I can't help you."

Lila dug into her bag and fished out a folded piece of paper. "Mr. Reimer, I'm Sebastian Kerr's granddaughter. This is a copy of my birth certificate. Look who my mother is."

She passed it to him. Reimer scanned the paper, then put it down.

"But the certificate is wrong. My father isn't Casey Hilliard. It's Dar Gantner."

He pressed his lips together as if to whistle, but no sound came out. Then he started to pace the kitchen. When he came back to the table, he looked down at her. "Miss Hilliard, I believe you. And I believe you want answers. For all the right reasons. But some things are better left alone. This is one of them."

"It's too late. You must have seen the news. They set fire to my house and killed my family. Shot at me and launched a grenade into my apartment. That's why I'm here. I need something that will stop them. Evidence to support . . . ," she paused, " . . . what I think you already know."

"And what is that?" His expression turned calculating.

"That Teddy Markham was one of the three who detonated the bomb."

Reimer tried to cover it, but she saw him wince.

"You know something, Mr. Reimer, don't you?"

Reimer eyed her again, as if making a decision. He sat down and ran a hand over his head. "I never thought I'd have to deal with this." He let out a heavy sigh. "Things happen, I told myself. It's the way things work. I couldn't do anything to stop it, anyway. I was a rookie. Practically a gofer. Understand? I took orders."

Lila nodded, not saying anything for fear she'd spook him.

"Tony Liotta took the lead. Made all the decisions."

"What decisions?"

He looked up. "All you need to know is that there is no proof. You won't find anything. Ever."

She clasped her fingers together so tightly her knuckles went white.

"Whatever was there was destroyed a long time ago."

"But there was something?"

"I didn't say that."

"I don't get it. If everything's gone, why do you sound so . . . so . . . worried?"

He let out another breath.

She pressed, "Look, Mr. Reimer, you're telling me to drop it, and I respect your opinion. But someone's trying to kill me. I need help, and I think you can give me that help. I'm appealing to your sense of justice."

He covered his eyes with his hand.

"There was something, wasn't there?"

He dropped his hand and looked up at her. "You never heard this from me."

She nodded. Her heart was pounding.

"A bracelet was found in the rubble."

"A bracelet?"

"One of those ID bracelets with thick metal links. The kind teenagers wore a long time ago. Guys gave them to their girlfriends . . . you know . . . to go steady." He paused. "It was broken apart, and part of it had melted, but you could still read the initials. TAM."

"Theodore Addison Markham," Lila breathed.

"It's not definitive proof, understand. It just proves he was at the store at some point. Could have been weeks before. He might have been shopping."

"But it puts him at the scene."

"It does. But no court in this country would ever find him guilty because of it."

"What happened to the bracelet?"

He snorted in contempt. "What do you think? The cop who found it entered it into evidence. A week later it was gone. Disappeared from the evidence locker. Along with any record of it."

She was afraid to breathe.

He shrugged. "It happens, Miss Hilliard. More often than you'd think. Someone knows someone. Applies pressure. Greases a palm. Presto. Magic. All gone."

"Who applied the pressure?"

"I have no idea, and if you know what's good for you, you won't try to find out." He shook his head. "All I know is that neither you nor anyone else will ever find that bracelet. Or any record of it. I'm sorry."

FIFTY

D usk cloaked everything with a mantle of silence as Lila climbed back into the Honda. Even the hum of traffic seemed hushed. The gloom matched her mood. All the energy she'd invested had come to nothing. Or, more accurately, to someone powerful using their clout. Making evidence disappear. She keyed the engine. What had she expected? That a piece of shiny, unspoiled evidence would be waiting for her just because she, Lila Hilliard, willed it?

She turned west on Touhy toward I-294. She wasn't going to make it back to Loves Park by dark. She'd better call again. Tell them what she'd learned. About Joanna Kerr, too. She spotted a pay phone at the side of a convenience store and pulled into the lot. The phone stood at the edge of a dimly lit alley. She got out and called Benny's. Still no answer. She decided not to be concerned. They were probably out getting dinner.

She hung up, so engrossed in her thoughts she barely heard the motorcycle engine that sputtered and then went quiet. She was starting back to the car, treading carefully around patches of ice, when someone charged her from behind.

Too late she realized she'd forgotten to check for a tail when she left Park Ridge. Before she could scream or even think of escape, her attacker slammed into her, knocking her off her feet. Then he grabbed her, pinning her arms, and jerked her upright. He crushed her so tightly around the middle that she gasped for breath. Instinct made her struggle. She tried pushing against him to pry herself loose, but she couldn't muster enough strength. The pressure around her middle tightened. It was all she could do to draw a breath.

As he dragged her toward the alley, she knew without looking that it was the man on the motorcycle. He was going to kidnap her and throw her into the rental truck . . . or kill her. She tried to dig in her heels. It did no good. She tried to kick out, but his grip was as powerful as a metal clamp.

It was dark, but stores were still open, their neon signs bright beacons in the winter dark. Rush hour traffic sped by. Passing motorists couldn't see her, or if they did, they'd be well past the store when they registered what they had seen. Enduro Man knew that. No one would be coming to her rescue.

Where did he pick her up? At Reimer's? Or had he been stalking her all day, just waiting to strike? Why hadn't she seen him? Suddenly the frustrations of the day seemed insignificant. She was just little Lila Hilliard after all. Unable to save anyone, including herself.

As he dragged her deeper into the alley, part of her wanted to surrender. Just get it over with. With luck the end would be quick. Then she snapped. What was she thinking? This man shot at her! Destroyed Danny's apartment! How dare he? Anger gripped her, and she remembered the HideAway knife. She'd attached it to her key ring that morning. But the keys were her bag. In the car. No . . . wait! She'd slipped her keys into her pocket when she got out to make the call. They were in her right pocket. If she could just wriggle her fingers into that pocket.

Although he was moving her down the alley, it required enormous strength to drag her and keep her body immobile at the same time. She needed an opening. A slight loosening of his grip. That's all it would take. She could work with that.

A second passed. Then another. The man's hold was an iron band. She was beginning to despair, then something shifted. It was subtle, but suddenly he didn't seem quite as sure-footed. Did he slip on a patch of ice? Didn't matter. His left arm loosened just a bit. It was enough. Lila wrestled her arm free and dug into her pocket. She grabbed the HideAway. His grasp tightened again, trapping her hand in her pocket. But she held on to the knife.

Now all she had to do was wait for his hold to loosen again. She'd only have one chance. She couldn't screw up. She tried to make her body go rigid so it would be harder for him to drag her. He grunted but kept going. They had almost reached the back of the alley. Despair mounted. It wasn't going to happen.

But then it did.

He stopped, and one hand dropped from her waist. He was going for his gun. She heaved and bucked and pulled the HideAway out of her pocket. Then she slashed at the arm that was still clutching her. The knife sliced through his jacket.

He let out a howl and dropped his arm. Lila wrenched away and spun around. He wore a ski mask. His eyes were the only features exposed, and they were staring at her in shock. His free hand cradled the arm she'd just stabbed. She lunged at him and slashed again, this time through his mask. Blood spurted through the wool. He screamed in pain. His free hand flew to his face.

Lila was free. She turned and raced back to the Honda. And wondered what she had become.

"Here it is," Benny said, in a muffled but triumphant voice. They were in the garage, the door firmly closed. Lila heard metal scraping, then a quiet plop. Benny slid out from under the Honda. He was holding a black rectangular object, slightly larger than a deck of cards.

"What is it?" Dar asked.

"A GPS tracking device," Benny replied. "Lets you follow a car from your computer. They're magnetic—I have a couple in the shop. Someone slipped it on the undercarriage . . . who knows when." He grimaced. "My fucking fault. I shudda checked."

Lila tried to reassure him. "You didn't know it was there."

"I shudda." He rubbed his knuckle below his nose.

"So they've known where we've been all this time?" Reba asked.

"Looks that way," Benny said. He turned to Cece. "You have any idea when or where they planted it?"

"It had to be when they were staking out the house," she answered. "A week or so ago."

Dar nodded.

"So now what?" Lila asked.

Benny's nostrils flared. "Well, first, I take out the batteries . . . " He turned over the tracker and started to open the back. "No." He went to a shelf in the garage, took out a hammer and pounded the tracker. Seconds later, it was in pieces. "That's better."

They watched Benny drop the shattered pieces in the garbage.

"Obviously, we have to leave," Dar said. "They're probably on their way. You need to protect yourselves."

"Don't worry about us," Reba turned to Lila. "But a HideAway knife ain't gonna be much help to you going forward. They'll be expecting it. You're gonna need something more . . . powerful."

"If you're talking about a gun," Dar cut in, "forget it."

Reba and Lila exchanged glances.

"Maybe you oughta go inside," Reba said to Dar and Cece. "Lila, you come with me."

"Too bad about that ID bracelet," Cece said when they were settled in the living room later. "Do you have anything else? Anything that proves Teddy Markham was involved?"

"What about that photo of the six of you in the park?" Lila asked. "The one I found on my father's computer."

"I thought it was destroyed in the fire," Cece said.

"Rain made prints," Dar said. "There could be a copy floating around someplace."

"A picture's not proof of anything," Reba frowned. "Just that you were all together when it was taken. What about the apartment in Old Town? Was

Teddy's name on the lease? Not that it proves much either, but it's something."

"Alix was the only one on the lease. And after we left, we moved around."

"Did Teddy have a job? Is there a record of him working anywhere?"

Dar shook his head. "He and Payton didn't work. Except for the Movement."

"What about when you assembled the bomb? Any chance he would have signed for anything—credit card receipts, for instance?"

"We didn't have credit cards. And even if we did, we weren't that stupid."

"It's no crime to buy fuel oil anyway," Benny said.

Lila stood up and started to pace. "We need something, damn it. We're running out of time."

"When did you first suspect that Teddy . . . wasn't who he said he was?" Reba asked.

"To be honest, I never did," Dar said, watching Lila. "But Rain never trusted him. She confronted me about him one night." He ran a hand across his forehead. "I thought she was being unfair."

"Maybe you oughta go see this Rain," Reba said. "Sounds like she might know something you don't."

"We can't," Dar said after a pause. "She's dead. Her car exploded on the highway a few weeks after she came to see me."

Everyone was quiet.

Dar stared at the floor. Then he straightened. "Hold on. Wait a minute!"

Lila looked over.

"I just remembered something!"

"What?"

"When I saw Rain the last time, she told me Payton had sent her something. Something to do with Teddy. She said I should know it was there if I needed it."

Lila's heart banged in her chest. "What was it?"

"I don't know."

No one spoke for a minute.

"Well, I reckon you need to find out," Reba said.

FIFTY-ONE

A few hours before dawn, Dar, Lila, and Cece started out for Brookfield, Wisconsin, a suburb of Milwaukee. Cece was driving one of Benny's beaters, an ancient Ford Econoline van that vibrated when they pushed it over sixty. Benny checked it for tracking devices; it was clean. Still, it was safer to drive in the dark, and they took back roads.

They found Rain's address on the Internet. She'd reclaimed her given name—Julie Bergman—and had operated a flourishing photography business. According to her website, she'd shot portraits, weddings, corporate galas, and bar mitzvahs. Seminal events.

"That was Rain," Dar said. "Always in the middle of things. Directing. Pushing."

From the shots on her website, she'd become good at it, Lila thought.

"She pushed your mother into making jewelry, you know. Alix turned out to have a flair for it. She made good money. Her own, not her family's." He yawned.

It occurred to Lila that if her mother had lived, maybe she would have become so successful she would have rejected her family's money. Which would mean that Lila's conversation with Joanna Kerr about her grandfather's will would have been moot. She realized she still hadn't told Dar and Cece about her conversation with Joanna Kerr; things had happened too quickly. But she could tell them now. She peered over the front seat. Dar was asleep.

When Rain's husband answered the door the next morning, he wasn't what Lila expected. Peter Hesky—Rain used her maiden name professionally—looked at least twenty years older than Rain. He was small-boned and stooped, with white hair and thick white eyebrows. His eyes, a watery blue, were rimmed in red, and the craggy lines on his face suggested his grief at losing Rain was still raw.

Surprise flooded his face when he saw the three of them parked on his doorstep. "May I help you?"

Dar explained who he was, and introduced Lila and Cece.

"So you're Dar." Hesky appraised him.

"She spoke about me?"

"Many times." A small smile curled his lips, a smile that said he might have heard more than he wanted. "She said you might show up here one day. And that if she wasn't here . . . ," he swallowed, " . . . I should help you. So . . . ," he beckoned, "come in."

"Thank you." Dar and Cece went inside, but Lila hung back.

"You're Alix's daughter. One of the twins."

Lila nodded.

"Rain mentioned you, too." He shooed her in. "It's all right. You're safe here."

What made him say that? Lila wondered. Did he know they were in trouble? Her senses went on alert. He closed the door and checked his watch. "Kind of early in the day for a visit."

Dar nodded. "We don't have much . . . "

"We're on a deadline," Lila said.

Hesky reacted with amusement. "Must be tight. You look like you haven't slept all night."

Dar picked up on it. "Do you know why we're here?"

"Before we get into that," Hesky replied, "I want to show you something. Upstairs." His tone grew soft. "Julie would have wanted this." He motioned for them to follow him and slowly mounted the steps.

They climbed up to a large room. Rain's studio. Three walls, painted a warm gray, were lined with large portraits. Couples wreathed in smiles, prim corporate executives, children looking by turns angelic and feisty, teenagers with self-absorbed expressions. One boy, wearing a tallis and kipah, was hunched over a lectern, brandishing a silver pointer over a Torah scroll.

The fourth wall was different. Painted white, it held a collection of black-and-white photos. Faces of weather-beaten farmers, migrant workers, black children from the inner city. Some looked to be in despair, others were hopeful. The effect was dramatic and stark. Very Dorothea Lange.

"This was her real work," Hesky said. "The pictures she loved to shoot."

Dar walked slowly past the wall, studying the photographs. When he reached the last photo on that wall, his breath caught. It was the picture of the six of them in the park forty years ago. It was larger and sharper than Dar remembered—Rain must have worked some technical wizardry on it.

There was Alix, long blond hair framing her face. Rain with her glasses and ashy-blond hair. Casey behind. Payton, looking intense and passionate. Then Dar, and next to Dar, Teddy, with a lazy smile as if he was in the middle of telling a joke.

Lila and Cece joined Dar in front of the photo.

"It's like stepping back in time," Dar said softly.

"She was beautiful," Cece said.

Dar smiled and slid an arm around her. Then he turned to Lila and cupped her cheeks in his hands. "You are so like your mother sometimes, it's . . . it's . . ."

"Painful?" Cece finished.

"No." Dar smiled, dropping his hands. "Wonderful. I am blessed to have you in my life."

Lila turned away, but he saw the makings of a smile.

Hesky cleared his throat.

Dar turned toward him. "Sorry . . . ," he hesitated, "I don't know if you knew, but Rain . . . Julie came to see me a few weeks before she died."

"I knew."

He pointed to Payton in the photo. "She told me this man had sent her something important. She said I should know that, in case I needed it."

Hesky didn't look surprised.

Dar's pulse sped up. "Did she tell you what it was?"

"No. But I know where it is." Hesky studied them. "In our safe-deposit box. But the bank doesn't open for another half hour. Let me fix you some breakfast."

Ten minutes later, the tantalizing scent of bacon filled the air. Lila couldn't remember the last time someone had cooked it for her. Gramum? Or Sadie? Hesky scrambled eggs and toasted bread as well. The smells blended together in a rich, hungry aroma.

"Who do I have to cook for anymore?" he asked, when they protested he was doing too much.

Dar and Cece wolfed down their food, but Lila only managed a few bites. She listened to Hesky's chatter. He'd grown up in Milwaukee. He met Rain at his niece's bat mitzvah—she was the photographer. They hit it off, but he didn't pursue her. He was divorced and thought their age difference too wide. A week later Rain came to his condo and said he couldn't get away from her that easily.

They married six months later. It was a perfect pairing—she gave him passion, he gave her stability. Two months after her death, his eyes still filled as he rinsed the breakfast plates and loaded them in the dishwasher.

Thirty minutes later they piled into the Econoline and drove a few blocks to the bank. The bank manager, a woman, seemed surprised to see Hesky with three strangers but greeted them politely. After he explained what he wanted, she led them down a flight of stairs to the sign-in area where Hesky filled out some paperwork. Then they went into a large room walled with metal drawers of various sizes and shapes. Three curtained-off booths occupied one corner. A waist-high counter ran around all four walls.

The manager took Hesky's key, matched it with another one, and removed a slender metal box from one wall. Number 7584, Lila noted automatically. Two-digit numbers. Separated by nine. The manager laid the box in a curtained-off booth and withdrew.

Hesky pushed the curtain aside and fished another key out of his pocket. The box wasn't large, about twelve-by-fifteen inches. He unlocked it and swung the lid up. Inside were papers and a few small velvet boxes that probably held rings or necklaces. But something else was there, too. Hesky drew out a clear, hard plastic container, slightly larger than a CD case. He handed it to Dar.

"I believe this is what you're looking for."

Dar took it to the counter. Cece and Lila crowded beside him. Dar opened the case, lifted out an object cocooned in tissue paper, and started to unwrap it. Lila couldn't breathe. Cece's lips were pressed together. Even Hesky craned his neck.

Dar held the object up. It was a small metal plate about the size of a dog tag, two inches long, and an inch wide. Dark smudges that looked like dirt marred part of the surface.

Unable to contain herself, Lila asked, "What is it?"

Dar studied the object, as though he was trying to make sense of it. Then recognition flooded across his face. His lips parted.

"Well?" Cece asked.

Dar picked it up by the edges. "I don't believe it."

"What?" Lila's voice tightened.

"It's the VIN from the van we stole."

"The what?"

"The ID plate from the van. Teddy tried to pry it off so it couldn't be identified. It didn't work, of course—the same number was on the engine mount, which wasn't destroyed in the blast. Turned out they traced the van pretty easily."

"I don't get it," Cece said. "Why is that important?"

"See these smudges?" Dar pointed to them. "Teddy cut himself when he tried to pry the rivets loose. This must be his blood. Or what's left of it."

A chill ran up Lila's spine. "And his DNA . . . "

"And Payton kept it. All these years."

"You know what this means," Cece said, looking at Dar, then Lila.

Lila felt goose bumps on her skin. "But how did Payton know it would be so important forty years after the fact?"

"Maybe he didn't," Dar said. "He probably just held on to it, not knowing why. Payton sometimes had a sixth sense about things. And, of course, we don't know if they can still get a viable sample after all these years." Dar carefully rewrapped the piece of metal, laid it back in the case, and then closed the cover. "Still . . . ," he turned to Hesky, "may we have it?"

"Of course."

"Payton was always the zealot," Dar said softly. "And yet he's the one who came up with the goods." He shook his head. "I wonder why he didn't come forward forty years ago. Maybe none of . . . "

Lila cut in, "Maybe he figured no one would believe him."

"Or that they'd charge him with murder," Cece said.

"Or maybe he knew it could disappear," Lila added. "Like the ID bracelet."

Dar nodded. "That is the way he'd think. But I still don't believe it."

But Lila did. She believed it all. She hugged herself. It would all be over soon.

FIFTY-TWO

They weren't all like Eichmann, even if they were SS."

Lila couldn't help eavesdropping on the couple in the next booth at Denny's that night. The woman was trying to convince her partner that not all Nazis were evil and was touting a film called *Black Book* as proof. Lila could empathize; she'd seen the film at an art house in New York.

"What's our next step?" Cece slipped a napkin into her lap. "How do we deal with Teddy?"

Lila forced herself back.

Dar propped his elbow on the table and rubbed his temples. "It won't be easy. We can't call. He won't take the call."

"And you can't show up at one of his campaign appearances," Cece added. "You'd never get through security."

A young African-American waitress wearing soft-soled shoes came over to their table. Her hair was braided in cornrows. "Take your order?" she asked.

Dar ordered meatloaf with the soup of the day, Cece a chicken Caesar salad. Lila, remembering the smells in Hesky's kitchen, ordered pancakes and a side of bacon. The waitress collected their menus and retreated. Lila waited until she was out of earshot. "We need to make him come to us."

"How?" Dar asked.

She leaned forward. "We may not have to do anything. His people are probably still out there, which means he must know I've been 'out and about.' He may even know I've been introducing myself as Sebastian Kerr's granddaughter. Hell, I'll bet it's driving him crazy."

"Driving him crazy and getting him to come to us aren't the same things," Cece said.

Dar threw up his hand. "Stop. Both of you. This is exactly what I didn't want."

"What?" Lila said.

"I don't want you involved. It's too risky. His people will get to you. Maybe they'll pump you first. But then they'll make sure you have an 'accident' just like Rain. And Casey. And Payton."

"You're forgetting something," Lila said.

"What?"

"The VIN. If the blood sample matches Teddy's DNA, it implicates him in the bombing. And changes everything."

"We need to stay alive until that happens."

Their drinks came, along with split pea soup for Dar. It looked so thick a spoon could probably stand up in it. Lila watched him ladle it into his mouth. The couple in the next booth blathered on about the Holocaust.

"Know thy enemy," the woman was saying. "That's what she did. Went right into the belly of the beast. Do you realize how much guts that takes?"

Dar's head tilted, as if he was listening to their conversation. A moment later he put down his spoon. "I have an idea."

"About what?" Lila asked.

"About how to get Teddy to come to us."

The sunset was a red smudge in the western sky by the time they arrived in Madison the next evening. It had been a quiet trip, Dar, for the most part, lost in thought, rehearsing what to say to Judge Stephen Markham, Teddy's father.

Cece got directions when they stopped for gas, and a few minutes later they passed through a wooded area and parked across the road from the Markhams' multi-level redwood and glass home on the shore of Madison's Lake Monona.

Cece whistled. "Pretty high end."

Dar thought the house looked smaller than it had forty years ago. And shabbier. The redwood needed a coat of stain, the glass windows a good cleaning. Still, it was imposing. Which, of course, was the point.

There was another difference, he thought as he surveyed the house. Forty years ago you could walk across the back lawn, all the way down to the lake. He remembered doing that with Casey and Payton while Teddy talked to his father. Now, though, a fence prevented access to the back. He pointed to it. "This is new."

"I thought Secret Service protection didn't kick in until after the election," Cece said.

"I suspect he's got private help," Dar said. "Stephen Markham is an old man. I doubt he can manage the place on his own."

Cece nodded. Lila didn't say anything.

Dar slipped his hands in his pockets. "Okay, here's the plan. I'm going to go up to the front door and announce myself. I think I'll get in. It doesn't look like an armed fortress."

"Then what?" Lila asked.

"I'll feel Markham out. See how far he's willing to go."

"He's not going to pick up the phone and call Teddy just because you want him to."

"Probably not. But as soon as I leave, you can bet he will."

"What's that going to do for us?" Lila asked.

"I'm prepared to tell them about the VIN. If Teddy knows we have it and we're willing to release it to . . . say . . . the *New York Times* . . . it might . . . open up negotiations."

"And if it doesn't?"

"Then we're no worse off than we were. At least Teddy will know we mean business. That we're not going to keep quiet any more."

"But *we* will be worse off," Lila argued. "They'll know where we are. And come after us." She shook her head. "It might be the right thing to do, but it's too risky. If you go in, I go too."

"No."

Lila drew herself up. "This is not the time to be stubborn. You need backup."

"I'm only going in to talk to the man. Which I can do on my own." He made his voice stern. "Lila, this is my business. Not yours. You stay here."

She blinked.

"If I don't come out in twenty minutes," he went on, "you and Cece drive like hell back to Benny's with the VIN plate. And if you don't hear from me within twenty-four hours, tell the world."

As Dar trudged to the front door, he remembered how Markham had patronized him forty years ago, in an effort to prove how little he knew about the history of class struggles. Dar had to remind himself that Stephen Markham was only a means to an end, the end being Teddy. He squared his shoulders and rang the bell. A perversely cheerful series of notes echoed inside.

The man who opened the door was squat and burly with a shaved head and a trimmed goatee. If he'd been taller and had an earring, he'd look like Mr. Clean. He kept one hand on the door, and the other on the doorjamb, while he looked Dar up and down. Something came into his eyes, something that said he could take Dar, if it came to that.

Dar nodded. "I'd like to speak to Mr. Markham."

"What about?"

"I'm an old friend of Teddy's."

The bodyguard squinted. "Name?"

Dar told him. Mr. Clean closed the door. It stayed closed so long that Dar thought he'd been refused admittance. Then it opened.

"He'll see you for five minutes," the bodyguard said coolly, but there was something new in his eyes. Caution. "But first I search you."

Dar hesitated, then nodded and stepped inside. While Mr. Clean frisked him, Dar's memories of the place resurfaced—the marble floor tiles, the windows overlooking the lake. He recalled the chatty black housekeeper who'd cooked fried chicken for them so long ago. She was probably dead now. For some reason that made him sad.

Mr. Clean led him down the hall to Markham's study. Inside, the light was dim, but it looked the same as before: heavy drapes, dark wood, oil paintings of ships at sea. There were two additions. On one side of the desk was a flat screen monitor, and on the other was a panel of about twelve buttons. Command Central.

The sour smell of old man permeated the room, and Dar could see that Stephen Markham had aged badly. His hair was colorless and wiry. Folds of skin flapped below his jaws as if the air had been let out of his face. Instead of a swivel chair, Markham now sat in a wheelchair. Only his eyes were the same, reflecting the intelligence Dar remembered. And the arrogance.

The eyes narrowed. "I've been expecting you. You'll have been out . . . what . . . about six weeks?"

Dar shouldn't have been surprised—he'd tried to anticipate what the man would say. Still, his stomach fluttered. With one sentence Markham had put him on the defensive. How did he know when Dar was released? What else did he know? Thank God Lila was safe outside. He motioned toward Mr. Clean who'd stationed himself near the door, hands behind, feet spread. The ready position. Like a prison guard. "This is a private conversation."

Markham glanced at his bodyguard, who shook his head. Surprisingly Markham overruled him. "You can leave, David. But stay close."

The bodyguard raised his eyebrows but did as Markham ordered, closing the door behind him.

Markham turned to Dar. "Now, what can I do for you?"

"I want you to call Teddy."

A tiny smile crossed Markham's lips. "Why would I do that?"

"We need to talk."

Markham steepled his fingers. "About what?"

Dar hesitated. His differences were with Teddy, not his father. Still, at this point, what did it matter if the father knew? "I have proof of Teddy's complicity in the bombing at Kerr's department store."

Markham went still for a moment. Then he cackled. Dar felt his cheeks get hot.

"You were always the smart one," Markham said. "Smart, but not shrewd." He waved a dismissive hand.

"What do you mean?"

"I knew at some point that one of you would claim to have evidence of Teddy's participation. And I'm confident I know what it is. Let me show you something." Markham picked up a remote from the desk and aimed it at the flat screen TV mounted on the wall.

Dar frowned.

Suddenly light flooded in through the window. "David!" Markham yelled.

The door opened and Mr. Clean hurried back in. Seeing the light, he ran to the window, opened the drapes, and peered out.

"What is it?" Markham asked.

The bodyguard shook his head. "Can't see anything." He closed the drapes and turned around. "Probably a rabbit."

"Damn system's too sensitive. Can't you fiddle with it? I don't need the goddamned lights and alarms going off every five minutes."

"I'll look into it, sir."

"Have Max do it."

"I will, when he gets back."

"Where is he? Teddy's people wanted two of you here at all times."

"He's with his brother. A personal matter."

"Well, get him back." Markham sighed. "All this new-fangled security and things still don't work." He gestured, the remote in his hand. "You can go."

After he was gone, Markham pushed more buttons. "Watch," he said to Dar.

The television lit up and a few bars scrolled diagonally. The picture settled on a video of Teddy at a campaign rally. He looked good: his temples had just enough gray, he was fit and tan. His smile was at full wattage as a man with a ten-gallon hat introduced him on camera.

Teddy stood beside the speaker, arranging the cuffs of his shirt so they extended just beyond his jacket. His hands fell to his sides, but then he raised his left hand and jiggled it, just the way he'd done forty years ago when he wore his ID bracelet.

Dar stared at the screen. Teddy's wrist was bare, but he still had the habit. Dar turned to Markham, who'd been watching him watch Teddy.

"I believe the evidence you're talking about concerns the ID bracelet Teddy owned. You lived with Teddy. You knew he wore it all the time, and you knew he didn't have it after the bomb. He probably told you he lost it."

He had, Dar recalled. In fact, Teddy had been obsessed with finding it. He and Payton had to restrain Teddy from sneaking back to the rubble to look for it.

Markham clicked the remote and the screen went dark.

"It's curious you bring up the bracelet, Judge. It almost sounds like you know what happened to it."

Markham's eyes went cold, as if Dar had scored an unexpected point. "There's not much about Teddy's career I don't know."

All at once Dar knew why he felt so uneasy in Markham's presence. Stephen Markham was the power behind his son. He was the one orchestrating events. "You . . . ," Dar said, "you set me up. Not Teddy."

"Teddy needs guidance. Always has."

Dar put it together. "The summer we lived together . . . Rain thought Teddy was an informer. She was right. You made it happen."

"One needs to protect one's children. You can understand that," Markham said. "Well, I believe your five minutes are up. If there's nothing else . . . "

Dar realized he couldn't tell Markham about the VIN now; he'd be giving up his only leverage. Better to let Markham think the evidence he'd referred to was the bracelet and get out. "It's clear that you've been controlling events for years. I salute you."

Markham tilted his head. "Maybe you are shrewder than I thought."

"Tell me something, Judge. Why didn't you have me killed in prison? You could have 'arranged' it. Like the others," he added.

Markham surprised him. "Now, why would I do something like that? There was no need for that. I fear you've picked up a healthy dose of paranoia, my friend. They say that can happen in prison."

"How fortunate for me." Dar wondered why he'd been spared. Was it Teddy's doing? Or did Markham assume that, because he was serving a life sentence, he couldn't possibly be a threat? That if he did implicate Teddy, his accusations would be dismissed as the rantings of a bitter convict?

Whatever the case, it didn't matter. Now that Dar knew the truth, Markham would never let him leave alive. Dar realized he had made another blunder. Lila was right. He should never have come. He looked around. Only one door. And the windows behind the drapes. Escape was impossible. His only choice was to brazen it out. And buy enough time for Lila and Cece to escape.

"Thank you for seeing me," Dar said. "I guess I'll be leaving now."

Markham pressed a button on his desk panel. As if on cue, the bodyguard came back in. This time he didn't stop at the entrance but planted himself a few feet from Dar.

"You didn't really think I'd allow you to go, did you?" Markham asked.

Mr. Clean took a step closer.

"No, I didn't." But the judge was right about one thing. Like him, Dar had a child to protect. He cleared his throat. "Judge, you and I will never agree about most things. But, for my daughter's sake, I am willing to negotiate."

"About what?"

"Call off the men who are targeting her. She's got nothing to do with us, or Teddy, or our history. Let her live in peace."

Markham's expression grew puzzled. "Targeting your daughter? I'm not doing that. I have no interest in taking this to the next generation."

"But your . . . the man on the motorcycle. And the rental truck. They're your men."

Markham looked at him. "What man on a motorcycle?"

"The man who . . . ," Dar's voice trailed off. The look on Markham's face said he was telling the truth. Markham wasn't going after Lila. But if he wasn't, who was?

The bodyguard cut in before he could process it further. "Matches?" He sounded almost eager.

Markham looked at Dar. "David has a trick which is quite effective. It involves lit matches and the tips of your fingers. I'm going to allow him to proceed. Unless you tell me what I need to know."

Dar thought about Markham, Teddy, and Lila. If Markham wasn't going after Lila, negotiation was moot. He shook his head.

"Changed your mind again?"

Dar kept his mouth shut. Markham shrugged and nodded at David. The bodyguard rummaged in a drawer and pulled out a box of kitchen matches. He advanced on Dar.

FIFTY-THREE

After Dar went inside, Lila went down to the water, circling around the fence surrounding the Markhams' property. Lake Monona was smaller than Lake Michigan, but tonight a frigid wind lashed its surface, producing explosions of tiny whitecaps out beyond the ice. She tucked her hands in her pockets.

"It's hard to wait, isn't it?" Cece joined her at the shore.

Lila didn't answer. She listened to the plop of the waves. Then she walked back to the fence and peered through it. Three balconies on different levels jutted out from the redwood walls, making a rough triangular design. The triangle was supposed to be the most stable shape in the universe, she recalled. That's why Buckminster Fuller championed the geodesic dome, a series of interlocking triangles.

The balconies were fenced off with slabs of redwood supported on iron bases. Behind each balcony Lila could see sliding glass doors. The rooms beyond the doors were dark. The only illumination came from the first floor. A large window was covered with drapes, but a narrow sliver of light seeped out where they were joined together. Was that where Dar was meeting with Markham?

The lowest balcony was about ten feet off the ground. Ten or ten thousand, it didn't matter. She couldn't reach it. Still, she wondered if the glass door was unlocked. That would never happen in her home—she always made sure all the doors and windows were locked. But this was an old man living next to a strip of woods on a tiny outcropping of land. The topography was a buffer. And Markham probably didn't get around much. He might not go into some of his rooms for weeks on end. There might be a chance the door was unlocked.

She found the gate to the back. Would there be some kind of alarm? Some buildings in New York and Chicago, post 9/11, had added them, but this was secluded property.

She tentatively pushed against the gate. It was unlocked. Had it just been installed? She opened it and stepped through, motioning for Cece to follow. They were creeping across the back yard when a set of floodlights kicked on. Lila froze. Motion sensors. Damn! Adrenaline surged through her, and she threw herself on the ground.

"Drop!" she whispered to Cece.

Cece did.

The drapes covering the first floor window flew apart. The shadow of a burly man appeared in the light, arms crossed. Lila held her breath. Maybe he wouldn't notice them. Maybe he'd think a squirrel or possum or some other animal triggered the sensors.

She squeezed her eyes shut. Please, God. Just this once.

A moment later the drapes closed. Lila took in a ragged breath, and tried to slow her heartbeat. But she didn't move. Someone could be coming. She counted to twenty. No one came, but the floodlights stayed on. Finally she stood up and took a cautious step forward.

Cece whispered, "What the fuck are you doing, Lila? Let's get out of here."

Lila shook her head. "Dar shouldn't be in there by himself."

"Agreed. But what can we do?"

Lila turned and went back to the Econoline. Opening the side door, she rummaged around on the floor, retrieved something, and quietly closed the door. She carried it back gingerly.

When Cece saw what it was, she inhaled sharply. "Where did you get that?"

"Where do you think?"

"Reba."

Lila nodded. "It's a .38 Special. She taught me how to use it."

"But you know what Dar said."

Lila didn't reply. She'd been swinging between confidence and panic since they'd started out for Madison. She was in pretty good shape. Or

315

had been before the grenade. And Dar Gantner, father or not, had risked his life for her. She slid the .38 Special into her jacket pocket, and returned to the house. Closing in on the lowest balcony, she beckoned to Cece. "If you give me a boost," she whispered, "I might be able to swing myself up."

Cece looked at the balcony, then at Lila. "You're not serious."

"Well, I can't very well knock on the front door and stroll inside."

"We promised Dar."

"I don't like the look of the guy who opened the drapes."

Cece shook her head. "Dar was clear."

"Cece, I can't do this without you."

"Jesus, Lila. What if something happens to you? Your father will . . . "

"What if something happens to him?"

Cece looked at the lit window, the balcony, then back at Lila. "Shit. What do you need?"

Lila explained. Cece bent over and locked her hands together. Lila stepped one foot into them. As she shifted her weight onto that foot, Cece grunted and collapsed. Lila fell to the ground with a thud.

Her heart hammered like the wheels of a runaway train. An eternity passed. Nothing happened. Lila slowly raised herself. "Let's try again."

"I'm not strong enough."

"You have to be."

Cece just looked at her.

"Use the side of the house to support your back."

Cece wedged herself up against the wall of the house and dropped to a squat. Locking her hands together, she nodded to Lila. Once again, Lila stepped into Cece's locked hands. This time they held. Lila tried to grasp the siding of the house to gain purchase, but there was nothing to grab onto. Splinters dug into her nails. Somehow, though, Cece managed to lift her a few inches. Lila stretched her arms over her head, reaching for the balcony's iron support base. She was close. Just a few more inches. Then Cece's upward motion slowed. Lila could feel the woman shudder. The strain on her back must be excruciating. There wasn't much time. She stretched again. Please, God.

Her fingers made contact with the post. She clamped one hand around it, then the other. Frigid metal stung her skin, but she held on. Remembering all the gymnastics classes Casey and Gramum made her take as a child, she swung back and forth to build momentum. Meanwhile Cece collapsed, gasping for air.

Lila swung a few more times. Each time her grip became sturdier, the arc wider. Then, with a Herculean effort, she swung herself up and through the gap between the slabs of wood fronting the balcony. She locked her legs on the lower slab, hoping it was strong enough to hold her weight. It was, and she hung, upside down, her feet curled around the slab of wood. She grabbed the top slab with her hands. Her muscles screamed. She wondered if she'd made too much noise. She carefully shimmied across it. Then she pushed and shoved and rolled her torso through the space between the slabs. She'd always been slim, and since her injuries she'd lost weight. She managed to squeeze through.

A minute later, she was lying on the floor of the balcony. Her back, arms, and legs ached. She would have bruises. She waited until she was breathing normally, then stood up and patted her pocket. The .38 was there.

She moved to the sliding glass door. If the door was locked, she would have a problem. There was no way she could climb back down. She'd have to smash the glass or shoot the lock off. Which would, of course, announce her presence.

Reaching out, she gripped the handle of the door and gave it a tug. Nothing. She tried again, pulling harder. This time she thought it budged. She tried again. The door seemed to want to move, but it was caught on something. Rust? Dirt and dust in the tracks? Either way, her spirits lifted. It was moving a little. Which meant it was unlocked. She braced herself, bent her knees, and pulled with both hands. The door slid open an inch. She kept pulling, hearing the scraping sound of metal on metal. The door gave, but in stingy increments. Finally it was about ten inches open. She slithered inside.

A guest room. Dark, but a mirror above a bureau reflected the floodlights outside. Lila could see a queen-sized bed with a heavy quilt, and a braided rug on the floor. The door to the room was closed. She crept to it and leaned her ear against it. At first she heard nothing. She pressed her ear harder. She became aware of a murmur, but it wasn't coming from the other side of the door. She cocked her ear, trying to pinpoint its source.

It came from back near the balcony door. She moved silently across the room. The murmur was louder. Still indistinct, but she recognized Dar's voice. Where was it coming from? The room with the gap in the drapes was below and to her left. Were they in there? She tried to concentrate, but the wind outside had kicked up and a draft whistled through the door. She couldn't close it; couldn't risk making more noise. What now? She realized she didn't have much of a plan.

She could still hear conversation. But where was it coming from? She looked at the floor. An air vent! She knelt down and put her ear against it. The voices were clear. Dar was talking.

"Thank you for seeing me," Dar was saying. "I guess I'll be leaving now."

A gruff voice. "You didn't really think I'd allow you to go, did you?" Markham.

A pause. Then Dar again, "No. I didn't."

Chills skipped up her spine. Lila straightened up, unzipped her pocket, and fished out the .38. She moved to the door. As she opened it, air blowing in from the balcony rushed through the room. But there were no other telltale sounds.

She stepped into the hall. After being in semi-darkness, the blinding light from a ceiling chandelier was disorienting. She blinked to adjust her vision. A flight of stairs lay to the right, flanked by a wide curving banister with carved spindles. A thick oriental carpet covered the floor. She took a step. No noise. The carpet felt cushiony. She took another. She made it to the top of the stairs. A voice rose from downstairs, more distinct than what she'd heard through the air vent.

Markham. "David has a trick which is quite effective. It involves lit matches . . . "

She tiptoed to the edge of the carpet. The steps were hardwood and covered by a thin runner. She'd heard somewhere it was better to tread on the edges, not the middle. Less noise. She took a tentative step down. No squeaks. She took another. So far, so good. She began to feel more confident and snuck down to the third step.

It squeaked.

Lila froze, the .38 in her hand.

At the same time she heard an intake of breath from downstairs. "I thought I heard something on the stairs." Markham sounded concerned.

"That's impossible." A low-pitched voice. Irritated.

"I tell you I heard something." Markham again, irritated as well. "Go see."

"What about him?"

Lila heard the sound of a drawer sliding open, followed by Markham's voice. "I'll handle it."

"A .22 won't do the job."

Markham's voice was impatient. "David, stop wasting time. I need him alive for the moment. Go check the noise."

Lila pressed herself against the wall. Whoever came out would see her, but she might have the advantage of surprise. She aimed the gun down the steps. Straightened her arms and her body. Tried to clear her mind.

The door opened. A beefy man with a shaved head emerged. The same man who'd opened the drapes. He pointed a huge gun her way. Lila's eyes widened, and she ducked behind the spindles of the banister as he fired. She saw a flash of light, heard two deafening cracks. Her stomach lurched. She didn't know if she'd been hit. Her ears were ringing. She smelled gunpowder.

"David!" Markham yelled. Querulous. Fearful. "What's happening?"

Chips of paint and plaster rained down the steps. But Lila was still alive. He'd missed. The shots must have ripped into the wall beside her. She forced herself not to panic. With the gun in front of her, she moved her aim slightly to the right between the spindles. The beefy man mirrored her movement. But before he could take another shot, she squeezed the .38's trigger.

The muzzle flashed, and the crack of the discharge slammed into her ears. The recoil made her arm fly up. The beefy man groaned, dropped his gun, and fell to the floor clutching his thigh. Blood oozed out, staining the floor and carpet.

Markham yelled, his voice edged with panic. "David, what's going on?"

A smell like firecrackers drifted through the air. Lila started to shiver.

"David, get in here. Now."

Her heart thumped in her chest, but it wasn't over. Clutching the gun, she stood and raced down the rest of the stairs. Stepping around the bodyguard, she pulled open the door to the room.

An old man in a wheelchair was aiming a gun at Dar.

"Drop your gun." She raised the .38. "Now!"

Markham twisted around. Confusion swam across his face, but then his eyes grew cold, as if he couldn't believe anyone, especially a woman, had the gall to confront him. He swung the gun from Dar toward her and pulled the trigger.

The shot went wide and plowed into the door to her left.

Out of the corner of her eye she saw a blur of movement. Dar threw himself at Markham's desk and leapt on top. Markham aimed the .22 at Dar. At the same time Lila hurtled towards him from the side and grabbed for the gun. There was another muzzle flash and explosion. The bullet pierced the ceiling, triggering a spider web design. Dar crawled over the desk, grabbed Markham, and wrestled him out of the wheelchair. The chair tipped over, and both men fell to the floor. Markham dropped the .22, and it skittered across the carpet. Dar rolled over Markham, clutching him until the man was on his belly with Dar on top. He grabbed Markham's arms and pinned them behind his back.

Markham moaned. "My arm . . . I think it's broken!"

Dar held on. Lila got up, retrieved the .22, and slipped it into her pocket. She kept the .38 trained on Markham. "Call Teddy," she said.

Markham shook his head. He was breathing heavily.

"Oh, I think you will," Dar said evenly. "You see, there is a piece of evidence I didn't tell you about. Evidence that puts Teddy squarely in the middle of the bombing." He explained about the piece of metal with the VIN on it. "It contains Teddy's blood. And his prints."

"You're bluffing," Markham said. "The DNA couldn't possibly hold up after all this time."

"Do you want to take that chance?"

Markham blinked.

"Your only option is how you spin it," Dar said. "If you do it right, Teddy can hang on to his respectability. If not, we'll expose him. His place in history is in your hands."

Markham squeezed his eyes shut. When he opened them again, something new was in his eyes. Defeat. "Give me the phone."

FIFTY-FOUR

S herry's Café in Loves Park did a brisk business, especially in the morning. That's when farmers, truckers, and people going to work stopped in for coffee and gossip and news. The news usually ran to who was arrested for a DUI, who was cheating on whom, whose kid was busted for drugs.

Lila, Dar, Cece, and Reba were lucky to find a table two mornings later. They were nursing cappuccinos and munching on bagels when someone turned up the volume on the TV on the wall. The screen proclaimed a special report was imminent. The broadcast cut to one of the network anchormen.

"In just a few moments Senator Ted Markham of Wisconsin will be announcing he is ending his quest for the presidency," the anchor intoned.

Lila jerked her head up. Dar, Cece, and Reba did too. A hush fell over the room. A blue box on the TV screen, behind the anchorman's shoulder, dissolved to a shot of Teddy in his Senate office. He sat behind his desk, hands folded. Two flags—one for the state of Wisconsin; the other, the American flag—flanked him.

The shot expanded to fill the screen. Teddy's face looked unnaturally tan, as if someone had applied too much make-up. But his navy suit was sharply tailored, his shirt impeccably white, his red power tie a perfect Windsor knot.

He nodded into the camera. "Good morning, my fellow Americans. Two days ago my father—and his nurse-companion . . . ," Lila and Dar exchanged glances, " . . . were seriously wounded when intruders broke into his house in Madison. The nurse was shot trying to defend himself, and my father's arm was broken. Both men, thank God, are expected to recover, but it will be a long recovery, especially for my father. He is not a young man."

The camera started a slow move into a close-up of Teddy's face.

"An investigation is ongoing . . . and I want to commend the Madison police for their diligence. They have retrieved evidence that I'm not at liberty to discuss. But there is every reason to think these criminals will be apprehended. And prosecuted."

Dar gave a little shrug, as if to say, "he had to say something." He and Lila had discussed what might happen if they were apprehended. Dar's parole could be revoked, and he could be charged with conspiracy to commit murder. Lila could be charged with home invasion, aggravated battery, attempted murder, and whatever else they could drum up. Lila shrugged too. She would do it all over again. She looked back at the TV.

Teddy dipped his head and brushed his hair off his forehead. "There are some who feel this incident was politically motivated. I want to state unequivocally that I do not share that opinion. However, I cannot tolerate any risk or potential harm to my family. For that reason I have reassessed my situation."

"He's running scared," someone in the café said.

"Shut up, Clarence."

"It was my father yesterday," Teddy went on, "but it could be my wife and children tomorrow. I would not be a good president if my attention was divided and I was constantly worried that harm might come to my loved ones. This country needs a president whose mind is focused solely on solving the problems of this great nation. And the world.

"For those reasons I have decided I can best serve the country by remaining in my seat in the Senate, creating legislation that will move us forward. Therefore, as of today, I will no longer seek the nomination of my party for president. It has been an honor to serve you, and I will continue to do so in the future as a senator. Thank you. God bless you, your family, and God bless America."

The broadcast cut back to the anchorman. "A dramatic development from the campaign—or former campaign—of Senator Ted Markham. Recapping his statement, the senator said . . . "

Cece turned her back on the TV as he droned on. "Nice spin."

"Hard to believe he's going to get away with murder," Lila murmured.

"I don't know," Dar said, "his father was the mastermind, not him."

"So they're both getting away with it."

"They're paying a stiff price."

"The authorities wouldn't be this forgiving. Why are you?"

"Maybe Teddy will be a better leader," Dar said. "You know, without the pressure to get elected. Or having his father on his back."

"That's crazy. The only reason he'll stay in line is that he knows you have the VIN plate," Lila said. "And if he comes after you, you'll expose him."

Dar considered it. "He won't. As I said, the judge was the brains, not Teddy. And he's been effectively neutralized."

Lila looked at her father. She would never be that magnanimous.

"There's a huge irony here, you know," Cece said.

"What's that?"

"Forty years ago you and Teddy and Payton were rebelling against what you believed was a corrupt establishment. Who knew Teddy would take it to the next level?"

"I'm not blameless," Dar replied. "I used extortion to get what I needed."

"But you weren't running for president," Reba countered.

"True," Dar paused. "Speaking of ironies, don't forget Payton."

Lila frowned. "Payton?"

"We always thought he postured. Went too far. In the end, though, he was the one who came up with the evidence."

"And redeemed himself," Lila said.

"I wish your mother knew. Neither she nor Rain ever trusted him."

"Her daughter knows," Lila said.

"Speaking of daughters, where did you learn to handle a gun?"

Lila eyed Reba. Reba looked at the floor. Comprehension dawned on Dar's face.

"I guess that's another irony," Lila said softly.

No one said anything.

"So . . . ," Reba finally said. "You going back to New York now?"

"I . . . I don't know. I still have some things to do here."

"Like what?"

"Like buy Cece a new car. We pretty much trashed the Honda getting away from the rental truck. Then I want to find Dar a place to live. And get something nice for you and Benny."

"Whoa, girl . . . " Reba pointed her spoon at Lila. "That's real nice and all, but you're talking serious money."

Lila pressed her lips together. "Yeah, well, there's something I've been meaning to tell you." She cleared her throat. At the same time the cough of a motorcycle outside chuffed, then quieted. Lila ignored it. "I got a strange message about a week ago. From a woman named . . . "

She stopped in mid-sentence as the door to the café swung open. A man stepped in. Solid, not tall. His hair pulled back in a ponytail. Graying at the temples. He was wearing a black leather jacket and matching pants. In his hand was a helmet with a visor. His eyes darted back and forth, taking in his surroundings. A scar snaked on his cheek, still red and raw.

Lila gasped.

Dar, whose back was to the door, spun around. "What the . . . what's he doing here?"

Cece frowned. "Shit!"

"It's Enduro Man," Lila whispered.

"That's crazy. Why didn't Teddy call him off?" Reba gestured to the TV. "The war is over."

"Maybe no one told him," Cece said.

"Markham's people wouldn't be that slipshod," Dar said.

"So he's a lone ranger?" Reba asked.

Lila slumped, trying to make herself small. "Whoever he is, how the hell did he find us?"

"It's gotta be the tracker," Reba said. "The last place he picked us up was at the house. He must have decided to hunt us down the old fashioned way." She looked around. "And this being the center of town . . . "

Lila's skin felt clammy. "What do we do? Call the police?"

"Sure. While you're at it, why don't you fill them in on what you've been up to the last couple of days?" Reba glanced behind the counter, then at Enduro Man, who was starting to turn their way. "Listen. You and Dar sneak out the back. Go to Benny's shop and lock yourselves up in the back room."

They all stood. Reba and Cece moved in front of Dar and Lila, shielding them from sight. Reba gestured to Sherry, the owner, who was walking by. "Sweetheart, these fine folks need to get out the back door. Pronto."

Sherry studied Reba, then motioned with her hand. "This way."

Reba gave Dar a shove. "Follow her."

Dar and Lila slipped behind the counter and disappeared through the kitchen. With the crush of people in the café, Enduro Man didn't seem to notice. As Lila retreated, she heard Reba say to Cece, "I need you to distract him. For about five minutes."

"Excuse me?" Cece said.

"Come on to him. Spill coffee on him. Whatever. Just give me five minutes with his bike."

Dar and Lila ducked out the back door.

They were in the back room of Benny's shop thirty minutes later when the front door jingled. Two sets of footsteps stomped on the floor. Reba's voice called out. "Hey Benny, it's Reba Whiteman."

Benny cocked his head. Dar raised a finger to his lips.

"Hey, Spivak. Get off your fat ass. I got some business for you."

Dar raised an eyebrow.

"Hold your horses. I'm comin' . . ." Benny looked at Dar and Lila and nodded once. They both moved behind the door. Benny opened it, closed it behind him, and headed to the front. Lila leaned her ear against the door.

"This here gentleman . . . what'd you say your name was?" Reba asked.

"I didn't," a tinny, nasal voice mumbled.

"Yeah, well, whoever he is, he got a flat tire over at Sherry's. I told him you'd fix it."

Lila ached with fear. Why did Reba bring him here? What if he spotted them? This was lunacy. She started to tremble. Dar rested his hand on her shoulder.

"What seems to be the trouble?" she heard Benny ask.

"Looks like the valve on his Enduro somehow came out. The central core is missing. No way to reinflate it without replacing the valve."

"How do you know so much about bikes?" Enduro Man broke in.

"I ride a Harley. Just not in this weather," Reba said. "It's bad for my skin." She giggled. It sounded artificial. "Well, you're in the right place. I'll be seeing you."

"Hey, Reba. Thanks for the business," Benny said. "I owe you."

Enduro Man grunted.

The front door tinkled. Then Benny asked, "So, you got a name?"

"You can call me Jergens."

"Okay, Jergens. Let's take a look."

The door tinkled again. There was silence.

"Who's Jergens?" Lila whispered.

"I have no clue," Dar said. He was still holding her.

"What do we do?"

"Nothing," Dar said. "Benny and Reba know what they're doing."

The door to the shop opened again. " . . . probably only take a few minutes," Benny was saying. "Why don't you go get a brew or some coffee while I work on it?"

"That's what I was doing when it went flat," the man called Jergens snapped. "I'll stay here."

Lila stiffened.

"Well, I need to work on it in my garage. And I can't have customers back there. Insurance."

"How do I know you . . ." Jergens blew out a breath. "Oh, fuck it all."

"Hey man, it's cool. Come back in ten. I'll have a new valve for you. And air in the tire." Even Benny sounded relieved.

FIFTY-FIVE

B enny found a valve for the tire and reinflated it. Jergens returned, slapped twenty dollars on the counter, and took off. Benny went to the back room and unlocked the door. Lila and Dar were perched on stacks of boxes. Lila looked pale and shaky.

"He's gone," Benny said. "But we gotta get home."

"Why?" Dar asked.

"Gotta fire up the computer."

"What for?"

"You'll see. By the way, I have his license plate number. I called my buddy at the DMV, but he's out till tomorrow." He shrugged. "'Course, it might not matter by then."

They crowded into Benny's pick-up for the ride home. Once in the house, he booted up his computer and clicked on a website. After fiddling with the mouse, he let out a satisfied grunt. "There we go."

Dar watched the monitor. A road map of northern Illinois with a flashing dot materialized on the screen.

"What's that?"

Benny grinned. "Jergens."

Lila leaned over the computer. "You put a tracker on his bike."

"Turn around is fair play."

Lila gave him a high five. "How did you manage it?"

"I snuck it on when I put the tire back on. It's inside the rim."

"Will he'll find it?"

"I used a miniature version." Benny explained. "Not much bigger than a quarter. And sure, there's a chance he'll find it. But hopefully we'll know who he is and where he's going by the time he does."

Dar started to put on his jacket. "Come on, Lila."

"Where are we going?"

"We're going after him. We have to finish this."

"But what if it gets ugly?"

"If anyone tries to harm you, I'll fight the devil in hell."

She gave him a small smile.

"I can track him from here," Benny said. "And let you know where he's heading. Just keep in touch."

"Tell Cece and Reba we'll be back," Dar said.

"Wait," Lila said. "I have to get something." She went into the spare room.

Dar knew what she was going for. He kept his mouth shut.

Lila drove east on I-90 in the Econoline. She put her cell phone on the dash. They were closing on O'Hare airport when Benny called.

"He's still on 90."

"Thanks." She disconnected and gazed through the windshield. The afternoon sky hung low with dark angry clouds. Every few seconds a snowflake drifted over the windshield. "I don't like driving in snow."

"Maybe it will hold off," Dar said.

"Right," she said doubtfully. "So, who is he? Is Markham giving him his marching orders?"

"Markham might be furious," Dar said. "He might want revenge. But he's not stupid. I can't believe he'd try again so soon. He waited years to find Payton, remember."

"What about Teddy? Maybe Jergens is working directly for him?"

"Anything's possible," Dar said. "But it doesn't feel right. Then again, I haven't been around Teddy for forty years."

Lila ran a nervous hand through her hair. She leaned forward. Then she leaned back.

"What is it, Lila?"

She cleared her throat. "I should have told you this before, but it never seemed like the right time. And we were pretty busy."

"What is it?"

"A few days ago, I checked my messages on my phone in New York." She held out a hand as if to ward off a scolding. "Yes, I know it was dangerous, and I shouldn't have. But someone named Joanna Kerr left me a message. She said she was Philip Kerr's ex-wife, and she needed to talk to me right away."

Dar looked over.

"When I called, she said my grandfather changed his will just before he died. That Danny and I were supposed to inherit the bulk of his estate. But that her ex-husband . . . "

"Philip Kerr," Dar cut in.

"You know about this?"

He nodded. "I got a letter from her when I was inside."

"She told me she wrote you but never got a reply."

"I didn't trust anyone with the name of Kerr back then."

"So you know what happened?"

"I went to see Kerr after I got out. He said it wasn't true."

Lila's eyes went wide.

"He said his ex-wife was making it up. To get back at him. A bad divorce. No kids, he said."

"And you believed him?"

"At the time . . . " Dar looked over. "Wait a minute. What are you trying to say?"

"Think about it, Dar. The only heir to a considerable fortune finds out his father changed his will right before he died. Two people he's never met are going to inherit half of his money. How would you feel?"

"Furious, but . . . "

"Bear in mind we never really understood why Markham's people were after me. You, yes. It was logical. But me? I had nothing to do with the past."

"Yes, but . . . "

Lila looked over. "There's something else. Joanna Kerr said the brakes went out on her car recently. She doesn't think it's an accident. She's in hiding."

Dar sat up straighter. "When? When did this happen?"

"She wasn't specific, but recently."

"But after I went to see Kerr."

"Probably."

Dar let out a groan. "Oh my god. That means there were two groups coming after us. Markham's people. And Kerr's."

"The rental truck. And the man on the motorcycle. Different people. Different M.O.s."

"But the same objective." Dar rubbed a finger below his nose. Then he nodded. "Now it makes sense."

Lila nodded.

More snow dusted the windshield. Dar leaned forward.

"I think I know where's he's headed."

FIFTY-SIX

The snow began in earnest as they advanced up the Michigan shore. The wind picked up too, and blowing snow obscured the view. Lila turned on the radio. The all-news station warned that a storm from the Plains was closing in. Ten or more inches were expected, and blizzard conditions were predicted.

Traffic slowed to a crawl. Lila hunched forward, peering into the blinding white. Flashes of red occasionally blinked—the hazard lights on the cars in front. She rolled her shoulders and cranked up the defroster. Uncomfortable as they were, Jergens had to be in worse shape. He was on a bike with little traction, no protection from the elements, and no heat. Unless he'd pulled off the road somewhere and was waiting out the storm. That would be the smart thing to do.

Despite the intensity, the storm was eerily silent, the quiet broken only by the thud and swish of the wipers. An early dusk descended, and the light turned blue, then purple, then disappeared. Swirls of white slanted sideways across the van's headlights. Lila's eyes grew heavy, and she blinked to stay alert.

"What do we do if we tie Jergens to Kerr?" Lila asked.

"We call the cops. Let them handle it," Dar said.

"Except that if Jergens is the one who took a shot at me, threw the grenade, and attacked me in an alley, he's committed to killing me. And since I cut him with the HideAway, it's personal. The police won't be any help. Especially if we catch up to him before they do."

Dar tightened his lips.

She yanked her thumb towards the back of the Econoline. "The .38 is on the floor back there. In my bag. I need it."

Dar twisted around, grabbed the bag, and stowed it under the front seat.

Her cell trilled. Benny confirmed that Jergens was heading north on 196 toward Grand Haven, but the signal kept fading in and out.

"Must be the weather. We're in the middle of a blizzard," Lila said.

She disconnected and slowed even more, trying to keep the car from skidding off the road. She felt exhausted and drained. Twenty minutes later she was about to pull over when her cell buzzed again.

Benny. "The signal's stopped. For about ten minutes now. At the junction of 196 and 31. Near Holland. Could be a rest stop. Where are you?"

"About twenty miles south, I think."

"Well . . . " Benny cleared his throat.

"Thanks." She rang off and told Dar. "So what do you want to do?"

The snow was unrelenting. It glittered in the headlights from oncoming cars, but the headlights grew fewer and farther apart. The defroster grew sluggish; Dar had to keep wiping the glass to remove the condensation. "I think we ought to call it a day."

Lila hunched her shoulders. "But we're almost there."

"It's time to call the police. Let them handle it."

For someone who'd fought the system for so long, he was putting a lot of faith in it now, Lila thought. "Let's just check out the rest stop. See if he's there."

"And then what?"

Lila didn't answer.

FIFTY-SEVEN

I t took almost an hour to get to where Routes 196 and 31 met outside Holland, Michigan. Just before the junction was a highway rest stop. Lila followed a ramp to a one-story building with glass doors. A row of parking slots in front of the building was practically full, and she could see a crowd of people inside. The interior was brightly lit, and heads bobbed as people chatted, faking a camaraderie they would forget once the storm subsided.

Lila slowed the van. "Do you see him?"

"No."

She looked around the parking area. "I don't see the bike, either."

"I'm going inside to check."

"I'll go with you!"

"No."

"Please, Dar."

"He won't do anything with so many people inside."

Dar opened the van's door and slid out. Lila watched him disappear into the swirling white. Her stomach churned. She leaned over to the passenger side, grabbed the bag he had stowed under the seat, and pulled out the .38.

A few seconds went by. There was no way she could stay in the car while Dar was inside. She started the engine, backed out of her spot, and cruised slowly past the row of cars. She was nearly at the end when she spotted the Enduro. She recognized the plastic bumpers extending from each end. Most of the cars nearby were covered with a thick layer of white, but the motorcycle was bare.

Jergens was here.

She had to find Dar. She nosed the van around, circled the access road, and headed back to the building. In her haste, she gave the Econoline too much gas and sent it into a skid. She wrenched the wheel to the right. The van kept sliding. She was going to plow into the line of parked cars! The van straightened out with just inches to spare. Gripping the wheel, she drove back to where she'd parked, only to find the space had been taken by another car.

She thought of leaving the van in the middle of the access road with the engine running, but decided that was a bad idea. For the second time she coasted past the row of parked cars, hunting for a spot. Finally she pulled into a space at the end of the line, ironically two spaces from the motorcycle. She slipped the .38 into her pocket and got out.

It was ominously quiet, the snow muffling all sound. She plodded steadily through it, but her nerves frayed with each step. Finally she reached the door and pushed through. She searched the throng for Dar. He was tall—he should stand out in a crowd.

She didn't see him.

She went to the vending machines—maybe he was getting coffee. Not there.

Maybe he was in the men's room. She walked over to the entrance and waited at the door. A gray-haired man emerged, then a man holding a little boy's hand. No Dar. Lila shifted. She would ask the next man who came in to check on him. She looked at her watch. Nearly ten minutes since he took off. She couldn't wait any longer. She took a quick look around. Seeing no one, she snuck inside.

The men's room was remarkably clean, with six stalls and three urinals. Thankfully, no one was at the urinal, but she did see a pair of feet in the second stall.

"Dar? Are you there?"

"Huh? Who's there?" a voice asked.

"Dar?"

"I sure as hell am not," the voice replied. "And what the hell . . ."

"Sorry . . . " She hurried out as another man entered. He gave her a bewildered look.

Lila's heart was thumping, and her hands shook. Dar was in trouble. She could feel it. She looked around. People entered the rest stop through a set of glass doors on either end of the building. Floodlights illuminated each door and the area around it; if not for the blowing snow, she might have seen all the way to the road. As it was, the visibility was barely three feet. Still, she doubted Jergens would try anything near the entrances. Too many people coming and going.

That left the sides of the building, which were shrouded in shadow. She huddled into her coat, felt for the .38, and went outside.

It was dark, and the snow was gusting so fiercely it was impossible to see. She stayed close to the walls and crept around the building. She kept her eyes down, searching for footprints, but saw only dizzying eddies of snow.

"Dar?" she called out.

The wind threw her words back in her face. She kept going. She wasn't sure how long it took to reach the entrance at the other end, but when she did, she saw nothing. No disturbances. No footprints. No Dar. She started around the other side of the building, the side that faced the exit ramp. It seemed darker here, but more protected, and the wind was less intense. She'd only gone a few steps when she saw imprints on the ground. She stopped. Snow was filling them in, but she could see two sets of footprints. One set stopped abruptly, replaced by long runnels, as if something—or someone—had been dragged.

She pulled out the .38, then started forward again. Suddenly she heard a growl. She pivoted around, but it was too late. Jergens was charging her, head down. She tried to dodge him, but the snow slowed her, and he rammed her up against the wall of the building. Her head snapped back and exploded in pain. The world started to spin. The .38 slipped out from her hand, and the ground came up to meet her.

Lila swam up from the void. It was becoming familiar, she realized hazily, although the darkness wasn't as deep or thick this time. Slowly she opened her eyes. She was on the floor of the Econoline. Her hands and feet were tied. An inert figure lay beside her. Dar. Was he alive? She squinted, saw the rise and fall of his chest. Relief washed over her.

A foul odor drifted down. She turned her head to the side. Jergens was kneeling over her, his gun nuzzling her cheek. Was he going to attack her? Rape her? Had he already? Her clothes were still on. Her coat, too.

"Time to get up. You're driving," Jergens said. He teased the barrel of the gun up and down her cheek.

She licked her lips. She felt heavy and logy. "My head. I . . . I can't."

He prodded her temple with the gun. "You can and you will."

She tried to sit up. Again she looked over at Dar. He hadn't moved, and she could no longer see his breath. Fear flooded through her. "What did you do to him?"

Jergens grinned. With his mouth open, his breath smelled even more rank. "Don't worry about him."

Keeping the gun on her, he slipped his other hand into a pocket and brought out a knife and cut the ropes binding her hands and feet. She considered kicking him in the balls and grabbing the knife, but he kept himself too far away.

"Now . . . you're going to get up. Nice and easy. Climb into the driver's seat. And don't try anything stupid."

She raised her head. A wave of nausea overwhelmed her. She choked it back.

"Let's go, let's go."

Lila moved slowly, stretching and contracting her muscles.

"Come on. Get into the seat."

She did what she was told. She felt clumsy and slow. She landed in the driver's seat with a thump. Jergens rode shotgun, keeping his weapon trained on her. The keys were in the ignition. He leaned over and started the engine.

"Now drive."

She gripped the wheel and slowly backed out of the rest stop.

By the time they reached the outskirts of Grand Haven, it was midnight. Tree branches bowed under thick blankets of white. The tracks of cars preceding them were practically filled in. The town looked deserted. It was as if they were the only souls on earth. As she drove, Lila caught glimpses of the lake. It was frozen solid at the shoreline, the ice covered by fresh snow.

Jergens directed her down a narrow lane where an iron gate blocked the road. On one side was a gatehouse. He made a call on his cell. "We're here."

A moment later the gate opened.

"Drive," Jergens said.

Lila inched the van down a winding driveway. Tires crunched on snow. The wind screeched. Lila could just make out a large structure at the end of the drive. She rolled to a stop in front of an imposing house that looked solid and ostentatious.

The driver's-side door flew open, and cold air whipped through the van. Someone aimed a blinding light at her face. She squeezed her eyes shut. Beneath her closed lids, she could feel the light hover on her face. Then it swung away.

"Out of the van," a man's voice ordered.

Lila slid to the ground. A man in a thick parka, wool hat, and boots stood in front of her. He was holding a high-powered flashlight in one hand, a gun in the other.

"Go around to the back of the van," he said.

She did what she was told. The beam of light followed her.

"Stop."

She stopped in front of the panel doors.

"Turn around."

As she did, the flashlight lingered on her face again, then swung away.

"You're Philip Kerr," she said. "My uncle."

He didn't answer. He didn't need to.

Jergens got out of the passenger seat, came around, and released the panel doors. Gripping Dar's legs, he began to drag him out. Dar groaned. Lila was relieved. The fact that he was making sounds, however pained, meant he was coming around. Jergens grabbed Dar by the shoulders and propped him against the van. Dar's knees buckled, and he went down. Jergens hoisted him back up and shoved him against the panel door. This time Dar managed to stand.

A gust of wind swirled snow around them. "Why did you bring us here?" Lila pointed to Jergens. "Why not shoot us at the rest stop?"

Kerr flung the light in her face. The glare was blinding. She tried to twist away. When she couldn't, she turned back and drew herself up. "Well?"

Kerr didn't answer at first. Then he made a croaking sound, a laugh, bitter and soulless. "You *are* your mother's daughter."

Lila was momentarily distracted. A longing that had been buried deep within her surfaced. How was she like her mother? Her looks? Her voice? Her mannerisms? She wanted to know. But this man was her enemy. He was going to kill her. She couldn't ask.

"There were too many people at the rest stop," Kerr said briskly, as if he'd never said a word about her mother. He looked briefly at Jergens. "And I need to make sure it's done right this time. Three times you tried to finish the job, but here they are. If I didn't know better, I might think something other than sloppy work was at stake." Kerr swung the flashlight to Jergens, who threw up a hand to shield his face.

"Maybe we're just good," Lila replied.

Kerr grunted, then motioned to Jergens. "Is that true, Jergens? Are they just good?"

Jergens scowled. "No man, it's not that. I did exactly what you told me. It just . . . well . . . it wasn't easy."

"It would seem not." Kerr aimed the light back on Lila. "You keep your gun on Gantner. I'll cover her." He turned to Lila. "Let's go."

"Where?" Lila asked. She had no weapons. No protection. Neither did Dar. But, maybe if she thought fast enough, was clever enough.

"Start walking." Kerr pointed into the storm.

She had to level the playing field. At least try. She glanced at Dar. He seemed fully conscious now, and was watching her with a curious expression. Was he thinking the same thing?

She looked at Kerr. "No."

He raised the gun. "What did you say?"

"My father can't walk with his feet tied," she said. "Not in this weather."

Kerr tipped his head to the side, as if considering the request. Then he motioned toward Jergens. "Untie his feet."

He shone the light on Dar's white gym shoes. They were soaked through. Dar had to be freezing.

Jergens pulled out his pocketknife, crouched at Dar's feet, and sliced through the rope. Again she thought about kicking him and grabbing the knife, but she knew Kerr would pull the trigger. Jergens straightened up and slid the knife back into his pocket. His left pocket.

Kerr motioned with his gun. "All right. Let's go."

Dar's hands were still tied behind him, but Lila couldn't think of any way to free them without reminding Kerr that hers weren't.

Jergens gave Dar a shove. He stumbled forward. Lila thought he might fall, but he stayed on his feet.

"Move," Kerr said.

They started to slog through the snowstorm. First Dar, then Jergens, his gun at Dar's back. Then Lila, followed by Kerr with his gun trained on her. Lila's gloves had disappeared somewhere back at the rest stop, and her hands felt numb. She made fists, then relaxed them to keep her circulation pumping.

Eventually they reached an open expanse. Lila guessed it was maybe fifty yards from the van. All she could see was a swirling, twisting veil of white, but in the distance she heard a smacking sound. The beach. With the waves slapping where the lake wasn't frozen. The snow cleared for an instant, and she saw the water. It was covered by a blanket of white that looked solid enough to walk on. Twenty yards away a pier jutted out over the ice like a bony finger.

Jergens slowed as they approached the pier. "Stop," he yelled to Dar. Dar halted. The snow closed in again, obscuring the view.

"What now?" Jergens shouted.

Kerr called out from behind Lila. "Onto the pier. Everyone."

Jergens shook his head. "Why?"

"Just do it."

They started toward the pier. The snow had formed drifts—it was up to her waist in some spots, barely over her knees in others. The cold stung her face. It was difficult to breathe. As they stepped onto the snow-covered planks, Dar stumbled and fell. Jergens either wasn't watching or slipped as well, and fell on top of him.

Kerr hurried out from behind Lila with his gun. "Get up, goddamnit. Both of you."

It took Jergens a moment to extract himself from Dar. He wiped a sleeve across his face. "Fucking ice."

"Get him up." Kerr's voice was hard.

Jergens pulled Dar up.

"Keep going," Kerr shouted.

"I can't," Dar shouted back. "I don't know where the pier ends."

That was the point, Lila thought grimly. Kerr wanted to walk them off the edge of the pier.

As if he'd read her mind, Kerr said, "Well, now, that's a chance you'll have to take, isn't it?"

Dar took a tentative step forward. Jergens followed and called over his shoulder. "He's right. We can't see shit."

Behind her, Kerr was breathing heavily. "All right, then. Now, line up."

He shoved Lila towards Jergens. Jergens pushed Dar. Father and daughter stood together on the edge of the pier. Lila snuck another glance at her father. His expression had turned bleak. She gave her head a slight shake. He couldn't give up.

Kerr took up a position in front, Jergens beside him. Both guns were aimed at them. Lila swallowed.

"Now you, Jergens," Kerr ordered.

"Huh?"

"Get over there with them."

An icy ripple edged up Lila's spine. What was he doing?

"Why?" Jergens asked.

"You'll see."

Jergens hesitated, clearly confused.

Lila started to get the bare outlines of an idea. "Better do what he says," she said.

Jergens closed in on Lila, pressing his gun against her temple. "Shut the fuck up."

"Take the gun away from her face," Kerr snapped. "I have her covered."

Jergens complied and stood next to Lila.

"Well now. Look who's here," Kerr said. "The daughter of my sister. Her birth father. And the man I hired to kill her." He turned to Jergens. "Jergens, it would seem that you've become a liability. Three times you failed to get the job done. I think I'm wasting my money. What do you say?"

"I told you. Weather complicated things."

"So does incompetence."

"I'll finish the job now." Jergens jabbed his gun into Lila's ribs. She flinched.

"I don't think so." Kerr raised his gun, aimed, and fired.

The bullet opened a hole in Jergen's chest. A look of surprise came over him, and he collapsed on the pier. Blood spurted out. As he did, the gun dropped from his hands and bounced on the snow-covered planks.

Lila froze, her mouth open. Time was suspended, but whether for an eternity or just a millisecond, she didn't know. Finally her reflexes kicked in. She dropped to all fours. "Get down!" she hissed to Dar. "Drop to the ground."

She felt rather than saw him drop beside her. She hoped the blowing snow obscured them.

"Shit!" Kerr snarled.

Jergens' body lay in a heap beside Lila. She quickly rifled through his left pocket and found the knife. Then she turned around, reached for

343

Dar, and cut his hands free. She held tight to the knife. Gusts of wind slashed at her. Snow pelted her face. She started to crawl toward the spot where she'd seen Jergen's gun drop.

Suddenly a foot kicked through the snow, connecting with Jergens' corpse. Kerr. Jergens' body fell off the pier. There was a loud thud as he hit the ice below. Then an ominous crack. Then nothing but the shriek of the wind.

Behind Lila a flash of light exploded. A crack split the air. Kerr was firing again. At Dar? Lila wanted to call out, but that would tell Kerr where she was. She backtracked to where she'd last seen Dar. He wasn't there.

"Fuck you both!"

Another flash. Another crack. Closer this time.

Still on her hands and knees, Lila scrambled in the opposite direction. As she advanced, she swept a hand in a wide arc, searching for Jergen's gun. Her hand made a shushing noise. She hoped the wind covered it.

A third shot. Much closer. Could Kerr see her? An icy gust of wind whipped through her. A buzz tightened her muscles.

"The fuck are you?" Kerr was behind her. Closing in.

She made another desperate sweep with her hand. This time her fingers closed around Jergen's gun. Thank God! It was larger and heavier than her .38. She looked for the safety, then realized it had to be off. She slipped the knife in her pocket, wrapped her hands around the gun, and flattened herself on the pier. She would wait for the snow to clear. Then she'd shoot.

She was still waiting when someone grabbed her legs. She screamed.

When Dar heard Lila scream he crept toward the sound of the scuffle. Two shadows loomed through the blowing snow. Kerr had Lila in some kind of hold. She was struggling, but it looked like her arms were pinned.

"Help. Dar!"

Dar dropped to the surface of the pier. He tried to crawl toward Lila's voice, using the planks as a guide, but a dangerous numbness was spreading up his arms, deadening his sense of touch.

"He won't save you," Kerr said. "He's too busy saving himself."

Dar snapped. He'd failed to protect Billy all those years ago. He wouldn't fail again. He stood up and lunged toward the sound of Kerr's voice. This time he connected, and Kerr fell on the pier. A gun went flying. Dar grabbed Kerr and rolled over on top of the man. Kerr tried to twist away, but Dar hung on. He clutched the man's coat, using his own weight to keep him down.

Lila yelled. "I've got the gun!"

Kerr heaved and bucked and managed to partially wriggle out from under Dar. If Dar was going to keep him down, he would have to roll over again. Dar grabbed him in a bear hug and rolled. Their momentum took them to the edge of the pier.

"Be careful!" Lila screamed.

Too late. He couldn't stop. The surface under him vanished. They fell off the pier and slammed onto the ice below. The force of the fall broke them apart. A searing pain shot through Dar's leg. He cried out.

"I'm coming!" Lila yelled.

Visibility was sharper on the ice. Dar spotted Jergen's body a few feet away.

Another shape lay near Jergens. Kerr. He wasn't moving. Was he hurt —or was it a trick? Either way, Dar couldn't let Lila come onto the ice to find out. "No. Stay there!" He yelled. "I'm . . . okay."

"But you can't . . . "

Lila's words were cut off by a low-pitched, creaking sound. Dar went rigid. A ping followed, then another creak. Louder.

Kerr moved, waving his arms and legs. "Holy shit!" he screamed. "The ice! It's breaking up! Help!"

Dar heard the slap of waves in the distance, but he couldn't tell where the ice stopped and the water began. He looked back at the shore. It was only twenty feet away, but he couldn't move—the pain shooting through his leg was excruciating.

Dar felt the ice shift. Kerr tried to crawl in his direction. "For Christ's sake, help me!"

The surface shifted again, and a large chunk of ice broke off from the spot where Dar lay.

Kerr was on it, Jergens' corpse next to him. "Fuck! Help me!"

"Forget him. This way, Dar. Come this way!" It was Lila. "Follow my voice."

"Keep talking, Lila," Dar shouted.

"I need help!" Kerr yelled.

"Over here, Dar," Lila yelled. "Come this way! I know you can."

Dar pushed with his arms—his legs were useless—but made scant progress. He was running out of strength.

"Please . . . Dad."

She called him "Dad." Her tone was intense. He angled himself toward the sound and pushed with his arms. He was inching forward when he heard another crack.

The ice floe Kerr was on tipped precariously. Kerr was on his knees, trying to keep his balance, but as the ice tilted, he slipped toward the water. He tried to grasp for purchase, but teetered. He screamed again, his voice edged with terror. "Fuck! Help! I'm drowning!"

Dar was only a few feet from the edge of the floe himself. He couldn't risk it. Water sloshed over his hands and feet, stinging his skin. Suddenly Kerr's ice floe rose up at an angle, and he plunged into the water. Jergens' corpse slid in behind him. Kerr flailed and thrashed his arms. There was one last scream. And then nothing.

"Dad! Are you all right?" Lila's voice was laced with panic. "Answer me!"

Dar gasped. He couldn't talk. He was past cold, past numb, but he had to move. The ice shelf he was on might break loose. He struggled to his knees. Unbearable pain knifed through him. He forced himself to crawl toward shore. He caught a glimpse of Lila, aiming the gun with both hands. Did she know he wasn't Kerr? He wanted to call out. No words came. He hoped she wouldn't shoot.

Then everything went dark.

Sparks rained down like the aftermath of fireworks, winking out as they drifted over the lake. A cigarette, Dar realized sluggishly as he opened his eyes. He was on a stretcher. Gray light suffused the sky. Dawn was coming. The snow had eased, but everything was still white. Why wasn't he cold? He concentrated on his body. He felt comfortable. Even warm. His fingers touched something scratchy. Wool. He was covered with blankets.

A man in snow gear flicked his cigarette into the snow. "You gave us a scare," he said. His face was partially hidden by a ski mask. "I'm with the Grand Haven paramedics. You're on your way to the hospital."

"What happened?" Dar croaked.

"You fell off the pier and broke your leg. Almost froze too, by the sound of it. But you'll be okay."

"How . . . who saved me?"

"Your daughter pulled you out of the lake. Then she covered you with her body till we got here."

FIFTY-EIGHT

Six Months Later

B etween the sparkling lakefront, the tree-lined parks, and the sunny Midwestern hospitality, Chicago was at its best in summer. Dar spent Sunday afternoon with Lila and Cece on the "new" Maxwell Street. He wanted Lila to know where her mother had sold her jewelry. Although the market had been relocated a decade earlier, he claimed the heady brew of smells, colors, music, and noise were the same.

They strolled past booths offering everything from food to appliances to clothes to tools. Cece bought an enchilada, Lila an Italian ice. She was licking her fingers when Dar stopped at a jewelry stall. He picked over several necklaces, finally selecting a silver chain with a turquoise charm.

When he held it up, Lila frowned. "That's weird. I found a necklace just like that in my father's . . . Casey's . . . safe deposit box."

"Billy was making one like this for Alix when he died," Dar said. "A surprise Christmas present. Casey must have ended up with it."

"It was supposed to go to my mother?"

Dar nodded.

Lila smiled. First thing tomorrow, she knew where she was going.

"How is the reconstruction going?" Cece asked.

"Not bad at all. We might be celebrating Christmas in the house." She laughed. "If you two will deign to come to Winnetka."

"Wouldn't miss it, " Cece said.

Dar didn't say anything. Cece elbowed him in the stomach.

"Of course, I'll be there," he said.

Lila laughed and checked her watch. "Sorry, I have to get back to Evanston. I'm making dinner."

Cece raised an eyebrow. "You're cooking?"

"Well, actually, Brian is grilling. . . . but I'm not half bad with salad." She gave them each a quick hug. "Call you later."

Dar watched her go, a smile playing on his face. Then he turned to Cece and drew her close.

Manufactured By: RR Donnelley
                              Momence, IL USA
                              November, 2010